CHRIS BUDD lives in Somerset
plays guitar in a band, runs the y
reads too many graphic novels a
cricket. In between this, he runs
planning business he started in 2(

Chris's debut novel, *A Bridge*
reviews. He is also the author of ...dueing *Book* and
produces the *Financial Wellbeing* podcast series.

GW01403334

Also by Chris Budd

The Financial Wellbeing Book
A Bridge of Straw

MANNERS FROM HEAVEN

CHRIS BUDD

SilverWood

Published in 2016 by SilverWood Books

SilverWood Books Ltd
14 Small Street, Bristol, BS1 1DE, United Kingdom
www.silverwoodbooks.co.uk

Copyright © Chris Budd 2016

The right of Chris Budd to be identified as the author of this
work has been asserted in accordance with the Copyright, Designs
and Patents Act 1988 Sections 77 and 78.

All rights reserved. No part of this publication may be reproduced,
stored in a retrieval system, or transmitted in any form or by any means,
electronic, mechanical, photocopying, recording or otherwise,
without prior permission of the copyright holder.

This is a work of fiction. Names, characters, places and incidents
either are products of the author's imagination or are used fictitiously.
Any resemblance to actual events or locales or persons,
living or dead, is entirely coincidental.

ISBN 978-1-78132-617-6 (paperback)
ISBN 978-1-78132-618-3 (ebook)

British Library Cataloguing in Publication Data
A CIP catalogue record for this book is available from the British Library

Page design and typesetting by SilverWood Books
Printed on responsibly sourced paper

Everyone thinks of changing the world, but no one thinks of changing himself.
Leo Tolstoy

Part 1

Breaking Down the Self

Chapter 1

The distant sound of a car engine roaring at a level far louder than necessary broke the spell of Schubert's 'Quintet'. Elliott Harmison stabbed at the car radio and changed channel.

A newsreader began to burble away in a voice devoid of emotion, describing events that could barely be imagined. Elliott turned the radio down to a level where he could not understand the words, waiting for the next programme to begin. He didn't need any more news in his life. Lucy said he was suffering from an overdose of perspective. A typical big-sister opinion.

The high hedges flanking the road obscured the autumn view, only sporadic five-bar gates allowing a flash of the iridescent yellow rape fields stretching away across the Somerset countryside.

Elliott slowed his car into yet another tight corner, peering ahead in case of an oncoming vehicle going too fast. Years of driving these narrow lanes told him that they created two distinct types of driver. The first accepts their fate; relaxed and easy-going in nature. They have no pressure on the time of their arrival, or they left in good time and appreciate the beauty of the countryside. They chose their car based on comfort and possibly gadgets. They were often keen gardeners and gave to charity.

The second driver type was perpetually frustrated. For them it was less about the journey, more the destination, their swift passage to which was so often impeded by a family saloon slowing down to admire the view. It was all about them. Always. This was the driver type that was concerning Elliott as he eased around another bend.

Elliott believed himself to be of the first type. Lucy had snorted white wine out of her nose when he had once made this observation over dinner. Phoebe, his niece, had admonished her mother, without effect. Lucy's mocking hadn't changed his opinion, but it did remind him to keep them to himself in future.

The slightly less distant roar of a car accelerating out of a corner suggested he was rapidly being caught up by a driver of the latter persuasion.

Elliott tried to restore the tentative feelings of happiness that had recently been starting to gain a foothold. He found it like being told not to think about breathing. His default personality position of being angry at the world was, at best, held in abeyance, a feeling of well-being just starting to nudge through the barren wasteland of his state of mind. There were times when he had wondered whether he would ever be party to such feelings again.

The time to move on felt within reach. A new life at thirty-eight. He checked the rear-view mirror. No more feeling angry – despite the existence of people who deliberately made their cars louder than necessary. He checked himself, resisting the temptation to feel annoyed at the fact that something had almost made him annoyed.

A fleeting moment of contentment constantly under attack from negative forces, their persistence itself part of the army of vexations that were lined up against him. He focused on happy times, when he and Naomi were on holiday in Sinai, enjoying mojito cocktails on the veranda of their hotel overlooking the Red Sea. A deep and shared contentment interspersed with flies landing on different parts of his body. That's how he felt now: determined to be joyful but pecked at by discontent. Seeking happiness despite the world, not because of it.

He glanced at the clock on the dashboard. He had concluded the last meeting of the week in good time in order to pick up Phoebe from school after her judo match. Being late was not something he allowed at any time, but especially not on her sixteenth birthday. Lateness is an option. Lateness is rude. Naomi would never have been late.

Elliott heard the car engine again, this time much louder. The throaty roar of an engine that did not need to be so loud. He looked in the mirror again to see a sports car of a model he didn't recognise exit the bend and accelerate towards him with alarming speed. Elliott's mood resentfully turned a few notches grimmer.

The car braked hard as it reached him, then, with no possibility of overtaking, took up residency so close to Elliott's rear bumper that he could not see its headlights in his rear-view mirror. He tried to concentrate on the road ahead and ignore the car virtually stapled to his rear end. He failed.

The sun reflecting off the windscreen meant that he could not make out the driver's face. The colour of the car was a strange variant on purple. Elliott decided it could best be described as puce. The proportion of time spent looking ahead and looking in the rear-view mirror was now tilting dangerously towards not sufficiently concentrating on driving his own car. A blind corner ahead forced Elliott to slow down to second gear and focus back on the furthest part of the road ahead in case of oncoming traffic. Still the car behind maintained its position as they entered a long, narrow straight with no chance of overtaking.

Now that the car was so close he could also hear a thumping bass drum. Elliott ostentatiously tilted the mirror. He was a tall, somewhat lean man driving a not-particularly-big car. The mirror was actually quite far away as the seat was pushed as far back as it would go. This allowed for a large amount of forearm to be plainly visible to the driver behind as he tilted the mirror downwards. The objective was not the tilting of the mirror itself, but for the driver to see him tilt his mirror. He surreptitiously flicked it back into position at the last moment, a practised move which meant the mirror was still in place but the point remained made.

The sports car made no attempt to move back to a safe distance. Elliott tried not to look, but even if he hadn't kept glancing in the side mirrors there was still that ridiculous exhaust, spitting and coughing like an asthmatic Alsatian straining to rip the head off some poor unsuspecting rabbit.

Elliott flicked on his fog lights. The sports car, thinking they were brake lights, slowed down suddenly and for a moment Elliott could see something in his mirror other than the colour puce. With a roar the car came right back up, and for a moment it seemed as if he might be rear-ended.

Each time Elliott renewed his car lease, and thereby took delivery of the latest model of the same car, one of his first acts would be to stick a pin in the passenger side windscreen washer in order to adjust the direction of the jet. Now he pulled on the stick to squirt his special liquid mix (three parts water, one part vinegar). The jet on the right squirted onto the glass, but the left squirted a stream of liquid over his car and onto the windscreen of the car behind. He gave a grim laugh of triumph as he watched the wipers jump into action and the car move back to an almost safe distance away.

A few moments later and the sports car seemed to be even closer than it had been before. Elliott slowed right down, breathing deeply to try and keep his anger under control. Ten miles an hour around a corner. Five, almost stopped. Coming out of the bend, he stamped on the accelerator. He tried to remind himself that the objective was to send a polite message that he didn't want to have a car right up behind him, that the ideal result was for this person to back off. And yet he couldn't resist the feeling of pleasure that the other driver would himself be getting a little annoyed. Serve him right, might learn a lesson.

Inevitably, the sports car also accelerated and quickly resumed its hassling position. Again, Elliott slowed down. It was as if there was a rubber band tying the two cars together. Every time Elliott sped up, the sports car would return as if it was being pulled. His many years of legal training led him to consider slamming on his brakes, causing an accident. The insurance company would certainly find in his favour. He felt his bile rising and had to admonish himself for even thinking such a thing as a serious possibility.

Coming out of another corner at ten miles an hour, he was busy looking in the side mirror and therefore failed to notice the road ahead widening. With a roar that caught Elliott by surprise, the sports car pulled out and sped past in a flash of vomity purple. Elliott accelerated, the two cars momentarily racing towards another corner. Although the sports car quickly moved past him, it still entered the next corner on the wrong side of the road, moving into the apex in front of Elliott, who gave a long and unsatisfying beep on his horn as he braked harder than he probably needed to.

Suddenly the sports car slammed on his brakes, forcing Elliott to come to a complete halt. The darkened window of the driver's side slid down and arm came out with the hand balled in a fist. The middle finger slowly unrolled into an obscene gesture, then the driver floored the accelerator and sped away, leaving a cloud of dark smoke from the exhaust as a parting gesture of insolence.

Elliott sat for a moment, consumed with rage. All thoughts of birthday teas and joyous yellow fields were banished in a tight ball of anger and injustice. Above all the other emotions screaming for his attention, it was that finger that held firm in his mind. The suggestion that it was he, Elliott, that was somehow at fault. What had he done? Who the hell was this person to act like that, and then tell him that *he* was the one in the wrong?

Aware that a car coming round the corner behind him might not see him in time to slow down, Elliott gripped his shaking hand onto the gear stick, put it into first and pulled away. He drove slowly, a myriad of thoughts growling at him, swirling around as if stalking each other, combining and conjoining to make a fractured sense of purpose united by the twinned senses of injustice and humiliation.

The road now started to wind its way downhill and entered a wood. Trees loomed high on both sides, some clinging to the bank as the road cut into the hillside. The new rift in his mind began to allow other annoyances to enter and take over his thoughts, creating a loop of negativity. The face of Paolo, Lucy's ex-husband, leered at him, offering him legal work in the same way that a cat likes to keep a mouse alive when bringing it into the house. The cyclist who, earlier that day, had shouted at him for turning right through a gap in stationary traffic even though the cyclist had been undertaking at the time. Why were there so many rude and stupid people in the world?

Still in the wood, the road levelled out, the trees dense and on the same level as the road. Elliott knew that the corner up ahead was a tight one. He slowed down to turn, and as he did so, he saw alien colours amongst the greens and browns. A mangled mess of puce, off the road and in the wood. It was as if two giants had taken the sports car and slowly pushed the front and rear ends either side of a tree, wrapping it round until the back end was thirty degrees or so at an angle to the front, and then flicked it just clear.

Elliott pulled up, got out of his car and walked quickly over. Music was still playing from the crumpled vehicle, and he could now tell that there wasn't much else other than the bass, or at least not to his ears. In fact he would barely have considered it to be music. As he got closer it occurred that he might be about to see something gruesome. The thought that it could have been him involved in that crash was not too far from his mind. This was all so stupidly avoidable. His cheeks flushed red as he slowed his pace and approached the wreckage.

He peered in through the open passenger window, the dark-tinted glass lying in pieces on the floor amongst the twigs and leaves like fairies' crazing paving. In the driver's seat he saw the profile of a man in his late twenties or early thirties, short dark hair and carefully cropped sideburns, the appearance of someone who held a close relationship with his barber. A dark grey suit jacket lay on the passenger seat. The man's eyes were closed and his head slumped, leaving his chin resting on a bright flowery tie. He was breathing, and was held in position by a seatbelt, which was putting creases into the cloth of a crisp white shirt. A limp airbag hung like a frozen pool of sick from a hole in the middle of the steering wheel.

Running quickly round the front of the car to the driver's side, Elliott put an arm through the hole where the window used to be and turned off the music. As the thumping bass was cut off Elliott became aware that the engine was still turning over. He turned the key in the ignition, the abrupt silence magnifying the sheer preventability of the situation. He tried to keep his focus on the situation in hand rather than allowing his anger to rise up at how easy it would be for this not to have happened. As he removed his head from the window he got a good look at the face of the driver of the car.

If there had been anyone watching from the other side of the road they would have seen what Elliott himself would barely remember doing. After he had stared at the driver for a few moments they would have watched him stand upright, preoccupation written over his face. If they were close enough they may have noticed the bright redness of his cheeks contract into two small circles. They may have surmised that his heart was pounding, that a roaring sound was in his ears and he was not really seeing anything despite the fact he was staring into the car. His eyes rolled slightly upwards and he cricked his neck, the overall impression being that he was sucking on a lemon.

Slowly, as if controlled remotely by a small child, Elliott opened the car door and prodded the driver in several places, on the arms and legs and then feeling round his back. It might have seemed as if he had some medical knowledge; the theoretical observer wouldn't be too sure. Then he stood again and turned back towards his own car, moving as if he had taken himself by surprise.

Elliott went to the back of his car. He opened the boot and removed several large files, placing them on the back seat. Leaving the lid open, he went back to the crashed vehicle and tried the driver's door, which, with some persuasion, he managed to open. Next he reached across the unmoving driver and unbuckled his seatbelt. He was braced awkwardly on his right leg for the man slumping forwards, and with one movement, rolled the inert body up and over his shoulder in a fireman's lift and stood up, banging the man's head on the door frame as he did so. The casual observer would have been surprised at the strength of the man, but would have noticed that the driver of the sports car did not stir.

That initial surge of energy did not seem to continue as Elliott stopped once or twice, first sitting on the bonnet of the sports car, then to lean against his own car. Eventually he reached his destination at the back of his vehicle. He bent his knees to slowly roll the man into the boot of the car, being careful not to bang the head again, then shut the boot. He stood still for a moment, that thousand-yard stare returning. Then he opened the boot again and patted the man's trouser pockets, searching for something.

He returned to the driver's side of the still-steaming car, pulled the man's jacket out through the window and felt inside. He took out a mobile phone from one pocket, a wallet from the other. He put the phone in his own pocket but returned the wallet after a quick look inside. He placed the jacket back on the seat, using two hands to ensure it was lying flat and would not crease.

The observer to the incident would then have seen Elliott ease himself into the driver's seat of his own car, start his engine and drive off. They might also have later reported that his expression was somewhat blank, but as he went off he looked like someone waking with a terrible hangover, slowly remembering the sordid details of the previous night.

Chapter 2

Meanwood Towers had been built some five hundred years before Elliott and Lucy's parents had moved in with their young family. It was big enough that brother and older sister had grown up aware of each other, rather than alongside. The space afforded by the house allowed friendship to eventually outgrow their sibling rivalries despite the six-year age difference.

As part of a school project, Elliott had once charted the entire history of the house, right from the moment the first tentative priory was built near to a small hamlet in 1150. Discovering the secrets of his home revealed as much to Elliott of the machinations of his own family as it did of the history of the house.

The priory had originally been called Milkwood. Then, as now, it sat staring at the local wood, which lay the other side of what was then the main route between the cathedral towns of Wells and Bristol. The milk came from a solitary cow, which was donated by the local hamlet. It was a poor priory and something of an embarrassment to the local abbey. The priors felt that being sent to Milkwood was akin to punishment, although this seemed a little odd to the young Elliott. Surely punishment and unhappiness came as part of the job of a religious devotee in the Middle Ages?

The locals began calling the building Meanwood as a reaction to the bitter priors. When the abbey was dissolved in 1538 the priory became independent for a decade before being purchased by a pious local landowner, James Chesterton, and the nickname stuck. Chesterton embarked on a building spree including a rather foreboding turret which overlooked the hamlet, and the name Meanwood Towers was complete.

The turret stood as a monument to folly and hubris. It included a circular room at the top of a spiral staircase from which Elliott would look up from his studies to gaze out over the giant leylandii trees bordering the grounds, and onto the roofs of the village which had grown out of the original hamlet. In the housing estate which now bordered one side of the property lurked two types of children: ones who weren't interested in Elliott at all, and those who were interested just enough to bully him. As he laboured over his project, sitting in the turret which his parents had set up as a simple study, he felt a kinship with the very last prior, trapped, unwanted, unsure of his place in the world.

By the time Chesterton died the house boasted a great hall on the ground floor, which was separated from the kitchen and pantry by a screens passage. A buttery, for storing wine and barrels of beer, was down a few steps off the kitchen. As children Elliott and Lucy had loved those hot evenings when they would serve drinks and olives to guests at the annual garden party their parents threw for the wide circle of friends in the village, many of whom lived in the neighbouring estate. Elliott would pour the wine as if it was some ancient elixir, then scurry back to the buttery and hide with Lucy, listening to the thrilling gossip and conversation. For some reason people spoke more freely in the kitchen than in the lounge, especially when they didn't know they were being listened to by two excited children.

These had been Elliott's happiest moments, when Lucy seemed like a second mummy and had not yet grown old enough to see her little brother as an intrusion instead of cute, a change effected through no fault of his own and one that he would find hard to come to terms with.

Then came the day when the gossipers turned their idle bile towards the hosts of the party, even as they drank the free wine. The children had put the empty bottles in the bins outside, then ran around to the side of the house, laughing, happy, joking with each other about the fancy dresses and shoes they had seen. They went into the buttery through the back entrance at the side of the house, down the steps, across the stone floor and back up the steps on the other side to take up their usual position behind the door to the kitchen. There they listened in mounting horror and shame as their family's true position in the local community was revealed to them. They discovered the prevailing view was not as the beneficial feudal lords of their imagination, but the subject of scorn and envy and malice. Ridicule was directed at the notion of an annual garden party, as if they were landed gentry allowing the servants a once-yearly treat. The seven-year-old Elliott did not understand as the mean-spirited words ran through him like a sword, piercing both his simple view of the world and the hitherto unchallenged position his father held as an impregnable hero. It all became clear as to why the other children were so consistently mean to him at school.

The main room between the kitchen and the turret, which Elliott knew as the lounge, was originally modest. It was Chesterton's son who had taken down the screens passage and extended the room into a sizeable chapel, including a grand fireplace. The Chesterton family had continued to practise Catholicism, at first discreetly, but when Queen Elizabeth banned the Roman Catholic faith Chesterton engaged the assistance of the great designer of hiding places, Nicholas Owen. The altar was dismantled and the chapel turned into a large room of quiet contemplation, the vestments and crosses hidden underneath a secret trapdoor in the floor. A seminary priest would come to stay and worship with the family, but such acts were fraught with danger and punishable most severely.

The fireplace was so large that a person could duck underneath the lintel and stand up on the other side. Owen built an opening halfway up the chimney, accessible by discreet footholds notched into the wall. A visiting priest who needed to hide quickly could scamper up inside the chimney, onto a small ledge, crawl through a hole in the wall and into a room nearly a metre deep. His nose would be almost touching the stone wall, hardly daring to breathe as the house was searched by the queen's men, the pursuivants employed to seek out the accursed priests.

As a child Elliott loved to creep into that priest hole. The silence was almost overwhelming and he liked to imagine the fore-bears that had stood in that same spot, pressed against the cold stone, life or death hanging by a breath or a whimper as the cramp set in, urine pooling at their feet. The priest hole seemed to be made to measure for him. Lucy would walk round the room calling loudly, "Where could Elliott be?", creating a shiver of excitement as he imagined that he had fooled them yet again. That it was the most obvious of hiding places he eventually came to realise, teenage hindsight leaving him embarrassed at the overuse of the one place in the house no one was supposed to know about. A large dried flower arrangement now occupied much of the hearth, a moving-in present from Lucy. It had been more for Naomi than Elliott, all three of them knew that, but he just hadn't got round to getting rid of it now that he was on his own.

When Lucy and Elliott had been forced to turn the house into three flats on three floors after the sudden death of their parents, he had chosen the ground floor because of the access to the turret. These days the secret door spectacularly failed in its attempt at subterfuge, the only efforts at concealment being that the skirting board at the bottom of the wall continued across the door, as did the wainscoting about four feet from the bottom. The lower part was painted purple and the upper part covered with wallpaper in keeping with the rest of the room, the intention being that the door would appear to be part of the wall. However, the fact that there was a knob in the wall and a black door-like shape cut into the wallpaper rather gave the secret away.

The not-so-secret door from the lounge opened into a small room. From here one stepped onto the spiral staircase, which took up the entire width of the turret. An old and rather incongruous stairlift sat rather guiltily at the bottom of the stairs. The turret had been used as an observatory by the previous owner, a rather crotchety old actor who retreated up the stairs in order to get away from his wife. It was he who had installed the stairlift and fitted thick metal shutters in the top room in order to keep out any excess light and noise.

The stairs wound gently upwards with only arrow slits in the thick stone walls, ever darker as they ascended up the three floors and the light from the window on the ground floor dissipated, arriving on a small landing with a door through which one emerged into a circular room bathed in light when the shutters were tied back. Windows were all around, and as a child Elliott used to stand with his eyes wide open and spin, the view changing dramatically from one moment to the next. He could see over across fields towards Bristol and Wales and the Brecon Beacons in one direction, the roof of Meanwood Towers in another, more fields and the edge of the village, and then turn once again to see over the leylandii trees and across the modern rooftops of the housing estate.

As a child Elliott made the turret his den, firstly full of Lego that he never got told to tidy away, then a model railway that would run endlessly round and round on a shelf that his father had built for the purpose. The shelf would detach across the door to allow access and so a lock had been built into the door, allowing Elliott to go inside, fix the train track back together and then lock the door to make sure no one came in unexpectedly and broke the shelf. This only enhanced his feeling of joyous isolation and protection from the outside world.

As a prepubescent he would sit on a chair and divide his summer holidays between reading books similar to but never quite as good as Tolkien and sitting at a desk painting tiny models of postmen, ladies with pushchairs and other villagers who would line the tiny railway track, politely waving at the engines in perpetuity. Those models didn't make fun of him for being clever, for being different. In the turret he felt truly safe.

On occasion he would allow himself to be distracted from his attempts to construct a perfect world in miniature and embark on a crusade, such as the happy hour he spent adding an 'e' with a permanent marker pen to all the packets of Blu-tack he had brought back with him from school. In his early teenage years he would sit on the same chair and stare out of a window facing the broadest vista, no longer seeing the view but instead lost in anger at the iniquities of the world, at the cruel things that people could do and say to each other. As he neared adulthood his visits to the tower became fewer but more meaningful, an opportunity snatched to hide from the ignorance of the world he was being forced to become a part of. But the view, and his reaction to it, never changed.

*

Elliott now turned off the lane leading out of the village and into the drive to Meanwood Towers. He stopped for a moment to wait for the electric gate to open, fingers drumming on the steering wheel. After what seemed an eternity he finally drove along the gravel driveway that went past the side of the house and opened out into a parking area at the back. Two outbuildings that had once been a stable block stood at right angles to the house, the left building now sporting a modern-looking door with oak frame and frosted glass panels. Next to the door was a rather ostentatious gold plaque bearing the legend 'Elliott Harmison Legal', then underneath, in case anyone might be in doubt, 'Solicitor'. The smaller right-hand block gave no such clue as to its contents but was actually full of gardening equipment for the enormous vegetable patch that occupied the space behind the outbuildings.

No cars meant Lucy was at work, Phoebe was still at school and Pru Hutton, his secretary, had left for the weekend. Only Benny Daker, the musician and retired art dealer who rented the middle flat, could conceivably be home. A glance up at his flat showed that the windows were shut. Benny always had the windows open when he was at home. So. No one was around.

Twenty minutes later and Elliott sat in the lounge on a black leather sofa, cradling a glass of single malt whisky. Just a sharpener. His hands had almost stopped shaking. The hum of a washing machine came through the kitchen from the buttery. He had changed out of his suit and thrown the now-sweaty shirt into the white plastic washing basket along with a variety of socks, underpants and shirts from the wicker basket in the corner of his bedroom.

He absorbed the peaty aroma from the whisky glass, exhaling just as slowly. His eyes scanned the shelves of books that surrounded him as if looking for some kind of inspiration. They skipped across the carriage clock, a wedding present he didn't like but couldn't bear to throw away. Leaving in five minutes. He had texted Phoebe that he would try to get to the last bout itself and would definitely be there to pick her up. He had apologised profusely in the text for missing the whole match. She had responded that it was fine. As he knew she would.

Finally his gaze moved across the books. The Biggles paperbacks that he had read as a small boy. His prized first edition of Franz Kafka's *The Trial*, whose works he devoured as his teenage world view became darkened by loneliness. A copy of James Joyce's *Ulysses* that he had tried to read four times and given up each time. His eyes stopped on a book about the practices of the Korean military. He stared at the spine as he recalled the methods within, flipping through the chapters in his mind as if it were a filing system. It stopped on Chapter 8. He had daydreamed occasionally about its contents, never so much as considering that he might actually put the theories into practice. But now fate had intervened, sticking its fingers into the fissure in his mind and pulling it wide to present an opportunity. A solution to the question of what the hell he was going to do with the man now tied up in the room at the top of the turret. An idea that had surely begun its formation in the dark recesses of Elliott's mind a long time ago and which now began to piece itself together like a film shown backwards of a wine glass smashing on a concrete step.

One slightly-too-fast drive later and Elliott was walking briskly across the school car park. His swinging arms gave so much momentum that he had no choice but to break into a jog. Phoebe was due on for her last bout at five o'clock, just a few minutes away. Being late is a luxury chosen by the ignorant. He made a mental note to write that line on the whiteboard in his office.

He ran a little quicker, then opened the door and entered the hall, closing the door carefully and quietly behind him.

The tournament seemed to be in between bouts. From the size of the girls lined either side of the judge Elliott guessed that he was in time for the under-sixteen age group. Phoebe saw him and gave a surreptitious wave, just one arc of her hand across her body. A narrowing of her eyes told him he was wearing his tension on his face. He smiled and gave her a thumbs-up, then took a position at the back of the hall, preferring to stand behind the rows of seated parents with smaller children playing on phones or attacking bags of crisps.

The judge called out Phoebe's name and she hopped upright, walked round the side of the matting in her bare feet, turned and paused before bowing at the same time as her opponent. The black frizzy hair that normally covered her shoulders was tied into a bundle on top of her head, revealing a hard, determined face, the lack of make-up giving her eyes an open quality that accurately suggested an intensely loving, loyal nature. It was a face that suggested that if you were to mess with her family, she would mess with you.

The order and etiquette of the moment calmed Elliott briefly. The other girls seemed huge in comparison to the small, wiry frame of Phoebe, despite her being old for her year. Had Elliott not seen Phoebe fight before he might even have been worried.

The bout did not last long. The other girl clearly *had* seen Phoebe fight before. After a minute or so of avoidance techniques from her opponent, Phoebe managed to take a firm hold of the girl's lapels, throw herself backwards to the ground, putting her foot on her opponent's chest as she did so, and roll backwards. The other girl was dragged forward onto Phoebe's foot and then propelled into the air, landing on her back on the mat with a thud and a whooshing of air leaving the girl's body that that brought an equivalent 'ooh' from the crowd, like an owl answering a mating call.

Jumping to her feet, Phoebe ran back to her position on the mat, energy seeming to crackle from her fingertips. The other girl slowly wheezed back to her feet. She didn't need to bow as she was already bent over double, trying to get her breath. Phoebe bowed deeply and slowly, backed out of the mat area, put a finger up towards Elliott to indicate that she would only be a minute, then skipped out of the hall and into the changing rooms. Thirty seconds later she burst out again, now with earphones in place.

Reaching Elliott, she grabbed his arm and dragged him towards the doors.

"Wow," he said, trying to keep up with her pace, "Phoebe, that was brutal. You don't hold back, do you?"

She took out an earphone. "Huh?" she said. Elliott heard a powerful but tinny female voice over a mighty string-based racket. In answer to his quizzical expression she pointed the ear-piece towards him and said, "Katzenjammer."

"Of course it is," he replied. "How could I not have guessed?"

"'Cause you're an old loser who listens to classical music?"

24

He put up his hands in an admission of guilt. "I said," he then continued, "that was brutal. That last bout."

Phoebe leaned in to him, and he bent down slightly so that she could whisper in his ear. "She's a total phoney. And she fancies Mikey. I hate her."

"Don't use the word 'hate' please, Phoebe. Naomi always told us off for using that word."

"Sorry."

Elliott gave her a friendly punch on the arm. "You are a nasty piece of work, Phoebe."

Her eyes sparkled up at him. "Thanks!" she said, beaming. She hugged his arm a little tighter.

As he held the door open for Phoebe a young man, a student, approached from the car park. They both stood back and allowed him to enter the building. He walked past them without a word.

"Thank you," said Elliott at the back of the young man as he walked away from them into the building, sarcasm dripping from every word. Then, a little louder, "Don't mention it. Oh, you didn't."

As the young man rounded the corner at the end of the corridor he turned to look at them with a 'whatever' look on his face. Elliott tutted and almost pushed Phoebe out of the door before him.

Phoebe walked quickly to the car and stood by the passenger door, glaring, arms folded with such intensity that it seemed they would never again hang by her sides.

A few moments later Elliott reached the car and glanced over the roof at Phoebe's demeanour. "He was rude," he said, deflecting the intensity of the stare with a shrug. Then, after a few moments, "Okay, and I may be a bit tense."

"*You're* tense?" Phoebe looked at him quizzically, the forgiveness immediate. "I'm not sure what you mean by that. Tense for you is like snow to the Inuit."

They got into the car and Elliott started the engine. "You may care to expand on that sentence. Or you may not. Use your judgement."

Her irritation had dissipated as quickly as it had arrived. Phoebe spoke quickly, words tumbling out as if she expected to be interrupted at any time and therefore needed to make her point as fast as possible. "Well, the Inuit have over two hundred words for snow. Powdery snow, ice, three-day-old slush – you know, lots of different ways that water just exists, and they have a word for every nuance. Well, you're like that with being tense. You have so many different ways of being uptight about things. There's the way you shout at adverts, which is different thing to how you silently fume…" (he loved the way she extended 'fume' for emphasis, giving it several extra Us) "…when shop assistants talk on the phone while serving you, which again is different from how sarcastic you are to people when they don't say, 'Thank you' when you think they should. So you saying, 'I'm tense' is like saying to an Inuit, 'It's snowy.' There isn't enough information in the statement to give a clear outline of the true situation."

Elliott drove out of the car park in silence. At the end of the lane he waited to turn into the traffic. Eventually a car slowed and flashed his lights. Elliott pulled out, putting his hand up high in thanks, palm towards the other car like a Native American in a bad Western about to say, "*How*". Eventually he spoke next, as they both knew he would.

"Firstly, the Inuit actually have a similar number of basic words for snow as we do. They join them together to make different meanings, but this is no different than us joining two words together to clarify meaning. Snowdrift would be an example."

Phoebe sighed. Elliott continued.

"But I do take your point. So I shall elaborate. I am tense because I have had a rough day, and it's given me a problem that is occupying my brain."

"And this problem is making you tense?"

"Yes, sort of. I mean, tense in that I'm both excited and worried in equal measure. Is there a word for *that*, I wonder?"

"I don't think there is," said Phoebe. She took a large chocolate bar out of her bag and began to unwrap it. Elliott was about to tell her not eat this close to having her tea, then remembered that he had made a similar observation last week, which resulted in a severe reprimand for the interjection first by Phoebe, and then by Lucy, who had also been in the car. "Maybe we should invent a word for it," continued Phoebe. "Something that describes how you want to regain control of a situation. How about you feel contratious about it?"

Elliott laughed. "I like that. I'm feeling contratious. Okay, how about this one? I want to turn right, there is stationary traffic on the opposite side of the road, the cars move forwards, and someone pulls up and closes the gap, stopping me from turning even though they can't go anywhere. What word would you use for how I would feel in that situation?"

"Well," said Phoebe, "knowing you, there would be a burning sense of injustice. But then that's your default position. You would also be angry, both at the inconvenience, but also at the selfishness and stupidity of the other person. Put that lot together. I reckon you would be feel...injusfish. Idity. Injusfishidity. That's what you'd feel."

Despite the knot in his stomach reminding him of where he needed to be, it felt good to spend a few moments with Phoebe. She had the knack vested only in those for whom love is blind to remind him of the good that existed within him. Collecting Phoebe from school was never a chore. But for once it was also not where he wanted to be right now.

Chapter 3

Stage 1: Assault on Identity

Thursday, 6.30pm

Elliott sat on an upturned bucket, chin resting on his hands, elbows leaning on his knees. Not that he could see his knees; the darkness was absolute. The old actor had been very thorough when installing the shutters.

With only half an hour to re-familiarise himself with the methods of the Korean military, the contents of Chapter 8 had absorbed him totally. As he stared into the darkness he worked over his plan once again, thoughts flitting between good and evil, solution and problem. How he could challenge the core belief system, a set of ideals around which actions could be legitimised.

Somewhere in the Middle East a group of men had sat down together as a committee, discussed how they could improve their community, and agreed that killing all the children in the local school would be the most appropriate solution. A government had decided that the best way to help the disabled and disadvantaged would be to reduce the amount of money they received from the state in order to incentivise them to find work, whilst an hour later agreeing to increase their own pay by three times the rate of inflation. A schoolboy in America had shot all twenty-five of his classmates because he had not been invited to a party. Everywhere Elliott turned, people were doing horrific things to each other, and each and every one of them could provide justification for their actions.

He rubbed his eyes with his fingers, massaging the eyelids before moving on to the bags under his eyes, round and round, probing, as if searching for something. This turret had been his bolthole for such a long time, a sanctuary, and yet also remained as the symbol of his loneliness. It was in here that he sought refuge when he had got into trouble at school for the only time in his life. Which was also the last time he had allowed Alan to make a full appearance.

He had been fourteen years old. A group of boys had begun teasing him in the playground as he had sat quietly with his one friend, a boy from Japan called Daisuke. Also quiet and bright, the two of them had been put together by their maths teacher and quickly formed a timid but ultimately firm friendship based around the shared isolation of the dispossessed.

Joey Davison was the ringleader of the gang, one of those boys who was old for his year and who always seemed to be a foot taller than everyone else. Captain of the school rugby team and bottom of the maths class, it seemed to Elliott that Joey spent his break times hitting anyone cleverer than himself. It was tempting to point this out, but Elliott had by now learned that in the playground, discretion was the better part of intelligence. As Daisuke had once said to him, in Japan kids think it is cool to be clever and nice to people. In England the cool kids are the ones who are thick and mean.

On this occasion they had stolen his briefcase – he was the only boy in school who actually carried a briefcase – and had commenced drop-kicking it to each other across the tarmac. Elliott had felt the rage rising inside of him. Alan. A harmless, silly name his father had given to that beast within him, that uncontrollable surge of blood and fury. His father had held him one time until the shaking stopped and the sobbing was under control, just stroking his hair and holding him tightly so that he would always know that at least his parents loved him. His father had made it clear that his temper was not acceptable but, being a man of passion himself, recognised that the boy needed assistance. And so Alan was invented, an attempt to make something real in order that it could be referred to directly and thereby controlled.

"Go away, Alan," Elliott had repeated under his breath as Joey Davison managed to kick the briefcase over his head. "Sod off." It would have worked had one of the clasps on the briefcase not broken. Joey Davison laughed and kicked the case one more time, hard. The case flew open and the contents were strewn across the playground.

Schoolbooks, his old Rupert the Bear pencil case, all went scuttling in various directions across the hard ground. The bookmark flew out of a copy of *Nineteen Eighty-Four* as it hit the ground. A small crowd had now gathered and a gasp went up as individual pieces of homework, lined paper covered in neat handwriting, were whipped up into the sky by a sudden breeze.

But it was a metallic scraping sound that proved to be the trigger for Alan to take over. The Class B17 Barnsley toy steam engine had cost six months' worth of savings, pocket money that Elliott had earned by washing the windows and then saving in his piggybank shaped like an ivy-covered cottage. He had brought the beloved engine to school to show Daisuke, who had held it as tenderly as Elliott himself as they admired the pristine green paintwork, the fragile wheels, the steam dome, the smokebox. It was a work of art, to be cherished and loved. And there it was bouncing across the playground, bits flying off in every direction.

"He's got a toy train!" someone shouted, and everyone started laughing. They didn't understand beauty. They wanted to destroy everything they didn't understand. Elliott felt Alan rising inside him. Only this time, the cause felt just. Right was on his side. He allowed Alan to take over.

It was the testimony of some of the younger children that saved Elliott from being expelled from school permanently. They explained that Joey Davison had said something to Elliott and laughed. Nobody heard what it was; Joey Davison wasn't telling and Elliott couldn't remember – it was Alan who had heard the comment, not he. The children reported that Elliott had moved his head in a funny way and then launched himself at Joey Davison with a force that took everyone by surprise. He seemed to be in the grip of an uncontrollable fury. He knocked the bigger boy to the ground, quickly knelt on his arms and began pummelling his face. Elliott was reported to be mute during the attack; indeed the whole playground was stunned into silence by the swiftness and ferocity that was so out of character. The baying crowd now stood frozen to the spot by an exhibition of such naked anger, the chant of "Fight, fight, fight" now stagnant on their lips as they saw the real impact of their goading.

After thirty seconds or so a teacher barged his way through the silent crowd and picked Elliott up by the shoulders, lifting him clear off the ground, arms still swinging punches for a few seconds like a chicken running around with its head cut off.

Elliott was immediately suspended from school, and when the report came back that Joey Davison had a broken eye socket it seemed likely he would be expelled. He spent the week of the investigation in his turret, brooding, angry. Sometimes he would try to repair the engine; often he would close the shutters and sit in the dark, trying to make sense of a world that didn't seem to like having him in it. When the full facts of the situation came to light thanks to the younger boys, it was decided that Elliott could return to school, provocation providing the mitigating circumstances for his behaviour.

That week he had spent in the turret remained with him. His mother would bring him lunch; his father would sometimes sit with him and help with the engine. Neither rebuked the boy. He wouldn't talk to them, just scowl. The world was so full of injustice. The words 'it's not fair' kept going round his head and yet were so impotent in describing the monolithic slab of wrongness that seemed to surround him like a shroud.

Elliott was left alone after that incident, his years of being the target for bullies finally over. Even Daisuke was wary of him for a while. Joey Davison soon returned to the school and confined his violence to the rugby pitch, where it seemed to find its natural outlet.

"Where the fuck am I?" The croaky voice sliced through the darkness. Elliott was hauled unceremoniously out of his reverie. "Hello?" the voice echoed. "Is there anyone there?"

Elliott jolted slightly in surprise, the bucket making a brief scraping sound on the floor. The ensuing silence was disturbed only by the heavy breathing of the man tied to a chair seated in the middle of the room.

"Who...who is there? Why am I tied up? Hello?"

"Hello," said Elliott. "How are you feeling?"

"What? What do you mean? What's happened? Where am I?

Hello! Talk to me – what the fuck is going on?"

"You had a car accident. You were driving too fast, skidded off the road and hit a tree. I found you and brought you here. Now, how is your head? Your neck? I checked you in the car and I don't think there's seriously wrong, just a few bumps and bruises."

"Nothing broken, I don't think, but my head hurts. And my arms. Why am I tied up?"

"I brought a bucket if you need the toilet," said Elliott, his voice as incongruous in the darkness as a torch beam. "I'm sitting on it, but I can get it set up if you need it now."

There was no answer from the darkness.

"What's your name?" asked Elliott.

The man started to answer, but his voice croaked and caught in his throat. Elliott had not taken his eyes from where he guessed the man's head would be based on his voice, and he now reached forwards and put his right hand against the man's cheek. Startled by the sudden touch, the man jerked his head away. Elliott took a firm grip of his jaw with thumb and forefinger and forced his head back to face front. The man fought to break free, but Elliott's grip was strong and his determination stronger. After a few moments the man's efforts weakened, then he suddenly started thrashing again, freeing himself from Elliott's hand.

In the dark could be heard the sound of something being unscrewed, then the clink of a bottle being put onto the floor. Elliott reached forwards with both hands and grabbed the man's face again, this time with greater force. His mouth opened involuntarily under the strain. Quickly Elliott grabbed the bottle of water from the floor and poured some into the man's mouth.

"It's water," said Elliott. "Drink."

After a few moments the man flung his head from side to side again in a panicky motion. Elliott lifted the bottle and began to gently pour the water over the man's face. Quickly he stopped squirming and positioned his open mouth below the water stream, drinking greedily. When Elliott could once again hear the splash of water on the man's face he lifted down the bottle.

"Okay," he said. "I hope that's better. Now, what's your name?"

"Fu-fu-fuck you."

"I would be really most grateful if you wouldn't swear. Come on now, what's your name?"

"Where am I? Who are you?"

"Look, I can hardly hold a conversation with someone when I don't know their name, can I? Tell me your name, and we can move forward. I'll explain everything. But I need to know your name."

There was a pause, then the man said, "Ian. My name is Ian."

"Okay, Ian. Great. Pleased to meet you."

"Ha. Who are you? Where am I?"

"What's the last thing you remember? Before waking up here, I mean."

"I-I had an accident. Skidded off the road. Am I...am I dead?"

Elliott laughed briefly. "Sorry, Ian, that's unkind of me to laugh. No, you are not dead. You survived the accident. I rescued you, actually."

"Who are you? Please. Just tell me where I am. What do you want from me?"

"We'll come to that. Do you remember what happened just before the accident?"

"I've been trying to think. How I could have ended up here. But I can't work it out."

"Just before. The accident. Any ideas?"

"No. I was driving along the road, just a normal day, nothing happened. I can't think why you've tied me up here."

"So you don't remember anything just before driving way too fast round a corner and skidding off the road? Nothing at all? Try this line of thought. Who might have been first on the scene of the accident? Hmm?"

There was a pause. Elliott thought he could hear the realisations snapping together.

"Some...body who was driving behind. That guy in the Astra. Is that you? The...pri...the person who kept trying to stop me getting past?"

"Almost. I'd prefer to say that I was the person you were harassing. Let's get that the right way round from the start, shall we? My name is Bob. Well, it's not, but that's what we'll use. I don't suppose you could pick me out in an ID parade from the little that you saw of me as you screamed abuse while overtaking on a blind bend and almost killing me. Besides, we're a long way from there. So. Here we are. Now you remember. That's good."

There was no response from the void. Elliott could only imagine what the man would be thinking. How could anyone be expected to process such information in these circumstances? He paused, listening to the man wriggle and squirm in his chair, testing his bindings. Eventually, when only heavy breathing could be heard, he spoke.

"So," he said again. "Ian. I expect you're wondering why I've brought you here." He paused, then laughed. "Sorry, Ian, just kidding, I've always wanted to say that. I have said it a few times, actually, in meetings and things, but this is one occasion when it is actually the exact right thing to say. Couldn't resist it. Sorry." His laughter petered out.

"I'm sorry," said Ian weakly.

"What's that?" replied Elliott.

"I'm sorry."

"Sorry? What for?"

"I'm sorry I pissed you off. I apologise. Please let me go."

"What are you apologising for, Ian?"

"For whatever I did that made you...you know..." The next words choked in his throat, making them difficult for Elliott to hear.

"Kidnap you?" Elliott paused. "Is that what you were going to say? Kidnap? Yes, I suppose I have done that, haven't I? So what do you think you might have done that drove me to 'you know' you?"

"Well, I guess...look, I'm sorry, please don't hurt me any more. I can't see you, I don't know what..."

"What do you mean, 'any more'?" Elliott interrupted. "I haven't hurt you at all yet. Any injuries you have are self-inflicted by driving like a total moron. How's the head, by the way? Any better?"

"It throbs. Um, thank you for the water. It helped."

"My pleasure. Very good. Now, tell me what you think you did to make me 'you know' you."

"Um, well, I guess I drove a bit aggressively, didn't I? I'm sorry. I was in a hurry, I was late."

"Late? What for?"

"A sales meeting with my boss. I was taking a short cut through the lanes, didn't want to be late. He gets impatient and my job is results-based and not very secure, so sometimes I have to drive like that." Ian spoke tentatively, in bursts, as if his thoughts were starting to come together and he was working out the situation.

In the dark, Elliott silently leaned forwards so that his face was right in front of Ian's. His voice dropped an octave. "Well, you didn't get there much quicker, did you?"

Ian whimpered slightly. Elliott stood up and walked around the room, circling the chair in the centre. He extended his right arm, allowing the fingers to touch the wall as he walked. They made a drumming sound each time they scraped across a window.

"What do you believe in, Ian?" he said.

"What?"

"I need you to do a bit of thinking for me. I need to get to know you, understand you a bit. So talk to me. What do you believe in?"

"I-I don't know. I'm tied to a chair. My head is thumping. I, I can't think straight. What do you want me to say?"

"I want you to tell me what you believe in. That's all."

"Then will you let me go?"

"No."

The man whimpered again, making a sound not dissimilar to the one a cat once made in France as its kittens were being put down. Elliott had not enjoyed his French exchange experience.

Elliott continued to pace and drum. Pace and drum. After one more circuit of the room he turned and began to walk in the opposite direction. Drum and pace. Drum and pace. Eventually Ian broke the silence.

"Well, my dad always told me to expect the worst, then you'll always be pleasantly surprised."

"That's not a belief, Ian. That's a philosophy of someone unable to accept responsibility for their own future. What other bits of 'advice' did your father give you?"

"He told me to look out for number one because no one else in life was going to do it for me."

"Well, at least that's a borderline belief, I suppose."

"I believe in hard work," said Ian quickly, as if by giving Elliott what he wanted as quickly as possible he might be untied. "In being rewarded for initiative. Yeah, looking out for number one. Everything happens for a reason, just make sure the things that happen to you are the best things possible. I'm just a foot soldier, but I want to work my way up. Having confidence in what you do – self-confidence is the trait of winners. Encouraging excellence, expect it in yourself and in others. Don't rely on anyone else." He fell silent again. Elliott had stopped walking during the short speech, memorising each of the points being made. Once the last words wandered out into the darkness he continued pacing once again.

"And do you believe in God, Ian?" he asked.

"Not in the typical way," the disembodied voice replied from the darkness after a pause. "I don't believe in a supreme being who is controlling all of our destinies. You make your own luck in this world: if you want something you have to go out and get it. Whether there is a Heaven and Hell I've no idea. If there is a God, I reckon he's got a pretty sick sense of humour. Look at you, for example." He snorted to underline the point.

Silence filled the room again, aside from the tapping of Elliott's fingers. He waited a few extra moments before speaking again to ensure the inappropriate overconfidence of the last point was underlined.

"How would you sum up your cause, Ian? The thing you believe in so much that you would fight for it?"

This time the reply came without hesitation. "Freedom. Freedom of choice, to choose to live what life I want to live without being told what to do. Without being tied to a chair. For example."

"Hah, very good. Pithy." Elliott stopped walking for a moment, the last footstep echoing just for a moment on the white plaster walls. Then he began pacing again in the same direction. He was searching for something tangible to grasp on to, a belief system that he could deconstruct. "And what," he continued, "would you say to me if I suggested that all of what you have said is a total load of drivel? That you have taken a bunch of ideas, some of which are interesting, some not exactly thoroughly thought through, and combined them to make something deeply unpleasant? How would you react if I said that although I could agree – or for that matter disagree – with any of the policies of your personal manifesto, the overall ideology that it amounts to is one that is to be despised and reviled?"

"I-I don't know. You have me tied up and I don't know who you are. I don't know what you want from me."

"Do you earn good money, Ian?"

"Um, yeah, I do pretty well, for my age."

"You must do – that was a pretty nice car I dragged you out of."

"How is it? The car, I mean."

"Not in good shape, I'm afraid." A groan came out of the darkness. "Oh dear. You *are* insured, aren't you?"

"Of course," said Ian. "But that's the first set of wheels I've really loved."

"So get it fixed. Big deal."

There was a pause before Ian spoke again, this time a little more quietly, as if nervous of the reaction that might come from out of the darkness. "It's not actually my car. We…we have a bonus scheme at work: whoever has the best sales figures in the team at the end of the month gets to drive the sports car for the following month. I've had it for the last four months." Was that a glimmer of pride showing itself briefly?

"Nice incentive scheme," said Elliott insincerely. "And now you're feeling embarrassed that you're the idiot who wrecked it." He presumed that Ian nodded. It wasn't easy to hear a nod. It was more like he could feel its presence. "That motivates you, does it? Being able to drive a flash car?"

"Well, yeah, of course. I get respect from my work colleagues. It's recognition from my boss that I've done a good job."

"And when you drive it down the road, do people look at you, in your expensive car? That isn't actually yours?" *Rat-a-tat-tat* went Elliott's fingers across the shelf upon which a toy train once ran, as he walked slowly round and round the room. Something was forming. The car. The earnings. The belief in hard work. Was this something he could pick apart? Was it a sufficiently robust belief system for him to remove bit by bit?

"Yeah, they do look at me, actually," replied Ian.

"And what do you believe they might be thinking, those people, when they look at you, roaring past?"

Ian paused, as if he was unsure of himself for a moment. Elliott quickened his pace ever so slightly.

"I don't know. Not really thought about it. I suppose they might be admiring the car."

"That's possible. They might be car enthusiasts. Do you think they are admiring you?"

"I guess that's possible too."

"What is it you like about that car, Ian?"

"It's nice to drive."

"Is it? That's interesting. See, I've no idea about cars. I'm an A-to-B kind of guy. I don't even really understand what the phrase 'it's nice to drive' actually means."

"It's got poke," said Ian. "Accelerates well."

"And that comes in handy, does it?" Asked Elliott.

"Well, no, but it is fun. Got past you pretty easily, didn't I?"

"Yes," said Elliott, an emotionless bark. "Ha. Yes, you did, didn't you?" *Tappity-tap.* "Ian, do you mind if I make a suggestion?"

"I don't have a great deal of alternative, do I?"

"No. No, you don't, do you? I've an observation on that to make as well, actually. But first, a thought about you and that car. I'd like to suggest that when you drive around in that expensive car, a car virtually designed to ensure that everyone *knows* it is an expensive car, what you are enjoying is the very fact that everyone knows you are in an expensive car. It is the equivalent of standing in the middle of the town centre," Elliott stopped walking and turned in the dark to lean towards the man in the chair, "and shouting at the top of your voice, 'I've got more money than any of you, you bunch of losers.'"

Spit flew from his mouth as the words screamed from somewhere deep inside him. He wiped his mouth with the back of his hand and took a moment to compose himself before continuing to speak in a tone that was abruptly calm once again. The pacing recommenced, this time in the opposite direction. *Tap-drum-tap.*

"The irony of all this, I find, is that the reaction you elicit in other people is actually the precise opposite of the one you are trying to achieve. What people are really thinking when you drive past is, What a complete tosser. What a show-off, a braggart, a deeply unpleasant individual. Isn't that fascinating?"

Elliott paused, but no reply came. He began pacing again, his fingers taking up their position on the wall.

"Showing off is such bad manners, don't you think?" he continued. "Never beat another person's story. Basic rule of dinner party conversation. And yet sit a man in a car which is specifically designed to show off, and he thinks that he is actually more important than other cars on the road. Even if – and this bit I really love – even if it's not actually his car and he's only borrowing it so that his boss can get him to sell more stuff to make his boss more money. I don't know about you, Ian, but it seems to me the ironies are rather piling up on themselves here, are they not?"

Tap-tap-tap. No answer from the chair.

"You are here for a reason, Ian. Everything happens for a reason. Wasn't that one of the Christmas cracker philosophies you told me ten minutes ago? Well, would you like to know what that reason is in this instance, Ian? Why you are here, specifically?"

Elliott's fingers passed over the door. He continued walking another half the circumference of the room, then turned left, took two silent steps forwards and leaned forwards so that his face was positioned directly behind Ian's head. He spoke softly into the dark.

"You're going to have to work with me a bit here, Ian. Okay? I need you to contribute. Get involved." No response. Return to the wall, continue to pace, fingers trailing and tapping.

"Okay," whispered Ian eventually, in halting reply.

Elliott stood and continued talking from behind Ian. "I made a cake once, Ian. I did. I'm not really a cake-maker, if truth be told. But I made this cake. I had flour. Eggs. Sugar. Butter. Vanilla. Chocolate. Lots of delicious things. And when I took it out of the oven, do you know what? It tasted awful. How can you put such lovely things together and end up with something awful? You are awful, Ian. You are a rude man. You are impolite. And that cannot be allowed to continue. Would you like to know why?"

"Yes please."

"You are not a defender of freedom, Ian. You are not a foot

soldier in the free market economy. You are a show-off. A rude person who has insufficient respect for other people. You are a fraud. You live a lie, driving an expensive car that is not even yours but enjoying the feeling of false respect that you mistakenly think it gives you. You are a shallow, insignificant little worm and you are now entirely dependent upon me. As well as your arms and legs being bound, the door is locked. The windows are locked. Even if you could open them, we are fifty feet up at the top of a tower. We are in a soundproof room, so shouting and screaming will make no difference. You are no longer driving in a car being unknowingly derided by everyone you pass. You are now in a room being openly derided solely by me."

Time for a pause. Elliott shut his eyes for a moment, then opened them again. Was there any difference between shutting your eyes and keeping them open when in a completely dark room? He tried it again. Other than the smell, the sound of Ian's breathing was the only sensory impact within the room, yet it seemed to be louder when his eyes were shut. He thought this strange, but could not find an explanation for the phenomenon.

When he felt he had given enough time for his words to have sunk home, Elliott spoke again.

"I'm going to leave you now, Ian," he said. "I'm going to go out of the room and not come back until morning. It's about 7.30pm now. We're going to be here for a while, you and me. Because the good news is that although you are virtually beyond contempt as a human being, I have not given up on you. I am, in fact, here to help you. I am your saviour. I am here to show you where your beliefs are flawed, to break down the infrastructure of lies that bind together to become your world. You and I will then put them back together in a way that will make you a decent human being. In short, Ian, I am going to teach you some manners."

Elliott felt his way to the doorway. He pulled the door open and stood facing inwards, knowing that the man slumped in the chair would be able to see only a dim silhouette.

"Your actions have created this situation for yourself. You are responsible for your current circumstance. What could you have done to bring about such an extreme reaction in me?

40

"We're going to talk again, Ian. There are things that I need you to understand. Be patient with me. Help me to help you, and we can get this over with quickly." He smiled into the dark.

"See you in the morning," he said brightly, and closed the door.

Chapter 4

Thursday, 8pm

Using tea tree shower gel had been Naomi's idea. It tingled in all the right places. Before meeting his future wife Elliott had been a strictly Marks & Spencer's own brand soap kind of guy – shower gels were for the breed of unrealistically handsome men who appeared in perfume adverts. Now he felt cleansed of both the grime of the day and the doubt in his head, his sense of purpose rebooted.

He dried himself with a warm towel hanging on the bathroom radiator. "I'm clean!" he said out loud to the bathroom tiles.

Next he put on a clean pair of boxer shorts, green corduroy trousers, a light blue cotton shirt and navy blue cashmere jumper. He chose by habit, his thoughts elsewhere. After spreading the towel back on the radiator, he picked up the old clothes and placed them in the laundry basket.

The project would succeed only if something primeval was achieved; if some common ground was established. It wasn't about imposing his own beliefs, but establishing some fundamentals. Values are like bacteria, there are some that you simply must have. So it had been for Elliott forever, instilled in him by his mother.

By the age of seventeen Elliott had managed to hold on to the few relationships that had transformed into tenuous friendship. There were seven of them in total, a disparate bunch bound together by a common social awkwardness. The three young women and four young men would sit in the same corner of the sixth form common room every break and every lunchtime, whatever the weather. They might play Risk, discuss homework, sometimes one might just read a book quietly, but they always lounged in the same area like a pride of rather diffident lions.

There was even a brief period of five weeks where Elliott could honestly say that he had a girlfriend. Jayne was Elliott's only real equal in history class and had the quiet determination of someone who was very rarely wrong about anything. She excelled in her ability to imply. Pretty when you got to know her, hair aggressively tied back with a multitude of grips. Her parents lived in a large house with a swimming pool in another village. Jayne invited the gang over one Sunday afternoon when her parents were away and surprised everyone by producing a keg of cider. The others had been rather bashful about the alcohol and Jayne would have drunk most of it if Elliott hadn't kept her company for some of the time. She had begun flirting with him from the moment he had arrived and it felt as if he was being dragged along by unseen mystical forces.

She had taken Elliott in hand that afternoon, awkwardly in her parents' bedroom, before vomiting in their en suite toilet. At school the next day it was assumed by the rest of the gang that the two of them were now going out with each other, and so they continued to act the part. After five weeks of a relationship in which Elliott would have best described his role as passive, Jayne decided to bring matters to a close one day at school. It was his birthday, and each of the others had given him a card and in some cases a small present, but when it came to Jayne's turn she not only had no card, she told him that she was not around that weekend as they had planned, and anyway it was probably best if they didn't see each other any more. Elliott was inwardly heartbroken, outwardly nonchalant.

It so happened that Jayne's birthday was two weeks later. He sought the advice of his mother on how he should respond to her snub. Her wry smile at the question and wise counsel reminded Elliott of the position the family held with certain parts of the local community. That lunchtime in the common room Jayne opened her cards and presents. When it came to Elliott's turn, some of the girls tried to change the subject, to save him (or was it themselves?) the embarrassment. However, instead of making a show of not getting her a present as everyone expected, he boldly reached into his briefcase and brought out not only a card, but also a single red rose. He kissed her on the cheek and wished her a happy birthday.

His mother had reminded him of their core values and he had simply done the right thing.

He carried the laundry basket through the lounge and into the kitchen, avoiding the stares from around the room as he went. Opening the door to his right, he went down the few steps into the buttery. Amidst the stress of getting Ian in place he had forgotten to empty the last load of washing. He hung up the wet clothes then put in the next bundle, but did not start the machine. Next he took a bottle of wine from the rack screwed into the wall. Removing the cork, he poured a small glass to settle his nerves and took it through to the lounge where he sat, perched on the edge of one of the black leather sofas.

Naomi watched him from out of one photograph. There were eight stares in total throughout the flat, six of which came from pictures of his wife. There was one in the bedroom, two in the hallway which led from the bedroom to the lounge, and three in the lounge itself. Four of the pictures featured Elliott and Naomi laughing together. The other two were of Naomi on her own, including one larger studio portrait that she had given to him shortly after the cancer had been diagnosed as terminal. This took pride of place as the largest photograph on a bookcase in the lounge and was the one they had agreed that he would talk to after she had gone, that he would think of as a hotline to her whenever he needed it, and it was this one that he particularly did not look at now.

The eighteen months since Naomi had been taken from him had been rather blank. It was as if his sense of purpose had been put on hold. Someone had pressed the pause button on his life, gone to make a cup of tea and forgotten to come back. Now he had a cause, a chance to make a real difference. He needed to see it through even though he knew Naomi would not have approved. Hah. That's putting it mildly, he thought. She had always told him to stop complaining and to take action, but breaking the law was never something she would have condoned.

Flanking Naomi were his father on one side and his mother on the other. The black-and-white studio portrait of his father, all sideburns and lapels, staring purposefully into the lens and out the other side, ending up in Elliott's heart where it inspired love and longing in equal measure. Elliott didn't speak to this photograph too often, but it did speak to him. He had loved his parents equally, but Mother was the rock, something upon which to rely, whereas Father had been the inspiration.

On the end of the bookcase, as if protecting the photographs from falling off the edge, was a foot-high brass bust of Mahatma Gandhi, a birthday present from Naomi. It had been a running joke between them that Elliott was like the Indian solicitor-turned-politician. They both wanted to change the world for the better without making it worse in the process. She would tease him that there were only three differences between the two of them: a religious belief, a good pair of trousers, and the fact Gandhi had actually changed something. On the bookshelf below sat his autobiography, resting incongruously next to an eight-volume biography of Winston Churchill. The bookcase was lined precisely against the edge of the door to the turret, taking the level of secrecy from not really very secret at all to maybe just a little bit secret to the chronically unobservant.

Elliott removed a book from the shelf, placed it on the table in front of the sofas and opened it at the bookmarked page on brainwashing. He read for the fourth time that day the section on adding guilt to the (hopefully) now established identity crisis before draining the glass and walking out to the lobby where his shoes awaited him.

He climbed the first flight of stairs, past Benny Daker's front door, and on up to the top flat where Lucy and Phoebe lived. The door had been left ajar for him and as he entered the smell of cooking surprised him. The layout of the flat was very different to his own, but nonetheless familiar. He went down the hallway and turned into the master bedroom that had been converted to a kitchen when the house had been split into flats by Elliott and Lucy. His timing was perfect. Lucy was approaching the large table that dominated the half of the room that wasn't kitchen, carrying two bowls of carbonara made with linguini.

Phoebe jumped out of her seat and threw her arms around his waist.

"Perfect timing, Uncle E," she said, squeezing. Elliott ruffled her hair in return.

"Nice top," he said to Phoebe. "Is it new?"

"What, this old thing?" Phoebe replied, giggling and pulling at the bottom of the top so that she could show it without wrinkles. "Thanks again, Uncle E, I love it." It was a plain grey sleeveless top with a scoop neck. A bland item of clothing that the lady in the shop had called timeless. It was therefore an ideal present for Phoebe that fitted with everything in her existing wardrobe. He had simply to hand the scribbled piece of paper Lucy had provided to the assistant.

As they sat down at the table, Elliott turned to Lucy. "I thought we were having lamb curry," he said in a voice pregnant with disappointment.

"Oh, I'm just back in," said Lucy, handing a bowl to Benny. "I promised Joey I'd have the new change management plan ready for his board meeting on Monday. So I've whipped up a quick but, I can assure you, delicious carbonara. So much to do, ha-ha." The anaemic laugh betrayed a subtlety of communication between brother and sister that no outsider could hope to penetrate. Familiarity does not breed contempt, but layer upon layer of experience and adjustment. Elliott sat down at the table.

Benny took one bowl from Lucy and passed it to Phoebe, then took the other and placed it in front of Elliott. "You sit down. I'll get the others," he said to Lucy, almost pushing her into the remaining chair, then went into the kitchen to get the remaining two bowls.

"Where's the Parmesan?" Benny called.

"In the fridge," Lucy called back. "I grated some into a bowl." She began to get up out of her chair.

"Got it!" called Benny.

"But I was looking forwards to lamb curry," said Elliott. The bottom of his lip pouted almost imperceptibly. Lucy sighed, settling back in her chair and looking pointedly back at him.

"I know," she said. "I *was* going to do that. But *then* I thought I'd do a quick carbonara instead." She glared at her brother. Then she turned and smiled at Phoebe. "I know you like carbonara too, darling, so I thought it would be okay." Lucy picked up a bottle of wine and poured some into Phoebe's glass, who didn't tell her 'when'. Lucy stopped at half a glass, ignoring the stare from Elliott.

He had always thought his sister to be rather plain, but others seemed to find her attractive. She was barely over five feet tall with long black hair which she kept in a practical half-up, half-down style, framing her strong jaw. Her teeth didn't fit together properly, two snaggle fangs giving her a face an appeal that Elliott just had to take other people's word for. The overall effect was of a teacher you might fancy but wouldn't admit it to your mates, but when you did you then discovered that they all fancied her too.

"When exactly did Joey Davison actually ask you for this change management plan?" asked Elliott.

"This morning," replied Lucy, filling her own glass. "Joey has been a very important client for me, Elliott, you know that."

"This morning? Ridiculous. That guy was a bully at school and he's a bully now. Lucy, you should tell him where to get off. That's not fair."

"Well, this carbonara is absolutely delicious, my dear," said Benny.

"Change management," chuntered Elliott. "What a load of nonsense."

Lucy spoke with the voice of a patient mother who had seen it all before. "Well, obviously it is not nonsense, otherwise I wouldn't be doing it. We're using a new personality profiling system. It's very interesting."

"I'm not a fan of personality profiling systems," said Elliott. "They try to define people. I don't think you can do that with a few questions on a computer."

"Yes, well," said Lucy, "that's the typical initial response of someone with your personality type."

"No it's not, it happens to be what *I* think. You always try and put people in boxes."

"People like you hate being put in a box."

"Stop saying, 'people like you'! I am me, unique, we are all infinitely variable and changeable. Stop trying to define me!"

Lucy looked straight ahead, at the wall. "Hmmm," she said. "Clearly 'dominant'."

Benny raised his glass to the middle of the table. "Would it be loquacious of me to propose a toast?" Elliott glanced at his watch.

"I think the word is procacious, Benny," said Elliott kindly, pouring red wine into Lucy's glass. "But no, it would not. You fire away."

Lucy, Elliott and Benny all lifted their glasses towards Phoebe. "To a delightful child, now coming of age and becoming a woman. Phoebe, you are the utter embodification of what Chuck Berry had in mind when he wrote 'Sweet Little Sixteen'."

"Oh, Benny, do you mind?" laughed Phoebe.

"Okay, that may have been stretching the simile a little far. Suffice it sufficiently to say that if I had a daughter, I would be twice the man I am if she were half the woman you are turning out to be."

"Thank you, Benny," said Phoebe, lifting her own glass and nodding a smile in his direction. The four wine glasses met in the middle of the table and clinked, producing different notes that seemed to mesh together in a chord.

"Do you know," laughed Benny, "I do believe we just made an F sharp minor!"

"Is sixteen the coming of age?" said Lucy, ignoring the bait. "I thought it was eighteen. When you get to vote."

"Surely," said Benny, "it is the reaching of sexual maturity?"

"Um, hello?" said Phoebe. "I am here, you know."

"I think you'll find," said Elliott, "it's a religious thing. Like the Jewish bar mitzvah, which happens when children are thirteen. It's about being accountable for their actions. It's all in the Bible."

"Actually," said Phoebe, "for girls it's called the *bat* mitzvah, and it is age twelve. So I came of age four years ago. Thanks for noticing."

"Well, I think the coming of age varies for everyone," said Lucy with finality, drinking her wine. She paused, then, "Having said that, I agree with my dear brother, it's all about taking on responsibility. Something we need to discuss, judging by the state of your bedroom floor." Lucy bent over her food as Phoebe glared at her, unnoticed. Elliott looked at Phoebe, his eyebrows raised in a warning which she reluctantly heeded.

"Well, whatever you now are," said Benny, "I think you are peaches clean, a simply splendiflerous young lady, and I am proud to know you."

"Oh, Benny," laughed Lucy, "the phrase is 'peachy keen'. You really are such a phoney. Where did you drag that one up from?"

"Firstly, Phoebe, my utter darling, I am not a phoney. John Lennon was a phoney – I happen to think Mark Chapman was right on that score, even if his punishment was somewhat unrepresentative to the crime. *I* mean every word that I say." Benny held a forkful of pasta, which he intermittently pointed at Phoebe as he warmed to his theme. "There are certain people in this world who could be classed as thinkers – take your uncle, for example." The fork was flicked in Elliott's direction. A small piece of pasta flew across the table and landed with an indiscernible *plop* in front of Elliott. He stared at the morsel. It was wrong. It was out of place. Elliott silently tried to pick it up, the slimy spiral pasta squirming out from his fingers three times before he achieved sufficient purchase. He finally lifted the offending item and placed it carefully on the edge of his bowl, far from his own uneaten carbonara, which seemed to shrink away to the other side.

"Certain people like to think over things," continued Benny. "They think over them a lot. They think over and they overthink. They mull, they ponder, they coagulate. And where does it get them, when they have thunk everything there is to be thunk? Into an ever-decreasing cycle of introversioning, down and down into a pit of unanswerable half-thought-through theorems. They are never happy with the present, instead constantly searching for something different than their current state. I am not so burdened. I have no truck with philosophy, with deep thought. I am anchored by froth. It is the garnish of the world which sustains me, which provides my pabulum."

"Pabulum?" said Lucy, laughing. "Oh come on, Benny, you're just making it up now."

"No," said Elliott. "That one's right, actually. It means intellectual nourishment."

Benny pointed his fork at Elliott, said, "Thank you, dear boy", then finally put the pasta that remained on his fork into his mouth. He continued to speak, the words now slightly muffled. "You see, I am an optimist. Which is actually a very difficult thing to be. It's the rebellious streak in me. My mother was not an optimist. She was downright bloody miserable in fact. If you asked my mother whether the glass was half-full or half-empty, her answer would be, 'Why are you using that glass? That's our best glass, that is, why don't you use a plastic cup? Honestly, Benny, you're always causing trouble.'"

Phoebe giggled happily as she took a sip from her wine, trying to hide the fact she didn't like the taste, Elliott noticed. He risked another peek at his watch. He needed time to prepare before the next session in the morning.

Benny leant towards Phoebe and spoke with a conspiratorial air. "I have also found that people are less inclined to be judgemental if they believe me to be inconsequential." He picked up a sprig of parsley from the top of the pasta, flourished it at the table in general, then popped it into his mouth. "Little life tip for you on your sixteenth birthday."

Elliott absorbed the happy domesticity of the scene for a moment. The tight coil of fear and excitement inside him loosened for a moment. Phoebe's cheerful gurgles especially were like a tonic to him, and he accepted the distraction eagerly.

"Elliott," said Lucy as a quiet descended over the table, "what time can you be around tomorrow?"

"I should be in the office most of the day, so available. Why?"

"I just need you to let someone in." Lucy continued to eat her pasta with a relaxed manner that Elliott did not trust.

"Into your flat?" he asked her.

"No," she replied, "yours."

"And why would I want to do that?" he said with a flatness that turned it into a statement.

"Don't be dramatic, Elliott. Please just do as I ask and let them in. They won't be long."

"Lucy, who are 'they'?"

"It's just a photographer. It's no big deal." She plunged the final forkful of pasta into her mouth, placed the cutlery silently into the bowl, a feat requiring no little skill, and pushed the plate fractionally across the table, away from her.

Elliott eyed his sister suspiciously. She seemed to go out of her way not to return his gaze, but instead looked out of the kitchen window, over the converted stables, past the wooden fence marking the end of their world and across the fields of barley that stretched away from the house and into the part of the world he thought of as 'not home'. He had read once that an older sister loves her younger brother until the brother becomes bigger than she is and is thenceforth able to hit back. Elliott hit back with words. He had always felt able to outwit his sister. And yet somehow he seemed to always end up losing the argument.

"Lucy, why would a photographer need access to my flat?" Elliott spoke with a studied offhand inflection, a manner he had heard so many families use with each other in his offices over the years, trying so incredibly hard to avoid offence and confrontation that an argument became almost inevitable.

"It's for a thing." She paused, then seemed to accept defeat. "A valuation."

Elliott did not speak. Yes, it *is* a big deal, he did not say. Because if you want a valuation, he didn't continue, yet have no interest in selling the house, the only explanation is that you are going to offer the building for security on a loan. This would mean that if the loan could not be repaid, then your share of the house would go to who-ever loaned you the money, who could then force the sale of the house in order to release their cash. But then why tell me that you are getting a valuation? You wouldn't need me to know if you used your half of the house as security – the three flats are under separate legal title, with Benny's flat owned jointly. Unless the loan was bigger than the value of just your flat. But you are more sensible than that, so there must be some other reason why the estate agent wants to come into my flat as well as yours. And why do you need a loan of a size that needs security anyway? Finally, you have raised the issue in front of the others to make sure I can't quiz you further, which means there is factor that I cannot yet fathom. He stopped not talking.

"I'm not letting a photographer into my flat," he said.

Phoebe had been eyeing the two of them. Elliott could tell her antennae were up. "Is this something to do with my dad?" she asked her mother.

"Of course not," said Lucy, poking at her pasta in a way that made it clear she was lying.

51

"I knew it," said Phoebe. "What does that fucker want now?"

"Phoebe!" said Lucy. "I will not have language like that coming out of your mouth. Your father is a...well, he's your father, and you should show him some respect."

Phoebe didn't answer for a moment. Elliott watched her battling with her emotions. Any mention of her father brought a response that only the truly ignored could recognise.

"Well, for one thing it is my birthday," said Phoebe quietly. "And he is not here. Again."

"Would you want him to be here?" asked her mother.

"Yes," Phoebe replied, with a tremble that betrayed her calmness. "I would love it if he walked in right now. So that I could tell him to fuck off."

Elliott stalked the periphery of the conversation, biding his time. He knew only too well that Paolo's business activities were based on a combination of bullying, bribes and backhanders. If a highly successful and extremely dubious businessman like Paolo Brice had something to do with his house being used as security for a loan, then Elliott had cause to be very concerned indeed.

The four of them sat in silence for a few moments. All Elliott could hear was the sound of Benny chewing.

"So," said Lucy brightly. "How was school, Phoebe? Haven't seen Mikey for a while. When are you going to bring him round again?"

Phoebe rolled her eyes in Elliott's general direction, her head tilted to one side at a forty-five-degree angle. "Lucy," said Elliott, "Phoebe hasn't been seeing Mikey for two weeks. They are just good friends now."

"Oh. Yes, of course, sorry, sweetheart, I did know that. Of course I did. Ooh, that reminds me, how did judo go today?"

"Fine," said Phoebe.

"She's being modest," said Elliott. "She totally pulverised her opponent." He leaned towards Benny conspiratorially. "A girl who just happens to be trying to go out with Mikey. Not that he wants anything to do with it, he's still obsessed with Phoebe."

"Hoo-hoo, nice one, Phoebe," said Benny. "That'll learn her. Don't mess with the Phoebster."

Elliott put down his fork into an empty bowl. "Lucy, that may not have been the lamb I was hoping for, but it was delicious. Thank you." He lifted his chair back without a sound.

"You're not going, are you?" asked Lucy.

"I'm afraid so. I have a lot to do tomorrow."

"But it's my birthday," said Phoebe.

"I know, darling, but you're sixteen. You should be going to the pub with your mates, not hanging out with old gits like us."

"Excuse me!" said Lucy.

"Okay, old gits like me and Benny."

"Old, gitty and proud," announced Benny, tugging at an imaginary cap.

Elliott lifted his arm and looked at his watch longer than was absolutely necessary to read the time from it. "Oh, maybe I have a few more minutes," he said. "After all, we probably need to discuss this." He took a white sealed envelope from his back pocket and threw it onto the table in front of Phoebe.

His niece looked at the envelope, then back up at him. "What is it?" she asked.

"Ah," he replied. "Just a little something."

Phoebe ripped open the envelope and looked at the front of the card. As she did so, two tickets fell out onto the table. She picked them up quickly, read even quicker and let out a yelp. Pushing back her chair, she ran around the table and hugged Elliott round the neck, saying, "Thank you thank you thank you thank you." Lucy shot him a 'What's going on?' smile. She leaned over to read what was on the tickets, then looked at him again, none the wiser.

Phoebe finally let go of Elliott's neck. She picked up the tickets and brandished them at her mother and Benny.

"Katzenjammer! My favourite band! Two tickets for the London concert!" Then she picked up the card. "And Uncle E has offered to drive us there and back!" She jumped up and down on the spot and squealed, "Oh my God!"

"Nice work, Elliott," said Benny, and offered him a fist bump. Elliott looked at it for a moment, then grabbed the fist with his hand and shook it.

"Who are you going to take with you?" asked Lucy.

"I don't know yet. Penny, maybe. Or Mikey. So excited!"

"Well," said Elliott, spotting his opportunity. "As the party seems to have climaxed, may I be excused? Lots of work to do tonight." Lucy eyed him suspiciously, but before she could quiz him as to why he was working in an evening, Phoebe spoke up.

"Of course, Uncle E. Thanks for my wonderful presents." She gave him another big hug. Elliott absorbed the love as if he was a car refilling its tanks at a petrol station.

He finally left the kitchen with a round of modest goodnights and strolled slowly down the hallway, calmly opened the front door, and walked onto the top of the stairs, shutting the door gently behind him.

As it clicked shut he turned and shot down the stairs two at a time. He bolted past Benny's front door and jumped the last four steps down into the large porch area behind the front door to Meanwood Towers. Unlocking the door to his own flat, he went in, put the keys in the ceramic bowl painted with green chillies that sat on a table in the hallway, kicked off his slippers and walked quickly into the lounge.

The not-so-secret door was shut. Good. He hadn't really expected to find anything different, but an overwhelming urge to make sure had come over him, presumably fuelled by the image of a photographer walking round the flat. Which was *not* going to happen. Walking over to the door, calmer now, he bent down and examined the edge. The hair that he had licked and placed across the gap was still there, a trick he had learned from an old James Bond film. For a moment he wondered if he should go up, even though he knew that to do so would be a mistake.

Instead he he stood in front of the bookshelves, which covered the far wall from floor to ceiling. Behind him was a dining table, beyond which two sofas were positioned at right angles to each other, one a two-seater and the other a three-seater. Each was covered in a thickly striped burgundy-and-cream fabric. The furniture was doing its best to surround a wooden coffee table, on which a cushion awaited his swollen foot. The larger sofa faced the huge open fireplace, although not even lying down on the sofa allowed a view of the priest hole.

He went straight to the book on the Korean military and took it to the armchair. A bottle of sixteen-year-old Lagavulin Scotch whisky that a client had bought him as a thank-you present was on the table, as was a glass that had already been used for the purpose. He opened the book at the marked page and simultaneously poured a drink.

Chapter 5

Stage 2: Guilt

Friday, 8am

Elliott paused for a moment at the top of the stairs to catch his breath, putting the tray of food on the floor. He regretted bouncing up the steps quite so quickly after consuming such a large breakfast himself. As he stood facing the white door he realised, rather to his own surprise, that the sharpness of his breathing was as much due to the nerves clashing around his stomach as it was to a lack of physical fitness.

He had been awake since 6.30, excited like a schoolchild at the prospect of getting stuck into a really fun project. A night's sleep had for a long time now consisted of a series of naps interrupted by attempts to fool his mind back into inactivity. As middle of the night turned into early hours of the morning the periods of fitful dozing would start to become as long as the periods of sleep, until eventually one idea would sneak through the defences and his mind would begin whirring into action, even as he told it not to. The concept of closing his eyes at night and then being awakened by the alarm in the morning was as alien to him as not saying 'thank you' to a bus driver. Finally, this morning at 6.30, he had admitted defeat and allowed the ideas to flood up, bursting out of the inspiration he felt from the challenge sitting upstairs waiting for his attentions.

There was a physicality in the presence of Ian. There was a man up there. An actual person, all flesh and blood, passions and ambitions. Sitting in his turret. The stark reality kept pestering him, trying to gain his attention.

He had gone to the kitchen and begun kneading dough. Ideas and strategies rolled around his brain.

These early stages were crucial in setting the rules, establishing the relationship. It was no different than dealing with a new client who might come to see him requesting legal representation. They all came so loaded with preconceptions, pumped up with umbrage and indignation. The first job was to unpick the often-warped logic and unswerving sense of right that was embedded in the mind of a person stuck in an argument, to make them aware of the rules of justice, that it wasn't simply a question of telling the other side why they were wrong. A strategy was required to make the law work correctly – which was generally interpreted as meaning to be in their favour.

Centring himself as he paused outside the room, he once again ran through the process he was going to follow in order to bring Ian to the state of mind necessary to be broken down; the part he was going to have to play. He imagined himself as Spencer Tracy in *Inherit the Wind*, about to go into court, about to potentially change if not the course of history itself, certainly the future of one man's life. A few deep breaths, release slowly, heart rate easing, regaining control.

Holding the tray with one hand, he grabbed the handle and walked into the darkness, kicking the door shut behind him. For those few moments as light filled the room he could see Ian close his eyes and turn his head away. He was still tied to the chair, and for a moment Elliott realised he was relieved.

"Good morning. Did you manage any sleep?"

Ian didn't answer.

"I brought you some food. I'll feed it to you. Full English. The sausages are lamb and rosemary, I made them myself."

Elliott put the tray on the table, then went back to the door and opened it slightly, just enough to let in a small amount of light. Then he dragged the stool in front of Ian so that his back was to the light, reached over to the tray, and picked up the fork.

Ian seemed for a moment to wonder whether he should accept the food, but his hunger got the better of him and he took each proffered forkful of scrambled eggs or sausage, draining the glass of orange juice in one visit. Neither man spoke during the meal, Elliott using a tea towel to carefully wipe away the orange juice moustache from his captive's face. At one point some of the scrambled egg fell from the side of Ian's mouth, and Elliott tutted, picked the egg carefully from Ian's shirt so as not to leave a stain, and put it back on the plate.

When the food was all gone Elliott put the tray outside the door on the floor, then returned to the room. He closed the door behind him, being careful at all times that Ian would not to be able to see his face clearly. He put his hands behind his back in the darkness and leaned back against the wall, palms pressing against the cold plaster. The darkness amplified the sound of a man who had just finished a meal, running his tongue around his teeth, cleaning out any rogue morsels stuck there. Eventually Elliott spoke into the newly restored blackness.

"Tell me about your father, Ian," he said.

"Why?" replied Ian.

"Indulge me. You're tied to a chair. I'm the one that tied you there. How about you just do as I ask for a bit, hmm?"

"What do you want to know?"

Elliott paused for a moment, sighed loudly, then continued in the same cheery tone. "Tell me about your father, Ian."

"He's a good guy. A bit too good, if you ask me. He owns a pub, where I grew up. Had me quite old, my mum was his second wife. Works really hard, turned seventy last year, never had enough to set anything extra aside. Dad always taught me to stand on my own two feet, don't rely on the charity of others. He'll probably die in that pub. So I look after number one, like my dad should have done a bit more."

Ian stopped talking abruptly. The words seemed to have tumbled out from him, as if they were not under his control. His voice had risen slightly during the short speech, and was that an occasional wobble Elliott detected?

"So. Ian. Do you recall the homework I left you with? Do you have any thoughts for me?"

"Plenty," said Ian. Elliott thought he detected a note of defiance in his reply.

"Care to share some with me?" said Elliott.

"Not really. They're pretty predictable. You've locked me in a tower overnight. I don't know why. I've pissed myself because I had no other choice. I can only guess that you are mentally deranged. I'd like to go now, please."

"Oh dear," said Elliott. "Is that it? After all I said to you last night?"

"Look, I get that. I was being an arse. I understand. You've made your point. I'm really sorry. I shouldn't have been so impatient. It wasn't my fault, I had my stupid sales manager on my back. But I am sorry I upset you, I really am, genuinely. Now please, let me go."

The note of defiance had a pleading edge now. Elliott ignored it. "So you are sorry because you upset me. Is that right?"

"If that's what you want, yes." His voice was tainted by a rising sense of panic. "Tell me what you want, and I'll give it to you. Do you want money? I have some money. You can let me go, blindfold me, drive me somewhere and dump me, and I wouldn't have a clue who you are or where I was kept. You can get away with this. Just let me go now. Please. I'm sorry I upset you. I've learned the lesson, I really have. I won't drive so aggressively in future. My arms hurt, my legs hurt, my whole body hurts, I'm scared and I just want to go home."

Elliott stood with his hands pressed against the door behind him, waiting. He counted to forty-two before pushing himself away from the door. He took up pacing around the room again, speaking as he went.

"That's an interesting idea, Ian. Letting you go. Getting away with it. I'll give it some thought." Having made a circuit of the room, he turned and went back the other direction, as if unwinding himself.

"But first, let's talk about you. You're a self-centred, arrogant person. That much is obvious. But then, we all are. But this has come as a surprise to you, as you thought you were pretty cool. You are not cool. Because cool is a status other people award you. And other people think you are self-centred and arrogant. Therefore, that it what you must be. Are we in agreement so far?"

No reply from the chair.

"The interesting question for me here is *why* you think you are cool. I've been thinking about you, Ian. Trying to understand you.

How can someone who seems to be reasonably intelligent be so wrong about themselves? It's like you swallowed a cliché as a young man. Let's recap. Last time we talked about what you believe in. Do you recall what you said?"

"I believe in freedom," Ian answered quickly.

"Ha, yes, nice one. What kind of freedom, Ian?"

"My freedom. Right now."

"Yes, yes, very droll. Why don't we assume that you cannot have that freedom unless you actively engage in conversation with me, indeed that if you don't engage in conversation, then matters might actually get worse for you? If we accept that hypothesis, let us ask the question again. What do you actually believe in?"

Elliott could hear Ian sigh resignedly. "I believe in hard work," Ian said eventually. "That hard work and talent should be rewarded."

"Yes. That's right. You said that yesterday. Rewarding hard work. Which in turn means punishing those who don't work hard, even if just by not giving them rewards." Elliott turned around and continued pacing round the room. "I wonder if it's a coincidence that you believe in something which benefits you."

"What do you mean? Everyone believes in hard work. How can you argue against that?"

"Do they? How do you know everyone believes that, Ian? Have you asked them all?"

"Alright," said Ian eventually. "Alright. Um, free market economics. That's what I vote for. If people can't be bothered to work, why should I have to pay? If a company is too expensive or its product is rubbish, it should be replaced by a better company through competition. It's like nature, a self-righting system, totally sorts itself out."

"Okay," replied Elliott. "That makes sense. I get that. The beauty of the free market. No barriers to entry for new companies, the collective good that comes from individual self-interest, Adam Smith's 'invisible hand', encouraging the entrepreneur, breaking down anything that prevents a truly free market such as strong unions and government intervention." Turn; walk anticlockwise once again. He spoke to the ground, as if he were a professor delivering a lecture. If he had been wearing a gown he would have hooked his thumbs into the lapels. "How does that sound to you, Ian?"

"That's about it, yeah. If I think I can run a company better than the one I work for, I should be able to take my clients with me and set up in competition. Government policy should encourage entrepreneurs, encourage competition. Keep the state out of it."

"Okay. That's all good stuff. So, I am presuming that means you would also agree with inheritance tax being set at one hundred per cent?"

"What? No, of course I wouldn't. Don't be stupid. There's no way the government should get whatever money I make."

"Who should get it, then?"

"My kids. I hand it down. Certainly not the government."

"Okay, how about to a charity?"

"No! It's my money, I choose where it goes. It's for my family, when I have one. For my kids to buy a house, or start a business. Like I would do if only my dad had anything to leave."

"But that means that your children will be given a large amount of money, which they might use to set up a business. And yet my kids, if I have any, won't receive any inheritance because I plan to spend it all. So your kids would have an unfair competitive advantage over mine. The free market would be distorted. It would no longer be the best and most talented that survive and thrive, but those who have rich parents. That breaks the free market rule, doesn't it?"

"But it's my money. I'd've spent my whole life building it up. I should be allowed to choose where it goes."

"Sorry, Ian, but that's inconsistent. To believe in a free market, you also have to believe in a barrier to passing accumulated wealth down the generations."

Silence settled on the space in the centre of the room that Ian inhabited. Elliott left sufficient time to allow for a response and only continued when he felt certain that none was coming.

"Well?" he said.

"I...I don't know. I'm disoriented. I've been in here such a long time, in the dark."

"The point here is not that your politics are wrong, but that they are founded on self-interest. Don't pretend that it's the best for everyone. You think a free market economy is for the common good? That a game of winners and losers means everyone is happy at the end? No. You believe in it because you think it would be good for *you*. Why do you think the middle and upper classes tend to vote right wing and the lower classes left wing? Because one lot want to protect what they have and the other lot want to get a piece of it." Elliott moved forwards and crouched in front of his estimate of where Ian sat. "You are a selfish little shit, Ian, who goes through life thinking that other people are in your way and who does not give a moment's thought to anyone but yourself. Including – perhaps especially – now." He bounced on his haunches like an overenthusiastic motivational speaker.

"Let us recap for a moment, Ian. We are agreed that your behaviour is unacceptable, that you are not a pleasant person. We are agreed that others see you that way, so it must be true. We can deduce from this that how people perceive you, and therefore how you actually are, is entirely down to you."

"Yes. Alright. Jesus, I said I agree."

"Do you work hard, Ian?"

"Yes."

"And your high salary and expensive car are just returns on your efforts?"

"Yes." The response was a little too quick and a little less confident.

"And if I offered to buy enough from you right now to achieve your entire next month's target, would you continue to work hard?"

"I…"

"No, you wouldn't, would you? So you are rewarded for results, not effort. If we were all rewarded for hard work then miners would be paid a lot more than bankers. But that's not how it works at all, is it?"

"I don't see anything wrong with how I'm rewarded, as long as I get the sales in. That's what I'm paid for."

"Nothing is necessarily wrong with that, Ian. But do not try and tell me that you believe in hard work when that is not the system you operate within and from which you benefit. To do so makes you a hypocrite and a sham."

In the absence of a response the point hung in the air like a foul accusation, not admitted and yet not denied. Elliott shifted on his haunches, moving the weight from one leg to the other. The silence marched onwards, the argument percolating like a festering sore. Eventually, he resumed his haranguing.

"So you believe in hard work, although not when it applies to you. What else do you believe in, I wonder? Freedom, you said. Freedom for the individual to make their own choices, perhaps? That sounds like one of your father's, I reckon."

"Look, are you really keeping tied up in a darkened room just so that you can have a political argument with me? Let me go, you nutter."

"Oh dear. Hello, rudeness, goodbye, freedom. No, that's not going to help. You see, you still haven't got the faintest idea why you are here, do you?"

"No. I've apologised for driving like an idiot. I do accept that was wrong. What else do you want from me?"

"You know it was wrong, do you? So you won't do it again, then?" He received an eloquent silence in response to his question. "Quite. I imagine it is something you do often, just 'how you drive'."

"Well, you could have pulled over," Ian snapped back at him. "You didn't need to do all that stupid slowing down and speeding up crap." It was said with indignation, like a dog reacting to being prodded by a small boy holding a sharp stick.

"Why?" said Elliott. "Why should I pull over?"

"You could see I was in a hurry."

Even though Elliott could not see Ian's face in the dark, he could imagine the sideburns, the slightly snubbed nose, the narrowed eyes betraying a lack of conviction in his argument. The face of a person who is using someone else's argument to fight their way out of an impossible position. His legs were aching now, so he stood, knees cracking as he rose.

"You just don't get it, do you?" he said. His arms were folded in an indignant posture, subconsciously using body language to underline the point even though they were in pitch darkness.

"No, really," said Ian. "All you had to do was pull in, I would have got past, and none of this would've happened. So why not just pull over? It was obvious I was in a hurry. Just let me past. Why cause an argument?"

"Because, Ian, if I had pulled over to let you past, you would have won. You would have succeeded in bullying me off the road. And that would not have been right. That would have been very, very wrong."

Ian warmed to his theme, righteousness creeping up to sit nervously on his shoulder. "What if I was on my way to hospital? What if I had an emergency and your pig-headedness was stopping me from getting to the hospital on time? You could have caused the death of a person, or a child to be born in the back of my car."

"Were you going to hospital?"

Pause.

"No."

"Well then!"

"You didn't know that."

"This isn't about me, Ian, is it? It's about you. That is why you are here, Ian. Do you not realise that? Do you think I have kidnapped you, tied you to a chair, locked you in a room at the top of a soundproof tower in order to have a debate with you about who was right and who was wrong in a road traffic situation? Is that *really* why you think you are here? Hmm?"

It seemed from the lack of a response that Ian was beginning to understand when to not reply. Elliott caught his breath for a moment. He felt hot in the face and needed to keep calm, to maintain control. This was no time for Alan to make his presence felt. He breathed in, waited, and…breathe out.

"Let me tell you why you are here, Ian. The answer should interest you. Partly because you are tied to a chair in a darkened room, but it is also very relevant to who you are. What you believe in. You see, the fact that you don't know what you did that so upset me is the very thing that shows you up for the bad person that you are."

Stop. Turn around. Continue pacing. Try to make the sound of the pacing confident and threatening, not dragging and weary. Having a weary footstep does not add to an aura of menace.

"Ian, the thing you did that made me so mad was not that you drove your car dangerously close, as if you were the most important thing on the road and I should pull over to let you pass. It was not that you overtook on a bend, thereby putting my life at risk. To be fair, both those things got me angry. They also fly in the face of your own belief that talent and hard work should be rewarded. You clearly felt more important than me on that stretch of road, in that car you had been loaned to show off in. And yet you knew nothing about me. I could have been the most hard-working person in the world, but at that time, your actions revealed that you thought you were better than me."

"I was just late," Elliott protested.

"Yes, you said. But how do you know I wasn't late as well? That *I* needed to get to a hospital?"

Elliott stopped walking and knelt on the floor behind Ian. He reached into his pocket and took out a small, flat oval implement made of silver with a round hole in the middle. Reaching forwards, he took hold of the middle finger of Ian's right hand. Ian tried to move his hand away, but he had no freedom, no give in the rope. Elliott bent the finger back so that it stood separately from the other fingers, and slid the cigar cutter down over the finger.

"Do you know what this is, Ian?"

"N-n-n-no."

"It's a cigar cutter. Like a little guillotine. Clever little contraption. One uses it to chop the ends off those big Cuban cigars."

"Look, for Chrissakes, there's no need to—"

Elliott leaned forwards so that he could whisper directly into his right ear. "You see," he continued, "this is the cheeky little fella that upset me so much. This middle finger here. Do you remember what you did with it?"

"Yes, I'm sorry, I know, I'm sorry, it was rude, please don't—"

"What this represented, this finger, is the total lack of respect that you have for the rest of the world. You don't respect hard work in others. You just want rewards for you. What this finger shoved so aggressively towards me at the moment you finally managed to force me into the side of the road in order to get past said to me was, 'I am right, you are wrong. I deserve to be in front, you were in my way, but now I have won.' And yet, as we have agreed, the reverse was actually the case. *I* was the innocent party. *I* was wronged. Not you. If we had crashed and then gone to court, you would have been the one they would have found to be at fault. And so my annoyance turned to rage when *you*," the word was shouted, "had the nerve to make an obscene gesture at *me*."

Elliott was breathing heavily now. He thought may have sprayed spit onto the man's ear, he couldn't be sure. He was in control of himself. With his right hand he took out a handkerchief from his pocket, left hand still holding on to the cigar cutter, and wiped the ear clean.

"Do you see, Ian? All that you hold to be true is a lie. You believe in things not because they are righteous but because they suit you. You are rude, ill-mannered and arrogant in the pursuit of something that turns out to be a sham. This finger, this gave you away. This showed you for the bad person you are. And you know what? You're not even a good driver, because you crashed two minutes later! Ha-ha-ha-ha-ha-ha-ha-ha. You are a complete mess! A total hypocritical shambles. Do." Elliott prodded Ian's back with his spare hand. "You." Prod. "See." Prod. "What." Slightly harder prod. "I." Poke. "Mean?" A slight pressure on the ends of the cigar cutter, and the metal edges pressed onto the skin of the finger.

"Yes, yes I do, I'm sorry, I totally understand, I'm sorry I gave you the finger, I didn't realise that was the thing that upset you so much, I'm sorry, I can see what you mean, I'm sorry, don't, please don't, I'm sorry, I was wrong, I really…" Ian breathed hard and swallowed, then tried to speak more slowly. "I really should not have given you the finger. It was rude and disrespectful and rude and, and, please, don't cut my finger off…" The last words caught in his throat, and he swallowed hard again.

"Let me ask you the question that I asked you yesterday, Ian. And this time I would suggest you think carefully before answering. The future of your finger may depend upon it. What are you sorry for?"

"I'm sorry for being so disrespectful to you," Ian spluttered quickly. "I was acting like an idiot, you are right, and by showing you the finger I was being doubly arrogant and rude to you. I am sorry, I really am."

Elliott made no movement. He waited. He could hear the breathing of the man in front of him, gasping for breath as he waited to find out if he said the right thing.

"Ian?" Elliott said.

"Y-y-y-yes?"

"Do you know the most important part of what you just said?"

"No, no, I don't."

"What was notable was the speed with which you said it. You didn't think. That's the first thing you have done or said since we met that wasn't completely stupid. I almost believe you might have actually understood some of what we've talked about today, Ian." Elliott slid the cigar cutter back over the middle finger, and replaced it in his pocket. Then he stood and walked to the door.

"Let's get one thing clear," he said, pausing at the door. "I am yet to be convinced that you really are sorry for what you are. Sorry *is* 'I should not have done that thing I did.' Sorry is *not* 'I apologise if I upset anyone.' That's what footballers and celebrities say. It is petulant and insincere. You might as well say, 'I am sorry I got caught.'

"What I would ask you to think about for the rest of the day is all the other things you have done in your life that are as equally in contradiction with your supposed beliefs. Consider how people think of you, and what you have done to elicit that response. We'll chat again later." He put up one thumb and placed a smile behind it, even though he couldn't be seen. "I'm rather looking forward to our next session!"

Chapter 6

Leaning forwards on his dark blue cotton ergonomic chair, Elliott glanced at the Beethoven clock. Pru would be leaving shortly. He was torn between wanting to get back into the turret, and knowing that the last session needed to percolate in Ian's thoughts. He turned his attention back to the computer and the document he was drafting.

The clock had been a present from Pru three years ago to mark five years' service as the only employee of Elliott Harmison Legal. He had remembered to buy a large bunch of flowers mainly because Pru had written the date in his diary. She had then presented him with a limited edition bust of Beethoven wearing a pair of Vuarnet-style sunglasses with an LED display of the time; the hour digits in the left lens, the minutes in the right.

He looked around the offices that were once stables. The conversion had involved removing completely three of the horse bays to create a feeling of space. The wooden walls of the last three bays were removed and a frosted glass wall used to create a large meeting room. Elliott's office occupied what used to be the middle three bays, and Pru had her desk in the final two bays nearest the door, positioned so that anyone entering from outside needed to talk to Pru and could not see Elliott.

Elliott heard Pru's chair scrape on the flagstone floor. He leaned forwards, elbows resting on the green leather of the desk, ready to greet her for the last time this working week. She turned the corner into his bay with her eyes on a document in her right hand. A sheaf of loose papers fluttered ominously in the other. For a moment Elliott glanced at her feet and wondered if she might have actually started to wear a groove in the floor where she had made that same short journey so many hundreds of times before.

"Right," she said, the London twang of her North Surrey accent shining through and ensuring that the 't' remained silent. "This is the letter to Stan at Cooksons about the thing with that woman. You know, the one with the hair." She handed him a letter, which he signed and handed back. "This one is for that chap from the accountants thanking him for supporting the charity dinner thing you organised. Well, I organised and you paid for." She handed another letter, he signed, she took it back. "These three are to the executors of Mr Sandini's estate about their donation from you as a school governor." Pause while he signed the three letters. "And this one is a birthday card for me."

She handed him the card, he signed it, then looked at the front. It was an old-fashioned black-and-white photograph of two women in their fifties who were sitting under giant plastic hairdryers in a hairdressing salon of the 1960s, clinking two wine glasses.

"That one on the left actually looks like you," he said as he reached into his pocket. He pulled out his wallet, took out three twenty-pound notes, put them in the envelope with the card, sealed it and handed it back to her. "Happy birthday, Pru. Why not take Jim out for a nice meal?"

"Oh no, he wouldn't appreciate it. Might be able to repair the dishwasher now though." He knew she was joking, she knew that he knew she was joking. Working together for long periods of time will do that to people. "Thank you, my darling." As far as Elliott knew, Pru even called her cat 'my darling'.

"As if I'd forget your birthday. Especially after you go to all that trouble to leave so many hints around for me. Like a large note in my diary." Elliott reached down and pulled open a drawer in his desk, put his hand inside and returned it, holding a bottle of Veuve Clicquot champagne. "Happy birthday for tomorrow, Pru," he said, eyes twinkling as he handed it to her. "It seems we've run out of wrapping paper, can you get some more on Monday?"

"Oh my," said Pru, taking the bottle. "I've never heard of that brand before. Ooh, I might have a little drop of that when I get home. Better make sure Jim doesn't see it though, don't want to waste it on him. Ooh, thanks, Elliott, that's really kind of you. Aw, bless you, thanks." When Pru spoke his name, it sounded more like 'Ellia'.

He smiled at her, and said, "Have a nice weekend, Pru."

"Oh, I will now," she said. She walked back round the corner towards her desk, clutching the bottle to her chest like a newborn baby, staring at the label.

Five minutes later and Pru called a cheery, "Have a nice weekend, Ellia" as she left. He returned the sentiment with interest, then walked to the door and listened for the shutting of her car door and starting of the engine. The crunch of gravel, at first loud and then fading down to nothing as her car turned the corner of the drive and disappeared round the side of the house. He counted a few further moments to allow for the electric gate to open, then he left the office, got into his own car and guided it towards the edge of the house, peering through the windscreen and round the corner to make sure Pru had gone.

The gate was just shutting as the rear of her car turned right into the country lane that brought her through the village and off to her beloved Jim.

Easing his car down the drive with a disproportionate degree of caution, he clicked on the remote gate opener and waited. As he waited the interminable ten seconds for the gate to fully open inwards, he noticed a young man in black jeans and a black donkey jacket leaning against the gatepost on the other side. His face was buried so far into his book that it was obvious he had been watching Elliott leave the property.

Elliott wound down his window as he nudged the car forwards, clear of the gate now closing behind him. "Hello, Mikey," he said.

The young man gave the worst impression of someone being surprised that Elliott had seen in a long time. "Oh, hello, Mr Harmison, didn't see you there. Ha-ha." He held the book by his side, thumb marking the page.

"What are you reading?" asked Elliott.

Mikey brought the book in front of him as if it was the first time he'd seen it. "This?" he said. "Oh, it's a manga book. *Deathnote.*

Not exactly highbrow stuff, ha-ha." He shuffled his feet. Mikey had a way of occupying any space apologetically. Elliott tried to put him at his ease with a smile, but it only seemed to encourage the awkwardness.

"What are you doing hanging round, Mikey?"

"Oh, I just thought I'd wait for Phoebe. I missed her after school." The eager smile that lit up the young man's face and the head that nodded and bobbed so optimistically reminded Elliott of a puppy wagging its tail just before it was tied up in a sack and thrown into a river.

"It's not easy being your age, Mikey. The objective of being a teenager is to reach adulthood with as few moments as possible which, twenty-five years later, will cause you to suddenly stand still during a dog walk and shudder with embarrassment. May I give you a word of advice, Mikey?" Nod-nod, bob-bob. "There's an old saying. Not sure where it comes from, but it might just be appropriate here. If you love someone, set them free. If they return then they really love you. If they don't then…well, then they probably don't. Something like that." The nodding slowed and the gaze sank into the middle distance as Mikey processed the words.

"See you, Mikey," said Elliott, and he turned left onto the country lane, leaving the boy smiling vaguely.

Two miles later and Elliott turned right onto the main road. Something was drawing him back to the narrow country lane, to return to scene of the accident. As soon as he had closed the door to the room at the top of the tower that morning, Ian had moved from reality to myth, like the light in the fridge or the falling tree in the wood. Ian only existed if Elliott were in the room with him. Something was telling Elliott to see the car, see the broken tree, as if to confirm that he had indeed embarked upon this crazy project.

When Alan had taken over that day at school, he knew that it was wrong, and yet he felt no guilt, no personal blame for what had happened. He was not in control; Alan had been. Someone else, Joey Davison, had made Alan appear, not him. Alan was a reaction, like hives from a stinging nettle.

Strangely, the name his father had given to his temper had helped. By making Alan seem real he also became manageable, like an annoying classmate who loses interest when he stops getting a reaction.

A wash of brake lights ahead woke him from his trance, the red glow shining off the road still wet from an afternoon shower, as if making a declaration that none shall pass. The clouds were grey and there was an autumnal coldness that seemed destined to prevent the world from ever drying out.

Roadworks.

Elliott groaned. He could see the temporary traffic lights around eighty metres ahead. To make matters worse, he could see his turning ahead a dozen or so cars away but he had no way of getting to it.

A car coming the other way began indicating to turn right, then slowed and stopped. Elliott guessed that the queuing cars had not left a space, meaning the oncoming car had to wait. Traffic backed up behind it into the roadworks, meaning the queuing traffic could not go forwards to make the space for the car to turn, meaning...gridlock.

Elliott rubbed his eyes with the thumb and forefinger of one hand, bringing them together and pinching the top of his nose. He took the car out of gear and pulled violently at the handbrake. "Why are people so bloody stupid?" he muttered under his breath. Up ahead, cars in front of him moved forwards carefully to try and make room to uncork the bottleneck.

In his rear-view mirror Elliott could see a lady aged fiftyish in an open-top sports car, the roof down despite the gloom. She wore a scarf, a thick jumper and a large pair of sunglasses. A second pair was on her head, holding her highlighted blonde-and-orange hair back from her face. Her car was so close to his that there was virtually no room for Elliott to move back. The cars in front were now edging backwards, only a little more and the car could turn. The traffic lights had gone from green to amber, to red, to red and amber several times round. The lady behind was drumming her hands on the steering wheel, arching her neck to monitor developments.

Finally the car managed to get through the gap. Elliott imagined a 'pop' as cars streamed past him. Up front the gap was once again filled and all the cars moved forwards one car space until there was a gap in front of Elliott. Knowing that they would either move forwards in a few minutes when the roadworks were clear, or have to move back when another oncoming car wanted to turn right, Elliott stayed put.

After twenty seconds or so the bip of a car horn from behind drew Elliott to look in his rear-view mirror again. The lady was gesticulating, pointing. She was suggesting with some vigour that he might want to pull forwards, to fill the one car gap. Elliott stared back at her in his mirror.

This time he saw her lean on the horn. She was shouting as well now, arms waving. Elliott arched an eyebrow.

With a final flourish she slammed her car into reverse, the crunching sound echoing off the road. She backed up slightly, changed gear again and then pulled out with the clear intention of going round Elliott to fill in the space in front of him. As she did this, Elliott moved his car slowly forwards.

The sports car came to an exaggerated and abrupt halt. Looking to his right, Elliott smiled benignly at the now-incandescent woman, who was shouting at him through his closed window. He brought his elbow onto the sill and rested his head on his hand, looking at her impassively as one might consider an ape in a zoo. In his side mirror Elliott could see that the white van behind had not moved forwards to fill the gap. The driver and his mate were chuckling heartily at the scene unfolding in front of them, and even held out a 'be my guest' arm as the sports car reversed back into the gap it had only recently vacated.

Finally the traffic was able to move forwards and Elliott travelled the short distance before turning left. He didn't bother looking in his mirror as he turned, leaving the anticipated two-fingered salute from the sports car unrequited. Instead he steered his car down the narrow lane.

It felt like a bobsleigh run, this road, the edges of the tarmac seeming to merge into the foliage. He had been down it hundreds if not thousands of times before. The hedgerows were dark and impenetrable, solid-looking, like a tube. As a child he would lean his chin on the window and imagine a motorcyclist doing a series of death-defying tricks, one moment up the bank on one side, then zooming across the road in front of his father's car and then up the other bank.

The road ahead took a sharp left. On the bend was a five-bar gate leading into a field of sunflowers. They were bowed over at the end of another hard day, the seeds taken some weeks previously, leaving the heads dark and ghostly. They looked to Elliott like the photographs he had once seen in a book in the school library, of prisoners in a work camp in Japan during the Second World War. Row upon row of defeated, forlorn flowers, resigned to their fate, without strength or hope. Elliott had recently been feeling an allegiance with them but now they felt incongruous with his renewed optimism.

The road wound slowly downhill, entering the wood, the trees creating an archway then meeting at the top to form a tunnel. He saw the flash of police tape ahead and slowed down. There seemed to be no one around as he approached the crash scene.

Beyond the tape was the car, out of place amongst the foliage. Much of the surrounding shrubbery had been trampled or cleared away, leaving the scene looking more like an art instillation than the aftermath of an accident. He wasn't sure what it was that he had come to see, and now that he was here, an uneasy feeling came over him. For all he knew, it may even have been self-doubt. He pulled up the handbrake and took in the scene of his kidnapping that was before him.

Winding down his window, Elliott barely recognised what he saw. Maybe that was why he had come back: to see the scene through his eyes, not Alan's. He could remember pulling up behind the car, but Alan had taken over from the moment he had looked through the window. Perhaps Alan was actually the braver side of him, the one who had the courage to take the extreme measures that seemed to be so necessary to make a better world. For a fleeting moment he even wondered if this was his destiny. But he knew that such a notion was just as seductive as doubt, and equally as diverting. He dismissed it accordingly.

"Can we help you, sir?" Two police officers suddenly appeared at the front of his car, a man and a woman. Where had they come from? They walked round to his window and Elliott had to resist the urge to put his foot down hard on the accelerator. Their tone was friendly but firm, no doubt the default position young officers used with people who stop to stare at crime scenes.

"Oh, ha, not really," called back Elliott in a light and airy tone which he immediately realised was a little too forced. He had been caught in the act, found out, like being at the school disco and loudly asking out a girl just as the music stops. He had never made that mistake again.

"Right," said the male police officer. The two of them stared at Elliott. He suddenly realised what a complete suspect he was making himself out to be. Now fully committed, he opened the door of the car and got out. Even as his foot stepped onto the ground he wondered what on earth he was doing. He just knew that to drive away would make him look suspicious, and that ploughing onwards was the only option.

"I'm a solicitor," he said addressing neither of them specifically. "In town. I just wanted to drive by to get the lay of the land, so to speak. In case any of our clients needed to, well, wanted to, you know, in case they'd seen anything and might be able to help."

"Right," said the lady police officer. "Well, that's very good of you, sir." She stared at him for a moment. He felt twelve again. "*Have* any of your clients mentioned the accident to you at all?"

"No, not specifically."

"Not specifically?"

"Well, you know, only small talk, that there had been an accident. Gossip. You know. When, um, are they going to take the car away?"

"Did you know the driver of the vehicle, sir?" asked the first police officer. His arms were folded behind his back, legs slightly apart, like a sergeant addressing the parade.

"I don't know, what was their name?" He hadn't been practising law all his life to get caught out by that trick.

"We aren't at liberty to divulge that information, sir. If you do hear anything, you be sure to let us know, won't you?" The policeman grinned with an amiable finality. Elliott was dismissed.

"Yes, of course. Well. There we are." Elliott smiled at them and nodded to each in turn, then climbed back into his car. Damn, why the hell had he come back here? What was he expecting to see?

He drove carefully away, glancing in the rear-view mirror to see the two police officers watching him leave. They would note down his number plate, he knew that. He might even be checked out, but that would be alright – he *was* a solicitor, highly respected locally. Ask anyone, they'd speak well of him. His years of service as a school governor and trustee with various charities had to be worth something.

The trip to see the car *had* been worthwhile, however. It had brought home the reality of the situation. There was only a limited amount of time in which he had to work. Perhaps that's what he'd been trying to do in driving back to the scene: to give himself a dose of reality, wake himself up. Time to get focused.

Phoebe was in the act of turning her key into the main door of the house. He bipped the horn and she turned, waving. By the time he had parked the car and entered the flat, Phoebe was already in the kitchen putting tea bags into cups.

He watched her from the doorway of the kitchen. He could clear up properly once she had left. With that knowledge he was able to mainly ignore the teabags left on the draining board and the spoon sitting on the side. And the lid left off the sugar bowl. And the milk not put back in the fridge.

There are certain basic values, in particular relating to how our actions affect other people. These must be consistent for a society to consider itself civilised. These core values are worth fighting for. There are other values which differ from person to person, and this is fine. Elliott was quite prepared to accept that other people would choose to live their lives according to different values to his own. As long as they didn't affect him, that was entirely acceptable.

Other people. What a better world it would be without them. The last time he had to live with other people was in his student days. He had ended up in a shared house in the third term of his first year by answering an advert pinned to the halls of residence common room noticeboard. A group of second-year students had a spare room and Elliott had not made any friends in his time living in halls strong enough to keep him there. He found the small room and shared dining arrangements stifling compared to the relative freedom of Meanwood Towers.

The housemates were a disparate bunch, including an art student who seemed to spend all his waking hours working, an English literature postgraduate who spent all her time reading, two mature students on a media studies course who were out all day and up all night and extremely immature, and a fellow law student who spent her days watching soap operas on television and eating crisps. Elliott was also out of the house for long periods as he became increasingly involved with the National Union of Students.

It was fair to say that they didn't all share his values regarding personal hygiene or tidiness. Or washing up. Or not eating other people's food from the fridge even when it was clearly labelled. Or slamming the door when leaving for lectures in the morning. But that was okay. A note pinned to the door helped. He purchased his own plate and cutlery and glasses and labelled them accordingly, politely. Possibly the lockable lunch box that he used to keep his food in may have been overkill, he could see that now, but at the time it was a solution to the problem of losing food and reduced the degree to which Elliott got annoyed.

He had not kept in touch with his old mates from university.

Naomi didn't count as 'other people'. Not from the moment he had met her during his first job as a trainee solicitor with a firm in London. He felt like she was supposed to be with him, like the missing part of his soul. She shared his core values.

Elliott walked back into the lounge. Stupidly, he had left the not-so-secret door ajar. He went past one of the two black leather sofas and the coffee table in front of the fireplace and put his briefcase on the floor against the wall next to the turret door. He watched Phoebe's back in the kitchen as he silently shut the door, turned the key in the lock and then put the key in his pocket. Then he scooted over to the smaller of the sofas, at right angles to the bookcase next to the door, and sat down just as Phoebe came out of the kitchen holding two mugs.

She placed one on a coaster on the table in front of Elliott. "Mum's not back yet," she said, by way of explanation. Elliott took both mugs from her and put them on the table. Phoebe went back into the kitchen and came out carrying a plate in one hand, on which were placed six chocolate biscuits. In the other hand was her mobile phone. She put the biscuits on the coffee table and sat on the sofa nearest the unlit fire, instantly sinking backwards. This was a sofa you didn't so much sit on as fall into. Elliott looked at Phoebe, her face partially obscured by the phone that was now being prodded in front of her.

"Mum's texted me. She'll be late coming home."

"Oh for goodness' sakes," said Elliott. "She should just tell Davison to sod off. Change management, my backside."

"He's alright, Uncle E, don't be so hard on him. I like him." She typed into her phone as she talked.

"You don't know him like I do." He looked quickly across at his niece. "Hang on, when did you meet him?"

"At least he's not a phoney," said Phoebe quickly. "He appreciates Mum's hard work. It's always depressing when people take other people for granted." Her phone announced another text. "Mum says that because she won't be here, can you show the estate agent round your flat and up to the turret?"

"Oh fer..." barked Elliott. "I told her I am not letting a photographer in here."

"I don't think you have much choice, Uncle E," said Phoebe, still tapping at her phone.

"I told her. You heard me tell her. Why won't she ever listen to me? What time is he supposed to be coming?"

Phoebe shrugged, her attention barely straying from the screen in front of her. "They haven't found that guy yet," she said.

"What guy?" said Elliott.

"You know, the one from the car crash. Come on, don't tell me you haven't heard. He just disappeared. Police don't have a clue what happened. It's all over the local news. Beth at school says her dad works with a guy that knows one of the police on the task force and they reckon he's been kidnapped."

"Ha-ha-ha-ha-ha. That's a good one, ha-ha-ha-ha."

"Well, it's possible, isn't it?" said Phoebe, slightly miffed. "I mean, he's just vanished. Not a trace, they said on the news."

"Oh, I suppose it's possible, just seems far-fetched. Probably a drunk driver, he'll turn himself in when he's sobered up. So, what are you doing now?"

Phoebe picked up another biscuit and dunked it into her tea. She turned her head sideways to get the biscuit into her mouth before it broke off. "I'm gonna meet Mikey in the park," she said through a mouthful of soggy biscuit.

"I thought you two had split up?"

"We're still mates. People can do that, you know."

"Don't lead him on, Phoebe. That's not fair. Don't make him think he's still got a chance."

Phoebe rolled her eyes. "I've told him I just want be friends. I like him. Just don't want to be pawed by him."

"And he's okay with that?"

"Sure, I guess. How are you supposed to tell with a boy? Anyway, I've got more important things to think about. I've got to finish my book for English."

"Is it *Catcher in the Rye* by any chance?"

"Yes it is, totally amazing book. How did you know? Have you actually read it?"

"Yes, of course I've read it. Everyone's read it. Do you know, he only wrote that one book, pretty much? The only one worth reading, anyway."

Phoebe looked at him, her mouth slightly agape. He loved her total immersion in whatever she had been reading. Last week she dumped Mikey the day after she had handed in her essay on *Wuthering Heights*.

"But it's brilliant. Why would he only write that one book?" Incomprehension was written over her face as she looked once again to Elliott for insight into the mysteries of her burgeoning life. "I don't understand. Surely he was a writer? How could he not write?"

"He never gave interviews, as far as I know," said Elliott. "I always assumed it was because he had said all he wanted to say. I rather respect that. If you have affected that many people with one book, why write another?"

"Maybe he was the phoney after all," said Phoebe. "Christ, that would be ironic. Maybe he was writing about himself."

"Or maybe he just wasn't very bright and got lucky. Wrote

one book that contained sufficient insight to allow it to be put on the syllabus for fifteen-year-olds. Becomes one of the most famous books of all time, affecting huge numbers of teenagers and helping them understand their place in the world a little better, and yet is a relatively simplistic piece of work. Maybe he panicked, how the hell do you follow that? Lacking in depth it may be, but what he wrote changed lives and still does. That's quite a responsibility."

Phoebe stood, pensive, as if trying to decide on how to react to this opinion, then stood and walked towards the kitchen.

"Phoebe?" said Elliott. She stopped and looked back at him over her shoulder, making the whites of her eyes so huge it seemed that they owned her face. She hooked a thumb into her hair, all curls and darkness, and carefully pulled as much as she could behind her ears, those brown irises now capturing his attention. Elliott had known that face since the day it had entered the world. With such familiarity he had no idea if one could describe his niece as beautiful, however her very being contained such an optimistic intensity, a passion that seemed to infect in everything she did, every move she made, that he understood why Mikey simply couldn't let go.

"Be careful of that book," he said. "It's easy to read things into it that aren't there. You know who was the real phoney in that book? Holden Caulfield. When he referred to people as phoney, do you know what he really meant? He meant 'people who are not like me'."

Phoebe looked at him with the half-smile that sat on her face when she was assimilating knowledge. She placed her cup in the kitchen – on the side, not in the dishwasher where Elliott would have to put it – then turned and walked slowly across the lounge towards the hall. "More people should read," she said. "I often think that when I'm reading a book. Like *Fahrenheit 451*. If more people read that book there wouldn't be so many wars. It would change them."

"Did it change you?"

"Well, no, but I already knew. It's other people that need to change."

"Yes," said Elliott. "It always is."

Phoebe stared at the middle distance between them for a moment with her mouth half-open, the look on her face the equivalent of a computer icon updating the user on how long until the software is fully loaded. Her shoulders drooped slightly as if some of the processing power of her body was redirected to her brain. She shook her head once, closed her mouth, then straightened and walked out into the hall.

"Can I use your coat?" she called back to him. "I can't be bothered to go upstairs for mine."

"Of course, sweetheart," said Elliott. "Oh, no, wait." Elliott sprang from his seat and ran towards the hallway. Phoebe was already wearing the jacket and was taking a mobile phone from one of the pockets.

"You've got a new phone! At last! And what a phone it is, that's really cool, these are only just out." She turned it over and over, inspecting it, pressing buttons. "You've got it powered off, you dummy."

Phoebe was just pressing the power button as he snatched it from her. The black screen showed the maker's logo as the phone powered up.

"Hey, okay, Uncle E, I just wanted a look. I hate it when people snatch things from you and you only want to have a look." The phone began making a strange yelling noise, like the mating call of a moose, repeated every few seconds. Phoebe looked at the phone quizzically. "You seem to have an awful lot of messages, Uncle E."

Elliott stabbed at the phone, trying to make it stop flashing and barking. It was as if the phone were shouting at him, demanding his attention like a bored child. "It's just Stan," he said, "we've got a big deal going down, it's nothing." He shoved the phone into his trouser pocket. "Right, see you later then." He leaned forwards to kiss Phoebe on the cheek, but she ducked under him and went back into the lounge, peering round the doorway into the kitchen.

"Yeah, thought so," she said. "Your phone is there, charging. Why have you got two phones, Unc? You can barely be trusted with one."

"It's this big deal," he replied quickly. "They've given me a special phone. Like a hotline. In case something happens and they need me urgently."

"Right," said Phoebe slowly. "And so you keep that phone

turned off and in your coat pocket. That would rather seem to defeat the purpose."

"Ha, yeah, I know, ha. I'm a bozo, aren't I? Thanks, Phoebe, you've saved the day again, now you carry on to the park. I need to get on to these telephone calls, okay?"

"Oh, yeah, sure," she said. Her quizzical look lingered on him for a moment, then she turned and left the room. Quickly Elliott took the phone out of his pocket, prised open the back and took out the battery.

Chapter 7

Stage 3: Self-Betrayal

Friday, 5.30pm

Elliott sat behind a desk lamp. The head of the lamp was angled downwards, creating a defined circle of light on the wooden surface of the small table. Elliott could make out Ian from the light reflected off the table, but he himself remained in complete darkness. A squally shower was passing and large raindrops thrummed against the iron shutters.

He watched Ian sliding back into consciousness. Having had his arms tied behind for such a long time Elliott could imagine there must have been a terrible pain across the shoulders and buttocks. After dozing for a while, Ian lifted his head, although his eyes remained shut, as if he was concentrating, a grimace of pain on his face. From the smell in the room, unpleasant but not yet unbearable, Elliott guessed there would be a need to loosen his bowels, and not doing so was surely causing stomach cramps. Clearly it was one thing for him to wet himself, but shitting his pants was another matter entirely. Pride could take a person a very long way, and Ian still seemed to have plenty left. That would need sorting.

The moment Ian's eyes opened, he became aware of the light. This was obvious from the way he blinked rapidly. Having seen no daylight since the seconds before his car hit a tree over twenty-four hours ago, it took a few moments for his pupils to contract sufficiently.

There was minimal illumination to the rest of the room, such was the targeted effect of the lamp. Ian's discomfort was all too plain. Elliott silently squirmed in his chair.

Sitting on the table was a bowl half-full of water, perhaps

a third of the size in diameter in comparison to the circle of light. The bowl was not half-empty. The water in this bowl had been put there very deliberately. There were two features that gave this away. The first was the fact that it sat the middle of the spotlight, perfectly in the centre of the pool of light, a circle within a circle. The second was the car battery with a pair of jump leads attached that poked its nose into the spotlight. A red plastic handle-covering clip was attached to the positive post, and one would presume that a black plastic handle was attached to the negative post at the other end of the battery. The leads that came from the battery disappeared threateningly into the pool of light and then out the other side, back into the darkness. To Elliott the look on Ian's face was exactly what he had hoped for. A combination of confusion and fear.

"What the...?" Ian muttered to himself in the darkness.

"With us again, are you?" Elliott's voice came out of the gloom, splitting the silence like a blast of cold air on a summer's day.

"Jesus," said Ian. "You frightened the life out of me. What... what's the bowl of water for? And the battery."

"You know," said Elliott, "I've been doing a lot of thinking. Have you been doing a lot of thinking, Ian?"

"Yes. Of course. That's what you asked me to do."

"Ah, good. That is good. Well done. And are there any particular thoughts or ideas that have taken hold?"

There was a pause. "I've been thinking about you."

"Ah. Well now. Thing is, Ian, this isn't about me. It's about you."

"Yeah. I do get that. But still. You. I've been thinking about what would drive someone to do what you are doing. You're obviously sick in the head, but you're also intelligent. So I think someone has pissed you off. That you've been rejected somehow. I reckon you're angry because something has happened to you."

Elliott did not answer straight away. He rested his left arm on the table and leaned forwards, remaining careful to keep his face out of the light.

"You have been thinking, haven't you? But not of the things I asked you to consider. No, you've been thinking how to get out of here. And about how you can unsettle me in order to get me to do something rash. Am I right?"

84

"Angry because of something that happened to you. Am *I* right?"

"I'm not playing your games, Ian."

"Games? You don't want to play *my* fucking games?!" Ian paused for a moment, as if reining himself in, reminding himself of where the power lay in this room. He took a deep breath before continuing. He seemed disorientated. Good. "Sure, I've been sitting here thinking. Not a lot else to do, is there, especially when you're in so much pain from where some nutter has tied you up. I've been thinking about what you said to me. That stuff about who I am is decided not by me but by other people, how they react to me. It makes sense. I actually think you've got something there. And then I got to wondering about you. What in hell's name drives someone to kidnap another person just to make them feel shitty about themselves? Just to teach them 'good manners'?" Elliott had the feeling that if it wasn't pitch dark in the room and if Ian had not had his hands tied behind his back, he would have been impersonating inverted commas in the air with his fingers. "I don't know you so I don't know the detail, but I'll bet it's something to do with the fact that someone broke your heart once. And you've never got over it. So you have to make someone else suffer. Am I right?"

"You know, Ian, you are so right that it is almost scary. Someone did break my heart once. And everything I do in this room is driven by that." Elliott chuckled to himself. "No, really, that's so prescient of you."

From his seated position behind the table, Elliott put his arm into the light. Slowly he moved his hand until it hovered just above the bowl of water. He flicked the surface of the water at Ian, splashing his face and body. The drops of water slowly trickled down Ian's face, glinting in the light of the lamp reflecting off the desk. Elliott flicked the water again. It was warm in that room, what little air there was flavoured heavily with the odours of Ian. The combination was to create atmospheric conditions that were both soupy and fruity. Ian shook his head like a dog in the rain.

"Here's a thing," Elliott said eventually. "What if it was *you* that had broken my heart? What if *you* were the one that had driven me to kidnap you? Wouldn't that be ironic? If you had done something so awful to me that I had to go to such horrific and extreme lengths to try and right the wrong that had been done?"

"Wait, do I know you?" Ian said. "Have we met before?"

"Not specifically," replied Elliott. "And yet I know you. I know your type. Everyone comes across your type at some point. Our lives are worse for your existence. Imagine that, Ian. My life – and many other people's lives too – would be improved if you had never been born. What a concept. We are the people you brush aside as you go about your selfish life. We are left in your wake, unwilling to stoop to your level in order to make you aware of your idiocy, taking the path of least resistance so that our contact with you is minimal. Until now. I have sought to engage with you. I have had enough." Another flick, and more drops of water hit Ian in the face.

"Let's talk about your father, Ian. You've quoted him a few times. This morning you told me about him running a pub, not earning enough to save, still working in his seventies. Was he a big influence on you?"

"Is. *Is* a big influence."

"Sorry. Slip of the tongue." Elliott allowed himself a broad smile, safe in the knowledge he could not be seen. He poked his tongue out and wiggled his head around for a moment, then quickly put it away again, feeling a little foolish even in the dark.

"Of course he is a big influence. He's my dad. He had a tough life. I want to avoid the things that happened to him." He was speaking now in a strong, determined voice, his eyes burning with indignation, as if this was a speech he had given many times both in his head and out loud to anyone willing to listen – or unable to leave. It was not the kind of speech one imagined a listener asking for, but one that would be offered as evidence to back up a certain course of action. Usually a course of action which had recently been detrimental to someone else. Probably the listener.

"I think my dad is brilliant and everything, but I want to be in control of my life," Ian continued. "He instilled in me the idea not to be reliant on others, to stick up for myself. My dad just keeps working, keeps serving other people a good time, trapped by a system that won't let him go. Every day I'd go to school through the pub, through the stale smell of beer and cigarettes, of other people's good times. I vowed that I would be the one to determine my destiny, that I would never be a victim of life like my dad is." The last few words trailed off and the fire that had sparked briefly in his eyes once again dimmed.

Elliott drummed his fingers on the side of the bowl. The water rippled from the outside into the middle. Ian bowed his head and stared at a point on the floor. Elliott could see two small patches of red on the man's cheeks. It was rather fascinating to watch someone else's anger for a change. He recognised the symptoms in himself but had never realised just how obvious they would be to others. Eventually he spoke, dramatically, in a voice pregnant with portent intended to make it clear to any listener that this was an important moment. He stopped drumming his fingers only the moment before speaking.

"Ian, there is a contradiction that runs through you like the San Andreas Fault. Something about you that is so fundamentally flawed that I am amazed you are even able to function as a human being. And you are going to have to accept this flaw if we are going to be able to move forwards in our discussions."

Elliott paused to allow for a reaction from the centre of the room. There was none. "You say your beliefs are based on your father's principles. And yet you also say you live your life in such a way that you don't make the same mistakes that he did. You therefore have a set of beliefs and a way of behaving that are completely opposed to each other. To repeat what I told you yesterday, you are a phoney. A fraud. A contradictory mess. You have no manners and no regard to other people. You lack respect. This unpleasant person that you have become is entirely down to trying to copy your father and yet not wanting to end up like him. This leads me to one conclusion. If you are to improve as a human being – and that is, after all, why we are here – you are going to have to denounce him and all that he represents."

Reaching down behind the table, Elliott flicked a switch on an electricity socket, loudly, ostentatiously. He picked up the two loose ends of the jack leads and brought his hands under the spotlight. He touched the two ends together, the crackle resonating round the room for a moment. Then he put the leads down next to the bowl of water and walked over to Ian, keeping his back to the light source, his face in darkness.

"Relax. This won't hurt a bit." Elliott took a knife out of his pocket. "I'm holding a knife, Ian. But you can trust me." Then Elliott reached down and starting cutting through the material of Ian's trousers. He winced as the stench of stale urine entered his nostrils. Putting his fingers between the tear in the cloth he pulled, ripping a large hole in the trousers.

"What the fuck are you doing?!" said Ian, panic in his voice. "Christ, I'm sorry, I didn't mean to upset you with that 'broken heart' thing."

"Ian, please don't swear. In fact it's probably best if you just don't speak," said Elliott, as he removed the remnants of the trousers and started on the underwear. Next the knife carefully cut into underwear that used to be white, Elliott again ripping them apart. Ian whimpered as his genitalia became exposed. Standing, Elliott went back to the bowl of water and rinsed his hands, drying them on his trousers. "Well, that wasn't very pleasant for either of us, was it?"

"What are you going to do? What the f…what are you going to do now?"

"I just told you. You are going to denounce your father. I appreciate this might not feel especially natural for you, with your genitals exposed and everything, but do try and concentrate, there's a good fellow."

Elliott picked up the bowl of water, ensuring that all Ian would see were his hands entering the pool of light and grasping the sides of the plastic bowl. Then he turned, took several small steps in the dark towards where he knew Ian was, and poured half the water carefully over his exposed genitals. Ian gasped, at least partly, Elliott guessed, due to the coldness of the water.

Carefully placing the bowl back into the exact middle of the circular pool of light, Elliott unclipped the red handle from the car battery and placed it on the table. He then followed both wires with his hands until he reached the other ends, went round to crouch in front of Ian, and pulled at the surprisingly smooth but flappy skin of his scrotum. Ian whimpered.

"Okay, okay, alright, you've made your point," he said between gasps. "Okay, sorry, let's talk, keep talking, come on, you don't need to do this."

"Just give me a moment, old chap," said Elliott. Then he laughed and looked up at Ian, even though it was pitch black and neither man could see each other. "Old chap! Ha! That's a good one!" He flicked Ian's penis playfully. He grabbed the scrotum, pulled it forwards a little and attached the clip to it. Next he did the same with the other clip. Then he stood. Ian was crying now.

"There's an old expression," Elliott said. "It's rather coarse so it's probably American. 'When you have them by the balls, their hearts will follow.' I think it's meant to be allegorical, but I'm not great with that sort of thing, so I took it rather literally."

Back at the table, the red clip had fallen on the floor. Eliott reached down and felt for it, his fingers clasping onto the plastic covering of the clip itself, then brought it into the light. He moved it close to the positive post and held it there, a few centimetres away, arm outstretched so that his head remained out of the light. All Ian would be seeing right now would be an arm from the elbow with a hand at the end holding something that could inflict a level of pain he would not want to imagine.

"Now, Ian. Do I take it I have your undivided attention?"

"Yes, yes of course you do, absolutely."

"Good. I rather thought I might. You see, these 'good manners' you referred to earlier. That's actually what this is all about. There are different versions of good manners all over the world. In this country belching at the dinner table is rude, in others it is a compliment. In Thailand you mustn't show the soles of your feet. You and I may have different views on what constitutes good manners. But they all have one thing in common. Respect for others. That's what we're really talking about here, Ian. A respect that you simply don't seem to possess.

"Let's talk about your father. He was the one that told you to look after number one, to just take care of yourself and not worry about other people. Do you think he was right?"

"Yes, of course," said Ian, somewhat tentatively. "Yes, that's why I am who I am – he was right, you've got to look after yourself in this world, no one else is going to look after you."

"My wife looked after me. My secretary looks after me. My sister looks after me. I've got lots of people who look after me, Ian, who care about me. Do you know why?"

"No, tell me, please, tell me."

"Because *I* care about *them*. That's how it works, Ian. It's the opposite of nature, the complete reverse of the free market economy. We are people, not businesses. As far as you were concerned, I was just another car in your way. I should have moved out of the way to let you pass, Almighty King Lord Ian in his borrowed-for-the-month car on his way to do important things."

Ian's eyes were fixed on Elliott's right hand, waving about as Elliott gesticulated to emphasise his points, the movement making the clip hover around the negative post on the car battery. Several times it almost touched as Elliott's voice went close to shouting level, and Ian's breath went in sharply and his eyes screwed tightly shut as if that would provide some sort of defence from the pain that would shoot through his body.

"Your father was an ass," Elliott continued, spittle flying across the light. "And he was wrong. If you spend what precious time you have on this planet looking out for yourself, all that you will become is selfish and arrogant. What a waste of a life. We are judged by the sum total of our interactions with each other, because we are a social species. Why do you think we choose to live next to each other, bunched up in cities, rather than being spread equally across the planet? Show love to another and that love will be returned. *That's* how the world becomes a happier place. By respecting those you come into contact with. It's a system that works, Ian. It only gets messed up when people like you are so selfish and ignorant, looking out for number one and not caring about anyone else, sticking their oar in the water and pushing instead of pulling, then everything collapses around your ears, Ian. And all because *you* exist! My world, *the* world, would be a better place if you had never been born. My goodness, Ian, I have no idea how can you even live with yourself, how you can even put one foot in front of the other. Just think of it for a moment. The space that you take up makes the world a worse place. What a weight to carry on your shoulders!"

Elliott stood and pressed the clips, opening the metal jaws and placing them over the exposed metal post on the battery. He ground his teeth. He had this. Sod off, Alan, sod off, Alan.

"I should just let go. Why shouldn't I? Justice. Revenge. Retribution for the world. How many people would thank me, actually thank me if I did this? How many of your colleagues would say you deserved it?" His hand was shaking as he kept the jaws apart. "And all because of what your father taught you."

Ian's eyes were streaming tears but did not waver their fixed stare on Elliott's hand. The silence of the next few moments betrayed a stand-off, each man unsure of his next move, Elliott allowing a degree of calm to return to him, Ian's mouth forming unheard words as he sought for the right words to encourage Elliott to move his hand away from the battery. Or perhaps afraid of saying the wrong words which would see the clip snap back into place over the pin.

"I...I..." Ian swallowed; it sounded dry. "I had no idea. I am sorry. I had no idea. I have never tried caring, but I can, I shall, I can change. Please give me a chance, help me to care."

"Do you denounce your father, Ian? Do you denounce your father? Do you realise how and why he is so wrong?" Elliott's voice was even, quiet.

"Yes, yes I do, absolutely. I totally denounce him."

"In denouncing him, what are you accusing him – and therefore yourself – of? In your own words, Ian."

"Um, of drawing the wrong conclusion from his experiences. Of getting it wrong. He told me to look after myself and I realise now that I took that as meaning not to care about others, but I see now, that's now how teams get built, it-it's not the best way for the world to work. Free market, competition, it's not always the best thing, sometimes collaborating and helping each other is best. If we just care about ourselves ahead of caring for others then we... my father...yes, it's true, totally, and I know that I have brought this on myself by my own actions, I do know that." Sweat was pouring down Ian's face and he was breathing fast and deep. "Christ," he whispered to himself, closing his eyes for a moment. He took a slow inhale. Still Elliott's arm emerged from the darkness and held the clip, jaws apart, ready to snap shut. His wrist was beginning to tire. In his head he urged Ian to get on with it. Ian continued, more measured now. "If I showed more respect to others, they would show more respect to me. I denounce what my father taught me. He was wrong."

Elliott turned his gaze away from Ian and looked at his hand. Slowly he lifted the clip away from the battery and set it down on the table. He looked back at Ian and smiled in the way that a parent smiles at a child who has finally eaten all their greens and can get down from table thirty minutes after the rest of the family has already left the dining room. It was a smile he rather wished Ian could see.

He walked around the room to take up a position directly behind Ian and placed one hand on the man's shoulder. There was a twitch when Elliott squeezed gently. "It's okay," he said, as if calming a child after its first panicky attempt at swimming. "Okay," he said again, as he manipulated the knotted muscles. Ian's breathing started to regulate, the sobs becoming further apart. Elliott's fingers gripped the shoulder as his thumbs found the harder parts of the muscles and applied pressure. Naomi loved this. She would often sit watching a film as Elliott stood behind the sofa teasing out the stresses of the day with his hands on her shoulders and back. "It's okay now," he said softly.

Ian's head was now bowed and he seemed exhausted. Kneeling, Elliott reached down and undid the knot in the rope that was holding Ian's arms together, unwound the rope, and stuffed as much of the coil into his back pocket to make it stay there. As soon as his hands were free, Ian reached forwards in a panic and grabbed the ends of the clips, removing them from his scrotum. Then he reached down to untie his legs.

"Don't bother," said Elliott. "The rope that binds your legs is secured by a combination padlock."

Elliott walked over to the table. He knew his way round this room in the dark pretty well by now. "I'm going now, Ian. I think we made a bit of a breakthrough today. But before I go, let's remind ourselves of the ground rules. You aren't going anywhere for at least a few days, probably a week. The exact amount of time depends on your progress to rehabilitation. You're doing very well so far."

Picking up the car battery and leads, he continued. "I'm going to leave this bowl here, and I will leave your hands untied. That will leave you able to stretch and move about a bit, this can't have been very comfortable for you. Firstly, I suggest you use the remaining water to drink and wash yourself. You may then wish to use the bowl as a toilet. I will be up again later tonight to take away the bowl and bring some food. I will not speak to you at that point, as it is important that you have time to reflect on what we have discussed. I will not be leaving the house for a while now. If you make any noise whatsoever, I will come back up and tie your arms to that chair again. The house is situated one and a half miles from the next house in the middle of a wood, so there really is no point in you trying to make noise to attract attention. Nevertheless, if you do, I shall find it both annoying and a major step backwards, and treat you accordingly. I hope you understand what I mean." He paused. "*Do* you understand what I mean, Ian?"

"Yes. Yes, I get the idea."

"Excellent." Elliott paused in thought for a moment before speaking again. He unplugged the lamp and picked it up, then walked over to the door and grasped the handle. "I took the light bulb out while you were sleeping, so don't bother trying to turn the light on. You'll be out of here soon enough, I'm sure." Elliott opened the door and left the room, calling over his shoulder as he went, "See you later, then."

Chapter 8

The morning sun tried valiantly to make headway against the blackout curtains in Elliott's bedroom. He had not drawn them completely the night before, leaving a gap of just a few centimetres on one side which now glowed brightly as if a searchlight was being beamed onto his window from an army chopper hovering outside. The alarm clock did its job at 8am but he had been lying awake since 7.30, staring at nothing for at least half an hour.

The day stretched out in front of him like a threat. It held no promises, no commitment, no compulsion; a weekend free of demands on his time. And yet the potential, the possibilities that lay in front of him. The excitement of the unknown. There was a plan to follow, the ten steps. From the moment he had stumbled across the studies of Korean and Chinese prisoner of war camps in the 1950s, those idle moments of wondering 'what I'd like to do with you if I got you in a room on my own' gained real substance. If he ever actually had the opportunity for a prolonged one-to-one session with someone that needed sorting out, he now had a theory to apply. Furthermore, unlike the original military intention, he would use the techniques for good, to help a person to realise they were wrong and then present them with the opportunity to improve, to walk away a better person. The idea of using brainwashing techniques to improve the world.

Perhaps he might pull over to let an ambulance safely pass by, only for it to be followed by a car trying to beat the traffic queues. Or have to take an instruction from Paolo for the documentation on a business purchase that he knew was undervalued. Or, as happened only last week, to see the dark window of a huge four-wheel drive wind down and a bag full of empty burger cartons be thrown into the gutter. On each of these occasions he had allowed himself to daydream how he might implement the brainwashing plan on these people, show them the correct way to behave, not only teach them a lesson but genuinely change their outlook and approach to how they saw other people – extreme manners, he often thought of it.

But to have such an opportunity presented to him, just there, on a plate, he could hardly have hoped for a more extraordinary coming together of circumstance. The chances were so great, it felt like destiny, irresistible. But did that make it right? He couldn't falter now, the barriers against the naysayers in his head must be kept strong and firm.

As he stared at the cream, red and black horizontal stripes of the curtains he began to build a wall in his mind. His father had taught him the technique as puberty wreaked its havoc to help him keep focus and repel doubt. School was a sea of self-doubt, insecurity just a plastic cup slammed into the back of the head away. Like a child's game he would stack small blocks of confidence on top of each other, building himself up, until a dead leg from Joey Davison or a stinging rebuke from Stacey Hill would bring the whole tower crashing down again. Even his teachers seemed to avoid him.

Then one day when he had come home with his homework soaking wet because Joey Davison had thrown it in the school pond, his parents had finally found out the truth. He pleaded with them not to contact the school, desperate not to make a fuss and make everything worse. His parents had talked in the front room while he ate his supper on his own in the turret.

Later that evening his father had knocked on the door. They had talked in a different way than ever before, different words and a new tone of voice, and Elliott would recall the growing feeling of comfort that comes from having your fears taken seriously for the very first time. They talked about how tough life can be at times, how mean people can be. For the first time Elliott had a real insight into the adult world, and how it wasn't so different from school after all. His father knew there were people locally who spoke nastily about him, Elliott reeling momentarily from the revelation that his parents knew they were not liked and yet carried on regardless. They still invited the gossips and the meddlers to their parties – "Keep your friends close and your enemies closer," he said. Elliott's love for his father grew immeasurably from that moment as he saw this man as a real person for the first time.

They talked about bullies, not just the physical bullies like Joey Davison, but the clever ones who would make you look stupid as a way of feeling that at least someone was beneath them. Elliott had finally admitted that he didn't really have any friends. His father had smiled knowingly and Elliott had felt better.

Then his father explained his suggestion. At night, when he couldn't get to sleep and the doubts would force their way into his mind, he was to imagine that they were knights on horseback, these doubts, trying to attack him. The black knight was to be the thing he was most concerned about, encased in dark armour. He called them the Worry Knights, and Elliott should take time to dress them and imagine the colours of the finery draped over their horses, the bright fluttering standards. Next, his father told him, he was to imagine that he was inside a castle, and to take lots of time when building the castle in his imagination, make extraordinary gargoyles and stained-glass windows, and turrets just like the one on their house with narrow slits from which archers could shoot flaming arrows.

And when the castle was finished, the Worry Knights would charge. But by the time they reached the castle there would be no way to get in: the drawbridge would be up, the moat deep and green, the portcullis down, and the men at the top of the battlements ready to pour boiling oil on his doubts and worries.

Most nights Elliott would fall asleep while still building the castle, taking pleasure in creating the detail. There would be giant fireplaces with priest holes, secret passages that allowed escape from the castle in case of siege. There would be a trebuchet in the courtyard and hidden openings from which nasty things could be thrown and poured. By the time he would start to decorate the mantel of the fireplace with carved figures, sleep would have taken over.

Just occasionally, if he was very concerned about something, the castle would be finished and he'd still be awake. At such times he would allow the Worry Knights to attack. All his fears and doubts, whether it was Joey Davison or a girl or homework, were hidden inside the armour of these knights, and he would imagine them dying a painful death with an arrow through the eyehole of their helmet, or drowning in the moat dragged down by the weight of their armour.

His father's talk soothed him and would be one of the essential building blocks of their close relationship in adult life. When Elliott saw Joey Davison the next day at school his stomach had lurched. Walking round the corner of a school building into the playground to see Joey towering above two sidekicks, he had ducked back out of sight, closed his eyes, and built a quick mental image of his tormentor running away from the castle with an arrow stuck in his bottom. He had giggled to himself at the image, then walked out into the playground with his head held high, looking straight ahead. Joey Davison had scowled as Elliott walked past, but not done anything. It was as if the new confidence his father had provided for him had scared away the bully. He had actually done it; with only the force of his own mind he had changed something – someone – for the better.

Elliott got out of bed and pulled back the curtains to let the sun enter the room. Padding through the lounge and into the kitchen he flicked the switch on the kettle and stared across the lawn to the leylandii trees which bordered the front and side of the house. Lucy's car was still on the gravelled parking area.

A large, plain white mug sat on the surface next to the kettle. On the bottom lay a spoonful of sugar. In a line to the right stood a plain white teapot, a tea cosy that looked like a small bobble hat, and a tea infuser, already filled with loose-leaf English breakfast tea. They had all been placed there the previous evening, so that all he now had to do now was take the boiled water, pour a little into the pot, swirl it round, being careful to make sure some of the water went up the spout, pour the still-hot water out of the teapot into the cup, swirl it round the cup, pour the water from the cup down the sink, re-boil the kettle, dangle the infuser inside, pour the water into the pot before it cooled again, put the lid back on, pull the tea cosy down over the teapot, and wait.

He used the time to get dressed, and returned to the kitchen to pour milk on top of the sugar, stir it round, and pour the tea on top of the mixture before replacing the cosy back on the teapot. Then he took the mug and walked out of his front door, up the stairs past Benny's door, and on to Lucy and Phoebe's flat.

Letting himself in, he called a greeting which was answered from somewhere deep within. He followed the sound down the short corridor past the bedroom doors on each side, into the lounge and on to the kitchen. Originally the bedrooms of the house, this flat was laid out differently to Elliott's. The kitchen wall had been knocked down to create a flow into the lounge. In its place was an island extended from one end of the work surface, around which they would eat most of their meals. The fireplace was more modest than the ground floor flat's, but shared the giant chimney stack, as did Benny's fireplace in the middle flat. The tiled conical roof of the turret was visible from the corner window, the tip of the roof being the same height as the ceiling of Lucy's flat.

Whereas the décor in Elliott's flat was all black leather sofas and red furnishings, Lucy's taste was much more modern bohemian. Prints of English birds in black frames on a white background adorned the wall, a set of six pictures purchased on her honeymoon, a reminder of a happier time that she kept meaning to replace. A cream carpet was partly obscured by a black-and-white rug underneath an ancient low oak table. Two sofas surrounded the table, upholstered with materials Lucy had chosen, with Phoebe's help, from thirty-three different sample packs that the upholsterer had left with her for two months.

A bookshelf covered the end wall, just as in Elliott's flat, but in Lucy's case they were large books on art, design, and the history of art and design. Lucy had always been the kind of student who would never buy a novel if the cover was of a scene from the movie of the book. When she and Paolo had still been in love – those few years that seemed like another age – their favourite anecdote, told at every dinner party, had involved a waiter informing them that the house wine was an Italian pinotage. Elliott knew that Paolo still told the story, but that Lucy looked back at those times with a shudder.

Phoebe and Lucy were sat at right angles to each other, having breakfast on the end of the island that formed the centrepiece to the kitchen. The radio was on low, a DJ that Elliott thought he recognised but couldn't name burbling away enthusiastically. Phoebe sat back in her chair and pushed a plate of bacon, scrambled eggs and toast away from her.

"Wow, that looks good, Phoebe," said Elliott.

"Yeah, I don't really want it. You can have it. Mum's having coffee and toast. I find it kind of depressing when I have bacon and eggs and stuff and someone else is just having coffee and toast."

Lucy looked at Elliott and rolled her eyes. Phoebe ignored her, pushed her chair back and stood behind it like a waiter.

"Here you go, Uncle E, have some breakfast. It's still hot."

"Oh, Phoebe, I couldn't," said Elliott, sitting down. He placed his mug on the table. Phoebe pushed the chair in as he sat. "Really, sweetie, this is your breakfast, you should have it." He picked up the knife and fork. "You made this for yourself, come on, you sit down now. Mmm, wow, this is butcher's bacon isn't it?"

Phoebe kissed the top of her uncle's head, then picked up a mug of coffee decorated with a picture of a rabbit and the words 'I Love Flemish Giants!' "I'm going back to bed," she said. "Somebody shout in the unlikely event of anything interesting happening."

"I'll be going in twenty minutes, darling," called Lucy as her daughter paused at the kitchen doorway. "You got plans for the day?"

"Are you going to work? Oh, Mum, that's crap."

"Phoebe, I've told you before, mind your tongue."

"I'm not sure 'crap' counts as a swear word, really. And in any case, it *is* crap, isn't it?" said Elliott.

"That is *not* helpful, Elliott. I've told you, I've got to finish this plan for Joey. He presents to the board on Friday, and he wants to see it beforehand, make sure it's right. I should have it finished by teatime."

"Who the hell would take the family inheritance and buy a wheelchair business with it? How to make a successful small business: buy a successful large business and give it to Joey Davison to run."

Lucy slammed her cutlery on the table and glared at Elliott. "I will *not* have you talking about Joey like that." She seemed close to tears for a moment. "He is not the person you knew at school. He works very hard and his wheelchairs have helped thousands of people. He donates huge amounts to charity. At least he tries to do some good in the world, unlike some."

"What the hell does that mean?"

"It means you would do well to stop being so negative about Joey Davison. About people like Joey Davison." She was close to shouting now. From the corner of his eye Elliott could see Phoebe edging back into the kitchen.

"Lucy," he said, speaking softly and cautiously, aware that Phoebe was still listening, "bearing in mind the relationship that Joey and I enjoyed, or should I say endured as far as I was concerned, I'm hardly likely to go out of my way to say anything positive about him. Am I now?"

The tactical manoeuvre seemed to work. Lucy's flushed cheeks began to return to their normal lack of colour. "Well, maybe it's about time you tried." The last word on the subject delivered with a loving disdain that she did not bother to conceal.

Phoebe walked out of the kitchen and across the lounge. "I'm going to bed," she called brightly. "You two can carry on arguing without me. I find it too depressing to listen to."

"You haven't said what you're doing today," called Lucy as she watched her daughter's back disappear into her room.

The door opened again and Phoebe's head poked out. "I'll probably just go to Steff's. You still okay to take me to judo later, Uncle E? You could pick me up from Steff's house."

"Time?"

"Four?"

Elliott thought for a moment. Stage four was this morning, which would need the afternoon to have any effect, leaving stage five for tonight. That all worked out pretty well. "No problem," he said to Phoebe's head, which disappeared back into its room and was replaced once again by the door.

With a sigh Lucy took a bite of her toast. As Elliott began to speak, she raised her index finger towards him. He closed his mouth, but held out his arms, requesting her permission to raise an objection. In response her finger was raised a little higher and her head dipped in warning. Defeated, Elliott returned to Phoebe's eggs.

They sat in silence for a few moments until Lucy finished the last of her breakfast. She picked up her own cup of coffee and held it in both hands. They looked at each other, Elliott still eating, waiting, looking at her expectantly.

"I don't have any choice," she said eventually. "I need the money. It's not easy being self-employed, and I need Joey to tell people I've done a good job. His testimonial is worth a lot. He's well respected."

"He's an idiot," replied Elliott.

"So are you but I don't go on about it." Lucy picked up Elliott's empty plate and took it to the dishwasher. It occurred to Elliott that his sister looked tired. Emotionally drained. The last time she had looked so weary was after Naomi died. He had been so absorbed in his own grief he had forgotten that his sister and wife had become the best of friends. Lucy had double the burden, supporting her brother and at the same time grieving for a lost soulmate.

The realisation had only hit him some six months after the funeral at a dinner party to which they had been invited as a pair, as if they were a married couple. She had been patiently explaining the benefits of stakeholder communication in a change process to a fellow guest, a rather gnarled and cynical business owner whose company, Elliott knew, was being held back because the owner was incapable of delegating. As he watched the one-sided and rather pointless conversation he studied Lucy's face that was so familiar, and for the first time he recognised in her their beloved if rather serious mother. Was it the crow's feet around the eyes that he had not noticed before, or the way she did not seem to smile as she was talking like she used to? And suddenly the whole picture came into focus for a second, as if he'd been transported into his sister's body and seen the world through her eyes, a world view formed and influenced by her experiences, not his. He saw the pain of her failed marriage, the expectations of her daughter, the lack of support from her brother. The loyalty, the love, the pain, and for a moment her life seemed harder to bear than his own.

Strange how a desire to protect can result in strangulation, how one person's caring arms can lead to another's suffocation. He saw it then, as he watched her battle to get across her point to the ignorant man, and he saw it now in her slumped shoulders and the momentary pause as she stood at the sink with her back to him.

She kept her hair long; their father had liked it that way. Black and shiny. Elliott always thought it looked strong, unbreakable even. Her nose was their mother's, slim but somehow determined, a strong nose with a visible bump that added to her features rather than detracted from them. Her eyes came from their father. Ever expressive, they were not so much the windows to her soul as sliding glass doors. They showed her joy at the world, alongside the energy she brought to helping those who wanted to be helped. Those who needed to be helped but did not want it were beyond her reach, and she did not waste her time with them.

"You can get better clients than that," said Elliott. "I can help you find more clients if that's what you need. Just don't deal with people like him. He can't have changed from what he was like at school, no one could change that much. You didn't know him then."

"Have any of us really changed, Elliott?" she replied, turning to face him and leaning back on the sink. She virtually folded her arms *at* him. "Has the world become easier? Have I progressed in the last sixteen years? I lie in bed at night and realise that nothing has moved forwards, nothing is better, I haven't improved anything. It never used to be like that. When I was young everything was about change, about improvement. Being angry at the world for not getting better, constantly striving to make yourself better – it's all about change, that's almost the point of youth. You're told by teachers and parents to grow up, stop behaving immaturely, learn to think for yourself, improve, improve, improve.

"Then kids come along, and suddenly you grind to a halt, and all your change is foisted upon your children. Their rate of change is so fast, especially in the early years, that you can't keep pace, so you forget about improving yourself, let alone the world, and focus all your attention on the change in your children. And then they grow up. And then what? What changes then? You wake up and realise the world hasn't improved while you weren't watching, if anything it's got worse. And what are you supposed to do about it? You thought that the young ones behind you were changing it, like you once thought you were. But no, they've become selfish and feckless while you weren't watching, just like we did. And so it's all down to you again. But you haven't got the energy to change the world any more. It's been kicked out of you by the very process of helping the next generation, who don't seem to want to change things either. You're shoved back into the passenger seat and you hold on tight, keep things close, and just try and be a positive influence on the few things that fall close enough for you to grab hold of."

"Just tell him to sod off, Lucy. Joey Davison is not worth you getting this stressed out for. You don't need him. You're better than that."

"Oh, thank you. Just thank you. Is that what you really think of me? Someone that only does something because she has to? Is that what Phoebe thinks? Mum is a pushover, an easy touch? Has it ever occurred to you that maybe I am working with Joey because I want to? That he might just be the cause I have been looking for? I need him as much as he needs me." Lucy turned, filled up the kettle, and took two coffee mugs out of a cupboard. She put in two spoonfuls of coffee, every movement a statement, every item placed on the work surface just a little harder than it needed to be. The kettle noisily began its task as she stared out of the window over the fields. Then she turned and spoke to Elliott again, arms again folded, her face set back into her default expression of nurturing.

"You know what you need, Elliott? You need to get out of the house. Ever since Naomi died you have been brooding. Go and meet people. Get some of your old friends over for dinner."

Elliott scrunched his face back at her. "Who? Why? Who would want to come and see me?"

"Friends? You and Naomi used to socialise a lot. Just invite them."

"I don't think that's a good idea, Luce."

"Why on earth not?"

Elliott's face unravelled itself and he looked down at the table, making small circles on the linoleum cover with his finger.

"I suppose I always assumed that people who came to see us were really just coming to see Naomi. I never really thought of myself as having friends. Before Naomi they were people who let me hang with them while they waited to find a partner, and when I was with Naomi they were people who enjoyed her company and had to have me along as well."

Lucy laughed. "Oh, Elliott. That's how everyone feels. You're not alone. And it's not true. People do enjoy your company. Especially when you're not being a pompous knobhead."

The doorbell buzzed and Phoebe came out of her bedroom to open the front door. It could only have been Benny, as no one else could have entered the building. Instantly Elliott recognised his northern brogue as it rumbled in the distance, offset by Phoebe's bouncing and enthusiastic tone. They greeted each other and said something that Elliott couldn't make out, then the two of them entered the room, accompanied by two others: a man in his twenties with tight, curly hair, soft, easy-going eyes and a camera dangling round his neck, and an older man who looked like the younger man would look in twenty years' time. Elliott and Lucy stood in greeting.

"Elliott, my good man, someone is here to see you," said Benny. "Estate agent and a chap who wants to take some pictures. Rang my buzzer as you weren't in, thought I'd bring him up here. By a happy coincidink, here you are. All's well, et cetera. Eh?"

Elliott eyed the photographer suspiciously. "Take pictures of what?" he said.

"Your flat, Elliott," said Lucy. "He's done mine and Benny's, he needs to do yours and the turret. For the valuation."

"I'm sorry," Elliott said to the two men, "there's been a bit of a misunderstanding. I'm sorry to have wasted your time."

"Is it not convenient?" said the estate agent. "'Cause I'm kind of here now, you know. Will only take a few minutes. We're not looking to win any awards, ha-ha, just a few snaps for the valuation, and I need a little look around, won't be long."

"Well, I'm sorry," said Elliott, "but it is inconvenient. Sorry."

"Elliott, don't be silly," said Lucy. "It will only take him ten minutes. Won't it?"

"I can certainly be quick. Quick jog round, run up to the turret, that sort of thing," said the photographer.

"There you go. Come on, Elliott, let's not be silly."

"I can't find the key and the door is locked," said Elliott. "Not been in the turret for a while, it won't be tidy. It needs to be another day. Sorry."

"Oh, nonsense, Elliott," said Lucy. "Your flat is always tidy."

"I'm going out. Sorry. Excuse me." Elliott walked past the three people standing in front of the door. Lucy ran after him and caught him as he opened the front door.

"Elliott, please. This is ridiculous."

Elliott turned and saw Phoebe standing behind her mother. "I'm not letting anyone into my home," he hissed to Lucy. "End of story. So drop it." He walked into the hallway, Lucy scuttling behind him.

Lucy put her hand gently on his arm. "Elliott, you have to do this. Please. I need a written valuation of this house."

"Why?"

The weight of the world seemed to descend upon her shoulders once again. It was as if a moment that she knew was inevitable and yet had tried so hard to put off had finally arrived. She spoke quietly, clearly trying to keep Phoebe from hearing. "It's for security. I'm taking a loan."

"What for? Who from?"

"Why do you think, you moron? I need the money. You think this is easy for me, Elliott? Please, just go along with it."

Elliott felt something stir inside him. This was not a moment for Alan to appear. He had to get out of that place. "Lucy..." he hissed, the firmness in his voice borne from a determination not to get angry. He watched the reaction in her face, like a mirror showing him how bad he must seem to Phoebe right now. He tried to speak more calmly, but it just came out overly deliberate. "I don't know what's going on here, but I'm not having it out in front of Phoebe. They are not coming into my flat. Okay? Got it?"

He tore her arm from his, turned round and walked out of the flat, slamming the door behind him. The final thing he saw as he left was the look of hurt and shock on Phoebe's face, his darling Phoebe, the one person in the world who, up until that moment, had thought that she really understood him.

Chapter 9

Stage 4: Breaking Point

Saturday, 11am

Elliott ran into his flat, double-locking the door behind him, then through into the lounge where he opened a drawer and took out a light bulb. As he crossed the room to the secret door he grabbed the length of rope from the coffee table that he had placed there the night before, then went into the turret. He took the stairs three at a time, burst open the door at the top and almost fell into the room. Ian let out a squeal as the door bounced against the wall, then swung shut again with a bang.

The lamp was still on and was shining on the corner of the empty plate on which Elliott had brought a portion of home-made lasagne with chorizo the previous evening. It had been accompanied by green beans in lemon and garlic and a dauphinoise potatoes of which he had been particularly proud. He had placed a tray with the food, a plastic jug of water and a paper cup a safe distance from Ian inside the room, then left without a word. Now Elliott walked over to the lamp and switched it off. The darkness seemed even more absolute than ever before, even desolate, maybe.

"Place your hands behind the chair please, Ian," he said, still puffing slightly.

"It's okay, you don't have to," Ian implored. "Please. I won't do anything. It hurts. Please, you can trust me."

Elliott thought for a moment before speaking. "You're a thoroughly unpleasant person, Ian. I don't trust you. I don't trust your type. I don't trust that you have understood why you are here yet. That you are here because of the person you have been. Because of your own actions."

"I do, I really do get that. I promise, I've been thinking about it, I do." He was almost begging now and Elliott had to force himself to remain firm.

"Hands behind the chair, please. Then we'll talk about it."

He walked around the perimeter of the room, then took a pace forwards so that he was behind Ian. He felt in the darkness for the hands being offered to him, then took the rope and bound Ian's arms behind him once again. He took an extra moment to compose himself, closing his eyes and focusing his mind. He called on some of his legal training, dealing with clients – only enter an interview with a client when you know what it is you want to achieve. Think about the eventual outcome of these sessions, then think of the steps, then think where you are in the process, then what today must achieve.

Don't be distracted by Phoebe. What happens in this room is isolated from the rest of life, it is a play and he is merely an actor. Everything is Ian. It is all about Ian. He is the key. He is the one who will make everything turn out right in the end. This is where the focus must be. Stage four. The big one. Focus.

"So," said Elliott eventually to the back of Ian's head. "What are you waiting for? This isn't about me, you know. Why are you waiting for me to speak? It's about you. What have you got to say?"

"Okay. Um, okay, look, I'm not actually sure what I am supposed to do now. Can you help me, please? I'm not even sure who I am any more. You've made your point, you've showed me that my father gave me the wrong direction in life, which means everything I've believed in, either subconsciously or consciously, is wrong. Where does that leave me? Why are you doing this? What am I supposed to say next? I just want to go home." Ian began to sob violently and loudly. "Let me go," he shouted between gasps for air. "Just let me go, you bastard."

Elliott stood and walked back around to the door. He leaned backwards with one knee bent and the foot against the wall. He waited in silence for the crying to subside. It took a few minutes, during which his stomach knotted as he heard the man in front of him break down, and then slowly released as he reminded himself over and over that this was entirely what was supposed to be happening, that it was for Ian's benefit in the long run. He wondered if this was how a paramedic might feel with a dislocated shoulder. Shove it back into place, knowing the pain it would cause and yet also knowing that things would be much better once the anguish was overcome. He had to stay firm. He had to see this through. Short-term pain, long-term gain. He waited as Ian slowly regained control until all that was left was sniffing.

"Tell me something, Ian," said Elliott at last. "Do you think I am the one that is in the wrong? Eh? Am I wrong for what I am doing to you?"

"Um, I don't know. Yes, I think so. You have kidnapped me. That is wrong. Even though I deserved it. Maybe we are both wrong?"

"Hmph," replied Elliott. He snorted. "I'm very much afraid that I am in the right. You are in the wrong. In fact, you might say that this entire experience is about you understanding that I am right and you are wrong. Kidnapping is, as you say, wrong. That is unarguable. However, I have done it for the right reasons. The one trumps the other. The bigger cause wins out. I am righteous. And if you don't get that, if you cannot actually thank me at the end of this, we have a problem. A really, really big problem."

Continuing to pace around the room, Elliott took a sudden step inwards to position himself behind Ian, slamming his hands down on the seated man's shoulders. "Let us recap a moment," he said. "In our last session, you denounced your own belief system, you disowned the person who had created it, your father. You betrayed your father. You realised that all you believed in, and all the people you believed in, are fundamentally flawed. This proves that my kidnapping is, ultimately, the right thing to be doing. Because all that you are is wrong.

"I've been thinking about a comment you made. About letting you go. About me 'getting away with it'. You think it is possible to stop this process in which we are engaged, that releasing you is an option. This is due to the fact that you haven't seen my face. I've kept you in a dark room for about two days now, and at the end of all of this, I could blindfold you, drive you into the countryside and dump you, and you would have no way of tracing me. I could, as you say, get away with it. Because you haven't seen my face. Because you don't know who I am."

Elliott walked over to the table, reached down and switched the lamp back on. Next he took hold of the lamp and tilted it so that it shone upwards. Leaning forwards, he brought his face into the beam and looked at Ian.

Smiling broadly, he said, "Hello."

Stepping back, Elliott positioned the lamp so that it shone on the ceiling. From his pocket he took the light bulb. Reaching up on tiptoes, he screwed the light bulb into the empty light fitting, now illuminated by the lamp. Then he reached behind him to the wall by the door and flicked the switch.

Light flooded the room and Ian was forced to shut his eyes and turn his head downwards, away from the source. Now that Elliott could see him properly, he did look a mess. He had rearranged his trousers, and Elliott wondered what it meant when a man would seek to cover up his exposed genitals in a darkened room with no one there to witness. There wasn't a great deal of pride left in the man in front of him – that much was obvious – and yet he had attempted to protect what little he had left. That was probably a good sign, cause for optimism that this experiment might actually work. But shining a literal light on the stinking mess of a human that Ian presented right now gave that pride the lethal blow that was needed. It may have only been Elliott there to see it, but the light shone for everyone. Ian bowed his head, rested his chin on his chest and began to sob again.

Elliott leaned against the door. "It was an interesting thought of yours," he said. "The idea that I could get away with it as long as you didn't know who I am. But it occurred to me that it would become a barrier to progress. The idea that I might let you go because I could get away with it was making you think that the conclusion was not inevitable. It would prevent you from taking that next step. In order to truly accept the depth of your self-delusion and open your heart to a new way of being you need to understand the lengths to which I will go in order to help you. So, this is me." Elliott leaned forwards, put two fingers underneath Ian's chin, and lifted up his head. Two bloodshot eyes the colour of anxiety stared resignedly back at him as another sob forced its way out with a bark.

Some dried blood was smeared across one cheek, dissected by the tracks that his tears had taken. The man really did look dreadful. Elliott smiled goofily and gave a little wave. "Hi," he said.

With his free hand Elliott reached into his back pocket. He brought out a small card and held it in front of Ian's eyes. "And here's another thing, skip. My name's not Bob. But you probably guessed that. You're unpleasant, but you're not stupid. As you can read on this here driving licence, my real name is Elliott. Elliott Harmison."

Elliott let go of Ian's chin and, almost to his surprise, the head did not drop back. Instead it looked back at him with a slightly puzzled expression. Elliott continued to lean forwards.

"You see, Ian, now you know what I look like and what my name is, there's no going back. For either of us. If we start with the pretty safe assumption that I have no intention of being arrested for kidnapping you, there are only two resolutions to this situation. I'm a pretty determined fellow, especially where there is a moral high ground involved. Your time here is going to result in you being a changed man, realising how your view of life was self-centred, egotistical and arrogant. Either you walk out of this room actually thanking me for what I have done to help you, or you don't walk out of here at all. You might say that I've just raised the stakes. I'd prefer to say that I've just focused your mind. I guess Heaven takes care of fools and scoundrels, eh, Ian?"

He barked one individual laugh. "Ha!" As he did so, Ian's head slowly fell back down onto his chest, from where it bobbed up occasionally.

Elliott picked up the plate and put it on the tray along with the jug, picked up the bucket, and slipped quietly out of the room. He returned fifteen minutes later carrying the tray with one hand. The jug was once again full with water, a fresh paper cup next to it, and the plate held a croque-monsieur, freshly made béchamel sauce browned on top of the cheese. In the other hand he carried the bucket, now empty and clean.

Ian had not moved. It seemed as if he had been sobbing for the entire time that Elliott had been out of the room. Elliott put down the tray and bucket and lifted the other man's head, then turned it towards the food. The eyes were dull, uncomprehending, staring at the food without animation. It was as if all processing power was being used elsewhere and there was no energy left to move the muscles in his face. The eyes moved from the food to Elliott with an expression that suggested a similar level of understanding to a puppy staring at its master putting up a shelf.

Without speaking, Elliott took the jug, poured the water into the cup, then placed the tray on Ian's lap. Ian looked blankly at Elliott's face as if awaiting acceptance or permission. Elliott knelt down and held the toasted sandwich to Ian's mouth.

"Eat. It's good," he said. Slowly Ian moved his head forwards and took a bite. Ian ate, still staring at Elliott as if studying a painting that he couldn't fathom the meaning of. After two more bites Elliott held the cup to his lips and he drank in huge gulps.

When the food was finished, Elliott took the tray and put it on the table, then sat back on the table and folded his arms, as if waiting for Ian to speak.

Still Ian stared back at him like the blackened eyes of a Modigliani portrait. The edges of his mouth were stained yellow with the sauce and his tongue kept flicking out as if trying to take a taste away from his lips. He rocked slightly in his chair and deep sighs were slowly released, lifting his body straight, then allowing his spine to bend and the slump to return. He licked his lips one more time, and then he spoke.

"I'm sorry," he said. "I'm sorry I gave you the finger. I'm not proud of the person I am. I have brought this on myself by my own actions. I deserve this, this, this moment, this time here. I, I don't know what I am going to do next, I don't know, I…" He stopped speaking for a moment, and Elliott still did not move, not even a muscle in his face which might give any form of feedback or acceptance. "You are better than me," Ian continued. "Everyone is better than me. I realise that now. I've always known it, I just haven't admitted it to myself. I give up on me, I give up on my friends, I give up on my life, such as it was. And I have learned. You have learned me. I mean, you, I have understood much, many things. I just don't, um, I think, I don't know what, what…" Ian's eyes focused for a moment. "I don't know what I have learned. I don't know what to think any more."

"Ian," said Elliott, "you have come a long way. But there is further to go. We will take that journey together. Okay?" The smile that crept onto Ian's face was so grateful, so pathetic, that Elliott had to force himself not to untie him and give him a great big hug. This was a time to focus, to deliver the coup de grâce which would allow real change to flood in like air to a vacuum. Ian was blank. He was ready to be tempted by an alternative belief system.

"There is another way, Ian. You don't have to be the person you have been. Do you remember earlier on I said that you must leave this room thanking me? I meant that literally. Good manners. It might not sound like much, but if you show good manners you are revealing what is in your heart." Elliott thumped his chest. "It shows that you care about others more than yourself. It shows respect. And I think we can both agree that such a thing must be a prerequisite for a good human being, can we not?"

Ian nodded meekly.

"Ian, I have to go somewhere this afternoon. I will be gone for a few hours. I want you to use that time productively. I would like you to think about something for me. I want you to consider what characteristics make up the ideal human being. I've given you two clues already. First that your previous selfish and arrogant behaviour, and the lightweight philosophies behind it, will not appear on the list, and secondly that good manners will. You take it from there. How does that sound?"

"Okay. Okay, I can do that. I think I know what you want."

"*No!*" Elliott slammed his fist onto the table. "It is *not* about what I want, Ian. It is about what is right. It is about demonstrating that you are able to understand the difference between who you have been, and what you need to be. It is about demonstrating that you can change. Can you change, Ian? Can you really do this?"

"Yes," said Ian quietly. "Yes, I can. And I can tell you why. Because I want to."

Elliott could not help but break out into a broad smile. "Now that's the spirit! There might be a chance of you leaving this room after all!"

Chapter 10

Saturday, 3.45pm

Tearing metal, the sound of breaking bones and bodies twisting that should never have to be heard, then a brief silence before shouting and panic and pain and pain and panic and hands and help and helplessness.

Elliott opened his eyes. He had fallen asleep on the sofa. The television was shouting at him. The rugby match which had provided such a relaxing backdrop had now given way to half-time adverts. He could swear the adverts were deliberately broadcast louder than the programme. Those last moments of hazy sleep as he resurfaced had been disconcerting, unwelcome. It must have been a car advert but had now moved on to aftershave lotion, all string quartets and chiselled jaws. He reached for the remote control and pressed the well-worn mute button.

After downing a large glass of water from the kitchen, Elliott stopped by the front door to put on a pair of driving-and-town-walking-when-dry shoes. He kept that pair inside the flat, on a low rack next to the look-professional-yet-casual shoes. The off-road-muddy-walk, off-road-dry-walk, driving-and-town-walking-when-dry, acceptable-with-shorts and use-when-decorating shoes were all kept in the porch. If any of these five basic pairs of shoes wore out he would take them to the large shoe shop in town and say to the assistant, "Can I have another pair like these, please?" Shopping by himself had never taken Elliott very long.

Shopping with Naomi had been a far more pleasurable experience. Having met when they worked as paralegals at the same firm of solicitors in London, she had eventually given up hoping he might ask her out to dinner and instead suggested she take him to Richmond shopping. She offered to attempt the impossible: to bring his wardrobe forwards by at least a decade. He had eagerly agreed, taking the trip entirely on face value. Not for a moment did he imagine his secret desires for his work colleague could possibly have been reciprocal, and he had expected to spend the day mooning over her like a lovesick rabbit.

As a result he had bought everything she suggested including three pairs of new shoes, the style of which he had endeavoured to replicate ever since. He deemed her judgement in such matters incontrovertible, especially in comparison to his own agnostic approach to sartorial matters. Latterly, however, it was also because his footwear provided a direct lineage through to those original shoes and a day which was to become the most magical of his entire life as the realisation slowly crept up on him that it might actually be possible for someone to fall in love with him.

As he now left the flat, he tripped over an Adidas bag. Phoebe's judo kit. Had she been ringing his bell? He must have been in the turret at the time. There was a note saying she'd be in the park, and could he bring her kit and pick her up at 4.45? He carried her judo kit out to his car and drove to the park.

Phoebe was sitting on a swing, not moving, arms folded and hair forwards. Mikey was adjacent to her, allowing his swing to rock, feet fixed to the ground. They looked awkward, uncomfortable, like they had argued and no one had won, but neither wanted to be the first to leave. It was a sight that made Elliott feel sad. Young love should be filled with happiness and excitement, all the promise of the future, all the potential of love yet to be experienced. The thrill of discovering that someone likes you, which might lead to being in love with you, yes, you, of all people, who never thought anyone would think of you in that way, who had wondered on many a rainy Sunday afternoon what love was and how you could change yourself in order to make people like you more, even as you knew you must be true to yourself, only to eventually discover someone who got flustered when you spoke to them and you hadn't even been trying to impress them. The endless boundaries of love first found, after so many years of thinking it could never happen, of waiting and watching and hoping and tricking yourself into not caring and then caring oh so very much but only briefly, only long enough to allow the possibility before the inevitable lack of response and long trough of living life in the waiting room that is life without love. Oh, Elliott knew all about love, both its fragile presence and its gaping absence. He beeped his horn gently, almost apologetically. Phoebe got up from the swing and walked over to him without a word to Mikey and got into the car.

From the glimpse of her face that he managed to sneak through her hair he guessed that she had been crying. Elliott knew better than to enquire. Not only would she not tell him, she would get annoyed that he had pried. Instead he told her a joke that someone had sent him in an email, and although Phoebe said she thought it was pretty lame, it seemed to lift her spirits.

The judo match was taking place in an industrial estate in an area known locally as the Trestles. One of the units had been converted into a gymnastic centre and was used as home by a local judo club. As they drove Phoebe turned on the radio, flipping the channel away from Radio 4 until she found a song she liked, playing on a local station. She stared out of the window, singing quietly to herself. When the song finished the news bulletin began. The lead item was the disappearance of a local man.

"Let's have some music," said Elliott, and tried to change the channel, but Phoebe blocked his arm.

"No!" she said. "I really want to hear this, it's totally freaky."

The report told of a local man, Ian Talbot, who was missing. When his crashed car had first been discovered on Thursday the police had suspected drink-driving, especially because his wallet was found at the scene, although his phone was not. They had initially wanted to find Ian Talbot in order to question him but now, two days later, he had still not surfaced and his family were getting worried. Further examination of the crash site revealed a second set of footprints and tyre tracks, and the police were now treating the disappearance as suspicious. The bulletin concluded with a police appeal for anyone with any information whatsoever to contact them, and gave a dedicated telephone number. Phoebe took her phone out of her pocket and tapped in the number.

"Who are you calling?" asked Elliott.

"No one, just putting that emergency number into my phone. You never know, I might see something that could be useful." Phoebe returned to the passenger window. Elliott remained silent as six different ways of changing the subject flew through his mind. He slowed the car down to allow another car to pull out in front of him.

"I wonder what happened to him?" she continued. "It's funny when something happens so close to home, it makes it so much more real. Maybe he ran away to start a new life, to leave behind mounting debts and a nagging wife. Or maybe he was kidnapped and the police are going to get a ransom note, perhaps wrapped around one of his fingers to prove they really do have him."

"Phoebe!"

She giggled. Almost a woman, he thought to himself, and yet still a little of the child remained in her. He hoped that giggle would never leave, with its betrayal of the joyful outlook that was the very essence of her soul. She didn't know it, but charging towards her was adulthood and its bitter exposure to the true nature of the world. She was changing, had been since the moment that she was born, but the changes had been getting gradually smaller, as if the refining process required less and less to be removed as she got older. But there was one big jolt left as the moulding process would be put to the test, and he only hoped that the final leap into maturity would not squeeze from her that joyful innocence and glee.

They approached a row of cars parked on either side of the road. A car ahead slowed and flashed its lights, inviting Elliott to pass first. He lifted one finger from the steering wheel to show his appreciation as he passed.

"When we get there and see the programme, do you mind if I don't stay for the whole time? I'll watch your first bout, but then I'll probably go and come back at the end, is that okay?"

"Oh. Okay. Sure."

"I haven't missed many of your fights, Phoebe," he said.

"The only competition you missed all of was two years ago in Chatterton village hall because you were poorly and Mum wouldn't let you go, and you missed two fights on Thursday. Other than that you've seen them all since I started judo."

"Well then, can I ask that such unswerving dedication on my part by rewarded with a bit of time off for good behaviour? Only an hour or so."

Phoebe looked at him, and eventually smiled. "I guess so." She continued to look at him, her gaze intensifying. He glanced at her, almost feeling the glare burning his cheek. He glanced again, then laughed awkwardly. "What?" he said. "What are you staring at?"

"I've just figured you out," said Phoebe, her eyes narrowing. "I've just sussed out what's going on here. You bastard. You sneaky little bastard."

"Mind your language please, Phoebe," said Elliott.

"You've been acting very strangely the last few days, Uncle E, and I've just worked out why. You are such a phoney. That wasn't your phone I found in your pocket at all, was it?"

"Of course it was, Phoebe, who else's would it have been? Don't be so silly. You're imagining things."

"No, wait, it all fits." She turned in her seat to look at him. He kept his eyes fixed on the road ahead, feeling her stare burning into his cheek. There is no stare more loaded with judgement than that of a teenage girl. He didn't need to turn his head to know he was being scanned. "Yeah, I get it," she continued at last. "You were all flushed and stressed when I saw you on Thursday after school. You could barely wait to leave my birthday tea. Then I find that mobile, with dozens of messages on it. You were getting all stressy about that photographer going into your flat this morning. I've worked it out. I know what's going on." She folded her arms and continued to look at him. He took his eyes off the road only briefly, darting a look in Phoebe's direction. Her face was impassive, eyes narrowed in thought.

"Look, Phoebe, I—"

"No, no, don't say anything. I have to get my head round this."

He stole another glance before looking back at the road and saw her lips were pouting, as if chewing over the last few options before a conclusion began to draw itself. Now he became acutely aware that she had turned her head and was staring at him.

"Phoebe, I really—"

"Look at you! You're going bright red!"

"Okay, that's enough. I don't know what—"

"Ha! It's true, isn't it? I've found you out! You've got a girlfriend, haven't you?!"

A teenager on a bike had been riding along the pavement and now hopped into the road in front of their car. Elliott instinctively stamped on the brake, his left arm swinging out across Phoebe's body to protect her before the seatbelt had a chance to do its job. He shook his head silently, put the car back into gear and carried on driving. A few hundred metres later he began indicating left to turn into the industrial estate.

"You sneaky—"

"Yes, alright, Phoebs, I don't think we need to hear that word again."

"I'm right, aren't I? You've got a girlfriend. Why so secretive, Uncle E? It's great news. Me and Mum have been saying how we wished you'd get a woman back into your life. Time to move on from, well, you know. Get back on the bike."

"I'm not sure that's the most charming phrase to describe falling in love, Phoebe."

"I'm right! You *have* got a girlfriend! And she stayed over last night! Oh wow!"

Elliott laughed a little too loudly as he pulled into a parking space and turned off the engine. Phoebe didn't make any move to leave the vehicle, but continued to face him with an intensely contemplative glare.

"So what is it? Why the secrecy? Is it someone we know? Is she ugly? Or fat?"

"Political correctness doesn't apply to teenagers, does it? Look, it's not really any of your business, Phoebe. Drop it, please. Look." With comedic effort he furrowed his brow and pursed his lips, then with a raised finger pointed to his face. "See this? Serious face." If anything her eyes narrowed even further and the smirk grew a little wider.

"Do you know what I envy about you, Phoebe?" he said. "It's not necessarily the optimism of your youth, but the absence of it in me. You see good everywhere, don't you? Even when you were a toddler you spent the entire time trying to work out where you were going to have fun next. I walk around with a fug in my brain wondering how the hell I got to be where I am. If something happens you embrace it, poke it a bit to see what you can do with it that might be a giggle, then squeeze every last drop of joy out of it. I tend to duck and throw my hands over my head, waiting for the worst. It's why I enjoy your company, Phoebe. You make me forget to be miserable for brief periods."

Elliott opened his door and got out of the car. Phoebe quickly did the same on the other side.

"Stop being dramatic and changing the subject," she called on tiptoes across the roof of the car. "Are you going to meet her now? Is that why you're not staying?"

"Enough, girl," he laughed. "You're barking up the wrong tree. Now come on, concentrate on beating people up." He walked into the sports hall and she bounced alongside him, asking questions which were met with his grinning silence.

After Phoebe won her first bout easily, Elliott left the hall, leaving with a discreet 'thumbs-up' and receiving a strange hand signal in return that he didn't recognise. If pressed he'd have guessed that it rather looked like a charging bull with the shivers, although the meaning of such a gesture was lost to him. He assumed it to be positive by the broad smile that accompanied it.

He got into his car and pointed it towards town and a search for solitude and contemplation.

The cathedral held a similar attraction for him as the turret, only with greater pathos. As a teenager he would take the bus into town, sitting downstairs while groups of three and four boys ran upstairs, throwing a word of abuse or their rolled-up tickets at him as they went. He would then walk to the cathedral, take his favourite seat on a pew near the back, and just 'be'. Although the turret and the wood and fields surrounding Meanwood Towers offered isolation, he found a more fulfilling solitude was to be had in the middle of a building full of other people, insulating him like a fleece. He could mull and mope without fear of being interrupted, just himself and his thoughts surrounded by the shuffling noises of worshippers and tourists, clergy and cleaners. Sometimes he would study, resting a history textbook on his knee. Scattered figures bent over in prayer would sit quietly on neighbouring pews. Tourists would wander through, staring and pointing, whispering, the combined effect of all the low voices creating an ambient music that washed around him, providing comfort that his solitude was shared with others, giving his isolation a sense of purpose.

Having finally found a parking space Elliott walked the short distance into the square on the other side of which stood the cathedral. He walked past a few skateboarders who looked old enough to know better and whose day seemed to consist predominantly of sitting around watching each other fail to perform tricks. Pigeons scattered in front of him and he felt the usual pull from deep within his childhood to run after them. His father had once promised him ten pence if he could catch one, and the desire to complete the challenge still smouldered away.

A small silver caravan stood one side of the square, a large orange board across its brow announcing 'CarBucks – The Best Coffee In Town'. He bought a large Americano and a freshly made pastrami sandwich, then walked over to the other side of the square where it looked as if someone had dropped an assortment of filthy clothes. He placed the sandwich and drink on the floor, then gently kicked the bundle. A face appeared sideways as the head of a young man peeked out. It stared first up at Elliott, blinking, just awoken, then at the offering. Elliott turned and walked towards the cathedral.

"Thanks, Mr Harmison," called the young man in a croaky voice, sitting up gingerly and unwrapping the sandwich. Elliott waved over his shoulder, not turning round.

A woman approached him, studying his features as she neared. She was slim and tall, over six feet, with a long coat flapping around her knees and several scarves. Some might have described her as elegant, some would have disagreed. He noticed a teenage boy dragging his heels behind her.

"Elliott?" she said. "Elliott Harmison?"

He looked at her again. She was certainly familiar, and yet he couldn't quite be sure.

"Is that you, Do-nu…" He caught himself at the last moment.

"Yeah! It's me, Doughnut," she said. "God, I haven't seen you since school. How are you?" She was leaning back now, as if she had walked too close and needed to get a bit more distance in order to take him in fully.

"Wow," he said. "You look amazing."

"Aw, bless you. Thanks, mate. I lost four stone after I left school. You, I have to say, look no different. But then you looked middle-aged when you were a teenager, ha-ha!" She thumped him excitedly on the shoulder. Elliott resisted the temptation to yelp.

"Blimey, Do…no, it's no good, I can't call you that. God, did we really call you that name at school?"

"Aw, that's okay. It was my nickname. I didn't mind it. Everyone had a nickname at school – you just deal with it."

"I didn't."

"Yes you did! Although, thinking about it, you might not have known about them." She looked sheepish for a moment. Elliott made a point of laughing and her face visibly relaxed.

"Thing is," he said, "I don't actually know your real name. I only ever knew you as Doughnut. Isn't that ridiculous?"

"It's Sharon. I was Sharon Blunt then, now I'm Sharon Taylor. Got a couple of those." She jerked her thumb behind her towards the young man, who nodded his head at Elliott in response. She leaned towards him conspiratorially. "Believe me, with a surname like Blunt, only being called Doughnut was a flippin' relief." She hit him on the shoulder again and cackled. Her son's eyes rolled briefly.

Elliott had always liked Doughnut. She was still delightfully brassy, just as she was at school. Plain, straightforward, there was never anything complicated about her. And she was never mean to him.

"You haven't changed a bit, Sharon," he said, joining in her laughter.

"Oh, I haven't got time for changing, Elliott. Too much life to be getting on with. Hey, you remember maths class? We used to sit together. You always tried to explain things to me. Didn't have the heart to tell you I didn't have a clue. Never got maths. Didn't stop you trying to help me, mind. Bless."

"Do you know, I had forgotten that." They stood grinning at each other for a moment. Then a slightly longer moment. The young man leaned across and tugged the back of her coat, but

Sharon knocked his hand away without looking back.

"Anyway," said Elliott, "what are you up to? Where are you working?"

"In between jobs. Fifteen years working for the council, operations stuff, got made redundant two months ago. I can tell you, the novelty of spending time with your kids wears off very quickly!" That cackle, he used to love that cackle.

"What are you looking for?" asked Elliott.

"Anything. My husband earns okay, so I don't need masses, but I like to enjoy what I do, you know?"

"A client of mine runs a charity. I know he's looking for someone. I'd be happy to put you in touch."

"No way! Would you do that? You don't even know if I'm any good."

Elliott took a business card and handed to her. "You used to be nice to me at school," he said. "That's got to be worth something, hasn't it? Call me in a few days and I'll see what I can do."

They parted with a kiss on the cheek. As Elliott walked across the cathedral square he looked back. Sharon was still looking at his card, turning it over and over.

As he reached the door of the cathedral, an elderly couple came out, the gentleman straining to push the huge door open from the inside to allow his wife to leave first. Elliott took the weight of the door and allowed them both to leave, accepting their grateful smiles as they went past. A noticeboard declared that the next service was not until six o'clock.

Elliott stood in the middle of the aisle, the vacant pews all round staring back at him optimistically. Did each of these benches really receive a regular posterior? There were so many, stretching out each side, with a few individual worshippers dotted amongst the naked wood. It was as if each empty place, with a hymn book hanging by a thread from the back of the pew in front, provided a permanent display of devotion.

The late afternoon sun shone through the stained-glass windows, casting a kaleidoscope of colours on the walls. Some pews were blue, others a golden orange, as if selected for a higher purpose. Over the centuries more wood had heard the sermons than human ears, an irony lost on the few tourists that now sauntered through the cathedral. Elliott heard the clatter of brass on brass as someone tossed their pound coins into the Perspex begging boxes, safe in the knowledge that no one would be checking whether they were actually donating the 'suggested minimum' of five pounds.

Taking a seat, he looked up at the extraordinary construction rising up in front of him, a sixty-foot-high carved wooden evocation of the last moments of Christ. Behind that huge edifice was the real action. He could hear the choir practising, the beautiful voices of the children soaring and echoing around the thick stone walls like angels sprinkling blessings. It gave the auditorium a magical quality that made him feel closer to a God that, he had to remind himself, he did not believe existed.

A pure light from a carefully designed window near the ceiling landed on the top of the high altar which separated the crossing from the apse. A construction consisting of maple carved into statues of the disciples, it was topped with gold effigies of the main characters from stories that he remembered from innocent days at school when these things seemed to matter.

He stared for the umpteenth time at the impressive sculptures, the supreme workmanship and expensive materials combining to instil awe in all who looked upon it. What must have gone through the minds of the people who decided to build such a shrine? To be filled with such absolute certainty of purpose as to interpret the teachings of Jesus as an instruction to collect money from the people of the land, buy gold with that money, and build a great big statue of Jesus with it.

A middle-aged lady walked past, talking to her husband. She was doing her best to whisper but the American accent still came across. She wore a T-shirt across her large bosom. The letters WWJD were stretched taut across her chest. What Would Jesus Do? Good question, thought Elliott. I could probably tell you what he wouldn't have done. He wouldn't have built a bloody great temple to his dad filled with gold taken from poor people.

What *would* Jesus do? The question refused to leave his mind. Would Jesus have kidnapped Ian in the same circumstances? Would he have continued to keep Ian locked up and threatened to torture him until he realised the error of his ways? He thought it unlikely. Jesus almost certainly had a slightly better control over his temper than Elliott.

And yet he knew that he had right on his side, that it wasn't just about losing his temper. There was more to it than that. Much more.

Jesus was an extremist. "I am the way, the truth, and the light." Margaret Thatcher was an extremist. "This lady is not for turning." Like them or loathe them, you could only admire what those two had achieved.

If the world was going to be changed, if the slide into an all-pervasive hatred of our fellow man could possibly be checked, did it not need someone to take a stand? Like Jesus had, whether or not he actually was the son of God. It was time again for a trailblazer who would show that the little things matter, like decency and kindness and holding doors open and trying to understand other people's reasons for doing things rather than judging them based on your own values, and that such principles knit together to make a society that is worth being part of. If he could change just one person, would they spread his message, like a virus, taking effect one by one, person by person, until the world started to realise that being nice to each other is where everything starts and stops?

Would someone one day be walking about with a T-shirt that read WWED? A smirk surprised his face. More like WWND. That's much more what he should be thinking about. What Would Naomi Do? He felt so bereft these days without the certainty to his actions that her presence had provided.

Without Naomi, who was left to impress? Who was there to reflect against, to give feedback? Life these days was like being on holiday in Vienna on his own. No one to share the memories with, to validate his opinions, to challenge and agree – or disagree – or to swap glances with when laughing together.

He was out of his depth. Ian represented an opportunity he had dreamed about but never truly believed could come to reality. Without Naomi to talk to, without even Lucy to correct him there was uncertainty as to whether he was doing the right thing. The only option was to continue stumbling through the darkness, trusting that his objective was good and that the path he had chosen was correct.

One thing was sure: there needed to be a conversion. When Ian left the turret he had to be a disciple, a true believer. He had to actually thank Elliott for kidnapping him. That was the challenge. He had taken Ian through the first four stages, destroying his character, now it was time to start rebuilding.

Just a few people milled around now, staring up at coloured windows and carved tombs of dead soldiers, silently respectful of something they did not understand. That summed up his own feelings. Impressed by the strength of their beliefs, envious, even, of their faith in the face of such overwhelming odds, but not actually understanding what all the fuss was about.

Programmed deeply within him was the assumption that he was probably wrong. In everything, all the time. Basically flawed. Life was a tiny path on which he had to balance his way, arrogance urging him to fall one side and self-loathing the other. And yet he had to allow for the possibility that he might actually be right for once. He didn't dare use the word 'destiny', but what if he *was* doing the right thing after all?

The organist started to play, presumably for practice as there was now no choir to sing an accompaniment. A single melody played fast, dense, complex. Elliott looked at the enormous instrument, gigantic pipes climbing upwards from the small wooden platform. The musician himself was hidden from view, as if he was part of the organ itself, built into the very infrastructure like a villain in a Spiderman comic. The number of melodies increased, one hand playing a series of bass notes, changing note once per bar – or was it one of the feet? Two seemingly unconnected melodies now began in the higher register – yes, the bass must have been the feet; actually, now he came to listen, there were two bass melodies too. When had that started? The whole thing was becoming a mess to Elliott's untrained ears, one endless melody having little connection with itself, the other chasing faster and faster, round and around a constant scale, the bass threatening to hold in one place, then changing again. He needed to keep his heart rate down, but this music entered him and was making him anxious. How could something be so damned difficult to play and yet sound so totally unfathomable? Why would someone want to create such a thing? It was music that was out of control.

All at once he saw the dichotomy he sought to expose. There was the invisible force driven by deep-seated values regarding doing what must be the right thing, the worship of Christ, the worship of music; the beloved dedication to a life of sacrifice and penury. Something pure surrounded him, in the very windows, showing nothing but sacrifice at every turn, dedication to a just and righteous cause that transcended values, rose above right and wrong, a cause so intrinsic to matter and being that it was as basic a human need as eating and breathing.

And yet here too was evidence of the idiocy of assumption. Follow this religion. It is the only one. Other religions will tell you theirs is the only one. But they are wrong, and we are right. And if you don't agree we will get bigger guns.

Is that what he was? An unknown soldier, fighting for good? Was he an extremist? But if he was fighting, that meant someone was on the other side, with their own version of good that they too were prepared to fight for. So whose values were right? Surely his was the defence of the most basic of values: treating others as you would be treated yourself. Good manners, respect. This was what Jesus had taught, but what Elliott saw before him proved that such a pure message could be twisted and turned, the ultimate show of confirmation bias.

Certainty of purpose versus empathy in thought. Indoctrination to a higher calling against an open mind. The only way that things change is through determination and sticking to a vision. The only way disputes are resolved is by listening and understanding.

And yet the argument was moot. His path had been set by a moment's decision, albeit one over which he had no control. And yet what was rage, what was Alan, if not the manifestation of his deepest-held beliefs?

The dials were set, the course determined, Elliott thought to himself. The only option now is to hold on and see where the journey takes me. Who is going to change: me or the world?

Part 2

The Possibility of Salvation

Chapter 11

Stage 5: Leniency

Saturday, 7pm

The evening sun was so low in the sky that it shone on the underside of the clouds, creating a mottled ceiling of orange looking down onto the world. The outside of the turret was ablaze with the rays of the setting sun. To anyone standing outside it could almost have seemed as if there was a fierce fire burning inside, making the bricks glow from the heat.

In the small room at the top of the turret Ian was oblivious to the beauty of the sunset, indeed with the shutters still closed he would have struggled to keep a grip on whether it was morning, afternoon or night. Elliott leaned against the table and observed his hostage carefully as he ruthlessly devoured a home-made beef and Stilton pasty that Elliott had taken out of the freezer the previous evening, dipping the end into the small pile of home-made piccalilli on the side of the plate.

In truth, Ian did not look great. This was a man who nature had intended to shave either daily or not at all. The stubble was patchy at best and already becoming fluffy on his upper lip. It created the appearance of a badger with alopecia.

The smell in the room carried an unwelcome depth to it. Elliott wished he could open some windows, however that was not yet an option. The aroma gave a strong suggestion of repeated issues in the trouser region. As Ian finished his meal, Elliott took the bowl back down to the flat and emptied it into the toilet, then rinsed it several times in the bath. He wondered for a moment if it would be possible to let Ian take a shower, but quickly decided that letting him see the inside of his flat at this delicate middle stage of the process would be dangerous.

Instead he took a bucket from the buttery, filled it with water, and took a flannel and a bottle of shower gel from his bathroom. He threw them into the empty bowl, grabbed a carrier bag bulging with clothes and went back up the spiral stairs. As he entered the room, Ian was standing, feet still chained to the chair by the bicycle lock, and was reaching across to put the empty plate on the table and take a drink of water.

They hadn't exchanged any words since Elliott had returned from the trip into town; he had simply handed over the plate of food and put the water on the table. It was as if Ian was not going to speak until Elliott addressed him. To be fair, he probably didn't have a great deal to offer. It was hardly the sort of environment in which to engage in small talk. Discussing the weather was out as Ian hadn't seen any for several days. The pace and direction of what happened was entirely in Elliott's hands, which was exactly how he wanted his captive at this stage of the process. Compliant and defeated.

Ian sat back on the chair and looked at Elliott, as if he were an old, faithful hound awaiting instruction. Elliott picked up the carrier bag from the floor and placed it on his lap.

"Okay," he said finally. "What's on our agenda this evening, Ian?"

"We're gonna discuss what makes a good person," Ian replied in a monotonous voice. Then, a little more brightly, "I've been thinking about it. I've got some ideas for you."

Elliott beamed an obvious smile, intended to provide his pupil with positive feedback. "Good. That's really good. First, though, you stink. Sorry to be so blunt, but you do. I think we should do something about that, don't you? In that bucket is some warm water, and in the bowl a flannel and some shower gel. I suggest you take off all your clothes and give yourself a wash. Put the clothes in here." He pulled out a second carrier bag from the first. "Then I've got some clean clothes for you. Look." He pulled out a pair of chino trousers, pants, socks, and a plain blue shirt, placing each one on the table in turn. "I guessed your sizes." A red jumper was the last to come out of the bag, and he held it up. "This is rather nice, actually. Hand-knitted." He looked at the label. "Masha. Not heard of them. Must be the name of the person who knitted it.

Nice. Rather wish I'd got one for myself." He placed the jumper on top of the other clothes.

"Okay," he continued, "this is what is going to happen. I am going to tie your hands together. Then I will tie your legs to the chair with the rope, using a bow knot you can easily undo. Then I'm going to take the chain from your legs. Finally I will untie your hands again so that you will be able to release your legs and move about freely when I am out of the room. I'm then going to go downstairs for exactly fifteen minutes. When I return, you will have washed yourself and put on these clean clothes, then sat back in the chair and tied the rope around your legs again. I will be able to look through the keyhole to make sure you are tied up. If you are not tied up in exactly fifteen minutes, I will take that as a sign that progress has not been as I would have hoped and react accordingly. Assuming your legs are bound, I will come back in, bind your hands, and put the bike lock back around your legs. Then, as long as that all goes smoothly and you don't do anything silly, we can talk. Okay?"

"Okay," said Ian. He smiled at Elliott weakly. "Thank you," he said.

"Great." Elliott clapped his hands twice. He knelt down and tied Ian's hands together, then his legs, took off the bike chain, untied his hands and left the room. Just before he closed the door behind him, he looked back into the room to see Ian stiffly reaching forwards to untie his legs. He locked the door and went downstairs.

Elliott had two favourite places to sit in the lounge. The first was the right-hand seat of the black leather three-seater sofa facing the enormous fireplace. Immediately to its right was a small circular wooden table on which sat a rather isolated coaster. The sofa had been positioned entirely with reference to two large floor-standing speakers encased in beech, which were situated a precisely calculated distance either side of the fireplace to ensure the perfect sound would arrive at a person relaxing in the right-hand seat.

At right angles was the matching two-seater sofa. With time to kill, Elliott sat down and immediately got back up with some effort. He entered the kitchen and returned with an open bottle of Coteaux du Languedoc 2007 and a glass already filled with some of the red wine. With the objective for the current session already clear in his mind, he chose John le Carré's *Tinker Tailor Soldier Spy* from the bookshelf, opened it at a random page and began to read. The restrained and patient approach of George Smiley immediately held itself up in contrast to his own breathless methods.

The characters in the novel were revealing their allegiances. They chose their sides. Each had a reason. Each had dignity. Each in their own way was right, and yet each one was just as equally mistaken. Their choices would be questioned on a daily basis. What roots did they really have to back up their version of reality? What alternatives were available to them: to carry on being on the side of good or to switch sides and...do what? Realise that the other side has God on its side as well?

Why was he caring so much when other people didn't? When the world didn't even care enough to keep Naomi free from cancer, when Paolo didn't care enough to show his daughter he loved her or simply to behave like a decent human being? Being on the side of good is a constant battle. Bad seems to come so much more naturally.

Before choosing a side you must first decide whether the game is even worth playing. Assess the stakes, decide whether the prize for winning is sufficient to warrant the risk of losing. Ian had at one point called himself a foot soldier, implying a dedication to the side of right and justice. And I am fighting too, thought Elliott. I am a soldier for good behaviour, for thoughtfulness, for manners, and for the better world they would bring with them.

Fifteen minutes passed and he had barely read more than two paragraphs. Replacing the book on the table, Elliott walked back up the stairs and looked through the keyhole of the door at the top. He saw Ian dressed and sitting on the chair. He looked carefully at the knot. It seemed genuine. If he was going to have any success in this project he was going to have to trust the process, to have faith that the steps he had taken so far would have destroyed Ian's ego to such an extent that he would now actually be appreciative of the small kindness that had been shown to him. Now was the time to put the process to the test.

He opened the door and walked into the room, feigning confidence. He walked around Ian, aware that the man could grab him at any time. As Elliott reached the back of the chair, Ian put his hands behind his back, wrists together. Elliott paused for a moment, considering whether to make a bold statement by walking back round and putting the bicycle lock around his legs again without first tying up his hands. What a moment of trust that would be, to kneel in front of the man knowing that his hands were free. Was it too early in the process? Was he brave enough to submit the very course of action he had embarked upon to such a stringent test at this stage?

As he deliberated, the idea of two hands forming one giant fist coming down on the back of his head suddenly filled his mind and any bravery quickly left him. He took the rope and tied the hands together, then went to the feet and tied them tightly to the chair with the bicycle lock, being careful to shield the code from Ian even though he didn't appear to be trying to see.

Standing, Elliott looked down at his captive. "Feel better?" he asked.

"Much. Thank you." Ian smiled back up at him. "I am so grateful to you for this. I know you could easily have kept me here like a pig in my own shit. I didn't even ask you to let me wash because it never occurred to me that you'd agree, so thanks, really. I feel heaps better."

"Good, Ian. That's really good. I feel sorry for you, you see. It cannot be easy coming to the realisation that you were a deeply unpleasant human being that nobody liked." Elliott paused for a moment, partly for effect, partly because he was watching Ian's face fall back into what looked like melancholy. If the process was working as the book said it would, his mind should be blank now, ready to take on the new reality that Elliott was providing to him. Ready to become a better person because he wanted to, and not just saying what Elliott wanted to hear.

To Elliott's surprise, Ian spoke, in a voice that seemed to carry an underlying desire to please.

"I know what a good person looks like," he said. "I want to say this before you tell me. I want you to know that these are my thoughts, that I'm not just saying it to you because I think it's what you want to hear."

"Go on," said Elliott, sitting back against the table. He folded his arms for comfort, then realised his negative body language and unfolded them again. Unsure where to put his arms, they hung limply by his sides like a scout's flag at a wet summer camp.

"A good person is someone who thinks of other people before themselves. It's not complicated. And I can do that. I really can."

Elliott cocked his head to one side. "Prove it," he said. "Where is the evidence to back up that statement?" Standard interview technique. He just never thought it would come in useful as part of brainwashing someone to be a better person.

"I had a girlfriend once," said Ian after only a slight pause. "I mean, I've had loads, but I was only properly in love once. And I wanted to be loved back. But I wasn't. To be honest, I didn't think I was lovable. Do you know what I mean?"

"Yes. Yes I do."

"Unlovable. That's me. And yet I know what she wanted. I just couldn't give it to her. I tried to be what she wanted, but I couldn't do it. Why not? Why could I not just change to be what she wanted me to be?"

Elliott wondered for a moment how hard Ian had been working on this answer. As he spoke Ian paused often to look to his right, like an actor delivering the big speech.

"I destroyed that relationship, Elliott," Ian continued. "I realise it now, I wasn't good enough for her. I think I set her free from me by being a dick, sabotaged the relationship. I'm not happy. I want to be loved. I want to be lovable."

"What makes someone lovable, Ian?"

"I don't know. I don't have these answers. I'm not a deep thinker like you. Help me, help me to answer your questions, I've never even thought about these things before."

"Well, what did you love about her?"

"Oh, she was gorgeous. And I don't just mean she was fit." Elliott winced. Ian noticed and carried on quickly. "I mean she was kind and caring as well as beautiful. When she smiled the tip of her nose would go up. I loved that. And she listened to me. Nobody ever listened to me quite like she did."

"And did you listen to her in return?"

Ian paused, and it seemed to Elliott that it was not so much in order to structure his reply but because he was reluctant to give up the answer. Eventually he spoke. "Not really, if I'm, honest. I don't suppose I really knew much about her at all. It didn't end well."

To Elliott's eyes the man sat in front of him looked as pathetic as he wanted him to be. He felt the urge to sympathise, to put his arm around Ian's shoulder, but he knew he must resist. The process, he must focus on the required outcome of the session to fit in with the ten-step plan. He had provided the kindness that this session required in order to instil a sense of relief and gratitude. Ian had responded as the book said he would, he was becoming a clean slate upon which his new, kinder, thoughtful character could be drawn. But now Elliott needed to once again remind Ian of the terrible person that he was, to continue the destruction of his personality that was necessary before the rebuilding process could begin. He had to keep the pressure on for a little longer.

"So I do know," Ian continued. "I am aware of the sort of person I have been, and I can see what I need to do more of. That's something I can work on." He looked to Elliott like a small child who had eaten all of his omelette and was waiting for praise.

Standing, Elliott walked around the room, stroking his chin, carefully exuding the image of being thoughtful, pensive. Ian's head rotated as he looked up at Elliott circling him, an expectant look on his face.

"In the time we have been together," said Elliott at last, "there is one thing you have not said or done. Something I would have expected from any decent human being. From someone with aspirations to be, as you put it, unlovable." He stopped pacing and looked at Ian, whose mouth was now opening and closing silently as he searched for something to say that would please his captor, to correctly guess what his latest transgression might be. His brow furrowed as if he was in the first day of acting classes for beginners and had been asked to appear thoughtful.

"Not once have you asked me to make contact with your family to tell them you are safe. Why is this, Ian?"

Ian's mouth remained open for a few revelatory seconds. His eyes darted to his left. If he had answered immediately Elliott could have believed the response. "But that's because I didn't think you'd have let me," said Ian. "You, you took my phone, so I just thought, assumed, you know, that you wouldn't let me."

Elliott put his hands on his hips. "Does your mother ever complain that you don't call her enough?"

"Um, well, yes, but don't all mothers?" Ian laughed nervously. Very nervously.

"I wouldn't know," said Elliott. "I don't have one any more."

Ian clamped his mouth shut. Standing in front of him for a few moments longer than would be comfortable in polite company, Elliott eventually turned, picked up the bucket and carrier bag containing Ian's dirty clothes and walked to the door. "You should be warmer now with the jumper. I will be back in the morning," he said without turning, then left the room.

As he shut the door he heard Ian calling behind him, "Wait, wait, *can* you get a message to my parents, please? They'll be..." The voice tailed off as he went down the stairs.

Chapter 12

Wearing his off-road-when-not-too-muddy walking shoes, Elliott walked out through the front door of Meanwood Towers. He gave the heavy door a perfectly weighted flick and it swung slowly back to click gently shut behind him. He walked out into the evening with tiny glow of satisfaction.

The evenings were starting to get shorter now but there was still enough daylight for him to see a beer bottle lying on the lawn by the row of trees that provided a screen from the road. Since as long as he could remember it had been a game for the local youths, a challenge to see who could get an empty bottle over the top of the leylandii trees bordering the posh house on the edge of their estate. If this one had been successful, there were probably several more buried halfway up. He walked across the grass and picked up the bottle, then climbed over the main gate and into the lane. A quick walk along the verge showed no other cans or bottles were visible.

He put the bottle on the wall by the gate, then crossed the road and entered the wood. As a child he had explored little. Never the outdoor type, the forest had scared him. It had only been as an adult that he had begun to appreciate how the comforting snug of solitude could be enhanced by the lack of walls. The wood was not thick and had been carefully managed over centuries. Although these trees did extend for several miles, creating a blanket around the shoulders of the village, the only wildlife to be found were some deer, assorted small mammals and a multitude of dog-walkers.

As he walked he felt the nervousness of his youth returning. A huge laurel bush cast darkness across the path as if it were hiding an ogre ready to pounce, creating a boggy area that had held out against the long summer. Walking on, the dusty path opened again into a hesitant brightness. He was now surrounded by a combination of huge trees half-empty of leaves and strong saplings trying to make their way in the world. He felt frustrated that he could not name any of them.

Everywhere stood either reverence or renewal. One huge tree – he wanted to think it was pine because of the needle-like leaves – had a trunk that looked as if it was made up of thirty individual walking sticks which had been bound together, placed in the ground and had a magic spell cast upon them. It rose fifty – or was it more like a hundred? – feet into the sky, its grandeur and majesty only diminished by the fact that hundreds of equally magnificent specimens stretched out as far as he could see. In fact, they *were* as far as he could see.

Directly underneath each tree was death. Branches broken off in the recent storms were strewn around as if the aftermath of an explosion. Stripped of foliage, they looked so tired and worthless, shorn of purpose. He could not even be sure which branch came from which tree.

There was no concept of right and wrong in nature, no requirement for justice. There was only survival. It made Elliott feel at once proud and slightly foolish. These were the things that elevated the human mind above the animal: sapience, abstract thought, the ability to tell right from wrong. His work with Ian was a very human intervention, to have appointed himself judge and juror, to be the enforcer of politeness and good manners. His was an unnatural response to a human disease which surely had no mirror in the natural world.

He saw something strange up ahead, off to the side. It looked like a small child facing the path, kneeling and praying up to the sky, face upturned in hope. As he peered closer he realised it was just the base of an upturned tree stump.

Not for the first time he wondered if there was a body buried somewhere in these woods. On the other side of the combe the land rose again, much higher, and on the top was an Iron Age hill fort. Was he now stood in their burial ground? Mossy mounds surrounded him. How many human remains were underneath him right at this very moment? How many bashed-in skulls?

Suddenly he became aware of a movement to his right. A young doe deer stood only fifty metres away, nibbling on a laurel bush. It had lifted its head and was now looking straight ahead, its attention focused on potential danger that could be heard or smelled. Without looking at Elliott it seemed to become suddenly aware of him and darted in the opposite direction. The white fluffy tail bobbed as the doe bounced, zigzag fashion, through the forest.

The last deer he had seen was in Richmond Park, in London. He and Naomi had been walking off Sunday lunch one May afternoon, discussing whether it was time to leave the capital and return to his family home now that they had both qualified as solicitors.

City life had been blissful, not least because it coincided with their exploration of each other, physically and emotionally. To their mutual delight they discovered that the initial attraction gave way to a depth and a truth that neither had thought possible – an admission that had marked the end of the initial frenzied period that they had expected to look back on and talk about for fifty years. An equally enjoyable period of mutual discovery followed, nuzzling into the relationship yet still able to surprise each other.

There had been regular visits to the theatre and occasional trips to the opera. Sundays at Camden Market, or spent at home with hot chocolate, Sunday papers and Schubert. But as they strolled through the park Naomi had observed that they hadn't actually been to the theatre for six months. Perhaps now was the right time to move on, to begin phase three. To nestle.

The marriage date was set. Elliott's father had offered the newly refurbished stable from which to operate his new legal practice. Naomi had secured a good job in town. They found a house to rent until they decided on a more permanent location. They had even whispered nervously to each other about children. Elliott sometimes lay awake at night, scared that he didn't deserve such happiness and imagining what it would be like to have it all taken away.

Naomi had not so much changed his personality as given it a complete overhaul. He had always presumed that four lonely years of university followed by one at law school would lead to further solitude as he studied as a trainee solicitor. Instead his life had been turned around through being the subject of a love that, unlike the only other love he had known, was not unconditional. He could never really believe in her love and would have to be told by Naomi repeatedly until he came to accept it as a fact whilst never completely comprehending. For Elliott the idea that someone could be in love with him was as mystifying as the concepts of infinite space or string theory.

Naomi had played in the company netball team, which gave Elliott a direct line into a social network, a new experience that he discovered he rather liked. After a while he even came to wonder if one or two of their friends actually became fond of him in his own right, as well as accommodating him as an appendage of Naomi. Through being with Naomi he learned how to speak with people, how to hold conversations rather than provide information. She taught him how to ask people about themselves, then turn their answer into a discussion. When to offer an opinion and how to notice the moments when an honest observation is not appropriate. He discovered an ability to make people laugh, which took him completely by surprise. At first he thought people were laughing at him, but the way they looked at him made him wonder if there might not be something more to it. His humour was dry, ironic and sporadic, and all the more effective for it.

He had proposed to her that afternoon amongst the azaleas of Isabella Plantation within Richmond Park, the extraordinarily vivid purples, pinks and burgundies crowding round them as if to offer their congratulations. For a moment he had wondered if this was to be the happiest he would ever feel in his life, a high point that he could not imagine ever attaining again. For the rest of his life he would recall that fleeting thought as the realisation dawned that it had been accurate.

The path through the wood had taken him on a loop and he found himself heading back towards the house. The sky beyond the trees was darkening and he quickened his pace. The floor around the path was now covered in wild garlic leaves. A fallen branch broke through the green carpet here and there. He noticed a beer can poking out through the leaves. There were plenty of dens in the woods that the local teenagers used in the evenings, and he imagined one of them tossing the empty can aside in a moment of bravado as they walked home. He stepped into the leaves, picked up the can, then continued back to the house.

As he neared the road he heard a car horn being leaned on impatiently. Getting closer, he could make out through the leaves a black BMW idling in front of the gate to the driveway. A hand on top of a hairy wrist was waving vaguely from the driver's window, with the air of a customer in a restaurant attempting to call a waiter by clicking his fingers. He knew it was Paolo's arm because around the wrist sat a gold watch, below which was a white collar at the end of a pink-and-white striped shirt. It was too far away to see the cufflinks but Elliott knew they too would be gold. Another giveaway was the number plate, which read 'PAO10'.

He didn't know anyone else who had as much hair on his body as Paolo Brice. He had seen his wife's ex-husband naked only once, in happier times when they were getting changed the morning of the wedding. They had been friends then, of a sort. In a 'keep your friends close and your enemies closer' kind of way. He hadn't shared his opinion of her future husband with Lucy, the same way he had not shared his views on their inevitable divorce.

The car horn sounded once more, an instruction to anyone within earshot that Paolo demanded entrance. Elliott took out his key fob and pressed the button to open the electric gate. The beeping stopped and the hand gave a thumbs-up to its unknown saviour.

Paolo was not his real name. He wore his dyed black hair slicked back and held in place with copious amounts of gel. With permanent stubble that seemed to grow back two minutes after he had shaved and yet never turn into a full beard, he looked like a swarthy Italian from a second-rate gangster movie. He was actually called Joshua Brice, and was from Basildon in Essex. When he was six years old his father proudly announced that he just wasn't cut out for family life and joined the merchant navy, thereby ensuring Paolo would be an only child. He saw his father only once or twice a year after that. Elliott had gleaned this information on the night of the wedding, sitting out on the terrace of the hotel drinking the most expensive brandies and smoking the huge cigars that Paolo had insisted on buying.

Upon leaving school, at the earliest opportunity Paolo had joined a stockbroking firm in the City of London. Elliott knew of them by reputation and had it on whispered authority that Paolo's meteoric rise to the top was not entirely based upon hard work or good judgement. He had earned the nickname Whizz. When Elliott asked for the derivation of the name, Paolo had mumbled something about Billy Whizz, the comic character known for being super-fast. Accepting this without comprehension, it would be three months later while carrying out the recycling that Elliott suddenly realised with a flush of embarrassment that it was a reference to the large amounts of cocaine Paolo must have snorted during his ten years as an investment trader.

Lucy had initially been impressed by his naked ambition. When Paolo Brice wanted something, he invariably got it, and this extended to Lucy herself. They married in London and then shortly after moved to Somerset. They told each other it was a move that would improve their quality of life. For Lucy it had really been to put down roots near to her parents. For Paolo it was to trade up on the differential in property prices.

Paolo liked to tell people that he had downsized to a rural location, unaware of how patronising that statement was to people who had lived in the area all their lives. Indeed, Elliott sometimes wondered how Paolo could go through life not noticing the effect of his condescension on others. After buying a house bigger than they needed, Paolo took his swollen bank account and invested in a scaffolding business. This did well and eventually begat a dry cleaners, which begat a pizza restaurant, almost as if he chose the most obvious businesses for laundering money, hiding in plain sight. The birth of their daughter happened almost unnoticed by him, as if it were a minor business project that required his attention only at specific moments. Eight years later he had twelve businesses, one divorce followed swiftly by a much younger wife, had just opened his third restaurant and was officially considered by the local business network to be a real pillock of their community.

Like many self-made men, Paolo overestimated the degree to which his success was down to vision and hard work and underestimated the role that luck had played. Elliott had been involved in one or two of the deals and also noticed the considerable contribution of a willingness to do things others were not prepared to do. This approach brought Paolo just as many enemies as friends. As the business empire grew, so did the ego. Elliott always had the urge to prick his pomposity by pointing out that success was not measure in pound notes but by the number of people who turn up at your funeral. Instead he kept his thoughts to himself, an exercise in biting the tongue that was frustrating but pragmatic. He had seen others get on Paolo's bad side and it was not a pretty sight.

According to the divorce settlement Lucy received a monthly maintenance for Phoebe but little else, as per the prenuptial agreement Paolo had insisted upon. The inevitable move back to the family home had provided Phoebe with security through her childhood and the house had been easily big enough for the whole family, Lucy's parents adopting the role of grandparents with relish. Elliott knew that what would really burn Paolo up inside was that Lucy was the one thing he could not possess. Paolo had once bought a competitor company only to sack all the staff and wind it down just to remove it from the market, and Elliott would not like to witness him do the same to Lucy's new lover.

The gate was not yet fully open but already the BMW was nudging forwards. A thought crept into Elliott's mind as he watched from the other side of the road. Acting quickly before the chance was gone, he clicked the 'close' button. The timing was perfect as the BMW jumped forwards just as the gate reversed its direction. There was a loud scraping of metal on metal, followed by an even louder expletive from within the car.

Elliott quickly clicked the 'open' button as he hurriedly walked across the road. There was an excited knot in his stomach. He hadn't felt this animated since he had thrown a cheese and pickle sandwich at Darren Pearce, who had been teasing him for liking Sarah Pope, just as the geography teacher entered the room.

"Oh dear, Paolo, what happened?" he said as he approached his ex-brother-in-law, who was looking at the front of his car.

"Fucking gate just dented my car. Fucking bastard." Paolo kicked the gate with his heel, and it shuddered loudly in response.

"Well, why didn't you just wait a bit longer?" said Elliott, his tone one of the grandparent trying too hard to offer only positive criticism. "It was almost open, I think."

Paolo turned slowly and stood to his full height, still a good few inches shorter than Elliott even with the stacked heeled boots that he wore. He glared with his head cocked slightly to the side, and for a moment Elliott wondered which gangster film he had stolen that look from. He could imagine Paolo standing a few inches from the mirror for hours on end, practising his intimidating stares. And they worked, he couldn't deny it, although this time, for some reason, he felt the urge to laugh.

Elliott carefully placed the empty beer can on the bonnet of the BMW, then took three steps forwards so that he was now standing close enough to Paolo to touch the bald patch on the back of his head. If he so chose. There was a flicker of uncertainty in Paolo's eyes. Elliott suddenly grabbed Paolo's head by the sides and in one swift movement, leaned forwards and kissed first one, then the other cheek.

"*Ciao*, Paolo," he said. "Welcome to our home." He stepped back, picked up the beer can, took Paolo's elbow and pushed it towards the driver's seat. Paolo followed his elbow into the car. "Why don't you park out back, hmm?"

Slightly dazed, Paolo drove away along the gravel drive, swaggering back round the front a minute or so later. He had regained his poise, a combination of hubris and disdain. He walked like the fourth person out of six in the picture *The Ascent of Man*, head slightly hunched forwards, arms out wider than they needed to be. The defining element of his walk was his shoulders, dipping and rising as he strode. It was a walk that seemed to think it was being watched.

The standard operating procedure between the two of them was for Paolo to bark patronisingly at Elliott, who would listen partially, while thinking dark thoughts. He knew who was the better person out of the two of them, and he had no need to prove himself. Today, however, the world was going to be different. Paolo opened his mouth to speak, but Elliott got in first.

"Phoebe loved her present," he said sarcastically.

Paolo looked at Elliott, confused for a moment. Then he looked to the sky. "Aw, shit." Back to Elliott. "When was it?" "Thursday."

"Shit." He took his wallet from his jacket pocket and took out a roll of twenty-pound notes. He peeled off five and handed them to Elliott. "Would you give these to her for me?" he said.

Elliott arched an eyebrow. Sighing, Paolo counted another five notes and offered the pile to Elliott again. "Is that enough?" he said.

"Oh, Paolo. Money doesn't fix everything, you know. A daughter would rather her father remembered her birthday, and perhaps receive a card, than have money thrust at her."

Muttering an obscenity under his breath, Paolo took five more notes, stuffed the three hundred pounds into Elliott's hand, and said, "Alright, alright, I'll get my secretary to send a card and some flowers as well, okay? Just give these to Phoebe and apologise for me, right? Do your thing, Elliott, sort her out for me, yeah?"

Elliott held on to the notes as Paolo pushed past him and pushed Lucy's buzzer. When he got no response, he pushed Benny's buzzer.

"Hel-lo," sang Benny out of the intercom.

"Benny, it's Paolo, can I pop up? Want to leave a message for Lucy."

The door buzzed and Paolo stepped into the flat.

"You could just tell me?" said Elliott.

Paolo turned at the door, addressing his ex-brother-in-law with a cold stare. "Here, have you heard about the Pilling deal?" he said, brightening, opening up like a Venus flytrap. "You'll love this one." He leaned against the frame of the door, settling into his story.

Paolo Brice had been part of his life for such a long time that Elliott had become numb to his emotions towards the man; this person who begat a wonderful child he didn't have time for. As Paolo told his tedious tale Elliott saw aspects of his own life come into focus. Paolo was even standing on a step so he could be higher. It occurred to Elliott that he had become subservient to this man, initially because he was so happy with Naomi that he didn't care, but more recently because he didn't know any other way. Now he felt less inclined to be bullied by the likes of Paolo Brice. There is nothing more dangerous than an ignorant person with success, Elliott, thought to himself. Their achievements are so rare and therefore so fiercely protected. Even the story he was now sharing showed Paolo to be the oppressor – he was actually proud of it. A person who does nothing to create good but instead forces others to react, to defend themselves. Elliott stared at the face in front of him. A smug, self-satisfied face that considered success to be measured by the age of your wife. A tiny pool of frothy spittle was gathering at the corner of Paolo's mouth as he prattled on about himself. Was Elliott the victim of relationships such as that he had with Paolo, or the cause? Was it his fault that Paolo was able to trample over him? He had tried to make the occasional stand, pretending he was too busy to accept a job he thought might be a little too far into the shade. These things helped, but in the end they were only correcting the world, setting things back to how they were, not gaining ground. In the battle for what was right he was quietly maintaining the front line as best he could, but there was no advancement into enemy territory. And yet the experiment he was conducting in the turret showed that pushing back was possible. He could gain ground. He just needed to take extreme measures.

Paolo was snickering now and Elliott realised not only that he hadn't been listening, but that Paolo hadn't noticed that Elliott hadn't been listening.

"Anyway, he won't try that again," said Paolo, chuckling. "Barred from being a director for five years and had to sell his house to move into a flat. Tosser."

"What about his family?" asked Elliott.

Paolo shrugged. "Collateral damage. Shame, but all part of being in business. He knew the risks. Anyway, laters." Elliott watched the back of a man he hadn't realised quite how much he hated turn away from him and walk up the stairs.

A whim landed upon Elliott like one of the kite hawks he had watched so often from the turret, swooping from the sky to claim a small, unsuspecting rodent. Quickly, before his brain could talk him out of the idea that remained untested in his mind, he went round the back of the house to where four cars were parked. A series of large rocks formed a border between the gravel and the back of the house, several red lady berberis shrubs filling the gaps. He placed the beer can carefully on the ground, then selected a boulder small enough to carry but large enough to make a point, bent his knees as he had been shown during his brief teenage job in the local supermarket, and lifted.

The rock came up a foot or so before Elliott realised that the adrenaline coursing through him was also deceiving his judgement. He put it down again as slowly as gravity would allow, then chose a rather smaller rock, one he could lift with a little less chance of permanent damage to his spine.

Performing his version of the clean section of the 'clean and jerk' that he had watched in the Olympic weightlifting contest, he stood up slowly but deliberately with the rock now resting on his shoulder. Turning, he walked towards Paolo's BMW and, with an effort propelled by disgust at a lifetime of submissive behaviour, he threw the rock onto the windscreen.

The rock landed with a loud crash and not an inconsiderable amount of tinkle. Elliott stared at the thousand uneven fragments that were now all over the bonnet and the floor and the seat inside the car. It seemed inconceivable that these pieces could ever have been joined together to make one piece of glass that you could actually see through. He felt energised, excited, like a schoolboy again, or at least how he imagined a schoolboy would feel having done something naughty. He stood staring at the car. The rock had made quite an impression on the dashboard before rolling onto the passenger seat and then the floor. Frankly, it all looked rather expensive.

"What the fuck?!"

Elliott turned to see Paolo standing behind him. He had run round the corner, then come to a comedy stop as he saw the damage, heels skidding into the gravel. Benny walked casually round the corner behind him, his face a perfect summation of the phrase 'detached amusement'.

Paolo approached the car, leaving a vapour trail of muttered obscenities as he walked. He reached the door, opened it, saw the boulder in the footwell, then turned and looked at Elliott.

"What. The. Fuck?"

"I know," said Elliott. "I was inside the office when I heard the crash. I came running out, but the kids had already run off."

"What kids?" said Paolo. "I'll fucking kill them." He looked like he probably would too, his face turning the colour of a cheap Grenache wine and his eyes bulging.

"I don't know," said Elliott. "I just got a glimpse as they went round the corner." He pointed to the gap between the stable office and the house. "They probably climbed over the fence behind the trees back into the estate. Have you had any trouble with the local kids?"

"Well, there were some little bastards playing football in their road in the estate. Almost hit one of them as I came round the corner. Gave me the finger, so I got out and chased them. But they wouldn't have been able to lift that."

"Probably got their older brothers to do it. Maybe even their dads. You know what they're like round here, Paolo."

"Shit," said Paolo, staring at his car. "Little fuckers. How the fuck am I going to get this home?"

"Um, drive slowly, I suppose?"

Paolo shot Elliott a glance. "Are you taking the piss?" he said.

"No," replied Elliott, "of course not." He walked round to the driver's side, opened the door, leaned in and brushed the glass off the seat and onto the floor of the car. "I just mean you should take it easy, you know."

Paolo walked round to the driver's seat and slowly got in, not taking his eyes off Elliott for one moment as Elliott shut the door for him. Paolo started the car and reversed back towards the office, then drove slowly forwards, pulling up alongside Elliott. He leaned his elbow on the sill of the window and leaned out to speak. As he did so, Elliott leaned forwards, indicating it would be easier for Paolo if he just spoke through the glass-free windscreen. Paolo haltingly sat up straight again.

"Sorry," said Elliott, going back round to the side. Paolo leaned back out of the window irritably.

"Fucking stand still, will you?" he shouted, then, more quietly, "Jesus, what a waste of time." Elliott wasn't sure if he was referring to him or the visit. Paolo poked a finger into Elliott's face. "What

I said about that Pilling deal stays between us, right? Don't want you messing with my reputation." With one last prod of the air, Paolo brought his hand back inside the car. The engine of the BMW roared briefly and then shot forwards, wheels spinning on the driveway, before braking again ten metres later and turning round the house.

Elliott walked slowly to the corner and clicked the fob to open the gate, nodding a greeting to Benny, who turned and walked with him. The two of them watched the BMW as it waited, stationary, for the gate to swing open.

"Ah, the personalised number plate," said Benny. "God's way of telling the world that you are not giving enough money to charity. That man really is a prize knobber."

"He was a decent person once," said Elliott. "People said nice things about him when he and Lucy got married. Amazing what losing the love of a good woman and receiving huge wealth can do to you." He turned to Benny. "What was the message he left for Lucy?"

Benny hunched his shoulders forwards and started stabbing the air. Elliott laughed, and it felt rather good.

"Listen," said Benny, in a voice uncannily like Paolo's. "Just give Lucy a message, right? Can you do that, do you think, ya fucking moron? Tell her that the estate agent and a photographer will be coming round Monday morning. If she wants the money pronto, then I need the valuation pronto minus one. Savvy? This offer won't last forever, tell her to get on with it or I'll find somefink more productive to do with my hard-earned wedge than wasting it on her. This favour has a deadline. Right, son?"

"That's very good!" said Elliott, laughing. "It's like he was here."

"From the little I know of the man," replied Benny, "I'd suggest that if there were a Venn diagram of Paolo Brice showing the amount of times he was kind to someone and the amount of times he did something that was in his own self-interest, it would be a page with one circle on it."

Elliott did not reply. So it was Paolo who was lending the money to Lucy. He stared at the brake lights ahead, then winced slightly as the BMW roared loudly down the road.

"Right," said Benny. "Well. Plenty to do, I suppose. Got a gig tomorrow. Ought to do a smidgerooni of practice, I guess." He started to walk down the side of the building, then called back over his shoulder, "Oh, and nice work with the rock, by the way. Always wanted to do that myself." Then he turned the corner with a wave and was gone.

Chapter 13

Stage 6: Compulsion to Confess

Sunday, 8am

"I've always found it really difficult to tell what people are actually like. Do you find that, Ian?"

Ian did not respond. Even if his mouth had not been full of toast smothered in Manuka honey, there was something about the way Elliott was leaning back against the door, arms folded and staring at a spot on the wall, that made it clear his was a rhetorical question. Elliott continued talking at the wall.

"When I was at school, there were people I liked and people I didn't like. It was pretty easy to tell who was going to fall into which category. Some kids were nice to you, some were not so nice. Some kids let you borrow stuff, other kids wanted everything to be done their way. You could tell within ten minutes if you were going to want to be friends with someone. But it seems the older we get, the better we become at hiding our real selves. I guess we learn the art of deception.

"Take you, for example. You seem like a nice enough chap. You are polite, say the right things. And yet I know that you have a deeply unpleasant personality. You are selfish, arrogant, vain. There's only room in your life for one true love, and that is you. You are so smooth that you even fooled yourself that you are a great guy. But would someone know all that from meeting you? Probably not. It is like iron filings that disclose the magnetic field. It is my reaction to your ignorant behaviour that reveals your true nature.

"See, I think about this stuff, Ian. I think about it a lot. I bet you were one of the cool gang at school, weren't you?" Ian didn't make any attempt to answer, and Elliott did not give him the time to do so. "Yeah, I can imagine you at school. Good-looking chap, popular with your classmates, spent break time snogging girls and indulging in a spot of casual bullying. I'll bet you sailed through your exams with the minimum of effort, getting average grades. Reports that said things like 'could try harder', 'despite lack of effort, does show a good understanding of the subject', and 'popular member of the class'. How am I doing?"

"Got to be honest, you're pretty spot on," said Ian.

"Know what my reports said, Ian? They said things like 'excellent performance', 'genuine academic understanding', and 'should try and integrate better with the other children'." Elliott stood now, addressing Ian directly.

"I was a nerd at school, Ian. I don't mind admitting it. There wouldn't be much point denying it, because it was true. Some kids, like Joey Davison, they were cool. Always so bloody cool. The thing about being a nerd, Ian, is that other kids seem to feel the need to point it out. No one kept telling Joey Davison he was cool. He just was. But those same kids who worshipped Joey Davison kept telling me I was a nerd. Joey Davison himself delighted in pointing out my nerdy characteristics. I kept wanting to shout, 'I know! So what?!' But I didn't. Because that would have just made things worse.

"My point here, Ian, is that it was obvious that I was a nerd. When all the other kids were either playing football at break time, or if it was raining, inside playing table tennis with books for bats, I did my homework or played board games with other nerds. I *liked* to study. Lunchtimes were often spent in the library, partly because I was hiding from people like Joey Davison, but also because I wanted to. There's something about being in the thick of all that knowledge that I still love today. I was interested in the subjects they taught us. Christ, I might as well have had the word 'nerd' branded on my forehead." Elliott had started to walk a few steps to his left, then turned and crossed back to the other side of the room, intermittently talking to the wall, then the floor, then Ian, his arms flailing in emphasis. "Actually I did, once. In biro. Joey Davison did it in a field where the teachers couldn't see us. Never did like PE when we had to do cross-country running." He laughed once, although it sounded more like a cough.

"Would it be so obvious now? Probably not. I'm still a bit of a nerd. I like things done the right way. I think manners are important." He stopped and gestured towards Ian for a moment. "As you well know!" He laughed briefly at his joke, which was not reciprocated, then resumed pacing slowly, like Fagin, wringing his hands as if awaiting delivery of ill-gotten gains. "But would you brand me a nerd after spending an hour in my company? Would you link the person I am now to the boy with the briefcase? Probably not. That is because I have learned to hide my real self. As have we all. It is only in times of stress that the real 'us' resurfaces, at moments when our concentration falters. When we are pushed and prodded and kicked into reacting in a way that relies on instinct."

Elliott stopped pacing, turned to Ian and stood dramatically to his full height, placing his hands palms-up in front of his body, as if waking from a daydream. "Which is, of course, why we are here!" He grinned. "Because I reacted to your dangerous driving as the ultimate opportunity to help someone change for the better. In such an unusual circumstance as coming upon a crashed vehicle driven by someone I knew to be deeply unpleasant because of their actions, my real needs were exposed. It's really rather fascinating, Ian, isn't it?"

Elliott stopped talking at last, leaving the final rhetorical question echoing briefly around the room. He wondered for a moment if Ian had actually heard the speech or had actually drifted off halfway through. He sat back against the table.

The vivid silence extended. Seated, arms still free, head now on his chest, Ian inhaled deeply, and Elliott actually felt himself lean forwards imperceptibly in anticipation – was Ian about to comment, to show him some sort of progress? But after a few moments Ian exhaled and Elliott realised that he too had been holding his breath, as if they had spent so much time together their breathing was now in sync.

"Now," said Elliott eventually, crouching down in front of his captive and smiling like a gangster who has just been provided with an alibi. "I'm guessing that the situation you find yourself in is pretty stressful. Hell, you don't even know if you are going to be alive in three days' time!" For a moment Elliott considered a gentle punch on the shoulder, but decided that might be a step too far. Ian continued to not react. Elliott leaned in further, put his finger under the other man's chin, and raised his head so that those dull, lifeless eyes were staring back into his own.

"My natural reaction upon seeing you in the car was to try and help, Ian. Under pressure. What's your reaction going to be? Hmm?"

He felt the weight of Ian's head lift from his finger. He brought his hand away and stood up to the sound of cracking knee joints, then went back to the table to wait. It only needed a few moments.

"I'm…" said Ian, then stopped. "Why…?" His mouth hung open for a moment, as though the thoughts were taking a lot longer than usual to get from his brain to his mouth. "I feel better," he said eventually. "For being clean, I mean. Thank you for that, at least."

Elliott nodded his head in acknowledgement, but said no more. This time he would let the silence do the work. As if in response, Ian sighed deeply and raised his eyes to the ceiling.

"I'm gonna tell you something I've never told anyone," he said. "I was on this sales course. I was working for a company, big multinational. I was a salesman, new to it all. They had this big training place in the countryside, our own rooms to stay in, conference room, it was like our own hotel. The maid who cleaned my room was gorgeous. I passed her a few times in the corridor. I flirted a bit, she flirted back. I really thought she liked the look of me. So I set up a DVD of a porn film I'd brought with me, on the TV in my room. There was a scene with a maid. I paused the film at a pretty racy point, just when they were snogging and getting started, you know. It was hard-core, but this was just the start of the scene – she had surprised him in his boxer shorts and they were snogging. I turned off the TV, then put a Post-it note on the remote control which said, 'Thinking of you. Turn on the TV and press to play', and left the remote control on the bed."

Elliott refrained from comment, but it wasn't easy.

"I thought she'd get a hint, you know, that I liked her," Ian continued. "Instead I got called out of the seminar and told to go home. Sacked. Gross misconduct. I've always thought they overreacted, that I was only having a bit of fun. But I guess in the back of my mind I knew I had totally and utterly embarrassed myself. Just didn't want to admit it. Haven't thought about that for a few years now. Managed to erase it from my memory. Had lots of time to think about that sort of thing over the last few days, here, on my own. What that poor girl must have thought when she pressed play and saw that film. It was normal for me, that sort of porn, but I guess it wasn't for her. Jesus, what an asshole."

Bringing his head down, Ian now looked to the side. It was obvious to Elliott that the man could not look him in the eye as he spoke again. "I don't know who I am any more, Elliott. Who I am or who I want to be. I just am. It's like I exist in space, in a vacuum."

Elliott had his arms folded, but balled his hand into a fist and gently punched himself on the arm in jubilation. A breakthrough. It was the first time Ian had spoken his name.

"So, I like music, yeah?" Ian continued. "American rock. Music-wise, that's what I listen to. In the car."

A load groaning sound came from Elliott. It was as if he had just been made to watch a slow-motion replay of a footballer breaking a leg. His face was screwed up, contorted, and his body writhed. Ian looked worriedly at him.

"What?" said Ian, confused.

"Pleeeeaase don't do that," said Elliott.

"Do what?"

"Murder the English language like that. The suffix '–wise'. It's like nails on a blackboard to me. Ugh. You meant 'That's the music I listen to in the car.' It is not difficult to construct a proper sentence. It is actually one word less. Please do not ever use '–wise' in a sentence to me again."

"Oh. Right, sorry, okay." Elliott recognised the verbal shrug. "Well, so, American rock, I love it, especially when I'm driving fast. I sing it out as I'm going. Soundgarden, Pearl Jam, Audioslave. And one song I especially loved to sing in the car, by Chris Cornell, called 'Can't Change Me'. It was like my mantra, my theme song. 'She's going to change the world, but she can't change me'. Accept me, this is who I am, don't try and change me. Fuck me, what an asshole I am. What an arrogant fucking asshole. 'I'm the only thing I really have'. I'd pump the air with my fist out the window, shouting to the world, 'You can't change me!'"

The pitch of his voice was wobbling, and were those tears forming in the corners of his eyes? "All this time on my own, I've been thinking about things that have gone wrong in my life. I realise that I've been blaming everyone else. When we failed to land a contract it was because the company overpriced it. When a girlfriend split up with me, it was because she couldn't accept me for who I am. I got caught sending a rude email to a client who was being argumentative, and I actually blamed the person who shopped me to my manager rather than realising I was the one that used the abusive language and sent the email in the first place. Jesus Christ al-fucking-mighty, what a wanker." The last words could barely be discerned as the sobs increased in frequency and volume, rendering Ian unable to continue talking.

Elliott felt like he could kiss the man breaking down in front of him. It was working, it was actually working! The system, the process, it was all about the process. He had followed it to the letter, and now it was actually making this man come to terms with his own failings, creating the possibility of redemption, of salvation, of becoming a better person. He felt invigorated, excited.

Ian looked up at Elliott, tears on his cheeks stopping halfway down in some defiance of gravity. "Truth is," he said, "I don't actually like myself very much." The last few words came out staccato, the sobs preventing speech.

Elliott had the overwhelming desire to hug the man, to hold him as he cried, to untie him, take him out into the field and show him the beauty of the world and the logic of his place within it. Instead he stood. "I shall return later with some food, and we shall talk some more." He went out of the door, locked it carefully behind him, raised both arms in triumph and relief, and shouted a silent "Yessssss!" into the roof of the turret.

He looked at his watch. Nine-thirty am. Time for a celebratory breakfast. He turned and started down the stairs.

Chapter 14

The steps were descended one at a time but quickly, Elliott's knees pounding up and down as he rattled around the stairwell. He lunged from the penultimate step, crossing the landing at the bottom with a giant stride across to the door and grabbing the handle in one fluid movement that had been practised many, many times over the years.

As he burst through the door momentum took him two strides into the lounge before he was halted by an almighty scream that seemed to almost physically strike his chest. His head attempted to continue its trajectory, giving the momentary impression that he had run into a wire stretched across the room.

The source of the noise was Phoebe, sitting on the sofa with a mug of tea that had only moments previously been clutched to her chest to keep her warm. Now, however, the contents were spread over her pyjamas and making her hot in an entirely more immediate way. The shriek of terror and surprise stopped as she drew breath, and was replaced by a second scream, this time of pain as she slammed the mug on the table in front of her, jumped up from the sofa as she did so and clawed at her pyjamas to keep the steaming hot liquid from scalding her skin.

Regaining both his composure and his balance, Elliott resumed his journey across the room and into the kitchen, returning with a tea towel moments later. Phoebe stretched out her left arm behind her at the same time as Elliott threw the cloth. She grabbed it and immediately began dabbing the large wet patches across her chest, cursing as she did so.

"Jesus, Uncle E, you scared the shit out of me!"

Elliott opened his mouth to admonish his only and most beloved niece, then decided he would allow her this one lapse given the circumstance. Well, technically two lapses – he didn't approve of the blasphemy either. The inconsistency of his own beliefs flared across his mind as he watched Phoebe stand and pat herself dry, his thoughts still half in the conversation he had just left. How could his disapproving attitude towards organised religion sit alongside an annoyance at anyone showing disrespect to that same institution? Was respect for the church ingrained in him through a childhood filled with subtle bombardment of religious dogma, through school plays and Christmas carols? He liked to the visit old stately homes whilst at the same time wishing there had been a more even distribution of wealth. There were almost certainly a plethora of such riddles and contradictions running through him like a course of veins, planted by the effects of experience and teaching beyond his control, values and judgements embedded by others, whether deliberately or by happenstance.

Was it really possible to escape the image we had been sculpted into? We are not robots, we are not automatons, we have the choice to be whoever we want to be. Surely. That must be true, otherwise he was wasting his time with Ian. This is what he was trying to achieve up in that room, to break a soul free from the baggage of the person it had been moulded into by experience. To allow Ian to choose the person that he wanted to be, to start again but this time develop himself by making his own conscious decisions.

Somewhere in the corner of his mind there was a noise, as if someone was shouting to him from far away. It was a nagging doubt that Ian was only being given the chance to make such choices because Elliott was guiding him there, and therefore it couldn't ever be a truly fresh start. Ian's new personality would be strongly guided by how Elliott shaped him, and therefore the new Ian would be the person that Elliott wanted him to be.

Phoebe had taken the towel into the kitchen and had filled the kettle again. She came back into the lounge.

"Sorry, Phoebe, I didn't know you were here," Elliott said after what looked like a few moments of allowing her to regain her composure. "You don't usually come down on Sunday mornings."

"Mum didn't want me putting the telly on because she's trying to finish off that stupid report for that stupid man," said Phoebe by way of explanation. Her tone provided the distinct suggestion that she might still be rather irritated.

Like an opossum playing dead in the face of mortal danger, Elliott stood still, only lifting his arm to catch the sodden towel thrown back at his head. He hardly breathed as the teenager slumped aggressively back onto the sofa, put her slippered feet on the table, folded her arms, and resumed her former activity of staring at the TV screen.

After a further period which seemed like five minutes but was in fact thirty seconds, Elliott walked as softly as he could round the sofa and picked up Phoebe's mug. He almost made it to the kitchen when Phoebe spoke again, without turning round or adjusting her position in any way.

"I thought you said you'd lost the key to that door. That's what freaked me out so much. You said you couldn't get up there, so I thought you were in your bedroom."

"Oh, I found the key," said Elliott. "Hadn't really lost it, just hadn't looked for it properly."

"So were you up there tidying it for the photographer, then?"

"Yeah, that's what I was doing. Tidying up. Anyway, sorted now, all done. What are you watching?" He nodded at the black-and-white film on the television in case she might not have realised what he was referring to.

"*Shadow of a Doubt*," she answered. "Seen it before. Just waiting for the local news really." She leaned forwards, picked up the remote control and changed the channel.

He went into the kitchen, the sound of closing credits of a national news programme wafting in behind him. The overwhelming desire to run in and lock the secret door was boiling up inside him. He kept peeking back round the kitchen door to make sure that Phoebe had not moved from the sofa. He couldn't hear the sound of the television over the noisy kettle, which seemed to be engaged in a battle with the water, but could see that the local news programme had started.

The kettle was one of many items round the house that he

kept meaning to replace. He knew it was possible to get kettles which hardly made any noise, but usually he didn't notice. He and Naomi had bought their kettle on a trip to Brighton one weekend; it was ridiculously expensive and looked like a miniature model of a spaceship, in some alternative universe where spaceships were painted lime green. But it was their kettle. And even though now, so many years later, it rattled and the timer function no longer worked, loyalty – to it and to Naomi – dictated that it retained its position as king of the kitchen.

As the kettle rattled and puffed its way to the boil, Elliott stood at the doorway, watching the back of Phoebe's head. She in turn watched the screen, but kept glancing at the door to the turret. The regional news had begun and the images commanded Elliott's attention for the first time. It appeared to be a press conference where a long table was covered by a white tablecloth, behind which sat four people. At first glance he wondered if the local football club had signed a new player. His heart leaped into his mouth as he noticed that the two people on the outside were police officers. In the middle was a man who looked around seventy years old. The woman was younger, maybe late fifties. They were grim-faced. The man was all but bald with a moustache creeping round the sides of his mouth and wore a smart shirt, the sort that he would have saved for a wedding or a funeral. The woman's hair was dyed with a blonde rinse that made it look almost gold in colour, and wore a light blue jacket with wide collars. No one was speaking yet; it looked as though they were showing the event live.

The kettle announced with a triumphant beep that it had completed its task, and Elliott quickly made two cups of tea and took them into the lounge. He handed one to Phoebe, who took it without looking at him but said, "Thank you" automatically. He put the other on the table in front of him and sat down next to his niece.

The woman on the screen – he assumed her to be Ian's mum – looked like she was trying not to sob. The man – almost certainly Ian's father – had his arm around her and was just holding her, not knowing what else to do. The policeman spoke first and explained who they were and what was going to happen, and that there would be a short appeal for the safe return of the couple's son. It looked to

Elliott as though neither of them had slept for several days. He felt as though he were being tested, taunted even, like Jesus being tempted in the wilderness.

Then the woman spoke, her short prepared statement coming out in staccato bursts as she broke down, emitting barking sobs as she tried to maintain control over her emotions. It was as if she was back at school and reading out loud in class, the correctness of the enunciation more important than the words that were being spoken. Each time a sob burst from her the room was lit up with white flashes, creating a strobe light effect as all the photographers sought to get that perfect shot of the grieving mother. They wanted tears and hurt and pain and suffering to be written large across her features. The first time it happened she was taken aback, and the flashes immediately stopped. Surprise was definitely not the emotion they were seeking. She continued but choked on the words "We love you, Ian", and the flashes jumped at her again, causing her to stop and collect herself. It was as if there was a chase between the woman trying to stop herself from showing any emotion and the cameras hiding in wait, ready to grab the slightest moment of weakness.

The words came through eventually as she appealed for her son, Ian, to come home and for anyone who might have any information, no matter how small or how insignificant it may seem, to please tell the police. She paused and one photographer jumped the gun, thinking that she was about to cry. A single flash apologetically filled the room, and Elliott could almost imagine he was a new kid on his first assignment, the other photographers turning to shake their heads at him.

Ian's mother tried to give out the telephone number but could not go on, the piece of paper she was holding in front of her lowered slowly to the tabletop as if her batteries had run out, all energy expended, and she stared blankly into the middle distance. Her husband took the paper gently from her fingers and read out the emergency line number, finishing with a plea straight into the main television camera for Ian to come home, no matter what he had done or what might have happened, they didn't care, they just wanted him back.

So his name really was Ian. He hadn't given Elliott a false

name, which would have seemed the logical thing to do in such a circumstance. What did that mean? Was Ian actually not that bright? Probably more likely that he had not had time to think or to formulate a plan when Elliott asked for his name. But still, it showed a degree of honesty. Something that might be useful.

"Jesus Chri-ist," said Phoebe beside him. Elliott frowned at her, but she barely noticed. Pick your battles. He turned back to the TV screen. The police officer next to Ian's mother stood to help her from the room and Elliott turned to look at Phoebe, who was herself in tears, wiping her nose on the sleeve of her pyjamas. Elliott opened his mouth to speak but no words came into his mind. Phoebe turned to look at him, her brow furrowed and one eye half-closed in thought.

"Uncle E," she said slowly. "Do you know anything about this?" Her finger pointed at the TV screen.

"What do you mean, Phoebe?" said Elliott, suppressing the nervous urge to laugh awkwardly.

"I dunno," said Phoebe. "It's just, well, you've been acting funny. And now you come out of the turret when you say you lost the key. And your face when that poor woman was trying to speak – you didn't look sad or anything, you were thinking about something. Like you know something."

"Oh, Phoebe," said Elliott, a quick, awkward laugh managing to escape. "What are you suggesting, that I've got Ian tied up in the turret?" He wondered if he could possibly have sounded any more contrived.

Phoebe head recoiled back into her neck. "What?" she said. "Don't be soft." She looked at him again quizzically, as if he had just made a joke out of someone's pet dying. "You're a solicitor, aren't you? I just wondered if you might be involved in the case, if the police were asking you for help or something."

"Oh," said Elliott, relief flooding into his stomach to replace the knot of tension that had been gathering there. "It doesn't quite work like that, Phoebe. I'm involved with company law, not criminal. I wouldn't get involved in something like this." Caring face, gently nodding head. "Now, don't you have homework to do?"

Phoebe stood and stretched. "Yeah, I might do it down here, if you don't mind. Mum's being a complete phoney at the moment, nagging me constantly. I hate it when people nag people constantly."

"Well, I'd rather you didn't, if I'm honest, Phoebe. I've, uh, I've got a few things to do. Work, you know. Stuff I need to concentrate on."

"That's okay, Uncle E, I'll work quietly with you." She stood and began brushing her clothes.

"No, Phoebe. Really. I'd rather you didn't. Just on this occasion. If you don't mind." He gave her his sweetest smile instead of the final "For me?" that he would have given her six years ago.

"Oh. Okay. Grumpy git," said Phoebe with a frown. She kissed him on the forehead as she went out, but as he watched her go he noticed the frown stayed in place a little longer than it might have usually.

At the sound of the front door shutting, Elliott ran over to the secret door, locked it, and put the key in his pocket. Then he flopped back down on the sofa and closed his eyes for a moment. When he opened them again, they were looking straight at the portrait of Naomi on the bookshelf, as if she had guided them there.

That day had been so absurdly emotional that he had become numb. He hadn't known at that time that the cancer would only give them another five months together. He had often wondered if she had known, within herself, and that was why she'd suggested the picture. It was all her idea, so typical that she would be thinking of him at the very time when all the attention should have been on her.

They had gone to the studio together with the intention of creating a picture for him to talk to. The photographer had set up the shot, with Naomi sitting on a chair, and Elliott sitting also, but next to the camera. And they had talked as the camera gently clicked away. Naomi had asked him to read to her from her favourite book, *I Capture the Castle*, and her eyes had sparkled and shone with a light that could never be snuffed out, that would live forever in his mind and in his front room. The smile that he loved so much had been frozen in time, a delicate half-smile that he knew meant she was engaged, happy, thinking, interested. That someone was actually interested in what he had to say.

He took the picture from the bookshelf and placed it on the writing desk, then sat in front of it. Placing his elbows on the desk and locking his fingers together, Elliott rested his chin on his hands.

"What have I done, Naomi?" he said to the photograph. "I'm sorry. I have let you down."

"You haven't let me down," Naomi replied. "You never could. I'll always be proud of you."

"You wouldn't have approved of this, I know," he said to her.

"I don't judge you, Elliott. I trust you. I trust you to do the right thing."

"But you always took the edges off me. Stopped me from going too far. Am I really doing the right thing here? His poor parents. I think I may have gone too far this time, Naomi."

"You have gone so far that you cannot go back, that's for sure. Looking behind at what you have done is going to be of no help to you. You know what to do for the best, Elliott, you always do."

"Hmm. I'm not so sure any more. What would *you* do next? If you walked in, right now? I know you'd give me a good telling-off for what I've done. But what next? Would you bail out and call the police? Or would you see it through?"

"I loved you, Elliott. Remember? I loved you."

"Yeah. Yeah, you did, didn't you? You actually did." The happiness in her eyes. The ache they shared in their heart. "I sometimes think you may have been the only person that ever really did."

He stood and held Naomi in his hands, then placed the photograph carefully back on the bookshelf as tenderly as he had held her in the hospice in those final weeks, just eighteen months after they had married. Everything in his life that was good was bookended into those four years, sealed like a coffin, never to be reopened. He gave a warm smile to her immutable stare.

Next in line along the shelf was a picture of his father. It featured both his parents, but it was his father that Elliott's eye came to now. Childhood had meant challenge and encouragement, but never help, never assistance – that was not part of the great plan. His father's method of teaching was to provide options and give endless encouragement while Elliott strove to find answers. That his father had loved him was without question. Why his father had loved him was a mystery that did not even allow for the question to be asked. Parental love was given not only without criticism but without condition of any kind. It had been as if both parties knew they shared a common objective, but without either knowing just what that objective was. His father's love was an invisible chord and it had only been late in life that he had noticed its existence, and yet the moment he did become aware of it, he also instantly knew it was something upon which he had always depended.

Was it just the emotional state he was in right now after seeing Ian's parents on the screen, or was the look in his father's printed eyes one of disappointment? He remembered the moment as if it were yesterday. The photograph was of his mother and father on holiday. His mother was laughing, as she so often was, on a beach in Devon. There was twelve-year-old Lucy in the background, throwing pebbles into the sea, and Mother had her arm around Father, the two of them just starting to bend double with laughter. They were effervescent, the life force that only seemed to exist when they were together simply bursting out as if it had no other choice, an elemental force of love that Elliott had only discovered three times in his life, each of them when staring silently at Naomi as she talked to others.

The object of his parents' laughter had been long forgotten. There was always the nagging doubt that he had been the source, perhaps his ineptitude in operating his father's expensive camera equipment. The scene gave him a slight blush of embarrassment, a reminder of a childhood he had been trying to put behind him for most of his life, and yet he kept the photograph because of the energy, the life force that was so seldom allowed to leak from his father. Mother was like a Roman candle, always bright, always present, always luminescent, but Father's energy was subtle, less specific, more machine gun than sniper rifle, more grass than flower.

Naomi had been taken from him. But the truth was that he had been expecting his parents to die for many years now. That's what parents do. They disappoint and then they die. He had been preparing himself for the inevitable for many years, getting his grieving in first. But in the end it hadn't been any easier, partly because of the way in which they were taken in the terrible car accident. There are some things that one simply cannot prepare for.

And the horrific mutilation of your parents in a hit-and-run car accident would seem to be one of them.

Next to the picture sat the automaton that he and his father had made together during that holiday. The North Devon coast had been battered by rain for much of the week, and they had used the time stuck in the caravan to make this moving model. A bald-headed cardboard man sat in his cardboard bath holding two cardboard oars. They in turn were atop a box with a handle sticking out the front. Father had done the cutting out with the sharp knife, Elliott all the assembly and gluing. He had asked for help on the tricky parts but only more encouragement had been forthcoming, another in a seemingly endless series of childhood moments of being allowed to learn from his mistakes when all he really wanted was for someone to do it for him, correctly. He picked up the model from the mantelpiece and turned the little cardboard handle. The man leaned forwards and the oars went back, then leaned back and one of the oars went down and forwards, propelling the bath. The mechanism inside was also made of cardboard and had been rather fiddly. Elliott had not managed to quite get both parts of the oar propelling section matched up, and so the other oar went forwards in the air. The effect, had the man been in water and not on top of his kitchen table, would have been for the bath and the man to have gone round and round in an endless circle.

Elliott walked slowly into the kitchen and turned on the oven.

Chapter 15

Stage 7: Channelling of Guilt

Sunday, 2pm

Watching Ian demolish the plate of lamb chops, mashed potato with garlic infused olive oil and broccoli with sea salt and black pepper, Elliott couldn't help but wonder if this was really a man in pain. A non-absorbent piece of meat was dragged around the plate in a vain attempt to soak up the last remaining vestiges of gravy. According to the process, Ian should now be consumed by doubt, confused, virtually a blank slate due to the knowledge that he had not only done wrong, but his very being was wrong. The way he was now gnawing at the bones did not suggest someone in the throes of a breakdown. But then again, how was someone *supposed* to eat meat whilst being in a state of wrongness?

That was the phrase from the book that described how Ian should be feeling right now. In a state of wrongness. 'The target should have seen so much that is wrong with himself by now that he will have lost any specific notion of why he is a bad person, he just knows that he is.'

Target. What a stark notion. An object to be aimed at.

"Please don't chew with your mouth open, Ian."

"Sorry," said Ian, wiping gravy from the side of his mouth with his sleeve.

"It really is disgusting watching someone else eat."

Ian swallowed and took a drink of water. "Sorry," he said again, before plunging his head back towards the food and forking some creamy mash the short distance that remained between the plate and his mouth.

Elliott let out a groan, then stood up from his position against the table and backed against the wall, as if the extra few feet away from the source of the offending sound would reduce the level of disgust. He placed his shoulders against the brickwork, then folded his right leg and placed the sole of his shoe against the wall, leaned back and crossed his arms.

Was this man really a blank slate? Had he reached the stage where he was so devoid of self-perception that Elliott could attach the non-specific guilt he should be feeling to the very specific set of values he had previously held? Had he been able in such a short space of time to associate those old values with the threat of pain? There was so much riding on this working; bridges had not so much been burned as blown to kingdom come. The state of vague but powerful wrongness that Ian should be feeling at the moment needed to be fastened to his previous way of behaving, in order to open up the way for a new behaviour to take its place and thereby for true change to have been effected.

Placing the knife and fork back on the plate, Ian stared at Elliott with a look of a dog that has been let back into the house after being banished for urinating on the carpet. If Ian had been able to control his ears, they would have been flat against his head. As Elliott took the plate, Ian automatically put his hands behind his back, meekly allowing Elliott to truss him once again. Instead Elliott just said, "No." He watched Ian begin picking bits of lamb out of his teeth with his tongue and fingernail and paused for a few moments before he spoke again.

"I saw your parents today," he said. Ian looked up suddenly.

It occurred to Elliott that only a few days ago that face would be filled with anger, but now it just looked pathetically grateful. Strangely the subservience that he saw in front of him, the lack of life force, did not translate into a feeling of power in himself. It would have been easy for such a transference of authority to take place, for Elliott's feeling of sovereignty over this person to have grown over the time they had spent together. But this was a benevolent dictatorship. He was determined to be conduit, a facilitator, someone who was merely bringing a process to bear that would provide Ian with the pathway to improvement. All Elliott needed to do was occasionally put his foot in Ian's back and give him a good shove, like any real friend would.

Elliott wondered for a moment if this was the right tack after all. It was one thing reading about the concepts and methods in a book; it was quite another applying them to an individual person's life and circumstances. You don't get to see the look on their face from the book. At the mention of his parents Ian's demeanour was one of a man thirsty from days spent in the desert. Elliott was reminded briefly of when he was allowed an aquarium as a boy, feeling helpless as one by one the fish became ill, making changes to the water and having to wait days and weeks to see any change, then waking up to see another fish lying lifelessly at the bottom of the tank.

"I saw them on the telly," continued Elliott in an offhand manner, as Ian continued to stare at him hopefully. "Making an appeal. They seem like nice people. Your dad looked like I thought he would, given your description. Funny thing, isn't it, unconditional love? That's what parents are supposed to give, isn't it? Unconditional. Without condition. Unaffected by what you do or say. They will still love you.

"Do your parents know everything that you do, Ian? Would they still love you then? If they knew about that video you left for the maid? How you treat people? How you drive? Would their love continue to be unconditional then? It's an interesting idea, is it not? What about a mass murderer? A rapist? Which would win in a battle between a mother's inherent love for her child against the shame and anger she would feel over the crime they had committed? Not something you can even imagine unless it happened to you."

Like a small child who realises the present is not for them after all, Ian removed his gaze from Elliott and allowed his head to fall back down until his chin prevented it from sinking any further.

"Judging by the look on your face," continued Elliott, twisting the knife in ever deeper, "I suspect there are things in your personal history that may be even more shameful than the ones you have already told me. Am I right?" No answer. "Thought so.

"Let's recap, Ian. Let us remind ourselves what you believe in. What are your core values? You told me that hard work and effort should be rewarded. Sorry, let's rephrase that. That *your* hard work and effort should be rewarded. You vaguely sought to apply that to the world in general, but actually it was pretty much just about you, wasn't it? We have realised that view is just a cover for the fact that you believe you are better than other people. Remember why we are here, Ian. You are not here because of something I did. No. I brought you here because of something you did. You showed me the finger at the very moment that *you* were doing something stupid and dangerous." Ian's head was rolling forwards, and Elliott stabbed the air with his finger in his direction. "*That* is why we are here. Because of *your* belief system, which holds *you* at the centre of its universe."

Elliott stepped forwards and kicked Ian's knees. "*Right?*" he shouted. Ian's head jerked back up and he nodded quickly.

Picking up the chair, Elliott placed it in front of Ian, as if offering something to put his feet up on, had his feet not been tied to the chair legs. Standing behind the high back, partly because that kept him directly in front of Ian and partly in order to provide some protection in case Ian lunged at him, Elliott put his hand in his pocket and pulled out a mobile phone. He placed the phone on the chair. Ian studied his every move. Next he reached into the other pocket and took out the battery for the phone, which he also placed on the chair. Then he put both hands on the back of the chair and leaned forwards.

"Recognise these?" he said. Ian nodded slightly, his expression difficult to read. Was he hopefully wondering if the ordeal might be over, or was he blankly waiting for his next instruction? Elliott only wished he knew. This test would be so much easier if he could only see inside that head to determine whether this process was really taking effect. "That is your phone. I had to take the battery out in case there might be some way that its location could be determined by the police. I did put the battery back in briefly, there were lots of messages. The first few seemed to be from your office, then your parents and the office ones stopped. Because it's the weekend, presumably. You're clearly not their concern at weekends."

Ian's blank face continued to stare at him, patiently waiting for a point to be made.

"I'm going to offer you a way out," said Elliott. "If you would like to, you may put in the battery and phone your father. You can't tell him where you are because you don't know, but I'm sure the location of your phone could be traced. The police will be round here in half an hour and you will be set free. I will be arrested for kidnapping you, and this whole exercise will have been a waste of time.

"If this is the course of action you decide to take, I will not stop you. But. Of course, there is a 'but'.

"If you do choose to return the battery to the phone, then you will have learned nothing. It is the choice that the old Ian would have made, the selfish person, the Ian that thinks the entire world revolves around him. The Ian that believes that everyone should be rewarded for their initiative whilst simultaneously believing in a system that preserves wealth for those who already have it. The Ian that thinks 'looking out for number one' is actually a positive attribute in that most social of animals, a human being. That thinks self-confidence is the trait of winners and that winners should be rewarded to give losers something to which they can aspire, while at the same time taking a job that requires little actual skill or talent but is handsomely rewarded. The Ian who clearly never had his head stuck down the toilet by the school bully. Who thinks you make your own luck in life and yet gives no credit to things that happen over which you have had zero influence.

"History is written by the winners. Big companies are run by the winners. Not the most competent, or talented, or skilled, or intelligent. The cream doesn't rise to the top in a big company, Ian, it is the idiots and the bullies, promoted out of one department in order to get rid of them. How many self-made business people admit that they are no more or less intelligent than any other business people, they just had a bit more luck?

"Ian, you told me you believe that if you want something, you have to go out and get it. Well, I want the world to be rid of people who think as simplistically and selfishly as you do. And so I'm going out there and doing something about it. Starting with you. Indeed, you should really be in agreement with me that you are in need of this intervention. Your very beliefs have brought this upon yourself. It's all rather neat, actually.

"It is those very characteristics that we despise which would drive you pick up that phone. So, you have a choice to make. This is a crossroads. Which Ian will decide the next move: the person that you were – arrogant, self-centred, rude, ill mannered, thinking everything is other people's fault if it goes wrong but down to his own brilliance when it goes right? Or the person you have the potential to be – humble, self-aware, modest, well mannered? Now is your time to choose, Ian. Do you wish to go forwards, or do you wish to go backwards?"

Elliott held the stare of the other man, arms still supporting himself on the back of the chair. Ian leaned forwards slightly, studying the phone and battery sitting side by side on the wooden chair. His eyes narrowed for a moment, then he sighed and looked back up at Elliott.

"I choose progress," he said quietly. "I choose enlightenment."

Careful not to show any expression that might suggest the surge in adrenaline that was at that very moment coursing through his body, Elliott slowly reached forwards. He carefully returned the battery to his right pocket and the dormant phone to his left, then turned and silently left the room.

Chapter 16

Sunday, 5pm

The sound of a buzzer pierced the silence and awoke Elliott from his nap. He sat up on the sofa, momentarily disorientated. The noise had come from inside his flat. There were three buttons at the gate to the property, just like at the front door, with a separate panel for those rare visitors to the office. Someone had pressed his button from outside the main gate. He was confused because he wasn't expecting anyone and could not remember the last time he had heard the buzzer go off in his flat.

The sound had been a common occurrence when Naomi was alive. After the wedding they had rented a flat in town. Their London friends promised they would visit, while expressing their concerns that the newly married couple would get bored now they weren't living in London. As far they were concerned London is a place that you move away from only when you have a specific reason to do so. You 'downsize', or you 'get out'. London is the centre of the known universe and everywhere else looks upon it in awe. There is London and there is Not London.

A few of their friends made the trip to stay with them but the numbers dwindled over the years. While Naomi found a job with one of the town's larger legal practices, Elliott set up on his own. His commute now took him from their flat in town against the traffic to the stables in Meanwood Towers. He was slowly building a small bank of clients. Some he liked, some he had no choice but to deal with in order to pay the bills.

He would lunch with his parents most days, Father generously handing out introductions to business acquaintances, Mother passing on even better introductions to her friends at the golf club. It proved to be something of an Indian summer in their relationship. The love and pride emanating from them both was revealed to him now that he was considering children of his own. He looked back over his childhood with a greater acceptance, memories refreshed from being back around the family home. Taking on board some of the extraordinary stoicism which his parents had used in order to find ways to cope.

The love generated by Naomi spilled out towards his father in particular. After being a willing student of life under the tutelage of Naomi he now was better equipped to recognise the guidance his father had provided. It couldn't have been easy, seeing his son and heir growing up in isolation, without friends, knowing his surroundings were contributing but unable to change them. Elliott realised how hard it must have been for his father to watch his only son plot a difficult path for himself, unable to intervene. Now they could spend time together he really began to understand the old man, to recognise the special place he held. For the first time ever he confided in his father, talked of the future and of his hopes and fears. To his delight and surprise his father not only listened with interest but did not jump to offer any solutions, his hands-off approach now a blessing where once it had been a frustration. He became a friend and a companion more than he was a parent, the metamorphosis of father and son learning to respect each other and finding a deeper love.

And of course his parents loved Naomi too. Everyone loved Naomi. How couldn't they?

Those early years of marriage had been a period of settling into their future, like the bean paste in a bowl of miso soup. If this was to be somewhere they would spend the rest of their lives, they wanted solid roots. Once again Naomi joined a netball club and friends ensued, although this time Elliott took more of a back seat, more confident in himself and less needing of the acceptance of others. His relationship with Lucy was able to repair and then build itself, and he loved spending time with Phoebe, their relationship burgeoning into something truly special.

And so life in their cosy flat, with thoughts of a family of their own, found its own sweet routine. It brought the calmness and order that Elliott had always sought, happiness blossoming from routine and structure. He knew it would not last forever. He still lay awake at night, but now the Worry Knights fought off the spectre of something being taken away from him rather than the worry of something he did not have. He even dared to consider himself happy in weaker moments. That was until the day that Naomi told him she'd found a lump in her breast.

The buzzer sounded again, longer, angrier, and this time Elliott shook his head, albeit carefully, focus slowly returning to his thoughts. It could only be an error or unwelcome. Either way he usually ignored it until the caller either went away or they bothered to read the names next to each button and realised that the top button was for the bottom flat, and the bottom button for the top flat. Only Benny had his name in the appropriate location to his home. Any genuine visitors that did come to Meanwood Towers these days were for Lucy, Phoebe or occasionally Benny, but never for Elliott.

He went across the lounge and peered around the corner of the kitchen door, sending a suspicious stare through the kitchen, out the window and across the lawn at the front of the house. The gate was swinging open and the chequered blue-and-yellow bonnet of a police car was nudging into the driveway.

He ran back across the lounge through the hall to the front door and clicked down the latch so that it could not be opened from outside. "No!" he muttered, moving the latch back up again. Lucy had a key to his flat, but if she tried to get in and couldn't it would be obvious he was hiding inside. "Think! Think!" He balled both fists and drove the knuckles into his forehead, closing his eyes at the same time. No matter how hard he pressed, nothing came, no ideas answered his call for help. The instinct for self-preservation would kick in as soon as he could shake off this paralysis. He couldn't be greeted by the police in his own flat, that much was clear; Elliott would try too hard to be nonchalant and end up giving it all away. These were thoughts of a panicky man, he knew that, but they were the only thoughts he had to go on. No one could know that Ian was here, it was too soon, Ian wasn't ready yet, wasn't fully prepared, changed, improved. This time would come but not now, not yet, and not here.

Returning to the lounge, he walked quickly over to the door to the turret. It was locked. He knew it was locked, but he tried the handle three more times. He took the key out and looked around for a hiding place. Behind some books, in a drawer, all too obvious. His eyes darted around the room and stopped on the fireplace. The priest hole.

Placing the key in his pocket, he ducked underneath the mantel and stood tall in the chimney, looking up. Through the stillness of the room behind him came the sound of another buzzer, this time from his front door. Why would they come to see him first when it was Lucy that had let them in? Oh Christ, what did they know? How did they know whatever it was that they knew?

He put his right foot in the first notch in the wall and lifted himself up. His left foot hit the sticks poking out of the top of the dry flower arrangement, sending it to the floor with the most gentle of crashes. As he started back down to right the arrangement the buzzer went again. That was bloody quick between rings. Impatient. They're not happy, they're in a hurry. A surge of panic ran through him and brought about a sudden change of plan. Rather than placing the key on the ledge he scrambled up the remaining holes, crawled on his belly through the small gap, and stood up inside the priest hole. He was breathing hard, and not from the exertion.

The tiny room was no more than one metre deep, three metres across – the same width as the fireplace – and three metres high. Sound didn't travel so well up into the small space; he would hear anything happening in the room, but not as far as the door. Heart beating fast, he leaned against the back wall and stared through the darkness at the wall he could barely make out in front of him as he forced himself to beat back the impending feeling of claustrophobia.

Voices. Female. Two female. As they got louder he could make out that one of them was Lucy. They were coming into the lounge. Before the second voice became clear Elliott could tell from the officious tone that it belonged to a policewoman. And the northern twang told him they had met before, at the scene of the accident.

Lucy's voice was the first to achieve clarity. "…understand it," she was saying. "His car is out back. He never walks anywhere from here. Well, there's nowhere to walk to. Apart from going for a walk. In the woods, I mean." What was it about the presence of an officer of the law that turned even his sister into a bag of nerves?

Lucy walked over to the secret door and gave it a rattle. "Locked," she said, as if the policewoman had not been watching her try the door. Elliott tutted silently at his older sister's constant requirement to be in charge.

"That's alright, madam." The policewoman pronounced it as 'allriot'. "We can come back later. Perhaps we could just go to your flat. I'd like to ask you and your husband a few questions."

"Oh, ha-ha," said Lucy. "Oh, we're not married, ha-ha, just catching up on some work, ha-ha." What the hell did *that* mean? Who was with Lucy upstairs?

"My apology. Well, after you, ma'am." Footsteps and the faint sound of the front door being slammed shut.

Were they really gone? That door had been shut very loudly, almost slammed. Suspiciously loudly. What would Elliott do in their shoes? If he were they, and if they did actually suspect, he'd pretend to leave, shutting the door so that the hider would be able to hear, then creep back in to catch them red-handed the moment they came out of their hiding place. Were they down there right now, tippy-toeing into the lounge, just waiting for Elliott to make his fatal move?

Lucy knew about the priest hole, yet she had not mentioned it to the policewoman. Did that mean she knew everything and was on Elliott's side? Had Phoebe guessed after all? Or did they not know anything and all was exactly as it seemed?

He was panicking. He didn't even know why the policewoman was here. Elliott got down onto his knees and put his head out of the entrance gap, listening for any sound that might betray their presence. He noticed the hum of his refrigerator for the first time in years. That was it. Birdsong was unable to force its way through the thick walls and up the chimney. Nothing came down the chimney from Benny's flat, but Elliott had no idea if it could have done. How did one listen for someone standing perfectly still?

Who had sat in this tiny nook before him? The priests, the outcasts, members of the English Catholic establishment now forced to cower in the face of the new order, hiding like a fox from the hunt, biding their time to rise again when the political situation was right. A force of belief and will in the face of ignorance as the soldiers ransacked the house below and above where he now sat. What would those priests have heard? Women being raped? Servants being stabbed? Trapped in the tiny space, unable to leap down and provide assistance in the knowledge that such an act would have put an end to the violence below by leading to their own demise. Sitting in the darkness listening to the screams, faced with a choice to either sit and wait for the ideals that they believed in to once again become the ideals of the many, or clamber down to try and help knowing that it would be futile, the soldiers of the state being all-powerful thanks to the law that resided in their swords and daggers.

Right had triumphed before, as it must always do. Then it was a fight over power dressed up as religious belief, now it was a fight for the survival of the very spirit of humanity itself, for the principle of accepting challenge and change. The soldiers and their paymasters had not learned, they had simply killed or imprisoned those who disagreed. Which side was he on now? Was he really carrying on the fight for understanding and a caring society, or was he yet another in a long lineage of forcible rehabilitation?

His objective was to open Ian's mind to new ideas, to knock him off what seemed an inevitable flight path to a closed mind and thereby empower free thinking. But free thinking with good manners, with respect, with empathy for his fellow man, to allow the possibility of a different opinion to his own without feeling the necessity to shut down all other lines of thought. Elliott's was a mission towards enlightenment, not away from it. He did not seek indoctrination into his own methodology but to an open-mindedness to all creeds. The police officer that may or may not be standing in the lounge holding her breath and waiting for him to give himself away was not a bad person in herself, but she did represent authority, with its determination to prevent challenge, to refuse the possibility of any other kind of thinking than the state would allow. Naomi had no choice. Cancer gave no options. And nor did the law. An inevitable course to which one must submit, without question, without challenge. There was but one path.

When did 'nice' become a bad word?

He twisted his body round so that he could sit with his back to the wall, head now a few feet above the entrance, feet dangling into the chimney. He wouldn't be able to hear a telltale footstep, but any talking as they gave up waiting would reach him.

What was that reference to Lucy's 'husband'? She had a man up there? On a Sunday? Phoebe was up there doing homework, for goodness' sakes. And yet the policewoman must have had good reason to mistake him for her husband.

For the next ten minutes Elliott spread his time between careful listening and worrying about his sister. Eventually he concluded that they really had left, and besides, his buttocks were starting to ache. Shuffling round onto his belly he put his legs back through the opening, feet searching for the holes in the wall. He stepped onto the floor of the fireplace carefully, then bent down and looked out across the lounge, heart thumping. To his immense relief, no legs greeted his eyes.

Ducking under the lintel, Elliott went into the kitchen and opened the door to the buttery. He turned the light on and went quickly down the stairs, closing the door behind him. Opening the hatch, he climbed out into the autumn evening, still warm even on this shady side of the house. To his right he could see the outline of the tower, ahead of him the side lawn and leylandii trees.

Keeping close to the wall, he walked round to the rear of the house. His and Lucy's cars were parked there, but no others. He knew Benny was out – had the police left as well? And what about the man in Lucy's flat?

He half-ran back to the front of the house, in the manner of someone crossing a busy road, wanting to make it look like they were making an effort without actually doing so. He peered round the corner. There was the police car, parked on the drive nearest to the front door. A flash of irritation went through Elliott that the police had such an inflated sense of self-importance that they couldn't even be bothered to use the designated parking area. If

Benny arrived home he wouldn't be able to get by. A tut emitted from his lips, unnoticed even by him.

The leylandii looked dense, however Elliott knew better. He walked boldly at the middle point between two trees and passed through relatively unscratched. Behind the trees there was a gap before the high fence that separated them from the housing estate. He walked down the side of the garden and onto the front road unseen. He then stepped back into the trees just by the front gate. Standing inside the trees like this he could see the front door, but could not himself be seen.

After a further ten minutes or so the door opened and the policewoman walked out. She turned to speak briefly to Lucy behind her.

They walked back to the police car and shook hands. The police officer then drove the way the car was facing round the back of the house. Lucy walked back down the path, then, when the policewoman came back down the driveway again, she wound down her window and called to Lucy.

"I didn't realise you had a car park at the back. How silly of me. Sorry!"

Lucy waved, then pointed her remote control at the gate, which made a whirring sound and started to open. The police car drove out and turned into the village, the gate shutting with a click and then silence.

Elliott forced his way through the thin branches back onto the road, brushed himself down, then turned left and walked the ten metres to the gate. He climbed over the gate and called, "Lucy!" to the closing front door.

The door opened again and Lucy stood looking at him as he walked nonchalantly up the driveway alongside the lawn. The temptation to cut diagonally across the grass had been quelled many years ago and even now, in a hurry so as to not keep Lucy waiting, he still did a walking run up the gravel and turned left along the path in front of the house to the main door where Lucy was waiting for him.

"Was that police I just saw?" Elliott said. "Coming out of here? What did they want?"

"To talk to you," she replied. "And me. Everyone. Where the hell have you been?"

"Oh, just for a walk in the woods."

"Horse poo. You never go for a walk. What's going on, Elliott?"

"Hey there, Tinkle, is everything okay?" said a male voice from behind Lucy.

Elliott did not get to answer Lucy's question. Instead he looked up at the face and shoulders of the man who came into view from over the top of Lucy's head. He was much taller than Lucy. In fact he was much taller than almost anyone Elliott had ever seen, perhaps six foot four inches tall. The face would have seemed large too, but the neck was wider than the head and seemed to slope down to his shoulders at a forty-five-degree angle on either side. The forehead had not seen hair for many a year, for it had receded like the parting tide into a semicircle which presumably extended all the way round his head. The mouth, nose and eyes seemed somehow to be a long way from the edges, a small face set into a large head. The overall impression was of a bowling ball sitting on top of a molehill.

Lucy stepped to one side to reveal the full extent of the man Joey Davison had turned into. Elliott could see that the years had been not so much unkind to his body – one that had been the envy of many a rugby team member – as positively cruel. The six-pack had been replaced by a weekend takeout; the barrel chest now extended to the entire torso. He looked like Desperate Dan if he had taken a career break and had spent the time eating buckets of chicken and watching daytime TV. The man exuded physical strength and a glorious past. It was as if someone had stuck a hose up the bottom of the teenager Elliott had once known and pumped him full of beer. This was probably similar what had actually happened, except it had been taken voluntarily and orally in small doses.

Elliott wondered when was the last time Joey's toes would have seen his nose. Elliott himself was able to see whether his own shoelaces were tied by just tilting his head forwards slightly. He suspected Joey would only be able to see his penis with the aid of a mirror.

Joey Davison stood in front of Elliott, more of a man than

anyone had any right to be. What he had been doing for the last twenty years since they had been at school together was written large – very large – all over his body. The teenage sporting prodigy had gone on to enjoy a degree of success at his chosen sports – second row during the rugby season and powerful middle order cricket batsmen in the summer – until a nasty knee injury from falling off a table while trying to drink a yard of ale curtailed any possibility of a professional career at either sport. Elliott had read about the accident in the local paper with a mixture of genuine sorrow and barely suppressed glee.

Looking at the giant of a man currently blocking out the view of the rest of the world, Elliott could guess how Joey's sporting activities would have progressed from that point. He would have continued to play at amateur level and be an enthusiastic member of the clubs. Meaning he would always stay in the bar after games. For a long time. He would have dropped down the rugby teams but still played for the social side, and gone from racing round the cricket boundary to being a permanent fixture at first slip where he would pluck speeding cricket balls out of the air, the natural eye barely diminishing with age.

Elliott realised that he had actually taken a step back. He was confronted by the man who had been his school bully. Whilst the word 'cower' may have been too strong, he had ever so slightly crumpled. He forced himself to stand up straight as the enormity of what Joey had just said sank in.

"Tinkle?" he repeated, looking at Lucy, who rolled her eyes in response. He couldn't decide which was worse: the word itself or what it revealed. "Tinkle?!"

"Elliott, you remember Joey Davison?"

The words came out before Elliott's internal censor had a chance to stop them. "Oh yes, I remember Joey Davison. Although more as a concept than as an actual person."

"Ha!" barked Joey. "Typical of you, that, Elliott. Always coming out with clever stuff. Even after all these years I still don't understand what you're talking about." He stuck out his left arm around the side of Lucy and put his right towards Elliott. "Good to see you again, mate."

The hand that was thrust towards Elliott was like a normal hand in every way except it seemed to be twice as big. The immediate image that flashed through Elliott's mind as he stared at the hand was how it would have comfortably been able to crush the skull of a small dog or a large cat. He stared dumbly at the hand. A hissed "Elliott!" from Lucy bounced off him. Many times when at school, and for many years after, he had daydreamed about what he would do if ever he met Joey Davison again. Silently turn his back on him, a devastating put-down – he had even fantasised about learning ju-jitsu in order that he could kick Joey's leg backwards to break his kneecap. Now that the moment was finally here his innate probity took over and he meekly placed his hand in Joey's, then readied himself for the inevitable crushing pain.

The grip was surprisingly light, however. It was the grip of a businessman, and of a man who knew his own strength as well as his position in the business world.

"Yeah. Sure," said Elliott uncertainly. He looked again at Lucy, this time slightly less aggressively. "Tinkle?"

"Yes," replied Lucy. "Tinkle. Short for Tinklebell." She looked at him as if to say, 'You know and I know that it's Tinkerbell not Tinklebell, but he doesn't know that and I haven't told him and he thinks it's a really sweet name, and if you say anything now I will not only never speak to you again but I will also rip your head off and use it as a sprinkler cover in my vegetable patch.' A lot of information can be passed between a brother and sister with only a glance.

"Would you excuse us for a moment?" said Elliott to Joey, who shrugged in return but didn't move. Elliott took hold of his sister's arm and walked her out to the front path with their backs to Joey.

"Is this loan for him?" he hissed. "Are you actually putting our house on the line so that you can give three hundred thousand pounds to that man?"

Lucy slowly removed Elliott's hand from her elbow, then turned gestured to Joey. He stepped down onto the path, then walked across to where Lucy waited with an arm for him to hook into.

"Come on, you," he said to Lucy. "I need to get home." Then, to Elliott, "I'm hosting the cricket committee meeting at my house tonight. Got to get the olives and balsamic onions out." The two of them walked arm in arm down the path. Lucy's elbow was at a right angle to her body, her head not quite reaching Joey's shoulder.

Chapter 17

Stage 8: Releasing of Guilt

Sunday, 10pm

Sitting against the table, Elliott held a pad of multicoloured sticky notes in one hand and a pen in the other. He would not have looked out of place in a teacher training college, seeking ideas from a room full of eager young students. He leaned forwards, all energy and enthusiasm. He had adopted the position five minutes previously upon entering the room and had immediately begun explaining to Ian what was going to happen next. On the door in front of Ian's eyeline was pinned a large piece of paper, taken from a flip chart.

On the table behind Elliott sat a half-empty bottle of Pinot Noir. There were two glasses filled with the red wine, one next to the bottle, and the other in Ian's hand. Also on the table was a bowl of parsnip crisps.

"And so, in conclusion," Elliott said, his left arm waving around to emphasise a point he had not yet made, "none of this is your fault. You have been formed by your experiences. It is a cycle." The top note showed a diagram hastily scribbled, the words 'Experience' then 'Values' then 'Learning' and finally 'Action' with arrows joining them to form a circle. "Every time we do something it creates an experience. This creates our values, which we draw a conclusion about. This affects our next action, which creates new experiences and so on. Many of these experiences are, of course, external, imposed upon us. This can skew our experiences and therefore our values. What has happened to you is that the external influences have not been good ones, leading to the unpleasant personality that we have been deconstructing. Do you see? Hmm? Do you?"

Ian nodded, looking up at Elliott with a blankly benign smile. Eager, obliging. For a moment Elliott wondered if this was what it was like to be a teacher, on the good days, when you had a child who showed genuine interest in a subject. If it was, and if those days were sufficient in number to outweigh the inevitable days of detention and discipline, then maybe it was a path he could have taken instead of the law. He felt at that moment an almost natural ability to impart knowledge. It was similar to landing a fish, he imagined, using the strength of the other against them, not fighting but working with them so that they almost didn't realise that they were slowly being reeled in. He had even rolled up the sleeves of his jumper.

"So you see, 'you' are not your fault. And that means you can change. So, what we're going to do now, Ian, is that you are going to tell me all the external influences that have created your patterns of behaviour, your belief system, that led you to the state where you thought that a lack of manners was acceptable. What are the acts that brought you to this room?"

"Driving like a twat?" said Ian without pause.

"Mind if I put 'recklessly' instead of 'like a twat'?" said Elliott, writing on the top note and sticking it on the flip chart paper pinned to the door. "Although that's really more an outcome," he pointed to the cycle, "an action that has come *from* experiences. I'm thinking more of the experiences that create the values in the first place. The people, the moments, the influences. Yes? Especially the people."

"Being rude to you?"

"Yes, yes, that's good," said Elliott, and another note was stuck onto the door. "But again, that's more of the product of your state of mind. What has happened to you which led to you acting in this way, do you think? Hmm? And by whom?"

"My dad, I suppose."

"Okay, okay, your father, great," said Elliott as he wrote 'FATHER' in capital letters, peeled off the note and stuck it to the door. "And what did your father do which led to you thinking rudeness is acceptable? Specifically?"

"Well, he didn't take any nonsense from the drunkards in his pub. He was very firm with them. At closing time he'd have everybody out by quarter past eleven, usually with a few swear words and sometimes a clip round the ear for the lads. He had a reputation for it."

Elliott wrote 'Sweary dad' and 'Dad's reputation for violence' and put them on the door as Ian continued.

"Mum was very intense. Struggled a bit. I remember she went away for a month. Everyone said she'd gone to the loony bin. Actually, she had. They took the piss…the mick out of me for it. Until I smacked one of them. Then they stopped. Really shut them up, that did."

'Ian's reputation for violence' went onto the door.

"My boss taught me the ABC principle of selling – Always Be Closing. She also showed me her favourite close, the alternate close, where you ask, 'So do you want it in the pink or the blue?' I've used those techniques for a while – tell the gatekeeper it is a personal call, that sort of thing – and even I'm starting to realise they may be a little naff."

Elliott stuck 'Aggressive sales training' on the door.

"They have worked, though – the fact that I am…was driving the sports car proves that."

Elliott wrote 'Motivated by sports car', stuck it on the door, then turned and folded his arms. He stared at Ian, who wore the frown of a child trying to decide between helping to empty the dishwasher or clean the car. Once or twice he opened his mouth and Elliott started to get the feeling there was something significant in his past he was holding back.

"Can you just write 'Mrs Jukas' on the door, please? I'd rather not explain."

Elliott wrote 'MRS JUKAS' in large letters and put it in the middle of the 'cycle of learning' diagram. He looked at Ian questioningly. Ian looked awkward.

"She was a teacher. In college. I, um, made a bit of a fool of myself. A formative experience, you'd probably say."

"Okay," said Elliott, "That's probably enough, Ian. Let's take a look at these notes. The people and the events that shaped you to be the person you are today. It's quite humbling, actually. The horrible person you turned out to be, entirely down to that lot."

They both stared at the door for a while, the time passing like an impenetrable maths exam. They sipped the wine and Elliott refilled their glasses. He offered the bowl of parsnip crisps but Ian declined, not averting his eyes from the history of his life in front of him.

Eventually Elliott went over to the door and took down the flip chart sheet, now covered in sticky notes of varying colours. Then, holding the paper at the top with both hands, he turned and held it in front of Ian, peeking over the top like a Chad as if to say, 'Wot, no manners?'

He reached into his pocket quickly and took out an object, the paper swinging down at one side. He grabbed it again on its second upward movement. A (much) younger version of himself would probably have said, 'Smooooth,' under his breath.

"Take this," said Elliott, and he threw a green plastic disposal lighter into Ian's lap, where it was caught and stared at. After a few moments Ian looked up again at Elliott, uncomprehending. "Do it," said Elliott, extending his arm as he took a step backwards, the paper remaining in the same place, hanging from his pinched thumb and forefinger. "Go on. Torch it. Destroy everything that has made you the person you are. Get rid of your old belief system. Clear the way for the new."

Slowly Ian reached forwards and held the lighter under one corner of the piece of paper. He took a deep sigh, then flicked. Nothing happened. He flicked again, and again, then shook the lighter. On the fourth attempt a flame appeared, which quickly spread itself onto the paper. Elliott waited a few moments until the flame was sure to consume the whole page, then moved to an empty part of the room and dropped the paper to the floor, kicking it closer to the wall. They both watched the flames consume both the paper and the notes stuck to it. The edges of the paper curled up and the whole became smaller and smaller. Eventually, with the paper still smouldering but blackened, all traces of writing obliterated, Elliott stamped on the flames, sending bits of charred paper into the air. When he was satisfied that the flames were all out, he walked over to sit on the table once again and turned to address his captive.

"Okay," he said, then coughed. He got up and opened the door, then returned to his seat. "Okay," he said again. The word was spoken calmly and ended in a smile. It was the sort of smile one might see on a politician being interviewed just after an unexpected victory in a local by-election. He held Ian's blank gaze. "You now have the opportunity to change. The old belief system has gone. You are *not* inescapably bad. Now that you have rejected your former identity you can begin to construct a belief system that truly reflects the person you want to be. How does that sound, Ian?"

The upturned face, so eager to please, so full of expectation. After a few moments it occurred to Elliott that he had not seen Ian blink for a while. He looked down at the man as if he were an exhibit in a zoo, examining his face. Still no blink came. Elliott began to feel rather unnerved.

"I said," he said, "how does that sound, Ian?"

"It sounds like a plan, Elliott," said Ian, staring, not blinking. More staring. More not blinking. It was really getting rather creepy.

As casually as he could, Elliott held the stare. "Shall we try and turn you into something that your mother can be proud of, Ian?" he said. "That Mrs Jukas would be proud of?"

Ian's mouth moved as if words were forming but unwilling to make themselves heard just yet. To Elliott's enormous relief Ian blinked. And again. Several more times, quickly. Something was happening behind the eyes. They were still pointed in Elliott's direction, but they were no longer seeing him. What was happening in there? Memories replaying moments of teenage embarrassment? Battle and conflict between unconditional love and personal values? The usual family politics?

The silence grew into something of consequence. Elliott felt he could do anything right now, that Ian was totally in his control, almost hypnotised. Yet because he did not understand the precise source of the paralysis, he dared not speak or even move. To speak now would be to spoil everything. The moment was Ian's. He needed to take it. Eventually, he did.

"She." Ian mouthed the word again silently. He swallowed. "Mum. She used to chase me around the house. With a wooden spoon. I had to hide in the toilet until she'd calmed down." The eyes snapped back into life. "I was a pain in the arse as a kid. I know I was. They told me often enough. Still joke about it now. In front of people. To each other. Bossy, always wanted my own way, Dad too busy, Mum too distant. Used to getting what I wanted. 'Difficult', they called it. Mum was strong-minded too. It was a battle between the two of us, that's what she says, a battle that she was not going to lose. That's what she says." Ian breathed in so deeply that little red spots appeared briefly on his cheeks, which disappeared as he slowly exhaled. The words tumbled out of him like water flooding through a burst dam.

"Did my parents love me? Yeah, I guess so. Mothers do love their sons, don't they? It's kind of inevitable. Unconditional, you called it. Not something I really understand to be honest. Maybe I will when I have kids of my own. Can you love someone you don't like? Is that possible? Someone who constantly annoys you? Can you actually love them?" The question hung in the air threateningly, as if it was daring Elliott to supply an answer. But there would be no empathy from Elliott at this stage.

Closing his eyes, Ian seemed to stop breathing. His mouth was closed too and the face was starting to go red. It seemed for a bizarre moment that he was trying to inflate his own head. Elliott wondered what on earth Ian was doing. Stubble had been making its way across his jowls and now provided a stark contrast as the fleshier parts of his face became crimson red. Suddenly he let out a anguished bark, thrust his face down into his hands and began a loud blubbing. It was so loud, so over the top that Elliott wanted to laugh, quickly clasping his hand over his mouth.

After about a minute the sobs subsided and the hands came away from Ian's face, wiping his eyes dry as he did so. The redness had gone and he took a few more moments to compose himself before continuing. "There's an old saying in sales," he said. "'You get what you talk about.' So if you've got ten different products but only tell people about one of them, that's what you'll sell most of. Ha. Bloody obvious now I say it out loud. Do you know, I've not thought of it like this before, but that's kind of how life works, isn't it? My parents told me so many times what a pain I was, I guess I turned into that person. I'm the same asshole I always was, just taller. My dad actually said that to me once. When I was a teenager. I thought it was quite a good line actually. He laughed, so did I. Bastard."

Time to step in.

"So if your parents don't really like you as a person," said Elliott, "but they love you because you are their son, why carry on being the person that you are? Why not become a person your mother *could* love?"

Ian stared, his mouth hanging open, like a photograph of someone captured in the process of answering a particularly tricky oral language exam. But no reply came. It was as if the wiring was wrong in his brain as two conflicting logical arguments bashed and clanged against each other, one embedded through confirmation bias and the other an interloper sent to agitate.

Elliott turned to the table, picked up the empty plate and glass, and quietly left the room. He looked back as he shut the door behind him to see Ian still staring at the spot which Elliott had just vacated, a tiny thread of dribble just starting to hang from the corner of his mouth.

Elliott sat on the edge of the bed and rubbed his eyes with his knuckles. He felt drained, his head thick, as if someone had put a tap on his temple and drained out the emotion. Or maybe the opposite: a plug to keep it all in.

Leaning back against the mattress, he pulled the duvet across with one hand, the other twisting his pyjama trousers back into position. His head gently landed on the stack of two pillows and his body nestled into his half of the double bed. A last-minute decision meant rolling onto his left side and therefore facing the vacant half of the bed, then a second twist of the trousers, legs stretched long then legs curled up, head buried deeper into the top pillow. Snuggling deep down into the welcoming sheets.

He felt safe, protected by the virtually bulletproof tog that smothered him. As his eyes closed he once again became aware of the space next to him that Naomi did not occupy. Thoughts ran around, vying for his attention, many of them old acquaintances but joined by some new upstarts, pushing their way to the front, demanding to be heard.

Climbing up the steps of the wall, Elliott put on his helmet as he reached the battlements. Looking out across the plain there seemed to be more Worry Knights amassed than ever before. Slowly and patiently he drew up plans for increased fortifications and traps to defeat the doubts that were trying to force their way in. Sleep overtook him as he began designing pits, the decision as to which man-eating animal was to be placed at the bottom remaining unresolved.

Chapter 18

Monday, 8am

One final squeeze of the teabag and it was carefully placed in the ceramic bowl along with six others from the previous day. It was only three small steps or one large one to the bin, but he had seen Lucy use the teabag bowl system and had decided to adopt it himself. He took the cup and walked past the bin to the fridge and poured into it the last of the milk. Another mental note amongst many: must get milk.

He and Naomi had always been teabag-straight-into-the-bin kind of people. No fussing with special bowls for teabags to save a few steps. The life they had been building together had been based on big ideas and tiny details. She had talked him down from his desire to change the world and instead focused his energy onto getting their tiny corner of it in perfect order. This meant applying the principles they had implicitly agreed upon to their new routine. It had been through their daily lives in London that their world views had merged, the everyday choices of life: which plays to see; which books to read; which newspapers to buy. A series of seemingly innocuous decisions had built up to an attitude that was uniquely theirs.

When Naomi had first received the diagnosis of breast cancer, it had been the small details to which they instinctively reverted. A conscious effort to concentrate on the routine, the minutiae of life, to make the illness fit around them. Bending to the illness would have represented weakness. Any alteration of their lives would mean admitting something was out of place. It was their way of battling the admission that something was, indeed, going very badly wrong with their lives.

The period of remission, going back to work, a continuity of life and all its joyous mundanity that screamed to the outside world, 'We haven't been beaten, we haven't had to change, we are carrying on as normal.'

And then the diagnosis and the hurtling inevitability of the finite nature of existence. The timescales, the percentages, the calculations of how much might be left and what should it be spent on. Naomi's friends wanting to be involved, desperate to do something positive, as much for their own benefit, or so it seemed to Elliott at the time. They would visit Naomi carrying large bowls of cottage pie, as if they had never noticed how much Elliott loved to cook. They were thoughtful and well-meaning and loyal and lovely and taking away just about the only thing Elliott could do to help.

Those wonderful Macmillan nurses, bringing with them comfort and companionship. There was an honesty about the way they avoided any suggestion of hope that he came to admire. Typical of Naomi, she loved to question them about their husbands and holidays while they poured morphine into her, enquiring how their lives were progressing even as she knew her own was becoming shorter and shorter. Palliative. Such a soft, gentle-sounding word with such a forceful and unstoppable meaning.

And then their story ended. The tale of Elliott and love came to a halt one Sunday morning. Quiet, peaceful and yet with the shattering, ripping, tearing effect of an earthquake as his world was rent asunder.

His parents had died in the car accident only a matter of weeks after the funeral, and for a while his entire existence was blank space, white noise. He was out of tune and out of focus. Somehow he managed to work. He was given time by loyal clients, deadlines wandering by unnoticed. It had been Lucy's idea to convert the house into flats and for Elliott to move back home. The familiar surroundings, and in particular the turret, had given him the new grounding that he needed to rebuild, but it had been Phoebe who had been the surprise package. They had always been close but now she went out of her way to look in on him and share her own ambitions with him, investing in him a sense of purpose for her future and thereby slowly coming to see that he may have one too.

He took the empty plastic milk carton and squeezed, the air rushing from the bottle like the sigh of a girl he had once imagined in days long gone when such thoughts were the first to enter his head when he awoke in the morning. Screwing the lid back on whilst maintaining pressure he watched the bottle carefully, then, satisfied that it was as small a shape as he could realistically be expected to produce, he added it to the rest of the recyclable plastic in the green crate that lived in the space next to the bin. They looked like a pile of white, stillborn dinosaur babies, fossilised and found in some mysterious, barbaric, ancient green pit.

He reached into a drawer and took out a black string net. He secured it over the top of the crate, fastening it around the edges. He did the same to the glass recycling box (three bottles that had once contained wine, a pasta sauce and whisky, which now looked back at him incriminatingly) and the paper recycling box (one newspaper from last Sunday, predominantly unread, and a paper bag full of shredded legal papers), stacked them on top of each other and carried them down the driveway to the front gate.

As he trudged back up the drive he heard the bip of a car horn. He turned to see Pru waving with the plastic control still in her hand as she waited for the electronic gate to open. She drove through, winding down her window as she came.

"Morning!" she called brightly as she drove past. It had the effect of lifting his mood, which he hadn't noticed had been black until put into contrast with Pru's. Only three people could have that effect on him. Naomi would purposefully and deliberately lift him out by pointing out the descending blackness. Pru knew him well enough to make a flippant comment at the right time. And Phoebe just had to be in the same room to make him feel better about life.

He returned to the kitchen for his tea, then walked round to the office. By the time he arrived Pru already had a brew of her own from the small kitchen built at the back of the stable and was listening to messages on the answerphone from the weekend. They didn't speak as he walked past and sat at his desk.

"Stan from Cooksons again," said Pru, coming into his office. "He really wants to talk to you, don't he? And one of the Sandini executors called. Ellia?"

He looked up. "Sorry, Pru. I *was* listening."

"Were you? Could have fooled me. What should I do then?"

"About what?"

"Stan from Cooksons and the—"

"Oh yes, sorry." he interrupted. "Could you call Stan and tell him I'm not well? Buy me some time." He ignored Pru's tutting. "Same with the Sandini people."

"Alright. If that's what you want." She hovered for a moment to demonstrate that she was not impressed, then went back to her desk. A few moments later Elliott appeared before her.

"Right, well, a pretty light post. I'm off out, I'll see you later."

"Where are you going?" Pru asked. "There's nothing in the diary. I should know, I'm the only one who looks at it."

Elliott was already halfway out the door. "I'll try and pop in this afternoon," he called over his shoulder.

As Elliott approached the front door to the house he heard Benny say, "It's true, Phoebe." He opened the door to see his niece standing with her arms crossed facing his upstairs neighbour sitting on the third step. She was on the threshold of his flat, leaning against the frame of the open door.

"What's true?" asked Elliott.

Phoebe answered. "Benny was giving me one of his yarns. He's such a phoney." She laughed and punched him gently on the arm. Benny winced.

"It's not a yarn," said Benny. "It's true. It's why I am a musician. My spirituality and impassionated nature were handed down to me through the gene pool. It was not serendipity or happenstance, this was my destiny from the moment Adolfo fell in love with Mary."

"Go on, tell him," Phoebe said, flicking her head towards Elliott, who began to protest but was drowned out by Benny.

"No, no, I really shouldn't, not again. Well, alright, it's all about my great-grandfather, Benito Contini," he said, all in one breath. "He was Italian and a bit of a hothead, a bit of a lover boy, you know. He grew up in a small town near Macerata, in the Le Marche region, on a hilltop. He was a shepherd, a sublimely talented musician, and in love with my great-grandmother, Mary, who was the daughter of the town mayor. She was equally besotted with him. But her parents favoured another boy, Adolfo, to be her suitor. Adolfo had been in love with Mary since they played together in the hills as small children. Benito and Adolfo had been friends at school, but when Mary's parents banned her from seeing Benito, the two young men found their friendship put to a great test.

"The young lovers continued to see each other but now furtively, an illicit affair. Mary would go out into the hills to be with Benito whilst he tended the sheep. Adolfo would often follow her secretly, at a distance, hiding behind one group of rocks and then another. And it happened that one fitful day Mary and Benito were making love under an olive tree—"

"See?" said Phoebe. "Isn't this ridiculous? It's like something out of *Don Quixote.*"

"...Under an olive tree," said Benny, a little louder. "Adolfo was spying on them. He was incensed at seeing his one true love in a flagrante situation, so he grabbed an olive branch, thick and gnarly, then ran up behind them and went to hit Benito over the head, to teach him a lesson. Now, as it happened, Adolfo hit Benito at the very moment of coitus, and—"

"Of what?" said Phoebe.

"Of coitus," repeated Benny. "He peaked. Blew his wad. The big O. He climaxed, dear girl."

"Oh. Ooh, I see."

"His body jerked backwards in ecstasy just as the branch swung down, turning what was intended to be a clip round the head into a full-blown wallop. The forced of the blow killed him instantly, just at the very moment that the sperm which was to become my grandmother entered Mary's body."

Phoebe's eyes looked like they might roll right out of her head. Benny's eyes were twinkling, arms flourishing the story with sweeping gestures.

"This is Contini family history, my dear. We know it to be true because Adolfo married Mary and took care of the child, as if he was his own blood. Adolfo spent the rest of his life trying to make good the terrible thing that he had done. It is believed that because his life flickered out at the very moment of ejaculation,

197

Benito's soul entered Mary's body that day, and that descendants of the Contini family have had part of that soul passed on to them, down through the generalisations. That spirit never changing, always present. Every generation of Continis has thrown an artist into the world. I am merely the latest incarnation."

Phoebe's arms were folded and she was leaning back from the hip, as if she were actually holding the baby herself at that moment. "With respect, what total bullshit, Benny. Why wasn't he arrested for murder, for example?"

"Phoebe," interrupted Elliott, "why are you not on your way to school?"

"Free period. Revision," she replied. "Thought I'd use your table. Mum's got her stuff spread out again."

"Right. Well. As pleasant as it always is, Benny," the two men nodded at each other like rival Elizabethan politicians on best behaviour while in court, "I need to crack on."

Elliott put his key into the lock and turned, Phoebe queuing behind him, folded arms across her chest keeping her books in place. As Elliott pushed and began to enter the flat, Benny called his name. Elliott turned, as did Phoebe.

"Don't forget," said Benny. His eyebrows were quivering high on his forehead, creating an expression that suggested Elliott needed to remember something that Benny would prefer not to say out loud in front of Phoebe. There was a pause followed by a sigh, indicating that Benny's plea had fallen on fallow ground. "The photographer?" he said. "The estate agent?"

Elliott stared for a moment, allowing the various pieces of fact and implication to sort themselves into some kind of order. Estate agent. Lost key to the turret. Found key. Phoebe. Photographer. Lost key. Right. Phoebe. Do not mix Phoebe with valuing people. He looked quickly at Phoebe, then back at Elliott.

"Yes. Good point. Ha! Thanks for the reminder, Benny. I was just going to tidy up, as it happens. Ha! Phoebe, sorry, can't study in here today. Got to let this photographer guy in. For your mum, you know. Lots to do, see you later." Elliott all but pushed Phoebe out of the doorway and into the porch, then shut the door with just a final glimpse of the annoyed and suspicious look Phoebe was giving him as the door clicked in place. Past her shoulder he saw a broad smirk covering Benny's face.

As he walked towards the lounge the buzzer from the outside gate signified the start of the countdown. Phoebe spoke into the intercom, undoubtedly bidding them a cheerful welcome. He had just a few minutes by his estimation to either lose that damn key again or alternatively not be there at all.

He felt the stress and excitement of the moment in equal measure. Neither were emotions he would normally experience. One part of him felt ashamed that a middle-aged man was running around his flat trying to hide from his sister. Again. But there was a hidden corner of him that secretly enjoyed the chase. This realisation came as something of a surprise and made him immediately more wary. This was a serious business. He remembered, when standing in front of the headmaster after the fight with Joey, having an uncontrollable urge to laugh. It was nerves, false and distracting as he waited for a solution to appear from the panic.

The sound of the front door to the house being opened was quickly followed by Lucy's muffled voice, presumably bringing the photographer and estate agent. Quickly he went over to the door to the turret that was now less of a secret than it had been in perhaps the entire rest of its history. As quietly as possible he went through and shut it carefully behind him, took the key from his front trouser pocket, then turned the key in the lock. He took it out again, aware that his sister could well look into the keyhole and spot that the key was in the lock from the inside. A twinge of shame echoed through him. A middle-aged solicitor, a man who commanded respect in his local community, cowering behind a door. And all because he was trying to make the world a better place, to just make a little change for the better. Where was the justice in that?

He leaned against the wall and looked up the stairs. He had always been judgemental, he knew that. Naomi used to tell him to be more accepting of the faults of others (and of his own, for that matter). Forgiveness. It was a subject he had found cause to dwell on over the years. He had always felt that it was only possible to forgive if that forgiveness came with contrition, with a desire in the person seeking forgiveness to change for the better. But did it matter if it was a genuine desire to improve; what the Catholic church called 'perfect contrition', or from a fear of the consequences; 'imperfect contrition'? And if the remorse was imperfect, was it then possible to forgive?

The voices grew louder as they entered the lounge, then they stopped. He put his ear to the door and jumped backwards as the handle to the secret door was violently twisted. He heard Lucy let fly a few curses in his favour.

"Can you do the rest of the flat first?" she said, presumably to the estate agent.

"Yep, Dave's on it, won't take too long, then we'll need to get up there."

"Well, can't you do it without? I can describe it to you, it's pretty boring, you know."

"I'm afraid not. Need to check it structurally, you see. Sorry."

"Oh for...Phoebe, do you know where he keeps the key?"

"Sorry, Mum. It was in the lock last I saw it."

"Where the hell is he anyway? He must have gone out through the buttery and escaped. He's acting like a bloody little kid at the moment, what the hell has got into him? Well, you might as well start in the bedrooms..."

The voice faded, presumably as Lucy took the estate agent to see the rest of the flat. Elliott let his head fall back against the wall and closed his eyes, turning his mind towards the next session.

Step nine of the ten-stage process. The end was in sight. Progress and harmony, the penultimate stage. That was a joke! Harmony was about the last thing he felt at the moment. If he climbed those stairs filled with the doubt he currently felt he would never be able to focus on the carefully constructed reinvention of Ian that required all his energies. Finally this next stage would allow him to offer a solution. This was so much more his style: to give help and show the way, to produce answers, not to break and rip and fracture with unkindness. This was the stage he had been working towards these last three days, the chance he had hewn for himself to effect real change. He only hoped the first eight stages had worked and that Ian was the blank sheet that the process promised him to be, devoid of personal ego, riddled with uncertainty about the previous behaviour that had led him to this stage. Finally they were getting close to the stage where Ian would actually thank—

"Uncle E?"

Phoebe's voice came through the door and startled Elliott into jumping forwards and spinning round, his heart thumping. He barely breathed, let alone spoke. How long had she been listening, perhaps with her ear to the door herself? Had he made any noise? He had been so locked in his own thoughts that he couldn't remember. He may even have been talking to himself. Oh, don't spoil it now, Phoebe, not so close.

"Uncle E, are you there?" She spoke in a loud whisper, clearly not wanting her mother to overhear. "Uncle E? Please, you're scaring me. I don't understand what's going on. Why are you being so odd? Why won't you let us up into the turret? What have you got up there you don't want us to see?" She was crying now, and Elliott felt his pulse thumping in his ears, not only due to the fear of capture before his work was complete, but because he simply hated so much to think of Phoebe unhappy. All children have to realise their adult mentors are imperfect at some point and Elliott had been dreading that inevitable day even since she was a toddler, following him around everywhere, wanting to do everything with him, whether it was passing him a screwdriver or doing a jigsaw together.

"I'm scared, Uncle E. I don't want to think you have that man up there. But I don't know what else to think. If you can hear me but you aren't answering it means you have kidnapped him. But I don't know if you're there. Oh God. I love you, Uncle E, I can help you, just come out and let's talk about what you're doing." He could hear her blubs, the sharp catches of breath. How long would she wait and continue to torture him like this? He heard a sigh so huge she might have popped a rib. "I'm going to school now. Either you aren't in there and I'm talking to a door, or you can hear me but won't let me help you. Which makes me so fantastically sad, as I don't know where else you could possibly be."

A few more moments of silence and then he put his ear to the door and heard her heavy footsteps moving away. He heard more discussion, presumably Phoebe saying goodbye to her mother, followed eventually by the shutting of the front door.

He had always known that failure was not something that could possibly be allowed to happen. Now, however, that reality had just been placed in front of him in the form of the potentially lost love of the person dearest to him in the world. He slid down the wall and sat down to wait for his sister and his other 'guests' to leave.

Part 3

Rebuilding the Self

Chapter 19

Stage 9: Progress and Harmony

Monday, 10am

"It's called eggs Benedict," said Elliott, sitting on the chair and watching Ian shovel mouthfuls of ham covered in white sauce and egg yolk. He held a photograph in one hand. "I do it the American way where I fry the ham a little before covering it with the hollandaise. I made the sauce myself. Quite tricky, actually, it's all in the whisking."

He took a sip from his cup of coffee and was amused to notice that Ian immediately did the same. During yesterday's session he had experimented with body language. At one point he adopted three different positions with his arms and on each occasion Ian had, a few moments later, copied him. This told Elliott that they were finally aligned in their thinking, and the final stage of the process, introducing the new belief system, could now begin. It was time for the two of them to come together, to share something, for Elliott to open up a little and let Ian see there was good in the world. He was more hopeful than ever that the two of them could walk out of this turret as friends.

Ian mopped the last of the yolk and hollandaise mixture on his plate with the last piece of ham and shoved it breathlessly into his mouth, a morsel of sauce catching the side of his mouth. His tongue flicked it clean. Still picking bits of ham out of his teeth with his tongue, Ian put the plate on a tray, which he pushed across the floor towards Elliott as far as he could reach.

"That was lovely. Thank you," he said.

Placing the knife and fork together on the plate, Elliott opened the door and placed the tray on the floor outside, as if banishing its memory from the room. Then he returned to his seat opposite Ian and sat with his hands in his lap, still holding the photograph. He waited in silence, the two men staring at each other, until eventually Ian moved uncomfortably and placed his hands in his lap. Elliott, satisfied that the two of them were in sync, began talking.

"I'd like to share a memory with you today, Ian. To open up a bit of myself with you. So far it has been you who has been stripped bare, figuratively speaking." He paused for a moment, wondering whether to correct himself, then carried on. "Now I'd like to reveal myself to you." He leaned forwards slightly. "Don't worry, figuratively speaking again. Ha-ha."

Elliott held up the photograph and displayed it to Ian. He watched the other man's face. It became vaguely interested for a moment. The eyes narrowed, as if he was hearing a song on the radio but couldn't quite remember who it was by. After a few moments of studying the picture he looked back at Elliott blankly, awaiting an explanation.

"My father," said Elliott. "It's a picture of him when he was at university." Elliott turned the picture to himself for a moment. "Quite a handsome chap, in those days." Ian did not respond.

"Why am I showing you this, Ian? Well, my father is no longer with us. He passed away a year or so ago. It wasn't a very nice end. He was in a coma for two months before he went. I was with him for a lot of that time. If I was an artist or a writer I'm pretty sure those two weeks created enough neuroses within me to inspire a hundred pictures or poems.

"He wasn't in his body, you see. I sat there watching him. Sometimes talking in the hope that he was still in there somewhere. His breathing was almost tangible, each breath seemed to be a huge effort, often ending with a whistle or a rattle. It had an almost solid quality that made it seem to 'exist' in the room. And because it was so palpable, it also had the quality of being capable of stopping at any moment.

"To see his determination to carry on breathing, with all the effort his body put into the feat, was extraordinary. The life force that is within us, Ian, that drives us even in the darkest and most desperate of hours to continue forcing out each breath, one in every few seconds, one out every few seconds, breathing by sheer bloody-minded force of will. When it looked easier to give up, to accept that it was time, he was still making himself force the air into and back out of his body.

"After a while it just didn't seem to be my father any more. His body had, in effect, become a breathing machine, relentless and hard-working but only existing for one purpose.

"I realised that I was just sitting there waiting for the breathing to stop. Sometimes my sister was with me but often we took it in turns and I was alone, and the noise the body made as it pumped and wheezed would be the only sound in the room. I spent my time waiting for something to stop being, for a sound to no longer be present. It was endlessly repetitive – or so it seemed for a while – and even soothing. Yet its absence was the very thing that I was waiting for, the signal that my father had left the room. Listening for a sound to be no longer there."

Elliott now oblivious to whether his body language matched with Ian's. He was staring up and to the right, remembering words he had written down at the time and using them to express emotions that he had tried to bury. Tears would not come, but the occasional word caught in his throat.

"When I talked to him there would sometimes be a slight response. It is strange how I felt able to say all those things I'd been thinking over the years but never told him. I always believed he knew deep down, that those unsaid things didn't need spelling out. But now, when the words were spoken out loud, creating a second noise in the room, I felt better for it. Once he slightly changed his expression, almost like he wanted to reply to me. I like to think it meant he was hearing me, that he understood. It might have been a wince of pain, but I think he knew I was there.

"And do you know a strange thing? For some reason I reverted to calling him Daddy." Now a few tears came. "I hadn't called him by that name for at least twenty years. Where did that pop out from? The walls of mutual respect we built up over the years, the ways of dealing with each other, the burying of love when faced with life's tribulations, all that had gone and I now reverted to the relationship we had when I was a small child and he and my family were my entire world. I didn't have friends – the other children made fun of us. During his life my father had been my friend. He was also my colleague, my mentor, my adjutant, my hero, my playmate, my judge and jury. Now he was just my daddy again."

Elliott took a handkerchief from his trouser pocket and blew his nose. "I can't pretend I found it an easy experience, Ian, but it was humbling, to see life in all its fragility. I wasn't with him when he finally went, my sister was on shift, but it didn't matter – he had already gone before that, it was just a pump that finally stopped working."

The handkerchief was returned to his pocket. Elliott sat up straight, put back his shoulders and jutted out his chin, as if rebooting himself. "Well," he said. "There you have it. I have shared something with you. I wanted you to know that I do not consider myself better than you. I also have feelings, I am human too. Just because it has fallen to me to show you the atrocious belief system that was given to you does not mean I consider myself above you. We are one, you and me."

The two of them sat in silence for a few minutes, their body posture identical as if a magical mirror had placed in front of Elliott which reflected an image of the sitter as a stinky, scruffy unshaven person.

"So far," said Elliott eventually, "we have been focusing on the problem. What is the problem, Ian?"

Without skipping a beat, Ian took his cue. "That I'm a rude, ignorant person and have been made that way by a combination of the way my parents brought me up and the people I associate with, both at work and socially, since then. That belief system has been reinforced by my actions and reactions." His answer was clipped, well rehearsed, almost as if answering a question from his sergeant major.

"Excellent summary, Ian. The point we must remember is that it is not your fault that you are a despicable, revolting and ill-mannered person. You have been made that way. And if this appalling person was created by others, there is hope that it can be changed."

Elliott stood up at last, stretching his legs as he walked around the room. Ian was impassive, his back as straight as Elliott's had been a few moments ago, looking forwards, hands one on top of the other in his lap. Elliott almost felt as if he should stick a biscuit into his mouth and pat him on the head. Instead he walked round the room twice, slowly, looking down in concentration, watching one foot land softly in front of the other, ending up behind Ian. He stood for a moment, arms crossed, before continuing.

"Yesterday you told me you that you consider yourself unlovable. Yesterday. It seems much longer. Ian, we all consider ourselves to be unlovable. No one *expects* to be loved. Love is the most wonderful surprise. Love is a security blanket thrown over our heads from behind, catching us unawares. I have an aquarium at home, full of tropical fish. But it is not actually the fish I need to focus my attention on. It is the water that I need to care for. And so it is with love. You have to be a person that someone would fall in love *with*. To create the environment in which love can breed – flourish, even. That takes work, Ian, effort – it doesn't just happen. Being lovable, someone who could be loved, can be really hard work."

Elliott returned to his chair in front of Ian. He leaned forwards onto his elbows, then interlocked his fingers. He was aware of Ian staring back at him with a gentle eagerness. Elliott's gaze wandered and he allowed his eyes to defocus blankly at the floor by Ian's feet, allowing his thoughts to gather. He wiggled his fingers. What was that children's playground game? 'Here's the church and here's the steeple, look inside and here's the people.' He looked up at Ian who smiled carefully, patiently.

"You, Ian, have not been lovable. That much we have established. But you can be. In fact, you already are. Ian, *I* love you. I do. That is why we are here. Because I love you, I love your potential, the person I know that you can be. You see, this is your way out, your future. We know that your being here is not your fault. It is the result of you making an abusive gesture to me after *you* had endangered *my* life, so even my reaction by kidnapping you, even that was not actually your fault. It was the fault of your belief system. And in the last session we concluded that you could choose an alternative. You denounced your personality and all who made it. Now you have the chance to become a person even your mother could love. You can choose a new belief system of which you can be proud. The real you, the you deep within yourself, the you that looks back on how you used to behave with shame and anger. What do you say, Ian?"

Elliott held Ian's thousand-yard stare. He looked into those dull eyes, wondering what was going on inside that head, willing it to say what he hoped it would say. What he needed it to say. Was Ian ready for the next and final stage? Had all this sacrifice, this gamble, been worthwhile? He had put so much faith in the brainwashing process but he was always conscious that it had been used by the Korean military for evil, whereas he was trying to use it for good, to improve the world. He couldn't know if the process was suitable for such a noble purpose. There were only two ways out of this situation: freedom and enlightenment, or incarceration.

Finally Ian spoke. "I understand. I want to be a good person. I want to be liked. I want to be…polite. I am ready."

After pausing for a few moments to calm his beating heart, Elliott stood and walked round behind Ian. His hands were shaking slightly as they tugged at the ends of the rope that bound Ian's legs to the chair. He stopped and took a deep breath, then tried again. This time he successfully untied the ropes. Ian was now completely free and able to move around the room. To escape or attack. For a moment, neither of them moved.

Walking round to the front of the room by the door once again, Elliott stood in front of Ian, who continued to look at him benignly.

"You are free to move around the room, Ian. You have made a conscious decision, of your own free will, to choose the path of good manners, of respect. That is a major step. I will leave you now to consider what this means in detail, how you will behave differently in future. I will return early this evening when we will discuss this together, side by side, as colleagues, as peers. Please use this last amount of time on your own to really understand within yourself what it means to be a nice person. What sacrifices you may have to make, and what benefits it will bring you." Elliott left the room and locked the door behind him, the last noise from within being the clicking of Ian's knees as he stood up and stretched.

Chapter 20

Monday, 5pm

Opening the passenger door, Elliott placed a flask of Scotch broth and two buttered rolls in a plastic container on the seat. Not for the first time he wondered if Ian crashing in front of him had been serendipity or something more preordained, like some weird version of karma.

Elliott drove out of the driveway onto the road and turned towards town. Fifteen minutes later he had made it into town as far as the ring road, which he followed for a further ten minutes. He then turned off into one of the many small suburbs, following the signs to the industrial estate, which was home to Joey's office.

The road took him through a residential area. He saw a man ahead on the pavement, holding the hand of a small child in a shiny blue coat, hood up. They stopped and turned to cross the road. Looking up the road towards Elliott, the man seemed to make a quick assessment, then scuttled into the road, tugging hard on the hand of the little girl. In her other hand she held firmly to a small tiger.

Elliott had to brake hard in order to slow down sufficiently. As he approached he wound down his window and glared at the man, who was studiously looking down at his daughter, clearly trying to ignore the glare of the angry driver. Elliott was so astonished at the stupidity of the man that he struggled to choose his words. What *were* you thinking? You have a small child with you, shouldn't you be setting an example? Tell you what you could try: how about waiting for five seconds?!

The man and the girl were almost to the other side of the

road. As Elliott opened his mouth to shout at the man, the girl jumped with both feet together onto the pavement and stared up at her father for his approval. Elliott's words caught in his throat. The man looked down at his little girl and for a moment the two of them were the only things that existed for each other in the whole universe. Her face spoke that she worshipped her father, that he could do no wrong, that he was superhuman. One day that little girl would have the crushing realisation of all of her father's flaws, that her daddy was capable of making stupid decisions. But not yet. Not now. Not here.

Elliott put the car into gear and drove slowly on through the suburbs.

The first time that Naomi's cancer had been confirmed they had to make a decision whether to try faster or stop trying for children at all. They decided to stop. It didn't seem fair to bring a child into the world if there was a chance they might not have a mother. Elliott knew it was the correct decision and yet, and yet. In his imagination all the achievements of the children he and Naomi would never have were laid out before him. As a young man he had felt bloated by all the love within him that the world did not seem to want. Then Naomi had become a willing recipient and the pain of wanting to love had been released on her.

Yet after a few years of their marriage he realised there were untapped reservoirs still within him. This was a different kind of love; it included larger degrees of protection, of nurture. He had learned so much from Naomi but now he wanted to guide a child through life, to have that feeling of pride that comes from seeing a person react in a brave or caring manner and knowing that reaction only came about because of something you did, a lesson you taught, many years before and long forgotten by all but you.

He had begun to actively enjoy the time he spent with his mother and father, nourished by a love for him that was absolute, that did not request anything in return except existence. He wanted that feeling for himself, it was the greatest adventure that he and Naomi could share, to love each other more by sharing their love for children.

Elliott turned into the industrial estate, drove past Joey's building, then turned around and parked within sight of the front door.

Before the cancer, when they still thought children might be a possibility, he would lie awake late at night as Naomi drifted off to sleep. He would imagine his seed within her and wonder if this was the time, if life was at that very moment coming into existence in this glorious body that lay beside him. Then his mind would drift and he would ponder the adult that the child might become. He wanted a creative person, someone who would be happy as long as they were using their hands. Open-minded, interested in the world around them. As long as they were happy and willing to care. He knew deep down that such ambitions are beyond the reach of parents and that children become what they hell they want to become irrespective of our best attempts to steer them down channels of our choosing. But he clung to the innocent hope of the wannabe parent. He would drift off to sleep imagining laughter and happiness and play and pride.

Those thoughts, these memories of children that would never be, would continue finding their way into his mind after Naomi had gone, except now he would construct walls and moats in order to keep them at bay.

The front door of Joey's building opened as the staff left work for the day. Industrial estates on the edge of town always made Elliott feel like they had been designed by children using Lego blocks. Joey's building was identical to all the others except for the name on the top. Now workers filed out of the other buildings, got into their cars and drove onto the servicing road as if a factory hooter had blown announcing the end of the day. The line of cars then turned obediently away from where Elliott sat in his car and formed a long queue to the main road and towards civilisation. The rush hour would only last fifteen minutes each afternoon, a sudden burst of activity like a hoard of flying ants all leaving the nest on the same day in July. No one seemed to walk out of this estate. Most people's idea of a public transport policy is one where other people use public transport more often. Elliott shook his head, but didn't notice.

Three cars remained outside Joey's building. Next to – or was it beneath? – Joey's huge pickup truck splashed with mud cowered Lucy's Mini. Next along was a small car with the words 'Polt and Moore Garages Replacement Vehicle' emblazoned in yellow lettering on the two doors. It gave Elliott enormous pleasure to see that while Paolo's large BMW was being repaired, he had been provided with a Nissan Micra. He revelled in the image of Paolo turning up late at the garage, then shouting at the receptionist because there was only one replacement car left.

The three cars provided further evidence of the treacherous felicitations going on within. How could Lucy, his protector for so long, the one person who had always been unshakeable in her determination to improve and help him, how could she cross to the other side now, of all times? Betraying him not once, but twice?

And yet forgiveness had started to worm its insidious way into his mind. If Lucy could find it within herself to allow Joey into her life, could he? The ignominy of going through school with your own personal bully, of knowing that one person found you so weak that they would choose you, out of hundreds of other small, scared boys, to pick on; to be able to refer to someone as 'my bully'. It was as if they had a dark connection and were forever linked to each other. At the time had he not wished he could go to Joey Davison and say, 'I forgive you'? No, he hadn't. He had wished that he had an elder brother, not sister, a big, muscular elder brother who would go to Joey Davison and tower over him, frightening him, making him realise what it was like to lie awake at night wondering what you had done that was so terrible you had earned your own tormentor.

And now this very same person was being allowed access to his sister's life, her body. The same sister that had held Elliott's hand while he had cried and cried when he got home from school after spending the day bottling up his fears and worries. As adults they had stood firm through the abrupt loss of their parents, traumatic times, the slow, drawn-out but painfully inevitable loss of Naomi. Lucy and Elliott, side by side, supporting each other through things that he had once imagined could only happen to other people. All that comradeship and solidarity earned through bitter struggle and shared pain. Given up to be with a man she knew was the cause of continuing nightmares for Elliott, her brother.

And yet this in itself pointed to forgiveness. Lucy would not have allowed such a thing to come to pass without good reason. She must know something, she knew, always, she knew. There must be something that he did not know. As when he would stand in the priest hole, scared by the ghosts of the past, as when he would wait for her after school so that she could walk him home, his protector. As when he collapsed into her arms after the funeral of his wife when all other guests had left the wake, desperate and lonely in his realisation of the life that stretched out before him without the only person he had ever met that truly understood him. In all these times he had trusted his big sister, instinctively, deep down, where only Naomi had travelled. There something shone, a beacon that told him Lucy knew best.

From his vantage point, parked in a row of cars on the road at the exit to the industrial estate, Elliott would be able to see when the three of them left. He was not so much hiding as waiting. He glanced back up the road and saw a cyclist coming towards him on the pavement, doing bunny-hops and wheelies as he went. Elliott recognised the rider, who in turn recognised Elliott's car and immediately started riding properly. Elliott wound down his window.

"Hello, Mikey."

"Hi, Mr Harmison. How are you? Everything alright?" Mikey had stopped the bike but was balancing, stationary, as he spoke, occasionally doing little hops. Elliott could only image what he must be like in a school classroom; it must be impossible for his teachers to make him sit still.

"Mikey, I wonder if you could do me a favour."

"Sure, of course." Hop, hop. "Whatever you like."

"When you see Phoebe next, could you tell her that you saw me this morning just before school? Nothing too heavy, just that you waved to me as I was driving past or something?"

"Sure, yeah, of course, no worries." Mikey had finally put a foot on the floor. He looked uncomfortable for a moment, which in his case meant he nodded and smiled even harder than usual.

Elliott eyed him carefully. "Is that okay?"

"Yes, no, of course, not a problem, although, well, it's fine actually, but, well, I just haven't really spoken to her, you know, much, well, at all, since, you know, you, like you suggested I don't, so…"

"Oh, I see. What, not at all?"

"No. I avoided her this weekend. She seemed a bit annoyed, actually. I guess that's a good thing? Part of your plan and that?"

"Ah, well, by 'set them free' I didn't meant 'don't ever speak to them again', Mikey. Just don't crowd them too much. You are allowed to actually have a conversation with her. And then you could mention that you saw me. Would that be okay?"

"Oh, yeah, great, okay." Mikey got back up on the bike and hopped again, getting ready to go.

"But Mikey – you haven't seen me now. Not a word to anyone, okay?"

"Got it." He winked. He actually winked. And with a brief, "See you, Mr Harmison", Mikey sped off along the pavement, pulling a wheelie. Elliott watched him in the side mirror for a few moments. Oh, to be so uncluttered by the pressures of existence.

Picking up the almost cold and nearly empty Styrofoam cup of coffee, Elliott turned his attention back to the reason he had a full bladder and a sore backside. He saw Paolo, hunched in the front of his temporary car, pull out of the parking space and pause to turn right. Swiftly Elliott slid down the seat, his legs crumpling into the footwell and his head ducking out of sight as Paolo passed.

Slowly he raised his nose up and looked out. As his mouth cleared the doorframe his breath fogged up the window, and he made two small holes with his finger. Through these he could see Joey and Lucy walk over to her car. They kissed passionately, Joey leaning over and Lucy craning her neck back and standing on tiptoes as Joey's arms stopped her from falling backwards. They looked as if he could fall on top of her and they could become one entity. Elliott muttered, "Oh, please" to himself. Eventually Lucy extracted herself, got into her car and drove out of the estate.

After waiting for a few moments Elliott started his car and drove into the parking space that Lucy had just left. Joey remained standing in front of his office, arms now folded.

"Hey, Elliott," said Joey in greeting. "I saw you parked up there. Do you want to come up to my office? I reckon you probably want to ask me a few questions."

Joey led from behind, opening each door with his long reach

and allowing Elliott through first. Up the stairs to the right and Joey held open one more door into a small room.

Judging by the framed, signed England rugby shirt on the wall, Elliott guessed this was Joey's office. He walked round behind the desk and saw a photograph of Joey held in a headlock by an England rugby player Elliott vaguely recognised, both of them grinning inanely. On the other side of the desk was a picture of Lucy that Elliott had never seen before. She wore a shocking blue ballroom dress. Even though she was his own sister, he had to admit she looked rather stunning. He wondered briefly where and when the picture had been taken.

There were no documents on the desk, just a computer monitor. Joey was clearly one of those people who tidied his workspace completely before leaving. This came as a minor surprise.

Elliott sat on the leather office chair proffered to him by Joey, who then seated himself behind the desk, leaning back with his hands locked behind his head. They eyed each other for a moment, like two stags eyeing up whether this was a fight worth starting.

Without speaking, Joey leaned forwards and swivelled slightly in the chair to face the monitor. He pulled open a drawer and took out a wireless keyboard and a mouse. After a few clicks the printer behind him began to hum. He swivelled, then, after waiting a few moments to make sure everything had printed, he took the sheaf of printed pages, banged them into neatness on the desk, then handed the bundle to Elliott.

The front page was entitled 'Management Accounts: August'. Elliott took the pages and rested them on his lap.

"I'm guessing that's what you want to see," said Joey. "Your sister is trying to make me take a significant amount of money from her. She's wonderful, by the way. You are her brother and live in the house she is putting up as security for the loan from her ex-husband. If I were you I'd probably want to know what hell I'd done to cock up my business so badly that I'd need a loan of that size, and whether the business has got a future."

"I think that probably sums it up," replied Elliott, his expression unchanged.

Joey laughed. "Lighten up, old boy," he said. "I may be a bit thick but I have run this business for many years now. I've done plenty of deals and I reckon I'm a pretty good judge of other people's motives. Go on, take a look. Ask me anything you like. I'm offering you open season on old Joey."

Picking up the papers, Elliott set aside the cover sheet. Next was a single page profit and loss summary from the previous month. From a glance Elliott could tell that business was no better than okay. A very small profit in the month, but Joey was not currently taking a salary from the business.

Next came the balance sheet. It did not look good. Not at all. The company was very close to going bust. One line immediately grabbed his attention. It read 'Bad Debt Provision: Mackeson Charity'. Moving his eyes across the page, Elliott came to the amount. Four hundred thousand pounds. If that provision became a reality, then the company would be insolvent.

Joey stood up and paced the room. He padded nervously, arms dangling distantly from his sides as if he was carrying two rolled-up sleeping bags. If a vertical line were drawn down through his centre of gravity his head would be behind the line and his stomach in front, leading the way as if he were carrying the bass drum in a marching band. As he walked one foot was thrown out hopefully in front, bending from the knee, then found the ground, followed by the next foot in a repeated act of optimism. It almost looked as if he was walking backwards, moonwalking like a sumo Michael Jackson, and yet somehow he continued his momentum around the room. The arms moved only slightly with the sway of the body, their balancing purpose long since rendered obsolete by the bulk of his body. If God had intended man to be made in this way, thought Elliott, he would have given him gills. Joey's body shape was vastly different from the one Elliott remembered from school, and these days was less built for running with a rugby ball and more suited to wallowing in deep water, grazing on krill.

Elliott leaned forwards and placed the papers back on the desk. Joey picked them up, then fed them into a shredder next to his desk. He went back round the table and sat down in his chair, which sagged like a seaside donkey carrying a teenager eating an ice cream.

"Any questions, Elliott?" Joey said again. "You're family. I'll tell you anything you want to know."

Despite the years that had passed, despite all that had happened since he had last set eyes on his nemesis, Elliott still felt somehow intimidated by the hulk of a man spilling over the sides of the leather executive chair in front of him. He looked so less threatening now, despite taking up twice the space that Elliott occupied. All this time, all the things he had dreamed of saying and the wrongs that needed to be righted. And yet there was something vulnerable about the monster from his past that caught Elliott off guard.

Hang on a minute. Family?

"Joey, what are you talking about, family?"

"Well, not literally. Not yet anyway." Joey actually looked abashed as he started fiddling with a black piece of foam in the shape of a rugby ball. "But I think of you as family."

The past came tumbling out in a torrent. "Joey, you are not my family and never will be. You are the person who caused as much misery to me as anyone in the entire world. You were my bully at school. Have you forgotten? You can't just brush that aside. You made my life a misery for years and years. Because of you I have had emotional blockages that even my dead wife struggled to overcome. I have carried a burning hatred of you for...for decades. You really think I can just forget that in an instant? You were *my* bully, for Christ's sake."

"Yeah. Sorry about that," said Joey.

Elliott stared at the man opposite him. This could not be happening. All these years, all this time waiting for retribution, for a chance to get revenge on the man who, as much as any other, had created his deep sense of injustice at the world, and now, after all that had gone on in his head, he was sat just a few metres away looking genuinely contrite. No! This was not fair! He felt like a boxer cheated out of the world title because of a rigged judging panel, but who was then being refused a rematch. He was not looking for remorse from this man; he wanted somehow to put the past right, to change what had happened so that his own extended period of humiliation could be finally put away forever.

"Thing is," said Joey, "I was actually really jealous of you?"

His voice went up at the end of the sentence as if he was trying to deliver a joint statement and question. "I was good at sports and stuff, but you were always so brainy. You didn't say much, but when you did it was always something really clever."

"And so you thought the best response to that would be to thump me?" Elliott could hardly believe he was having this conversation. "Repeatedly?"

"Yeah. Guess so. I'm not that bright, so I guess it was what Lucy would call an emotional response. I felt threatened by you. That's what she reckons. And she's right about everything else."

"You've discussed this with Lucy?"

"Of course. Truth is, I've been really nervous about meeting you. Kind of embarrassed, really. I wasn't a very nice person when I was a teenager. Everyone thought I was some kind of hero, but all I did was sport. Not clever stuff, like you. I've tried really hard over the years to put things right. That's partly what's got me into so much trouble, Lucy says. But now I'm sitting here with you it's all a bit strange, isn't it? I haven't been anyone's hero for a long time. That's why Lucy makes me feel so good, I guess." He looked down at the table, and for a moment Elliott thought he might be about to cry; his face flushed. He looked awkward, embarrassed. Instead he shrugged his enormous shoulders and looked Elliott squarely in the eye in the way he must have done so many times before to an opposition prop forwards on the rugby pitch. Except this time the glint of steel was replaced by the sparkle of a tear. "So. As I said. I'm sorry, Elliott."

Elliott shifted uncomfortably in his chair. This was not how things were supposed to be. This meeting had been planned for decades. How dare Joey show remorse and seek forgiveness?! The man was clearly not the same person he had been at school. Why should he have been? It was now Elliott's turn to feel a little foolish.

There were not many people Elliott still knew from his schooldays. Most of his peers had moved away and then stayed away. And there was the fact that he had not known many other kids at school.

Those few peers who had returned with their university degrees to ply their trade back home had known of Elliott, and Elliott had known of them. But he would be hard pushed to call any of them friends. On the occasions they did meet it was as if they were part of a special club. Elliott would sometimes get invited to a lunch or networking event with other professionals, or perhaps to celebrate the completion of a deal. If he did find himself next to someone who actually remembered him from school, they would both act as if it was the most natural thing in the world to be sat round a table together. It was as if people could deliberately forget things that had happened between them and carry on as normal, both parties participating in a fraud, implicitly accepting that a big fence surrounded their schooldays. All the things they did and said to each other in the enclosed cauldron of school had been fuelled by lust and jealousy as their hormones fought for supremacy. Blinking in the sunlight of adulthood, they looked back with awkwardness at their teenage selves and quietly, unknowingly and en masse, agreed to never mention the worst of those days ever again.

Elliott had graciously complied with this subterfuge, introducing his best clients to people who had stamped on his briefcase and laughed at his jacket and tie. He had broken bread with men whose done nothing while his dinner money had been stolen. He had even bought lunch for one female solicitor who had a school history even worse than his own, a mother of three who had been a very popular fifteen-year-old girl behind the bike sheds. In the first moment of meeting they had acknowledged that they had known each other at school, followed swiftly by an awkward flash in the eyes revealing memories of each other long buried (although some of those memories were in a very shallow grave), then both silently agreeing never to mention school again.

If that lady could move on from having such a sordid reputation to now being so dignified, then surely he could find it within him to accept that his school bully might regret what he had done some twenty-five years ago?

Elliott stood up, pushing his chair backwards. Now he looked down on Joey. Now it was his turn to be in the ascendency, to have control. He felt the power as he looked down on this pathetic man, a riot of muscle and flab underneath his baggy shirt, a person who only five minutes ago would make him feel scared as if he were back at school and awaiting a thumping.

A man who was so transparently in love with his sister.

Elliott held out his right arm. The smile that crept across Joey's face was almost pathetically grateful. Joey stood, took the hand, and they shook.

They both sat back down, facing each other over the desk again. "Come on then," said Elliott. "Tell me about this debt. Who or what is Mackeson? If that gets called in you're done for."

Without saying a word Joey opened the drawer of his desk, took out a piece of paper, and handed it to Elliott. It was a letter from his bank requesting repayment of a short-term loan. The amount was four hundred thousand pounds.

"Okay. I get it. It *is* being called in. Lucy is offering security to a loan. And the money is coming from Paolo. Is that the nub of it?"

"Yes. Yes, it is." Joey studied his hands. There was a defiance in him, despite the facts now being out in the open for all to see, despite the humiliation.

"How did you get to this state, Joey?"

"It's all my fault. I was stupid. Naïve. A charity asked me for a batch of electric wheelchairs at cost price for a hospital in Bolivia. Four hundred thousand pounds of wheelchairs for cost price. Payable upon delivery. So I took a loan from the bank and signed the deal."

"And I assume there was no hospital?" Joey shook his head sadly. "How did you find out?" Elliott asked him.

"When the cheque didn't come and they didn't answer their phones, I went to the hospital, in Bolivia. It's a McDonald's drive-through in La Paz."

"And who was this charity? I assume they don't exist either?"

"Oh yes, they exist, they checked out okay, I'm not that stupid, Elliott. But the person I dealt with didn't work for them. That was the mistake I made. Had headed paper, business card, everything, totally convincing. But he was a conman. Must have stolen the stationery. Got me hook, line and sinker. And now Paolo seems to be the only hope. Oh, the irony."

"Joey, I had come here to ask you not to take the money. I can see this is very serious. There's something going on at the moment which is rather taking all my attention, but can I at least ask you to hold off for a few days? Something isn't right here but I can't put my finger on it, and I can't do anything about it just yet. I'm a lawyer, I know the local bank managers, I'll speak to yours for you, buy a little time. Just make sure Lucy doesn't take the loan from Paolo until the end of the week."

Pushing his chair back as he rose, Joey stood up, puffed out his chest even further and stuck out his hand. "Of course, Elliott. Anything for my new family."

"And you can stop saying that until it's absolutely necessary," Elliott replied.

Chapter 21

Stage 10: Final Confession and Rebirth

Monday, 8pm

Elliott stood facing the door behind which sat his future, a bucket of water at his feet. Everything about him sagged. Eyes closed, arms limp by his sides, face tilted upwards as if it had been gently rolled back on his neck. The shoulders were slumped as he exhaled through his mouth, but as he took in a deep breath through his nose his whole body lifted as if being filled with strength as well as air. He exhaled again and the body remained in its new drawn-up position, head returning level.

He reached out for the door handle, opened the door and looked inside.

Ian was sat very upright on the chair. His legs were clamped together, feet side by side and tucked under the chair. Arms in front of him, hands on the lap, fingers interlocked. He looked for all the world like a swotty teenager sent to the headmaster for a telling-off for the first time in his life. Elliott wondered for a moment how long Ian had been sat like that. Surely it cannot have been long? Had he made any noise coming up the stairs? He didn't think so. When he had unlocked the door from the lounge to the bottom of the turret stairs he had half-expected Ian to be hiding, ready to attack him. Instead the acquiescent scene he now saw filled him with optimism. He reached down and carried the bucket inside the room, placing it to the side.

The wooden chair had been tucked away under the table. Elliott took a grip on the top of the back and whirled it 180 degrees so that it faced Ian, a metre or so away. Close enough to be slightly intimidating. Also close enough that Ian could lunge forwards and grab him if he so chose. No backing out now. This was the final session. This was it. Where he found out whether the process had worked. Death or glory and all that jazz.

Sitting, Elliott placed his elbows on his knees, and locked his fingers together. He then slowly leaned his whole body forwards until his head rested on his knuckles. He stared at Ian's right eye, which continued to look at a spot on the wall over Elliott's head. Neither spoke, the room full of the atmosphere of expectation. Elliott was waiting for Ian to speak, while Ian seemed to be awaiting instruction.

They sat in silence for three full minutes, neither man shifting his position. Eventually, Ian spoke, still not returning Elliott's stare.

"I choose politeness," he said, in a formal tone as if addressing the school debating society. "I choose good manners and respect. No longer will my focus be entirely on myself, but I will also be more aware of how my actions affect other people. If I make thinking of others before myself the starting point of every day then I can see that only good will come from that. In a selfish way it will actually mean that I will benefit. But that would be only a by-product. The most important thing is to focus on being a nice person to other people. Because that is simply how we should be."

He stopped talking, as if allowing Elliott the opportunity to speak. The speech had clearly been practised all evening and, now it had been delivered, it was as if Ian did not know what to do next. His eyes flicked at Elliott. Once. Twice. On the third time he held Elliott's gaze, a twitch appearing at the side of his mouth. Elliott continued to stare at Ian's right eye, in the middle, straight through the iris and on down into his soul. When Ian began talking again it seemed to come from somewhere inside his heart rather than his head.

"I wasn't happy. I considered myself a failure. My father wasn't the type to show emotion. He once joked with the regulars in the pub that he wished he had a daughter. They all laughed, but I was eleven at the time and I believed him. In fact I think I probably still do. He never actually wanted me and what he taught me has made me unhappy. I reject it. I reject him. I choose good. I choose politeness."

225

Ian looked again at the spot on the wall. Still Elliott held his head on his knuckles and stared. Ian's eyes narrowed slightly, as if he were thinking what to say — what was Elliott waiting for? Another minute passed, Ian looking over Elliott's head, Elliott staring at his face. Ian's lips were moving imperceptibly and his eyes were darting around now as he searched and searched for the thing to say that his captor seemed to be waiting for. Suddenly he smiled, briefly, slightly, shyly, then looked at Elliott again, the smile quickly being replaced with sincerity.

"Thank you," he said. "Thank you for waking me up. Thank you for putting me in this room. This cannot have been easy for you, and you have taken a huge personal gamble, all to try and save me. I will forever be grateful to you for taking that chance, for investing so much in me. It is now down to me to repay your faith. Thank you for kidnapping me and making me realise what a horrid person I was. I am changed, and I thank you."

At last, Elliott's impassive face cracked. He leaned forwards and held Ian's hands in his own. He didn't speak, but smiled beatifically at him. After a few moments he sat back again.

"Ian, there are two final things to be done to complete the process," he said. "First, we need a physical manifestation of your newfound cleanliness, a little ritual, so to speak." He stood, turned, and walked over to the bucket of water. "This has been in the fridge all day. By pouring this over you the shock of the cold will imprint within you the importance of the new person you have become. You did this, Ian, not I. You are the one who has fought so hard to achieve redemption and change." He lifted the bucket and held it over Ian's head. "You are the one who should be thanked. You are the one who has banished the old, selfish Ian, and allowed in the real Ian, the one who understands the importance of respect and good manners. Congratulations, Ian, welcome to the rest of your life. I am proud to know you."

Elliott poured the water slowly onto Ian's head. He then moved the bucket backwards so that the water went down the neck, then did the same at the front. Ian gasped for breath as the cold hit him like a slap to the face.

"Let this water baptise you and cleanse you, ready for the new

Ian to take his place in the world." The last of the water went over the head, and Elliott put the bucket on the floor. "Welcome, Ian. Welcome to a world of respect and good manners where you will receive the same in return." Still standing, Elliott held out his hand. "I offer you my hand to shake as an equal, a peer." Shivering, Ian looked at the hand, then slowly stood up. He looked Elliott in the eye with a blank expression, then lifted his arm and shook Elliott briefly by the hand.

"Right," said Elliott, turning towards the door. "There is one last thing to do. Now that we have metaphorically cleansed you, I'm sure you'd like to do it properly. Eh? Come on, let's go downstairs now and get you into a shower and some clean clothes."

Chapter 22

Ian rose to follow Elliott as they left the room. He took the first stairs gingerly, gripping the banister tightly, nervously, blinking a great deal in the now bright overhead light. Elliott waited a few steps further down, poised to spring forwards and catch him should he fall, like a father watching a child take their first steps.

Confidence returned quickly and soon they were walking normally down the stairs, albeit still one at a time. Ian had always seemed to Elliott to be a two-steps-at-a-time kind of guy. When they reached the ground Elliott walked forwards and unlocked the door to the lounge, opened it towards him and stood back for Ian to walk through. Ian took a step, then stopped and turned to Elliott.

"After you, please," he said, bowing his head slightly and motioning Elliott into the room with his arm.

Elliott felt a surge of joyful adrenaline. He had done it. He had actually succeeded in turning an obnoxious, self-centred man into a decent, polite human being. There had been so many doubts, so many moments when he wondered if that crazy moment of reflex at the car crash, to allow Alan to take over for just long enough to do something he wasn't brave enough to do himself, had actually been the most stupid decision in the history of the world. But now, this – success, and everything once again seemed so clear to him.

All his life Elliott had tried to do the right thing, to let his actions speak for him. But no one had noticed. Everyone just ignored him at best, or rolled their eyes as if these things were not important. Gentle methods, persuasion, had not worked, had not brought about change, and so he had studied the law, used his profession to try and do some good, to bring about change from the inside. All that gave him was an increased sense of impotence.

Then Naomi had entered his life, given him the confidence to be himself at last, to recognise the wonder within him that he barely knew existed. Together they changed him for the better, moulded his personality inch by world-weary inch. His cynical attitude had dissipated, infected by her joyous world view. But when she was taken away the negativity returned, sucked backed into his life like a nail into a vacuum cleaner. Why was he the one who always had to change? No one noticed; he had no one to appreciate it. Even more, nobody else seemed to be making a similar effort. The rest of the world seemed to believe that their own lives, their own religions, their own politics were the only beliefs that could possibly be right and would spend all their energies on forcing everyone to agree with them. The right to be ignorant, the right to shove your hands over your ears, the right to know only what you currently know.

Violence on behalf of political groups, murder in the name of God and faith, fanatics refusing to allow others to live in accordance with their own beliefs and principles. Impossible for everyone to be right but no one allowing the possibility that they might be wrong.

Why couldn't more people be like Naomi, see the good in others and promote that instead of sticking to some inflexible doctrine? Everywhere around him people were ignorant of others' beliefs and feelings, treading all over their views and emotions. Get out of my way, stop doing that, don't tell me what to do, listen to me, buy this and you'll be cool, believe in that and you're stupid. If you dare to mock my dogma I will murder your children. The noise of the modern world, everyone telling everyone else what to do. It was too much.

What an experiment it had been. He did feel like some mad professor, pushing the boundaries of science, no one believing in him until the results proved him right all along, accepting the Nobel Prize for Peace with humility and dignity, resisting the temptation to score points over his detractors but instead using the platform to promote happiness and joy. Naomi sitting in the front row, her glorious smile beaming pride up onto the stage and through his body. She would not have approved of his methods but she would be delighted at the results.

And it had worked. It had actually worked. Here was the man who he had kept locked up, threatened with violence, mentally and emotionally abused – but kept extremely well fed, to be fair – actually inviting Elliott to go through the door before him. He felt like holding Ian's cheekbones in his hands and kissing him on the lips.

Instead he smiled broadly and bowed his own head in return. "Thank you, Ian, that is most kind," he said, then held his head high and walked through the door and into the lounge.

He heard a grunt behind him and then everything went black.

Part 4

Reprogramming

Chapter 23

Monday, 10pm

Elliott was awakened by a pounding in his head. The taste of iron filled his mouth – blood. He tried to bring a hand up to his face but couldn't move his arm. This was due, he realised, to the fact that he was tied to the chair upon which he sat. His own chair. In the turret. He raised his head and looked around the empty room. It was the same as when they had left it, the floor wet from the baptising. Him and Ian. Where was Ian?

The sound of someone taking the steps two at a time made him turn his head to the door. They were Lucy's feet. She had a way of taking a flight of steps as if it were an inconvenience. He tried to get his hands free, panic rising that she would discover what he had been doing up here. Straining to see his hands, he struggled in vain. The sound of the door opening made him snap his head back round and he looked straight into the eyes of big sister. As if by reflex she stood in the doorway and folded her arms.

"Lucy," he said. "Um. Hi. Ha. I, uh…" No words presented themselves as being appropriate to the situation. Eventually he said, "I seem to be tied up. Would you be so kind?" He gestured with his head.

"Oh, Elliott," she answered in a remarkably controlled voice. "You total idiot. What have you been up to?" She strode forwards and untied his hands. He rubbed them automatically, although in truth they didn't hurt and there was no mark. He guessed he had not been unconscious for very long. He looked at his watch. Ten o'clock. He had been out for half an hour or so.

"Lucy, I, uh, think I need to explain something to you."

"I'd suggest you don't say anything just yet," his sister replied tersely. "Just come with me." He tried to assess her tone but found it to be strangely neutral. No, the *result* was neutral, but it seemed to have been arrived at from a combination of two extremes. She seemed furious and yet compassionate, as if a blistering inferno had been put into a pool of ice and created a nice cup of tea.

She walked out of the room and began down the steps, half-looking over her shoulder maternally. As they reached the ground Lucy took a step to the side and he saw that the door to the lounge was open. He could see Joey Davison standing, looking through the door at him expectantly. The huge man lifted his right arm and waved at Elliott with just his fingers. Then he took a step forwards as if he was a nightclub bouncer opening the door for a glamorous fashion model.

"Come on in, Elliott," said Joey.

"I don't understand," said Elliott to Joey as he stepped into the lounge. "Where is...I mean, why was I tied up upstairs?"

"Because you're a fucking moron, that's why," said a voice to his right. Elliott turned to see Ian sat on one of the high-backed chairs. Arranged on the dining table in front of him were two photographs, of his parents and of Naomi.

"What?" said Elliott. "I don't understand, what's going on?" He stood dumbly in the middle of the room, arms limp by his sides, head still groggy. "My head is thumping."

Joey Davison took two paces to cross the rest of the room and stand in front of Elliott, who turned his head to face him.

"This chap here, your – what shall we call him: victim?" said Joey, looking at Lucy for confirmation that he had used the correct term. She nodded, and Joey continued. "Your victim gave you a right old tap on the bonce, Elliott. It must have hurt, he hit you with this." Joey pointed to the coffee table on which sat the brass statue of Mahatma Gandhi. He slapped the top of the old man's head, then picked it up. "Smacked the hard bald bit here right on the back of your noggin, knocked you clean out." He threw the brass statue in the air slightly and caught it again, as if testing its weight. "Nasty little implement, that."

"Oh wow," said Elliott. "My head. No wonder everything is so loud."

The world seemed to close in on Elliott for a moment as Joey leaned forwards onto his knees, his giant head now only slightly below Elliott's. He peered intently into Elliott's eyes.

"Take your time, Elliott," said Joey. "You've had quite a whack. I've dealt with plenty of these on the rugger pitch, we want to make sure you're fully with us, no serious damage. Tell me, how many fingers am I holding up?"

A huge hand forced its way into Elliott's eyeline. It looked like a bunch of fat pork sausages sewn onto an uncooked haggis. Joey spread his fingers and held the palm towards Elliott.

"Five," said Elliott irritably.

"No," said Joey. "Four. Thumbs don't count!" He laughed like a barking mule.

"Joey!" said Lucy. "This is *not* the time."

"Sorry. Sorry." Joey shone a small pencil torch into Joey's left eye, then right. Eventually he straightened to his full, considerable height.

"He's alright," he said, then collapsed slowly back into the two-seater sofa, which responded with a miscellany of noises that suggested it wouldn't be able to cope with such a weight descending upon it every day.

"What happened?" Elliott said to the room. Ian was crouched forwards in his seat, like a crow on a telephone wire. He was rocking slightly, nibbling at a thumb, and his right leg was twitching, bouncing up and down off his toes. "I don't understand," Elliott continued, this time addressing Ian. "We were leaving. Everything was okay. It was all sorted, completed. I don't understand."

"Oh, Elliott," said Lucy, handing her brother a glass of water. "You can be such an idiot sometimes. Ian here has been filling us in on what he's been going through for the last few days. What were you thinking, Elliott?"

Elliott downed the water. It felt like the first drink he had ever taken, washing away the clagginess from his mouth. His head cleared just a little. "But we had completed," he said again stupidly. "He was converted. A new life."

"Dream on, Elliott," said Joey. "He clocked you one on the head the first chance he got. Probably would have then gone straight to the police. Am I right, Ian?"

"Of course," said Ian, tearing another piece from his thumbnail, staring another hole in the floor.

Elliott looked crestfallen. "How could you hit me? After all we went through together? After all we talked about?"

Ian looked up at him, exasperation moving across his face from the bottom up, then rolled his eyes and returned to concentrate on his thumb. His right leg again took up its frenetic beat. It seemed to Elliott that Ian was staring at the floor almost specifically in order to avoid the photographs sat on the table on a few feet away. What about the experiment? What had he not said that he was supposed to have? Had he missed a crucial step?

"But I followed the instructions to the letter," he said, surprising himself for a moment that he words came out of his mouth.

"These instructions?" said Lucy, brandishing the Korean military book at him. "Oh, Elliott." She placed it on the dining room table next to Ian, who did not alter his stare. "I am almost speechless, Elliott. It's, it's like…You have done one of the worst things I could imagine. You have committed a serious crime. It is only because you have done something so…big, so…well, illegal, that I stop for a moment and wonder what the hell has gotten into my little brother that provoked him into such a heinous act. And then, of course, I realised who he is."

Elliott looked at his sister. There was empathy mixed with the fury, a shared knowledge of the difficulties of his life to date. "He knows why he is here, Elliott," she said, turning to Ian. "That's the only reason why the police haven't been called."

Elliott looked at Ian expectantly. He felt a relief wash over him in this moment of disclosure, the lifting of a burden like an infidelity uncovered or a love finally expressed.

The truth now needed – demanded – to be laid bare on the floor for all to prod, to study, to pick over. His catalyst, his cause, his kindling. The agitator that sparked a dormant righteousness into action. Now came the post-match analysis and he knew the critics would not be gentle with his choice of such an extreme action.

Still he stood dumbly in the middle of the room, watching Ian gnaw at his thumb. Joey shuffled uncomfortably on the leather sofa, glancing at Lucy in case of instruction, the squeaking and squealing emanating from beneath him the only sound in the room. Lucy stood, leaning on the table with her other hand on her hip. She returned the requests for direction from the sofa with a tiny lifting of the eyebrows as if to tell Joey, 'Let's just wait a moment.' Elliott momentarily wondered how they had developed such subtlety of communication in a short space of time, then realised that it had not, of course, been a short space of time at all.

Eventually Ian straightened in his chair and rubbed his thighs as if acknowledging the combined weight of expectation. He looked at them each in turn, then to the ceiling. A deep sigh before finally breaking the silence. He spoke directly to Elliott.

"Of course I was playing your game. I'm not as stupid, actu-ally, as you seem to think. I was in control from the moment you turned the light on. As you said, there was no going back at that point, but I worked out that you were following some sort of pro-cess and realised that the best way to get out of there was to let you finish it. I decided to let you have your own way. It wasn't difficult to convince you that all your waffle was having an effect – it was obvious what it was that you wanted from me. And when I offered you to walk in front of me on the way out, the look on your face, honestly, anyone would have thought you'd won the flippin' lottery. So I grabbed the first thing I could get my hands on," he gestured towards the statue of Ghandi, "and clobbered you with it."

Ian paused for a moment, steeling himself. "You went down like a sack of spuds. I took you upstairs, tied you up, then sat down for a second to think, to work out what to do next. Then I saw this photo." He jerked his thumb towards Naomi. "I assume this was your wife?" Elliott nodded. "When did she pass away?"

"Eleven months and twenty-two days ago," said Elliott without hesitation.

Ian tried what seemed to be a benevolent smile. It almost worked. Elliott allowed it to wither without response. Ian continued. "There's something about you. About this house." He paused for a moment, looking around the room as if searching for something. "I've seen it before. A feeling of sadness in this home. Like something's missing."

"I changed the furniture when I moved in to try and help me get on with my life."

"Hmm. Well, it didn't work. And then there's your general anger at the world. I said that you'd lost in love, did I not? Nailed you there. I didn't realise quite *how* spot on I was, though." He tenderly picked up the photograph of Naomi. "She was very beautiful. I'm sure she was a special lady."

"She was," said Elliott, his soft voice carrying an edge that he knew Ian could not possibly have understood, that no one could ever understand unless they had walked through Elliott's life with him, suffered every slight and injury, had the promise of happiness given, then taken away.

Ian placed Naomi carefully back on the table and picked up the photograph of Elliott's mother and father. He held it up and stared at it for a moment. "And then I saw this photograph. I recognised it immediately of course. There was something about that picture of your dad when he was a young man that I couldn't put my finger on. But this picture, this was used in the papers. That's when I realised why you had kidnapped me. Because I killed your parents."

He continued to stare at the photograph as though he could bring the laughing couple back to life again, as if he could use the power of his glare to make the images move. The silence of the guilty filled the room, bringing with it an oppression that could only be lifted by the affected party, by the victim. Lucy spoke next to release Ian from the spell.

"That's when he buzzed our flat," she said. "Asked me to come down. At first I was obviously concerned that there was someone else in our house. Of course, not as big a shock as when he told us where he'd been for the last five days."

"I walked out of the flat in a bit of a daze, to be truthful," Ian said. "Hardly surprising. I was still planning to go to the police. I wanted to get help, in case you woke up, so I pressed the buzzers. As I was waiting for a reply I looked at the post to find out the address. Saw Lucy's name. I know you were both in the car at the time, it said so in the newspaper reports. I got...confused." Ian looked rather lost for a moment as he stared at the picture, then sat up straighter and looked at them, as if he had been caught doing something inappropriate. It occurred to Elliott that the man in front of him now was a different person to any of the Ians he had seen before. Had it really all been an act in that turret?

"Have you been planning this for a while?" Lucy said, addressing Elliott. "Have you been following him?"

"No," Elliott replied. "It was pure chance. He was driving way too close behind me in his flash car – that is not even his, by the way, he won the use of it in a sales competition – then overtook me on a bend. We were so very lucky that nothing was coming the other way. And then he gave *me* the finger, as if it was my fault! Then I came upon his car a few miles later, crashed into a tree. I went over to help, and saw his face. Recognised him immediately. I just could not believe that after he caused the accident that killed Mum and Dad he would still drive like that." His eyes implored Lucy to understand. He found no support from his big sister's body language. How did she manage to stay looking imposing for such long periods? He sagged just a little further.

"Where's Phoebe?" he asked. "Does she know I'm here?"

"No," said Lucy. "She's in bed right now. She's been worried about you, Elliott."

"She can't know," Elliott said directly to Lucy. "She mustn't know."

"It's okay. She's asleep. I think she might suspect something is amiss but doesn't know anything. She asked me yesterday if you were alright, said she was worried about you." Lucy finally lifted her hand from the table and stood up straight, but then folded her arms, which just made her look even more displeased. The sternness in her voice went up a notch as she continued to address her younger brother. "Why didn't you just call the police to the accident? Tell them who he was? You didn't have to kidnap the poor man." Elliott raised an eyebrow to a level beyond arch. "Yes, Elliott." She pronounced the final 'tt' of his name with extra vigour. "The 'poor man'." Elliott winced as she did the thing with her fingers in the air as inverted commas. "You kidnapped him. He was your *victim*, no matter how you look at it." She looked up at the ceiling and let out a guttural growl of frustration that struck directly at Elliott's teenage memories. "I know you, Elliott. I know how your mind works. This is all about that bloody starfish, isn't it?"

Ian lifted his head up from gnawing his nail and looked from one to the other and back again. "Hey, hello? I'm still here," he said. "Could you please tell me what you two are talking about? What has a starfish got to do with all of this?"

"Oh, Elliott," said Lucy. "I can't believe you haven't told him about the starfish." She turned back to Ian. "It's a parable. My brother's favourite parable in fact, and he knows a few. A man is walking along a beach and there are millions of starfish washed up on the sand, stretching as far as the eye can see. They are all dying because they are out of the water. The man starts throwing the starfish back into the water. One at a time. Now, a boy walks up to him and says, 'What are you doing?' 'I'm helping the starfish,' says the man. 'That's ridiculous,' says the boy, gesturing along the beach, 'you can't make a difference to all these starfish, look how many there are.' The man bends down and picks up a starfish, turns to the boy, and says, 'Well then, I'll just make a difference to this one,' and then he throws the starfish back into the sea."

There was the sort of silence in the room that demands attention. Elliott and Lucy both looked at Ian, who looked back at them one at a time in return. His mouth opened and then closed a few times. It seemed to Elliott as if the enormity and simplicity of what had just been said was having a profound effect on his former captive. Maybe all that he had tried to teach him over the preceding few days hadn't been in vain after all. Perhaps it was like a time bomb, planted inside Ian's brain just waiting for the right moment, for the right trigger to make it go off, and suddenly enlightenment would find him.

"So," said Ian eventually, "am I the man or the boy?"

"Oh, for goodness' sake," said Lucy, "you're the starfish."

"The starfish? Why am I a starfish?"

Lucy turned to Elliott. "Has he been this slow to catch on the entire time?" she said.

Elliott nodded sadly. "So it now seems," he said.

Lucy turned her attention back to Ian "The point," she said, "is that Elliott wants to change the world. He needs to be more accepting. But he has always maintained that one must try to make things better, no matter how small the change. That improving the behaviour of just one person would make all the effort worthwhile.

And that if we all had the same attitude then the world really would be a better place."

"And that's why you kidnapped me?" Ian spoke slowly as he stared at Elliott, his mouth hanging open. "To *improve* me? To improve *me*? You…you arrogant bastard."

"I just wanted to try and awaken you, to shake you out of the way you sleepwalk through life. You were *still* driving dangerously – I couldn't let that continue. I just wanted to do what is right."

"And you thought that kidnapping me was the right thing to do?"

"It was for your own good. For your betterment."

"That is not acceptable, Elliott. And I'm not buying it," said Lucy. "It was for *your* good. Because you had unfinished business. And because you got angry and couldn't control Alan."

Ian slapped himself on the forehead. "Oh, fer… Who the hell is Alan?!"

Lucy walked over to the sofa and perched on the edge next to Joey, who put his hands on her shoulders and rubbed tenderly. Elliott felt like he did when they were kids and she was trying to stop him breaking something while he was in an Alan-fuelled rage. She would pin him to the floor by sitting on his chest. Elliott could remember that feeling all too clearly. Her knees on his arms, which he could not so much as lift off the floor, her weight pressing down on him, the feeling of utter helplessness at first making him all the more angry, bucking and kicking to try and get away. Then calmness moving slowly through him, but a sullen, resentful calm borne out of a practical realisation that the only way he was going to get out from underneath his sister was by playing things her way.

And now she had taken control of this situation and he couldn't move. He would have to submit to her decision, whatever it was.

Ian continued to look from one to the other, his question remaining unanswered. Elliott avoided his stare.

"Look, can we get back to the point here?" said Ian eventually. "I *am* the one who has been kidnapped and tortured after all."

"Torture?" asked Lucy, one eyebrow cocked. "Really?"

"He threatened to electrocute my testicles and cut my finger off."

"It wasn't a threat," said Elliott. "I was quite prepared to do what I had to do. I would have chopped your finger off."

"No you wouldn't," said Lucy and Ian together. Elliott pouted.

"So what happens now?" continued Ian, addressing Lucy. "I need to contact my family, let them know I'm safe. What are we going to do about this nutter?" He jerked his thumb towards Elliott.

Lucy pushed herself up from the sofa, took two strides forwards and slapped Ian hard across the face with her hand. He barely reacted at first, as if he knew it was coming, as if it was the logical thing for Lucy to do. "Ow," said Lucy to no one, blowing on her fingers. She lingered over Ian, breathing heavily.

Ian breathed heavily and wiggled his jaw, trying to get the feeling back into his face.

"Now listen here, you arrogant little man," Lucy said to him. She somehow managed to tower over Ian despite her diminutive stature. "Don't go thinking you and me are on the same side. My brother has been very, very stupid. But you *did* actually cause the death of our – of *my* – parents, by driving dangerously. You clearly did not learn your lesson and continued to drive like that. So I think it would be reasonable of us, in the spirit of fairness, to agree that he was under some provocation. As am *I* right now. Would you agree? Hmm? Would you?" She poked him firmly in the shoulder. Elliott almost felt it from across the room.

"Yes," said Ian, wincing. "Of course. Sorry. I-I've been under a lot of strain. It's all a lot to take in." His expression betrayed the two sides of Ian's personality flickering in and out of view. It seemed to Elliott as if there was an internal battle raging as to which would eventually dominate.

"Okay," said Lucy, sitting back onto the sofa, her arms out in front of her with the palms facing down at forty-five degrees, as if trying to ward off a ferocious canine. "Let's take stock here for a moment. This is the time for calm heads. You've both done very silly things. Ian, you ran away. You then continued to drive irresponsibly and did not face up to what you had done. Elliott, you of all people should know that two wrongs don't make a right."

"Okay, just, hang on a second here," said Ian. His own hands were out in front as if in defence to Lucy. He looked as if he were

242

pushing at the backside of a particularly stubborn bull. "I deserve a telling-off, fair enough. You two must want to strangle me for what happened. But to say I actually killed your parents – is that really fair? It was an accident. I was a significant contributor to that accident, I'll accept that, but people drive like I do all the time. It was just an accident. I don't think it's fair to heap the entire thing on my shoulders, that's all I'm saying. Okay?" He spoke to Lucy in a way that Elliott had stopped doing at the age of twelve. That was the age at which he accepted that she was a lot smarter than he. He often thought it might have been the wisest moment of his life.

"No," replied Lucy, raising her voice just slightly above the level that Ian's had achieved. "It is *not* okay. Justify your actions to yourself, but not to us. That accident need never have happened. Our parents might still be here if not for you."

"But you can say that about millions of things," said Ian, his voice adopting an imploring tone that Elliott recognised. He wondered how often in life Ian had needed to talk his way out of a situation. "If I'd had an extra coffee that morning and left the house twenty minutes later our cars wouldn't have passed. Shit happens in life, okay, and a lot of it has happened to me, but I don't bitch and moan about it, I don't try and blame things, I get on with life. I make the most of things. I regret what happened, massively, but it's time to move on." He looked at each of them, his hands now open like a welcoming Jesus, only slightly more desperate.

Lucy studied him for a moment, as if reaching an important decision. "We can move on when the two of you make up with each other and say sorry," she said.

"What, are you going to knock our silly heads together?" asked Ian. "Then make us shake hands and say, 'Make friends, make friends, never, never break friends?'"

"She's always been like this," Elliott said to Ian.

"Actually, chaps," said Joey, "given that you've both broken the law and are in deep doo-doo, I'd strongly suggest you shut up and listen to her. She does tend to be right, I frequently find. What do you say?" There was a tone in his voice that fleetingly reminded Elliott of his schooldays.

"Thank you, Joey," Lucy continued. She turned to Elliott. "Ian has shown some remorse. Not enough, but it's a start. Now it is your turn."

Elliott folded his arms and stared at the fireplace.

"Well?" said Lucy. "I'm waiting."

A few moments of silence, disturbed by a low mumbling.

"Louder," said Lucy. "Apologise properly. Come on."

"Okay, okay. Ian, I'm sorry I kidnapped you and threatened you with torture," said Elliott, arms still folded. He looked sullenly at Lucy. "Okay? Happy?"

"Why, Elliott?" said Ian, the question bursting forth almost against his own wishes. He thrust his arms forwards, demanding rather than requesting an explanation. Elliott barely recognised the acquiescent individual of the last few days. "Why did you have to do this to me? There were other ways you could have got back at me: you could have told the police, you could have phoned an ambulance, then come to visit me in hospital and talked to me. Why this…this…stupid fucking brainwashing attempt? This has *not* been something I have enjoyed experiencing, *thank you very much.*" He paused, breathing hard, regaining control, both hands now resting on top of his head as if they had been flung there by accident. "Christ," he continued, calmer. "It's been awful. Trapped up there. So much time to think. To be at the mercy of another person, not even able to move. I had no idea…" He looked up at each of them in turn, no longer able to articulate. Elliott recognised how Ian would have smothered all memories of the accident, and his role in it, just as he himself had focused on the purpose of his mission in order to drown out the grim reality of what he had actually been doing. It was the magician's art of misdirection, tricking the brain into focusing on the righteous goal in order to drown out the heinous actions required to achieve it.

Ian's imploring stare scoured the room, a cry for insight into why the world had made this happen to him, why life had decided to twist itself in such a direction. Oh yes, Elliott understood that feeling only all too well. He would have plenty to say on *that* subject.

"This is all rather complicated," replied Lucy, speaking on behalf of her brother only in the sense that she had spoken first.

Elliott let his open mouth slowly shut. "It involves a rather difficult childhood, a belief in good and an overwhelming desire that people should do the right thing." She got up from the sofa, walked across the room to Elliott and kissed him on the top of his head. "Also a pathological reaction to arrogance. I'm only touching the surface, you realise. He's a complicated man, is my brother, and not always the best at handling a situation. You know how, when you see a squirrel and point to it for your dog to go and catch it, and the dog just stares at your finger? That's how Elliott approaches a problem. In short, he's just not very good at life. At least, not on his own." She looked at him with love in her eyes. "Which is probably the final reason for all this."

Lucy sat down at the dining room table and looked at Ian, resting her cheek on one hand.

"Everything can be justified," she said to him. "But that doesn't make it right." She paused for a moment. She peered at Ian, scrutinising, as if looking for secrets scarred into his features. "I'd like to talk about the accident," she said eventually.

Ian shut his eyes and nodded. Elliott started to say something, but Lucy held up her index figure to him and he remained quiet, an observer.

"I've only one question, really," Lucy continued. "Why didn't you stop?"

"I panicked, okay?" Ian replied, now staring at the table. "I saw the car go off the road in my mirror, but I had no idea how serious it was. If I had I would've stopped. I've thought about it a *lot* since."

"So why didn't you come forwards when you *did* find out about it?" Lucy glared at him, almost daring him to look her in the eye. Ian took her on for a moment, then looked away heavily.

"I wasn't aware that it was anything more than an accident for a long time. I don't watch the news — it's just too depressing. So many horrible things happening in the world that I can't do anything about, so I'd rather just not hear about them. Then one day I was paying for petrol and it was on the front page of the local paper, on the stand in front of the garage. Two pictures, one of the car — I'll never forget that car — and that picture of your parents." He pointed to the framed photograph on the table in front of him.

"I think one of them had died after being in a coma. I felt bloody awful as I stood there and realised the extent of what had happened, you've no idea how awful."

"I suspect we probably do," said Elliott drily.

"I thought it was just an accident! I didn't know people had died. And when I did it was too late to go to the police and besides, what good would that have done? It wouldn't have brought back your parents. So I just put it out of my mind. Tried to forget about it, get on with my life. I don't know what else to say to you. I am so sorry." He looked at them both in turn. "I am. So sorry."

The words were sweet to Elliott's ear. The risk he had taken in bringing Ian to his house. Everything had been put in jeopardy, the little that he had, a daring act of a man desperate to right a wrong. The potential sacrifice of Phoebe's love, surely the largest forfeit he might yet have to pay. His practice, the house, the respect of his sister. It felt for a moment as if all that he had staked on this gamble had been worth it for those few delicious words.

"And you can take that stupid look off your face, Elliott," said Lucy. "This does *not* mean your actions have been justified." Elliott removed his smile but retained his ever so slightly smug mood.

"Right," Lucy continued, standing. "This is all well and good, but it doesn't help solve our problem. Which is this. I have two stupid men in front of me that could – and one might say should – go to jail as a result of their control freakery. We need to work out a plan. And I need a coffee. Let's take a break."

Chapter 24

Tuesday, 2am

Elliott sat on the small sofa. He swilled a whisky round the glass to release its flavour. He took a sniff and then rubbed his eyes. So tired.

Lucy sat on the larger sofa, cup of coffee in hand. Joey sat next to her, his arm and hand on her thigh as if his very existence were dependent upon his remaining in bodily contact with her at all times. His other enormous hand was wrapped around his own glass of whisky.

Ian remained sat at the table, a third whisky in front of him.

Lucy spoke first, leaning forwards to sit on the edge of the sofa as if to announce that the meeting was back in session. "Okay. So. Where do we go from here?" she asked. "What are we going to do with you both?"

Joey leaned loudly back into the leather sofa. "Why don't we look at our options, send it up and down the road?" he said. "List a few ideas, see what we come up with. Run around the flagpole a bit."

"Ooh," said Lucy with a clap of her hands, "I know, I'll get my flip chart." She leaned forwards and used Joey's knee to push herself up to a standing position with an enthusiastic bounce. "It's in my study, I'll go and get it, don't start without me." She walked quickly across the lounge, away from Ian. They heard the front door put on the latch, then slam shut as Lucy ran up the stairs to her flat.

Joey and Elliott sat looking at different parts of the room, Ian staring alternately at each of them, mouth open. "You're not actually going to have a brainstorming session about this, are you?" he said. Neither man replied. "Seriously. You two. Come on now." Still they didn't respond, although each did shift their gaze to a different spot in the room, not looking at each other with all the practised ease of an Englishman on a crowded train. "Hello? I need to contact my family, people are worried. I could have just texted them hours ago, you know."

"Yes, old chap, but you didn't, did you?" said Joey. "So let's just give Lucy a little longer to work out the best way forwards for everyone. Alrighty?"

Elliott rose and, draining his glass as he walked, went into the kitchen and came back with a bowl of vegetable crisps, a second bowl containing Bombay mix, and the bottle of sixteen-year-old Laphroaig whisky. He placed the bowls on the table, filled first Joey's glass; then Ian's and lastly his own, then topped all three with a dash of water from a jug on the table. At no point did he look at Ian despite the exasperated looks he knew were being sent his way. He finally sat back down on the smaller sofa. Joey leaned forwards to scoop a giant handful of Bombay mix into his mouth almost before the dish touched the table. Ian remained staring at the two of them, occasionally shaking his head.

The front door shut again and Lucy reappeared, awkwardly carrying the flip chart. Joey jumped up to help her. Together they pushed out the back leg and stood the flip chart in front of the fireplace, facing the room. Then from her pockets Lucy took three pens, one blue, one red and one green. She looked at Elliott and gave him a broad smile. She rather looked as if she were enjoying herself. Then, taking the lid off the blue pen, she turned to face the three of them and said, "Right, where do we start? Let's list some options. First of all, Ian could go to the police."

She wrote 'Ian goes to police' on the flip chart.

"Well, that's pretty clearly not an option," said Elliott quickly. He looked around him. "Is it?"

Lucy pacified him. "Not really, but I want us to bring all the possibilities out. Get the obvious ones down, then the really innovative ideas will come forth."

"Oh, bloody hell," said Ian under his breath. "Problem-solving by management-speak."

Lucy made it obvious she was ignoring him.

"Okay then, how about we tell the truth? All of it. Why I did what I did."

"Don't be ridiculous, Elliott," said Lucy. "You would go to prison for kidnapping, probably for quite a few years. That's serious."

"Only if I pressed charges," said Ian. "Which I wouldn't. Not now I know why you did it." The three of them looked at him doubtfully. "Hey, I'm not taking this any further, Elliott. Lucy. It stays in here as far as I'm concerned. I am a man of my word, everyone knows that: if I say I'm going to do something then that is what happens. I have to live with what I did. I'll always have that accident hanging over me. Plus you could tell the police about me, so you don't actually *need* to trust me. But I'm telling you now. For me, this stops here."

"Okay, thank you, Ian," said Lucy. "However, it would still mean that Elliott's reputation would be completely finished. Who is going to use a lawyer who can't obey the law?"

"Solicitor," said Elliott. "Lawyer is an American term."

"I think you get my point, Elliott," Lucy shot back.

Joey chuckled, leaning forwards to grab another handful of Bombay mix, leaning his head back to throw the entire handful into his mouth.

There was a loud noise like a blocked sink. Joey leaned forwards on his seat, waving his arms around. His face started to go red and he pointed vigorously at his throat. Quickly Elliott jumped up and gave him a mighty wallop between the shoulder blades. Joey's head snapped forwards and with a final rasping sound a chickpea flew out of his mouth across the room.

Barely missing a beat, Joey's right hand, propelled by instinct, shot out and grabbed the projectile in mid-flight. He looked at Elliott, lowered his hand and opened his palm to reveal the offending chickpea.

"See?" he said to the room. "See those reactions? I've still got it, eh? Oh yeah. Still got it, baby."

Lucy closed her eyes and shook her head. Elliott thought she actually looked rather proud.

Joey threw the chickpea high up into the air and, in one fluid motion while leaning back into the sofa, caught it in mouth and continued to chew.

"May we please continue with the issue in hand here?" said

Lucy. Joey brandished his hand in a sweeping motion as if to say, 'Be my guest', then settled back, reaching one long arm across the back of the sofa.

"Right," said Lucy, "so going directly to the police is out. Our dilemma is that we need to deliver Ian into their hands in a way that does not implicate Elliott. If one goes down, you both go down. And therefore, safe in that knowledge, you must work together for each other's best interests."

"She said exactly the same to me when she was telling me which way I should vote in the general election," Joey said directly to Elliott.

"I was not telling you which way to vote!" said Lucy. "I was just trying to make sure you fully understood all the options." Joey looked at Elliott and winked. It occurred to Elliott that no one had winked at him in that 'matey' way for approximately thirty years. Paolo did occasionally wink in a conspiratorial way, it was true, and it made Elliott want to punch him every single time. It was a complicit wink that suggested they were in it together. That man needed sorting out.

"Could you write something else please, Lucy?" said Elliott, gesturing towards the flip chart. Lucy paused for a moment to decide which colour pen to use, opened her mouth briefly as if she was going to ask Elliott a question, thought better of it, then popped the lid on the black marker in readiness.

"We still have the loan from Paolo to sort out," he said. "We can't have Joey's business going bust now, can we?"

Lucy shot a glance at Joey, who looked sheepishly at his feet, then wrote 'Loan from Paolo' on the flip chart.

"Okay," said Ian, "bring me up to speed here, would you? Who is Paolo and how is he involved?"

"Paolo," said Elliott, "is my sister's ex-husband. Joey here rather foolishly," Lucy's glare turned on him, "ahem, should I say, very kindly, got involved with a charity. He borrowed a lot of money to provide wheelchairs for a charity who were then going to pay him. Rather unfortunately the charity didn't actually exist and payment was therefore not forthcoming. A fraud. His wheelchair-making business upon which so many people rely will go into liquidation unless it can repay that loan. Banks are no use if you actually *need* to borrow money, they'll only lend if you can prove that you don't. So Joey has to borrow from elsewhere in order to repay the bank loan. Up pops Paolo and offers to lend the money to Lucy, but only if she will sign over half the house to him as security. Lucy lends Joey the money, the business carries on, everyone is happy."

"Especially Paolo," said Ian.

"Quite," said Elliott. "The world turns once more and Paolo ends up with a little a bit more of it."

"It makes me so angry," said Lucy suddenly, her eyes shining brightly. "Why is it always the bullies that seem to win, with their showing off and shoving their success in your face? Why does no one notice the little acts of kindness? Every day people do things for each other without the need for thanks or payment or acknowledgement, just because it's the right thing to do. The world doesn't turn because of grand statements. The world changes slowly, it evolves, and it only happens because of the cumulative effect of a million thoughtful actions." Joey looked up at her from the sofa like a dog watching its master putting up wallpaper.

"Paolo is all front," she continued, addressing her wrath to the room in general. "He tricks people and bullies them and overcharges and prances around like he is someone that matters. He is known and respected – or at least feared – by all the important people in town. He gives money to charity and is the dinner party guest of the elite. And yet we all know he is only lending this money to Joey so that he has a hold over me, who he has never forgiven for rejecting him. He'd bet against his own daughter in a bare-knuckle fight. He is a vile and revolting individual poisoned by money and greed. I hate him so much." Her voice cracked for a moment. She pulled herself up before continuing.

"Joey, on the other hand, goes about his life being thoughtful and caring and doing wonderful things that nobody ever hears about. Did you know his company gave a ten thousand-pound donation to a homeless charity? No, you didn't hear about that, did you? Well, that was supposed to be Joey's bonus for the year, but he gave it up. He is a trustee of three charities. He picks up litter when he's walking down the street and puts it in the bin when no one is looking. He makes the world a better place. And nobody hears about it."

"Aw, Tinkle," said Joey. "That's sweet of you."

Ian looked at Elliott and mouthed the word 'Tinkle?!' Elliott rolled his eyes in response.

"Joey lost that money because he was trying to do something wonderful," Lucy continued. "I will not allow such kindness to be punished. The only way I can see Joey being able to keep his business is if I lend him the money, and the only way I can do *that* is by taking a loan from Paolo because I don't have the income history a bank would want. And if that means my life is a bit worse because I've got Paolo being smug all over me, well, that's a price worth paying to help a good man like Joey."

"Is that why you think Paolo is doing this?" said Elliott. "Because he wants something over you?"

"Of course it is," replied Lucy, spitting out the words. "I'm the one thing he can't have. We were genuinely in love when we got married. He was fun and exciting. He changed when he started to get successful, but I didn't. It wasn't even the money, it was the power that being rich seemed to give him over other people. He's never stopped loving me and he's never forgiven me because I stopped loving him. I wouldn't be surprised if he's had this planned for years."

"What if he had?" said Ian. The other three turned to look at him expectantly. Elliott imagined his eyes lit up in a similar way when the winner of the top salesman of the month award had been announced. Ian paused for a moment and looked at the each in turn before continuing. "I think I might have found us a way out of this situation."

Chapter 25

Tuesday, 4am

Elliott stood at the toilet, carefully aiming for the side of the basin. Four in the morning. A time for drug dealers, the incontinent and the sick. Who else is up at this time? Only someone with a compulsive reason to be out of bed and active around the house. An annoying bladder, an illicit encounter. The lack of noise in one's own home at four in the morning is somehow louder than at four in the afternoon. Elliott felt a tingle of impropriety, of being out of place, an enjoyable sensation that made him feel somehow worthy, as if not following accepted practice made him a slightly better person. Being up in the middle of the night, seeing his own flat at a time when he had never seen it before, brought on a different kind of excitement. Like a childhood New Year's Eve, being allowed to stay up past midnight for the first time, going past the latest time you've ever been up before.

As he shook he wondered if he had now been awake for every single minute possible on a clock. There were plenty of times when Naomi was ill that he had dozed on and off through the night, but he didn't really count that – it wasn't proper awake, it wasn't pointless awake, it was awake for a purpose. Five-thirty might still have eluded him. Six had happened often when he was working early in London and training as a solicitor. But he'd never stayed up all night at a party, nor been so disorganised that he had to pull an all-nighter to get an essay finished. This was certainly one of the very few times he and 4am had met.

Returning to the lounge, he picked up the whisky bottle and held it up to the one remaining lamp that was switched on. All the other lights had been turned off by Ian when Joey had begun snoring from the sofa. They had gently rolled him into a prone position, and Elliott had washed up Joey's glass, then refilled his and Ian's.

They had earlier listened to Ian's idea before talking it round for a while. Finally Lucy had approved the plan and then announced her exit for bed. Joey had wanted to stay up to join in the discussion of the details, even though he had very little to contribute. Now the plan had been fully formed the excitement had worn off.

While Ian took a turn in the toilet Elliott poured the last of the whisky into the two remaining glasses, added a dash of water, placed one in front of the single-seater where Ian had been sitting, then sat back into the remaining single chair opposite. Joey covered the entire sofa alongside them like a beached walrus who had accidentally fallen asleep on a Russian submarine.

Elliott had moved beyond the point of being tired now. The feeling in his head was a mixture of drunkenness from the whisky, tiredness from the lateness of the hour, and just a tiny bit of guilty pride that remained in place against overwhelming odds.

Ian was undoubtedly a different man to the one that overtook him a few days ago. Of that there was no doubt. The Korean army took months to achieve what he had tried to do in five days. Maybe extreme measures were the only way to effect real change after all.

A search for justice had been what drove him in the arms of the law in the first place. So many years studying the principles of decency and behaviour that society had agreed on through centuries of debate and reflection, only to find himself having to act on behalf of pseudo-gangster businessmen like Paolo Brice.

He smiled at Naomi across the living room. Her half-smile told him that she knew this was going to work out. Trust your instincts, it said. Be bold, it said. I believe in you, it said. Not for the first time he pitted his happiness from the time he had been allowed to spend with Naomi against the well of pain that her absence continually threw at him. On this occasion the joyous memories won the contest. It was not always the case.

Ian returned to the room and sat down in the armchair, rubbing both eyes with thumb and forefinger.

"You've changed," said Elliott.

"No I have not," said Ian, pride in his defiance shining out of the dimples in his cheeks.

"Yes you have," said Elliott. "You're wearing new trousers. Where did they come from?"

"Oh," said Ian. "I see what you mean. Lucy gave them to me."

"They're mine."

Ian smiled. "Well then, thank you." His hand slowly moved around his face, kneading the cheeks and stroking the beard that was just beginning to take hold over his chin. The unfamiliarity seemed to attract his attention as his fingers explored the new facial hair.

"Suits you," said Elliott.

Ian's hand stopped mid-stroke. "Sorry?"

"The beard. It rather suits you. I reckon you should keep it when this is over."

The stroking recommenced. "Hmm. Maybe."

"What were the main learning points from our sessions, Ian? I'm curious to hear from you, get some feedback, you know."

"We didn't have 'sessions', Elliott. You kidnapped me, remember? It wasn't fuc...it wasn't therapy."

"No, but something must have changed. Something got through, surely."

"Of course not. I was just playing along. I told you."

"Oh, do come on. You just don't want to admit it. There were signs, I could tell. You didn't take the phone, for example. You could have called your parents, but you didn't. That's because you knew I was basically right."

"No," said Ian in a tone of infinite patience, "I didn't take the phone because I could see it wasn't the right battery. It was a game. I assume you switched it with the battery to your own phone?" Elliott looked sheepish for the briefest moment. "Thought so." Ian shook his head. "Good grief. I figured out that if I did put the battery in the phone it would only set back your plan for my 'conversion', meaning I would have had to sit listening to your lectures for even longer. No, Elliott, the reason I didn't pick the phone up was because I knew the quickest way out of that room was to go along with you. To get to the end. And all that copying my body language thing. Really? I mean, really? I've had more sales training than you've had eggs bloody Benedict, Elliott. I know all about matching the client's body position to increase empathy. I was the one doing it to you, not the other way round."

Elliott sat back in the sofa and folded his arms. He studied Ian for a moment. There had been plenty of opportunity for escape. Just now, for example, while he was in the toilet. Ian could have taken his chances with the police. But he was still here, trying to turn his defeat into victory. Despite his posturing, Ian was going to help them resolve the situation, to make some kind of amends for his own failings. Surely that was telling in itself.

"You know the difference between you and me?" asked Ian through the silence in the room.

"I can think of a few," said Elliott. He was tempted to continue but instead kept quiet.

"Well, try this one on for size. You said at one point that I think everything is everyone else's fault. Which is rubbish, by the way, I'm quite happy to admit when I'm in the wrong. But I do reckon that *you* think everything is *your* fault."

Elliott laughed through his nose. "Alright. You've got me there!" he said, lifting his glass towards Ian just enough to underline the acknowledgement. He then turned to the photograph of Naomi and raised the glass to her as well. 'He got me there,' he mouthed to her.

Elliott allowed his neck to go floppy. His head fell backwards onto the top of the sofa and he stared at the ceiling. Ian *had* changed, just not in the way he had expected. It was a strange sort of victory. It came with a kind of satisfaction that he not experienced before. It was tempered. Like he imagined smacking a child would feel like. Wrong, and yet it achieved an aim. At least that's what his father had told him. Such measures were not allowed any more. Probably for the best, but he did wonder sometimes. Especially when those undisciplined children grow up and throw burger wrappers out of car windows.

He lifted his head and let out a long, weary sigh. It sounded like an airbed with the plug pulled out. He didn't want to take on the world; he'd rather just get on with his own life. Why did everything feel like such a battle? Why couldn't people just do what was right?

"Do you know," he said, "when a crowd claps along with a band, they always clap on the wrong beat? Benny explained it to me once. He lives in the flat above this one. They clap on the one and the three of the bar, rather than the two and the four. Almost every time. Why is that? Sit each person down individually and tell them to clap along to a song and they'll follow the drummer, on the two and the four. But put them together in a crowd and they get it wrong. It's like our collective decision-making is worse than the sum of the individual decisions. The world needs to change the beat. I just don't know how to make that happen."

"Maybe you're asking the wrong question," said Ian. "Why not try asking yourself why you think you are the one who has to take on that responsibility?"

Elliott stared at the bookcase, at the accumulated knowledge and wisdom contained in the books which coexisted in the world alongside ignorance and evil. The task seemed so great. Had he really thought that he could make a difference where *The Grapes of Wrath* had failed? Where *Catch-22* had done nothing for the world but entertain it for a while? At least the world was a better place for those books being in it. Could the same be said of him? If he had not been born, would the sum of all the joy in the world be greater or lesser? He had tried to make a difference, no matter how small. To contribute. That was his duty, was everyone's duty: to make a contribution. Society, culture, is the sum of an almost infinite number of parts, each person's behaviour contributing like molecules to a mountain. How much of a difference could one person make? And yet he knew that being good was not optional, that it mattered, just like 'every vote counts'. Could he ever hope to convert someone to the path of 'Doing The Right Thing' or was preventing them from doing the wrong thing going to have to suffice?

"I do forgive you, Elliott," said Ian. "I want you to know that. I forgive you."

Elliott continued to look at the bookcase, his eyes narrowing slightly. "Right," he said slowly. "Thank you, Ian." He could feel the other man looking at him.

"You don't think you need forgiving, do you, Elliott?" said Ian. The stare moved from intense to pointed.

Elliott weighed up his reply. It was over. What was the point in carrying on? They were at an impasse, neither of them able to further influence the other. He had taken on the forces of ignorance and won. Even a partial improvement in Ian's ability to think of others counted as a victory. Nothing could take that away now.

"Do you know the irony here, Elliott? Your brother-in-law, Paolo, he really gets under your skin, doesn't he?"

"Yes. He's a bully, and I can't abide bullies."

"You kidnapped me and held me tied up in a room. Does that not rather smack of the actions of a bully to you?"

"That's different. A bully just wants to wield power. I had a higher objective."

"Elliott, is it possible to have an opinion different to yours and yet still be right?"

Elliott looked at Ian through narrowed eyes and, like an experienced negotiator, ignored the question. "No, Ian. No, I don't think I need to be forgiven. You may not realise it yet, but I truly believe you are a better person for what I have done."

"You kidnapped me. How can you even try to justify that?"

"Ian, sometimes extreme measures are necessary to uphold a principle. Jesus said, 'I am the way, the truth, and the light.' He did not waver. Margaret Thatcher said, 'This lady is not for turning.' She never faltered. She also said, 'In order to achieve great things, to bring about real change, sometimes extreme measures are necessary.'"

"How about this one?" said Ian. "'Think a thousand times before taking a decision. But after taking that decision, never turn back even if you face a thousand difficulties.'"

"Exactly! Who said that?"

Ian cocked his head. "Adolf Hitler," he said.

Chapter 26

Tuesday, 11am

As Elliott walked into the office Pru was typing so rapidly that he felt for a moment as if he were entering the room to a drum roll. Whether she had been working quite so vigorously before the sound of his dark brown leather brogues crunching on the gravel signified his imminent arrival he didn't really care. Given that her output was all that he had ever asked for, he had no reason to think ill of her if she did a bit of online shopping while she waited for him to give her something to do.

"Morning, Pru," he said.

"Mor-ning," she replied without looking up. If the word had been played on a piano it would have been a B followed by a G. He had once worked it out. It was a word that said, 'I know you're late, you know you're late, but I'm not going to ask you why because it's none of my business, yet I still want you to know that I know so that you will appreciate the fact that I'm not asking you why.'

Elliott walked into his office and sat down behind the desk. As he knew she would, as she had so many times before, Pru stopped typing and came round to see him carrying a few yellow pieces of paper, each one a message.

"Right," she said, although her accent made it sound more like 'riot'. "Stan at Cooksons called. Apparently she's now unhappy with the wording. She thinks it makes her look too greedy. He says he knows she is greedy but she doesn't realise that and she is the one paying the bill at the end of the day." Pru looked up from the paper and looked at Elliott over her glasses. "Silly cow, if you ask me." She put that message to the bottom of the pile and read on. "Julie called, says Billy needs a contract. She's decided he's a keeper." To the bottom. "Some chap I'd never 'eard of called who says he's an old colleague of yours and wants to talk to you about writing wills for you. I didn't like the sound of 'im to be honest, think he might have been trying it on. Wouldn't leave his name and number, said he'd call back." Shuffle to the bottom. "And Paula wants to know if you fancy a coffee tomorrow morning. I tried to get out of her what she wanted, but she just said she had some interesting news about Freddy's knees."

"Thank you, Pru," said Elliott, both acknowledging and ignoring the messages in the same breath. "Now, I've got something I want you to do, please. I'd like you to call Paolo Brice. Tell him that Lucy and I are ready to sign the paperwork for the security to his loan. Please could he come over for two o'clock. Don't take no for an answer, it has to be today. Tell him if it's not today, no deal."

Elliott rather enjoyed the look on Pru's face. He didn't think his secretary was capable of being surprised any more; perhaps, more to the point, neither did she. But now her mouth hung open as she searched for the words.

"You're just gonna give in?" she said. "Just like that? Give up this place?" She gestured vaguely around her. "To that...to that..." This was getting priceless. Elliott felt himself lean forwards as he awaited the word. "To that...piece of shit?"

"Pru Hutton!" he said. "That's the first time I've ever heard you swear."

"Well. I just never thought you'd give in. Really." She had actually gone pale.

"Sometimes we have to take a step back to move forwards," he replied. Pru pursed her lips and stared right back at him.

"You look weary, actually," she said in a voice dripping with disappointment, then shook her head and walked back to her desk.

The meeting with Paolo booked, Elliott returned to the flat. He and Ian cleaned the turret together, removing all traces of occupation and placing the detritus carefully into bags. He fished the ripped and still-damp trousers out of the bin for Ian to put back on, then they sat nervously in the kitchen together, each with a cup of coffee made on Elliott's espresso machine that had been a wedding present from Lucy.

Ian quickly and efficiently made the two of them a salad with chicken and thinly sliced chorizo. They made an incongruous pair, Elliott in work mode of smart jacket, chinos and brogues, Ian in his torn trousers and traces of five-day-old blood still caked onto his face.

Eventually, Ian stood to leave. Elliott looked at him as he rubbed his jaw, shook his hands and took a deep breath. He looked terrible. Had he really changed, or just rebranded? New logo, new colour scheme, new photos on the website, but the same old shit inside the shop.

The next few hours would tell all.

"Come on then, let's get this done," said Ian, standing tall and flexing his fingers nervously.

"Is this really necessary?" said Elliott, remaining seated. It was the one part of Ian's plan with which he did not feel comfortable.

"Absolutely," said Ian. "You never actually laid a finger on me, did you? Despite all the threat of violence you never touched me."

"I just don't like violence. I was trying to make you see things differently, hurting you wouldn't seem to have helped in any way."

"You mean you're just a big girl's blouse?" Ian leaned forwards, jeering the words into Elliott's face. He smiled at Elliott's hurt reaction. "Oh, Elliott," he said. "I'm trying to wind you up, get you angry. Come on, get on with it. Smack me. Get rid of some of that aggression. If we're going to get assault included on the charge sheet, you need to do some proper damage."

Elliott stood and walked over to Ian, facing him about two metres away. Then he placed his feet about a metre apart, crouched slightly, put both hands in front of his face balled into fists, and leaned forwards. Slowly he began to bob up and down. He looked like a boxer would look if drawn by a five-year-old girl.

Ian placed his hands on his hips and stared. "What *are* you doing?" he said.

"I'm getting ready to hit you," said Elliott.

"Well, you look like you're trying to put off doing a poo in your trousers," said Ian. "Come on, stop acting like a constipated

Rocky Marciano and just hit me." Ian put his face forwards and tensed his jaw in anticipation, awaiting the slam of the fist.

Elliott let his hands go down by his sides. "I'm not in the mood."

"You don't have to be in a mood, you arse. Just give me some welly. Come on."

"I don't want to. I don't dislike you. I have no motivation."

"Oh for…" Ian took a step forwards, relaxing his body. "Look, this isn't about me," he pleaded. "This is about fairness. What is right. All the things you care about, ethics-wise. It's about getting—"

Elliott's fist appeared as if from the ether and slammed into Ian's face. Without the time to prepare for the impact Ian's head snapped backwards and he overbalanced. His brain was too busy dealing with the shock of the blow to send any signals down to his legs, and he fell heavily onto his backside. He spread his arms just in time to stop his head from slamming back into the floor. Blood was already cascading down from his nose and as he took time sitting on the kitchen floor to regain his bearings, Elliott leaned over and offered several sheets of kitchen roll.

"How was that, punch-*wise*?" he said, sarcasm dripping from each word like the blood from Ian's nostrils.

Joey came to pick up Ian at one o'clock, and with the flat finally quiet again Elliott took the opportunity for a nap. Despite the aching in a hand wholly unused to hitting people, it had been surprisingly easy to drop off. He fell asleep almost instantly, partly due to the late night, but also because of the sense of peace he felt about what was going to happen next. When the alarm beeped him awake at twenty to two he felt refreshed, like the inbox of his brain had been cleared out, allowing him to focus afresh on the task in hand.

If it had been ten days earlier, or perhaps if the two o'clock meeting had been with any other person in the world, Elliott would have walked briskly out of the house across the drive and over to office in time for the meeting at exactly two o'clock.

But now, after the particular week he had been through, with this particular person who would be sitting in the waiting area, he went into the kitchen, filled the kettle, put the teabag into the cup, poured in the boiling water, added the spoonful of sugar, took out the teabag being careful not to stir or squeeze it in any way, poured in a drop of semi-skimmed milk, then took the cup into the front room, sat on the sofa, turned on the television, and watched a daytime medical soap opera whilst flicking through a book on the origins of the First World War.

His mobile went off, Pru telling him that his two o'clock meeting had arrived. He told her he would be there in a minute, and asked her to make sure their mobile phones were switched to silent.

Walking across the gravel at 2.30, Elliott felt in control. He was late, and it felt good.

It wasn't really in Elliott's nature to not like people. To be annoyed by them, sure, that was different. He often didn't like what people did, what they said, what they didn't do, how they went about their daily lives with apparently so little concern for the impact of their actions on other people. And yet such self-preservation was just how things were and always had been, right from the first moment a caveman bonked a cavewoman on the head and dragged her by the hair back to his cave. Ian's 'look after number one' mentality was the default position of every creature on the planet. It was the natural order of things, the way things were and always had been and always would be. Elliott might have wished his species had developed beyond some primal instincts, had recognised by now what could be achieved by working together, by thinking of other people before oneself, but he couldn't find it within him to be annoyed when people acted in the way that evolution had taught them to. It was nature. And nature was one mean, badass mother.

But Paolo was different. It was as if Paolo went out of his way to make the lives of other people unpleasant while at the same time grabbing more than he needed. He didn't just look after number one, he seemed to take enjoyment in making sure the lives of numbers two, three, four and five were a misery. Elliott had never warmed to his brother-in-law, even in the early days when Paolo and Lucy had been dating. But big sister knew better, always, and so Elliott assumed it had been he that had the issues. Then Naomi had come along and the slow increase in his self-belief that only the love of a non-family member can create led him to wonder if maybe he was right about his brother-in-law.

As he walked into the stables Paolo was standing, hands behind his back. Sitting on the sofa behind him was Helen McSherrold, a partner from Ashbey Douche, a solicitor's practice from London whose corporate slogan was 'You're Business. Our Pleasure.' The mangled grammar would have been enough to make Elliott hate the firm and everyone who worked in it, but he had met Helen and a number of the other partners a few times over the years and had quite easily managed to form a dislike of them individually.

Elliott plastered on a broad smile, stuck out his hand, and walked towards Paolo. "So sorry I'm late," he said, shaking Paolo's hand and doing his best not to allow the pains shooting up his arm show on his face. "I was sat on the toilet and got stuck into a really interesting article on bees. Fascinating things, bees, don't you think, Paolo?" Elliott held his grip a few moments before allowing Paolo to let go. Paolo wiped his hand on his jacket, trying to be surreptitious but failing. He offered the same hand to introduce his solicitor, who was trying to sit up from the sofa with dignity but finding it a little softer and deeper than she had realised.

"Right," said Paolo. "Well. You already know Helen McSherrold, I think?"

"Yes," said Elliott, shaking her hand and smiling warmly as she managed to reach a standing position, smoothing down her grey cotton suit skirt as she did so. "Of course we know each other, don't we, Helen? I've been patronised by you on many a happy occasion in the past." The thick foundation make-up which made it so difficult to tell Helen McSherrold's age moved away from her mouth like a slug recoiling from a pile of salt as she tried uncertainly to process what she had heard. Elliott gestured towards the frosted glass of the meeting room and as the solicitor opened her mouth to reply, he continued speaking. "Shall we crack on? Pru, would you be so kind as to organise drinks?"

Pru sat behind her desk with her mouth open, staring at Elliott. "Pru?" he said. Then he took a few steps towards her, reached forwards, placed his fingers gently under her jaw and closed it for her.

"Right, right, yes, okay, so, uh, drinks, what can I get everyone, then, ha-ha, hmm?"

"That coffee would be good now," said Paolo. "Same for you, Helen?"

"Thank you," said the solicitor. "Cream, one sugar."

As Pru was about to speak, Elliott interrupted. "Ah, sorry, we only have skimmed milk and artificial sweeteners – I'm sure that'll do, will it not, Ms McSherrold? I'll have a tea. Shall we get on with that cracking on I mentioned? Yes, that's probably best, follow me."

Elliott walked down the building to the meeting room, his resolve to enjoy this meeting fuelled by the sound of the solicitor's heels scraping across the flagstones behind him. He shuddered, then turned as he opened the door, bowing slightly as if offering entrance to a room of forbidden pleasures.

Paolo walked round to the other side of the boardroom table and sat down, allowing the solicitor to find her own seat next to him.

"Where's Lucy?" said Paolo. "I at least thought she could make the effort to be here."

"I believe she has already signed. It's just me that hasn't. I thought it best that way, then she doesn't have to endure actually seeing you," replied Elliott with a smile. "Anyway, I thought you and me could have a little chat before the formalities."

Elliott took his seat. The two men stared at each other across the table for a moment before Paolo averted his gaze and looked around the room, his face a curious mixture of admiration and condescension. The glass door opened and Pru brought in a tray. On it was a cafetière with a mug, two white enamel cups and a matching sugar pot and two milk jugs. The teapot was emblazoned with the design of a Union Jack flag, and the mug with 'I'm The Boss' written across it was one that Pru had bought for him in a moment of irony on holiday in Corfu several years ago. She put the tray on the table and placed a cup in front of Paolo, who continued to look around the room, and the other in front of the solicitor, who nodded her thanks. Next Pru pushed the plunger down in the coffee, poured the brew into each of their cups, then placed one of the jugs and the sugar bowl between them. Then she placed the other jug, the mug and the teapot in front of Elliott, who looked up at her and smiled broadly. He winked, and Pru turned her head slightly away from the visitors to raise her eyebrows at him quizzically before turning to leave.

As Pru put her hand on the door handle to leave the room, Elliott spoke. "Just a moment, Pru." She turned and looked at him. Then Elliott addressed Paolo. "Don't you have something to say?"

Paolo ceased his ostentatious surveying of the office and looked at Elliott. "Hmm?" he replied. Elliott could tell he was genuinely confused because he was using his mouth to breathe instead of his nose. There was something about Paolo's mouth; it seemed to hang open more often than most people's.

"I think you have something to say to Pru," repeated Elliott. Pru stood by the door, her eyes beseeching Elliott not to be making such a fuss, but her boss continued to look expectantly at Paolo, who moved his hands slightly outwards and extended his neck slightly as if to say, 'What?' Next to him, Helen McSherrold leaned across and whispered something in his ear.

"You're fucking kidding me," Paolo said back to her in a low voice, as if wanting to give the appearance that he cared whether he was heard, but also wanting it made clear that he did not.

The solicitor whispered again, and Paolo looked at Elliott. "Jesus," he said again, not quite under his breath, more peeping round the corner. Then Paolo turned and addressed Pru. "Thanks for the coffee."

"No problem," said Pru brightly before exiting the room as quick as she could. Out of the corner of his eye Elliott noticed her try and give him a telling-off stare through the glass wall of the meeting room, but he was already turning his attention back to Paolo, who was now glaring at him.

"Let's cut the shit, Elliott," said Paolo. "She," Paolo jerked a thumb in the direction of the solicitor, "charges by the minute. You've already cost me money by these stupid games. I'm trying to do Lucy and her moron boyfriend a favour, so let's just get on with it." He flicked his fingers at the solicitor next to him without turning to look at her. Immediately she reached down into the briefcase at her feet and began placing papers on the desk.

"Doing them a favour, eh?" said Elliott. "Yes, I can imagine you might think of it that way." How long was this going to have to take? Timing was everything. There are only a few moments in a long-lived and, by his own admission, rather sheltered life that one might have the opportunity to create a truly dramatic moment. He didn't want to mess this up. "Shall we just talk about the favour you are doing them for a moment?"

"Hey, Elliott, come on," said Paolo, "let's get a shift on, dude. You and me, we've got better things to be doing."

"Actually, I'm not sure I have, Paolo. I think of all the places in the entire world that I could be, this is the one I would choose." Paolo looked back at Elliott, his eyes narrowed in displeasure at the way he was being spoken to. Elliott continued talking before Paolo had a chance to speak. "You see, I've been doing some thinking about this." He waved the partially signed contract in Paolo's general direction. "Why would you be lending your ex-wife and her boyfriend all this money? You're not exactly someone known for their largesse."

Paolo placed his hand on top of his stomach unconsciously. "No need to get personal, Elliott," he said.

"It means 'generous', Paolo," said his solicitor in a flat voice.

"Oh. Right. Well, look, I like to help people out when I can, of course. I'm on the board of several charities, I have a reputation for raising lots of money for good causes. I always make a point to buy something at a charity auction, always put my hand in my pocket, me."

"Yes," replied Elliott. He leaned forwards, elbows on the desk and chin cradled on top of his interlocked fingers. "All that is true. But if I may be so bold, you work with the charities in order that you can direct contracts for work towards your many businesses, and you always splash some cash at charity dinners so that everyone can see you. When you put your hand in your pocket, Paolo, it is invariably to play with yourself."

Paolo shifted in his seat. "What I do with my money is up to me. And right now, you are preventing me from lending it to my ex-wife." The finger came out and started jabbing the air towards Elliott. "I don't know why you have decided after all these years to start being rude, but it is not happening. Fuckin' get on with it, Elliott. I've got things to do."

Elliott glanced at the Beethoven clock on his desk. Any time from now. It could be one minute; it could be twenty. He had to hold the situation at a point of climax until the time was right. He toyed briefly with the idea of revealing all he suspected. But that was to come; the pleasure to be had now should not be sullied by the machinations he had lined up for later.

"Let's just recap, Paolo. You, an egotistical bully and a successful businessman, if we were to define success purely in monetary terms. You are wealthy beyond anything I would ever want and yet you still have a seemingly undiminished desire to make more money, although only if it is to someone else's detriment. You are offering to lend your ex-wife, my sister, four hundred thousand pounds which she will give to her current boyfriend – your replacement, if you will – in order to invest in his business. A business that needs this money because it has been conned out of that same amount of money by a fraudulent bogus charity. You require security for the loan in the form of this property, which you will then own if Joey's business cannot keep up payments. It will be in Lucy's name, so it will come from her share if it has to come at all, but I have to sign the paperwork as I am a joint owner. Correct?"

"That's about it." Paolo did not turn to his solicitor for confirmation.

"So, what are the real motives behind this largesse – this kind and thoughtful offer? This sudden burst of kindness, so out of character?"

Paolo barked a laugh. "I don't know what you are on about, Elliott, and I don't really care. But understand this – I am always me. I don't 'do' in character or out of character. What you see is what you get, take it or leave it. You can't change me. I am who I am. I've always been like that. Lucy thought she could change me – that's why the marriage didn't work. Well, one reason anyway. That and the fact she was frigid. People just have to accept me for who I am. You can't change me."

"Agreed. Maybe that's why you're still such an asshole," said Elliott. The solicitor sitting next to Paolo let out a snort of laughter and Paolo turned to glare at her. The solicitor offered a weak, apologetic smile before scrutinising her papers for the fourth time.

Elliott stood and began walking up and down the length of the room, all the time keeping the desk between him and the odious little creep opposite. If he was going to have to string this out a little longer, he may as well have some fun. In for a penny, and all that.

"You, Paolo," he continued, "are what is generally known as a tosser. Do excuse me if I get some of the words wrong here – I'm not really used to swearing or telling people what I think of them. Because we don't do that, do we? We're not a very honest race. We are a nation of tongue-biters. Mustn't make a fuss or hurt other people's feelings. But I don't think I could hurt your feelings, Paolo, could I? You know that we all hate you, you just don't care."

"That's not fair." Helen McSherrold had spoken, her voice firm in the practised way of the professional used to conflict. She looked at Paolo. "May I?" she said. Paolo nodded uncertainly. Elliott stole a further glance at Ludwig. He had rather hoped they would have arrived by now.

"It is true that my client is, as you put it, a complete knob-end," the solicitor began, sitting up even straighter with her hands folded on her lap. She spoke as if she were a schoolgirl in a debating class. "I think it's fair to say that in all my years of dealing in corporate and commercial law I have come across a large number of people, mostly but not exclusively men, who have had a significantly inflated opinion of their own abilities. Paolo is merely one in a long line of highly unpleasant people for whom I have acted."

Elliott wondered for a moment if the woman in front of him might actually be a robot. Relentlessly, she continued speaking.

"What motivates a man like Paolo Brice? Is it money? Undoubtedly. Is it the public interest? No, let us not kid ourselves. It is power. But in order to wield power, all parties need to see some benefit. He has to win and beat others to the prize, but he is also pragmatic. If he will permit me to speak on his behalf..." Paolo opened his mouth to speak, but the solicitor simply continued talking sotto voce, "...Paolo believes that lending the money to Joey Davison is in the interests of all parties. He expects a rate of return on his money, and your sister gets to help her beau. He saves his business, and there's profit for Paolo. A win-win situation. You, Mr Harmison, do not share this belief because of your lack of objectivity. You are unable to take the long-term and open-minded view that Mr Brice is able to take because you have an emotional investment in him as a person, and in this building. And that costs money. So, by charging you a rate of return substantially lower than he could achieve by, for example, investing in one of the many business opportunities that my firm is able to place in front of Mr Brice, he is compensating you for that emotional investment. May I therefore suggest that rather than have you listing a series of character flaws of my client upon which we could undoubtedly find agreement, why don't we just take those as accepted and move on to completing the paperwork. Hmm?"

The three of them sat in silence for a moment. Elliott looked at Helen McSherrold, Helen McSherrold looked at Elliott, and Paolo had his head facing Helen McSherrold but his eyes turned to Elliott. In the distance a police siren wailed. Elliott allowed a smile to creep around the edges of his mouth. Time to allow the climax to burst forth.

"I guess it must be nice having that much money just lying around waiting to be used," said Elliott, taking his seat and pulling the paperwork across the desk towards him. From the inside pocket of his jacket he pulled a fountain pen. "On the one hand I can't help but wonder where such an amount of money might have come from. Don't get me wrong, I know you are a wealthy chap. I've acted in enough deals involving you to know that. But I also know you borrow heavily when you invest. What is it you said to me once? 'Always invest other people's money, not your own.'"

"What is your fucking point, Elliott? Are you going to sign that fucking piece of paper, or am I going to have to walk out of here and tell Lucy that you preferred to make fun of me rather than allow me to save her boyfriend's company?"

"Please don't swear, Paolo, there is a lady present," Elliott replied. The sirens were louder now, as if they were going right past Meanwood Towers. "The thing is, I rather have my suspicions that there is more to this situation than meets the eye. It's obvious why you are making the loan: to gain a degree of control over your ex-wife, the one person in your life who represents failure. Indeed, I strongly suspect you engineered this entire situation. But how to prove it? That's the question. Half the people in this town know you are a crook. The other half also know you are a crook but don't care because you gave a donation to their charity."

"Elliott," said Helen McSherrold. "This is most unprofessional."

Paolo was now leaning back in his chair, arms folded, a smirk crawling unpleasantly around his face. "I dunno. I'm rather impressed, actually. The first time you've said anything with bollocks since I've known you. Course, it's going to cost you. The interest rate is about to go up two per cent." He leaned forwards across the table towards Elliott. "Is that an honest enough statement for you, Smelliott?"

The sirens had stopped and for a fleeting moment Elliott wondered if his timing was terribly off. But as he stared back at Paolo's smug face he heard the sound of tyres on gravel and car doors opening and shutting. Paolo had not yet seemed to notice. Elliott ostentatiously popped the lid off the pen and leaned over the document. As he pressed the pen to the paper to begin his signature, he looked up. Paolo was looking at him expectantly, revealing that this was something he really wanted. It was clearly the end of years of work, the culmination of many palms greased, many favours bought and won. Elliott looked directly into his left eye, marvelling for a moment at the beautiful patterns of the brown iris.

The sound of the front door to the office opening and the urgency of the voices that followed made all three of them turn their heads. They could not see anything at the far end of the office through the frosted glass, but four shapes began to form and then become more defined as they approach the meeting room. The door opened and was immediately filled with black uniforms and threatening authority.

Two of the police officers stepped inside the room, the other two remaining outside. Elliott suppressed a smile as he recognised the man and woman from his brief visit to the scene of the accident.

One of the officers stepped forwards and spoke directly to Paolo.

"Are you Paolo Brice, owner and resident of the Stud Farm in South Malting?"

"I am. What's this about?"

"Sir, I have a warrant for your arrest for kidnapping and violent assault. Please would you come with us? You do not have to say anything, but you should be aware that anything you do say will be taken down as evidence and may be used in a court of law. Come along please, sir."

Paolo did not move. "Sorry, what are you talking about?" he said, taking his mobile phone out of his pocket. "Shit," he said, and Elliott could see a string of missed call messages. Paolo turned to his solicitor. "What do I do?" he said.

"Well, if I were you I'd go with the police," she replied, smiling at the officers. "That much is plain." She put her hand on his arm. "Don't worry. I'll get one of our criminal solicitors to meet you at the station. We'll sort this out."

Paolo stood in a daze, then slowly walked out of the meeting room, his elbow held firmly by a police officer. Helen McSherrold scuttled behind him, already talking into her phone. Elliott put away the pen, folded the contracts then unfolded them, repeating several times until there was a definite crease. He then tore slowly down the line of the crease, held the papers ceremoniously over the bin, and let them fall.

Chapter 27

Tuesday, 7pm

"Parmesan?"

"Oh, thanks, Lucy, yes please. You are an egg. Or possibly a brick."

Lucy leaned across the table and grated some Parmesan cheese on top of Benny's bowl of salmon pasta. She gestured to Elliott to her left, who nodded and she repeated the action.

"Now," Benny said to Lucy, "back to our mutual friend Mr Cervantes. I fail to believe that you can be enjoying the experience. You simply have to be reading an expungigated version of the book. The full version of *Don Quixote* is virtually impermeable."

"Oh, Benny," said Lucy. "Do come on. I don't think 'expungigate' even exists. If you're going to use long words to impress us, you've really got to use the right ones."

"Oh, he knows what he's doing," said Elliott carefully. Benny raised his eyebrows in Elliott's direction like an elderly cat being threatened by a puppy. Elliott's eyes narrowed in return, fingers stroking his chin as he lined up his thoughts.

"Have you finally undressed me as a gongerist, Elliott, my old fruit and nut?" said Benny.

"That's actually very clever," said Elliott after a few moments. "Expungigate. It's not a word, but is a mash-up of 'expurgate' and 'sponge'. Then you used 'impermeable' instead of 'impenetrable', which is the opposite of a sponge, something that will not allow fluid to pass through it. Am I right, Benny?"

Benny did not answer, but instead nodded his head forwards slightly, closing his eyes briefly as he did so.

"Is this what you do, Benny? Is this how you get your mental stimulation? Constant word games?" Elliott shook his head in admiration.

"One has to keep the mind active," said Benny.

"You see, Lucy," said Elliott. "People are not always what we think they are. Sometimes they are better."

The sound of the front door slamming made Elliott look towards the hallway. It was followed by the sound of shoes being taken off without laces being undone and left in front of the door where someone was likely to trip over them. A few moments later Phoebe marched into the room and stood next to Elliott, arms on both hips in the double teapot position.

"What the hell have you been saying?" she demanded.

"What do you mean?" replied Elliott, placing his spoon and fork together in the bowl. "Saying to whom?"

"Come on," said Phoebe, "I know what you've been up to, sticking your nose in, trying to help. Getting him confused. What have you done this time?" She had the look of someone who had been telling herself to stay calm for so long that now the moment actually came, she could blow up in an instant.

"Phoebe, I don't know what you're talking about. What have you heard?"

"I worked it out myself, put the pieces together. You had to try and change things, didn't you? Had to poke your nose in and try and make him see things your way. Didn't try and understand things first, oh no, just get stuck in and make things how you think they should be. Why can't you just leave things alone, Uncle E? Why can't you just leave me alone?" Phoebe began to cry and thrust her face into her hands.

Elliott looked at Lucy desperately for help, but in return she gave a shrug and opened her arms with hands palms upwards and outwards as if to say, 'I've no idea how she found out, I didn't tell her.' Benny looked at the two of them, then quietly rose and left the flat, taking his half-eaten supper with him.

Waiting a moment for the sound of the front door shutting, Elliott stood in front of his niece and placed his hands gently on her shoulders. "Phoebe, I'm sorry. It's not what you think it is. We need to talk. Please, sit down."

274

"He told me, Uncle E. I know what you've been up to."

The look between Lucy and Elliott was now one of rising panic: the entire plan was about to be ruined and yet they had no idea how Phoebe could have found out. Had Ian never really been on their side, in the same way he had never intended to leave the turret? Had Ian pretended to go along with the plan a second time, had Elliott been a gullible fool twice? Elliott felt his entire world once again preparing itself to come crashing down around his ears even as Phoebe continued to sob and shake in his hands.

"Phoebe," he said softly. "My love. Phoebe. Please, let me explain. What has been happening is complicated, and for the best."

"How the hell do you know what's *best*, Uncle E?" Phoebe thrust her hands by her sides, fists clenched. Elliott took back his hands as if something he'd been about to pick up, thinking it was dead, had suddenly moved. "Why do you always think you know what's *best* for me? You think you understand how people work, but you don't. You're as big a phoney as the rest of them. Why do you always think you are the one who has to change the world?"

"The world," he began, conscious of needing to use exactly the right words, "the world is a messed-up place, Phoebe. There is so much that is good and yet so much that can be improved. The world doesn't change in one sudden burst, but by the sum collection of a million minor selfless acts. We all have to work hard each and every day to improve our little plot of life, and only then will the world start to raise its head from the downward cycle into mediocrity and selfishness. I did what I did not for you, not for me, but for the betterment of the world. For our future. Your future. Your children's future."

Phoebe was looking at him quizzically now. "And you thought you would achieve all that by telling Mikey to ignore me?"

"Mikey?" said Lucy.

"Yes, Mikey," said Phoebe, turning to her mother. "He hasn't spoken to me since Friday, then sent me some weird text about seeing Uncle E on Monday morning. So today in class I had him up against a wall and then he told me what you'd said to him. You told him to ignore me. Said it would make me appreciate him more."

"Oh lord, that!" Elliott's arms fell by his sides and hung there uselessly for a moment. "Mikey!" he said stupidly, looking at Lucy's accusatory stare. "I saw him the other day. I just told him the old saying. 'If you love someone, set them free.' I was trying to get him to back off a little." Lucy rolled her eyes and looked away from him. "Oh, Phoebe, I'm sorry if he took it the wrong way."

"He didn't take it the *wrong* way. He took it the way you said it. You shouldn't have *said* it at all. It's none of your business. Who made you judge and jury? Why are you the one who decides how people should behave? It's not fair." She turned and half-walked, half-ran into the hallway. For the second time in a few minutes they heard the slamming of a door, this time the one to her bedroom.

Elliott stared at the space that Phoebe had left in the room, his shoulders sagging under the weight of life. He took a step towards the door.

"Elliott," said Lucy, standing, her left hand steadying her on the table while the right rubbed vigorously at her eyes, "leave it, I'll go."

"No," said Elliott softly. "I've got to sort this out. To apologise." As Elliott turned to go he glimpsed Lucy staring at his back in wide-eyed astonishment.

He knocked softly on the bedroom door, as if anything louder would compound his guilt. Hearing no reply, he pushed down the handle. Unlocked. That was as good as a signal to enter.

Phoebe was sat on her bed. Her body was facing him, hands on knees, but her head was turned towards the wall, almost ninety degrees to the right, in order to avoid looking at him. It looked rather a painful position and he doubted she could keep it up for too long. He sat down next to her and she immediately performed a fast 180-degree turn with her head.

"Phoebe," he said to the back of her head, placing his hand on her knee. She did not move.

"Phoebe," he said again. "I'm sorry. I was foolish. I thought I saw the chance to help someone I love very much. But it was my solution, not yours. It was not my place to impose my views. Right intentions, wrong actions. I apologise."

Phoebe turned to look at him, a calmer but puzzled look across her face. "You told him to ignore me," she said,

"No, no, Phoebe, I didn't. I just quoted on old line to him. If you love someone set them free. If they come back they're yours, if they don't they never were. It means your love needs to be tested sometimes in order to prove its worth."

"He's a sixteen-year-old boy for goodness' sakes Uncle E. You need to make things an awful lot clearer to them than that!" Her eyes were shining now and Elliott knew he had not lost her. He wondered for a moment what he would ever do without the anchorage that her adoration provided.

"I'm sorry, Phoebe, I really am." He looked at her carefully, obviously. "You okay, Phoebe? With what's been happening? About Paolo?"

"That wanker?" She looked at him. He nodded to confirm that using a swear word about Paolo was okay. "Well, I can barely believe it, obviously, even by his standards. School has been shit, natch." She didn't bother checking this time. She probably didn't even think it was a swear word. "To be honest, I'm just glad they found that guy." She looked up at him. She looked relieved more than anything. Just how close he had come? Losing Naomi had torn the insides from him. If it happened a second time he really wasn't sure that he could survive. "I am," she continued, "I'm just so thankful that they found him. That's what matters. His poor family, worrying about him. The fact that my father did something like that – it's like it's not really real, that he is capable of doing something like that? I mean, he's always been a phoney and a really bad dad, but kidnapping someone? It doesn't seem likely – some other explanation will probably come out. Anyway, if he did do it, I don't actually care, I just hate him more than I did before. That's all."

Phoebe looked down at her hands. It clearly wasn't all. She had found a hairband from somewhere and was working with it nervously. Elliott waited. The longer the silence continued, the more obvious it became that she had something she needed to say. The only sound in the room was the ticking of the *Harry Potter and the Half-Blood Prince* clock on the wall that he had given her for a Christmas present, oh, four or five years ago. It occurred to him that he had not set foot in this room for several years now. The only other item he recognised was the Audrey Hepburn poster that

Naomi had given her the same year. There was a wet towel on the floor from that morning, or was it last night, and he had to forcibly restrain himself from picking it up. Her study desk was covered in papers and schoolbooks, and a particularly dubious-looking pile of clothes mouldered in the corner.

"Dad's a tosser," said Phoebe eventually, still looking down. "He always was. Even when he was my dad. But he's not my dad any more, Uncle Elliott, not as far as I am concerned. You are. I'm sorry things have been terrible for you over the last few years, but I don't want you to change. You're my rock and I want you to carry on being you. For a while I thought…I thought that you were the one, that you had…well, I was scared that you might be turning into someone I wouldn't have liked very much. Anyway, I know you are still my Uncle E and I love you very much." She looked at him and gave him a smile that made his heart leap and melt all at the same time.

Elliott reached out and took one of Phoebe's hands. Her black mascara was smudged and moist. "Thank you, Phoebe," he said. "I will always be here for you. Even when I'm not here physically I will still be with you up there." He tapped the side of her head gently. "That's what good people do. They get into your head and never let go. They continue to guide you forever because they always seemed to know the right thing to do."

"You could be slightly less judgemental, if I'm honest," she said, laughing. "And I'm still angry at you for what you said to Mikey."

"I'm not perfect, Phoebe. I'm human like everyone else, well intentioned but flawed. Okay, perhaps more well intentioned than most! I do make mistakes. Sometimes what we think is the right thing to do turns out not to be. That's what being human means. I'll be proud to be your rock, Phoebe. But do remember, even rocks get worn down over time."

Chapter 28

From his seated position on a stone bench at the side of the square, Elliott stared unblinking at the door of the cathedral. He had watched Paolo enter a while back. He wasn't sure how much time had passed. Five minutes? Fifteen? It didn't seem important. The arrangement had been to meet at 2.30, twenty minutes ago. There was no real need to be late. There was nothing more to prove. Not to Paolo. Not to Ian. Not to himself. There was just Naomi. There had only ever been Naomi.

He didn't see the door. He didn't see anything. Her face invaded and filled his thoughts. She was smiling, happy. It wasn't that she was proud, more that she wasn't not proud. What is the opposite of proud? Ashamed? Angry? Disappointed? That wasn't how she had ever seen him. He realised that now. Those thoughts had been of his own making. All those feelings of letting people down, not being what she had hoped he would turn out to be, the career that had not been as glittering as some might have predicted from his school exam results, the negative mindset that would overwhelm and engulf him, providing a destructive counterfoil to her optimism and light. These were never feelings that she had borne for him. That was how he had felt about himself.

One little starfish. He had loved that story when he first heard it. It spoke of doing some good in life, of helping others, of making the world a better place. They had been at a restaurant when Naomi had first told him the story. Her starter had been scallops wrapped in bacon followed by a mushroom risotto she ranked as the best that she had ever tasted. He didn't recall his own meal. Naomi had been telling him about a book she was reading, by a philosopher called Eiseley. He could recall picturing the scene as she recounted the parable, actually seeing the beach in his mind. Only now did he start to realise that the picture he had painted in his mind of the person standing on the beach was of a giant, Superman-type figure, holding the biggest starfish and talking to a small boy, looking up at him in wonder at his enormous chin and glowing intellect. He felt rather foolish as the picture came into focus for the first time. The beach had been golden (how could it be, it was covered in starfish?), the teeth were white, the starfish were grateful. What he had heard when Naomi told him the story was that he was to go out and change the world, one person at a time.

What had she meant when she told him the story? A goofy, slightly embarrassed expression dawned on his face. He got it now. Rather too late, but he got it. *He* was the starfish. Let me help you, she was telling him. You do not have to be the hero all the time, it is not you against everyone else. I am here too. I am your rock. You don't have to try and change the world on your own.

Now the picture shifted. Naomi was holding him, she had chosen him out of the millions of pale, grey, dying starfish as the one to which she would give life and meaning. To make small, incremental differences to the world. To treat people as you would want to be treated. To be polite, kind, to show good manners. Exactly what he had been trying to teach Ian.

Focus on the detail, do only what you can, and let the world come together through billions of tiny good deeds like the atoms that knit together to form a starfish. That was how Naomi would want him to live his life. Be a conduit. Believe in himself, believe in his beliefs, but don't be seduced by ego. Yeah, that would do as a summary.

She might not have agreed with his methods, but she would have approved of the results he had achieved. Because she had faith in him.

Perhaps that was her greatest gift to him, her real legacy. To simply love him. To see something in him that he had not seen himself. There would always be a hole in his life that was Naomi-shaped. But that didn't mean he had to pretend the hole wasn't there. He realised that he didn't even see it as a hole. It contained matter, substance, a sparkling, glittering residue of happiness and memory, of her confidence and belief in him. Memories of joy, the lingering element of a love which he had, at times, barely dared to hope might ever exist. He had nothing left to prove for her. The only thing that remained to do in order to truly honour her was to continue spreading her message of hope and good manners, of love and faith in doing the right thing.

She wasn't coming back. But in letting her go he was retaining something of her, something that death could not steal. The memory of their love for each other.

Standing, Elliott walked over to the cathedral door and went inside. He stood for a moment, enjoying the cool air and musty smell. He felt a calmness that came as much from the environment inside the virtually empty cathedral as it did from the moment of peace and clarity he had just found outside in the fresher air. There was no God. There was no life everlasting. There was no Heaven. And yet she persisted, somewhere. The idea of a better place was so irresistible, so comforting to him that he was also tempted to believe in it.

He spied the back of Paolo's head, seated halfway down on the left-hand side. Elliott had suggested this meeting place to ensure they wouldn't be overheard, but now it seemed an inspired choice. The childlike instinct not to tell lies or say rude words in a church might ensure that their conversation was a sensible one, with a conclusion that Elliott needed.

Instead of heading down the central aisle to join Paolo, he instead turned left and went round the side of the empty pews. He passed Paolo, who he was certain would have seen him, and went to the corner of the transept where an iron frame was situated. There were only two candles alight and a small pile lay in a plastic container to the side. He put a five-pound note in the box. The usual wry thoughts about the need to pay to be able to honour the dead approached but were dismissed. He wasn't interested in cynicism, not now.

He stole a piece of flame from another candle. The metaphor was not lost on him as he stared at the gentle yellow light in his hand. First there had been one flame, then there were two, both the same size, one as fragile as the other, a life given and yet a life that was so easily taken away. It could burn forever but only if it was shared. Left alone it would slowly fade, or with nothing more than a breath it could cease in an instant.

Placing the candle on one of the small metal holders he stood still, hands folded together in front of him. He felt the urge to say a prayer. But it was not a prayer to God.

"Goodbye, Naomi," he whispered. "And thank you." He paused. The sound of a volunteer putting out a table ready for an early evening concert echoed around the walls, breaking the silence. Now he came to listen, there were other whispers drifting through the still air, the precise words out of reach. But he knew what they were telling him. Go on, they said. It's okay. You can tell her. She can hear you. His stomach yanked and lurched. A tear dropped unnoticed from his bowed head onto the stone floor. "Thank you. For loving me. For giving me your soul and your heart and your life." The words caught in his throat now. He took a deep breath, then continued to speak, almost silently now as the whisper went beyond the need for articulation. "Thank you for believing in me. For giving me so much to believe in. For showing me how we should behave with one another. I will be your soldier. I will not let you down." He smiled at her memory and, although he did not know where she was, he knew she was smiling back at him.

Wiping his face with his sleeve, Elliott then blew his nose into a handkerchief. He was tempted to wait a few moments for his face to resume its pre-crying façade, then decided his emotional state might actually help what he was about to do. As he turned he thought he saw Paolo turn his head to look forwards, as if he had been caught spying into someone else's grief. Elliott walked over to him.

"Hello, Paolo," he said, sitting next to his ex-brother-in-law. "You look terrible."

"So do you," Paolo replied without looking round. Elliott expected him to say something further, something typically tactless, but instead he continued to stare in front of him. Maybe a night in prison had done him a bit of good.

"I know what you did," said Elliott. "I think I probably know why, although I've not entirely convinced myself that I care. But I do know that I don't want you get away with it."

There was a pause. Elliott wondered if Paolo was weighing up his options, calculating his next move in typical Paolo fashion. Or whether he was actually just a bit thick.

Paolo spoke impassively. "I don't know what you are talking about, Elliott. I have no idea how that man got into my barn. I have never seen him before. I don't know who he is or why he has ended up on my property."

"Oh, I'm not worried about that, Paolo. We'll come to that in a minute. I'm talking about your motive for lending Lucy the money." The expression on Paolo's face went from panic to relief then straight back to panic again. The poor chap looked like he had been through the wringer. Good.

"You see, Paolo, you are not the type to show kindness to an ex-wife. Why would you offer to lend money to Lucy in order that she could spend it on something that might make her happy – lending it to Joey? That's not like you at all. You buy businesses you don't need just to have power over people. You bribe town planners to give permission to build offices just to prove that you can. You can't even think of other people for long enough to give your own daughter a fleeting moment of joy. Happiness, Paolo, is not something you seek to create in other people. And especially when that person is Lucy's new partner, Joey Davidson. The man that she loves instead of you. Lending money to Lucy so that she could give it to her lover," he emphasised the word so that it almost dripped off his tongue, "would simply annoy you. Which leads us to only one possible conclusion." Elliott turned in the pew to face Paolo, who continued to stare forwards.

"You were the one that stole the money from Joey in the first place. You committed the fraud. You invented a charity in order to prey on Joey's good nature and convince him to provide you with eight hundred thousand pounds' worth of wheelchairs for only four hundred thousand, the amount it cost Joey to get them made. I don't know what you then did with those wheelchairs, probably sold them on for a profit like the low-level gangster you are. So you got one of your workers to pretend to act for a charity, and so when

Joey came looking for his money, they had never heard of him. Then when Lucy came cap in hand looking for help you were only too happy to step in, knowing that you were lending their own money back to them." He paused. "A nice touch, that, actually."

Elliott paused for a moment to allow Paolo to speak if he so chose. He declined the offer with silence and a face set as hard as a three-week-old bagel.

Still Paolo simply stared blankly. Elliott wondered for a moment if he might have had a heart attack. He craned his neck around to look at Paolo's impassive face. Nothing. No emotion, no response. It was like looking at a waxwork dummy of the man.

Elliott leaned further, almost far enough to get into Paolo's eyeline. He waved his hand in front of Paolo's face for a moment, but as he did so his bottom slipped off the shiny pew, polished by hundreds of years of worshipful posteriors sliding forwards to kneel in prayer, and his knees cracked on the stone floor. He let out a muted howl of pain which echoed briefly around the walls, and bent forwards, banging his forehead lightly on the back of the pew in front.

He quickly sat back and simultaneously stretched his legs and rubbed his knees with one hand whilst rubbing his forehead with the other.

"Elliott, you really are a fucking moron," said Paolo.

"You know what, Paolo?" Elliott replied, chuckling at his own clumsiness. "You may well be right. And once upon a time it mattered to me that you might think that. But not any more. Not now. Now what I care far more about is that you mind your language. You are in a house of God. Please have some respect for other people's beliefs. Show some manners for once in your life."

At last Paolo turned to face Elliott, eyebrows raised into a mask that itself could deliver a severe telling-off without the need for words. Once, maybe as little as a week previously, this would have been an instruction that Elliott would have obeyed by turning to look into his eyes, drawn in like an uglier and more ostentatiously wealthy version of Medusa. But now the spell was broken. Like a stag taking up the challenge, Elliott simply stared back. He saw the flicker of uncertainty in the other man's eyes for a moment, almost a flinch. Slowly, ever so slowly, Elliott leaned his body forwards from the waist, his head moving towards Paolo, maintaining eye contact the whole time. His neck began to extend until their noses were almost touching.

"Boo," he said. Paolo flinched, uncertain.

"I'm not afraid of you any more, Paolo," Elliott continued, sitting up straight again. "Not since that moment when I threw a great big rock through the windscreen of your car." Elliott rather enjoyed the pinch of red that suddenly appeared on Paolo's cheeks. "After the week I've had, what is right and what is wrong, and perhaps more importantly, how one should go about fixing things when they are the wrong way round, is a lot more clear to me. You are the wrong way round, Paolo. I know that much. You can't simply go about bullying people all the time. I won't let you. No more saying whatever you like to people. No more nastiness."

He leaned in closer. "You are a bully, Paolo. A rude, ignorant bully. And chickens are coming home to roost. You are rude to people. You have committed fraud. You are going to spend time in prison for kidnapping—"

"I didn't kidnap anyone."

"…and after you get sent to prison for kidnapping and torture your reputation will be up for grabs without you around to threaten and intimidate people. I will make sure that your reputation is not only left in tatters, it will be taken apart, dissected, analysed and buried in a hole so deep that you'll never be able to find it again even with an army of giant digger trucks. You won't only be unable to resume your business activities, you will be lucky to get a job stacking shelves. There are plenty of people sick of you and your muscle, just waiting for this day. You've made a lot of enemies, Paolo. That's what happens when you are a bully. When the time comes to fall, you fall hard."

Elliott cocked his head and watched the other man struggle to hold in his anger. The moment was exquisite, delicious. He wished this slice of time could last forever, and he made sure the expression on his face illustrated he feelings very clearly. Now he was the one that held Paolo's gaze, now the power was *his* to wield.

Eventually the time came to show just how power should

be used. With kindness. The very best way to show a bully how to behave. Not with force and threat, not with hubris, but with compassion. Even if it was an approach brought on due to a lack of any alternative…

"Luckily for you, Paolo, I have a solution to your problems. It's not a proposal, exactly. More of an instruction. Would you like to know what it is that you are going to do next?"

The waxwork dummy remained mute. Credit where it's due. At least the man knows when he's beaten.

"Do you know why we are meeting here, in the cathedral? You know I'm not a religious man, Paolo. I could never go for all that pomp and circumstance. But Jesus always seemed like a pretty decent bloke to me. Live your life according to his basic principles and I don't think you could go far wrong. So I got to thinking what Jesus would do. And it was obvious in the end. He always did the same thing. He forgave. Every time, without fail. Forgive, forgive, forgive. You have done horrid things to my family. But if you just say one word, I will forgive you. One word that even a child could say. Perhaps a child who was born with cerebral palsy and needs a wheelchair." Elliott reached over and prodded Paolo in the side of the head. The other man flicked his arm up and knocked Elliott's hand away.

"You are also a nasty piece of work, Paolo. The type that would take my forgiveness and use it against me. I'm not going to let you hang me out to dry. So my forgiveness comes with terms attached. You know what they say: you can take the man out of the solicitor but you can't take the solicitor out of the man. Or something. So. This is what you are going to do, Paolo. You are going to gift the four hundred thousand pounds to Lucy. No security, no interest payments. It will be a gift. You are also going to give me the paperwork that proves that you committed fraud against Joey. We'll call that my insurance."

"Why the fuck should I do that?"

"Paolo, I've told you once, stop using profanities in this place. You do that once more and I'm walking out of here and bringing a ton of trouble down upon your head. Do you understand?"

Stare.

"I said, do you understand?"

Stare. Stare back harder. More stare, but wavering now, around the edges of the eyes. And then, meekly, quietly, "Yes."

"Good," said Elliott. "You do, however, ask a perfectly good question. What are you going to get in return?" He paused. Was he milking this a little too much? Oh, possibly, but come on, who could blame him? Paolo would have done the same thing in return. Look at his face. Terrified. And then Naomi popped onto his shoulder. Careful. The power he had felt in the room with Ian had been seductive. Don't allow yourself to be tempted into those arms again. Be a conduit.

"Those three things are only really undoing the bad things you did in the first place. So you can think yourself lucky that you got off so lightly. And in return? In return Ian will not press charges against you for kidnapping him."

That picture, the look on Paolo's face, could be regurgitated into Elliott's mind upon request for the rest of his life. It was not only the moment when a bully received his comeuppance. It was the moment when Elliott finally achieved something worthwhile. He had changed someone. Or at least stopped someone from doing bad things. That was good enough. The world was infinitesimally a better place than it was ten seconds ago. Another little starfish had been saved.

"What the hell do you know about that?" said Paolo, raising his voice.

"I am a solicitor, Paolo. I went to see him. I talked to him. I can make this problem go away for you."

"You're a commercial lawyer, not criminal. What have you done, you conniving little—"

"May I stop you there, Paolo? Before you utter another rude word and I have to leave. It doesn't matter why I was able to go and see Ian. And I am a solicitor, not a lawyer, that's American, I don't know why you can't tell the difference. I was allowed to talk to him, he was willing to talk to me. All you need to care about is that circumstances have dealt you a way out.

"I am offering you a chance for redemption, Paolo. A chance to really change, to become a better person. If you do give back the money you stole I will let you keep your businesses and houses, you can go about rebuilding your reputation. It might even be enhanced. You have a blank page. You will be in the spotlight. People will look at you and wonder to themselves, 'What if it was true?' So you have the chance to show them. To do more for charity. Stop dishing out bribes." Was that a twitch in Paolo's left eye? "Don't be a trustee for a charity just for show and use your business contacts to do some good. All of these things are now possible because everyone will be watching you and wondering if you really did kidnap and torture that young man. Or maybe, possibly, you might reflect on how incredibly lucky you are and how close you've come to being unmasked for the deeply unpleasant individual you are and change your ways." Elliott leaned back and folded his arms. "But most importantly, give Lucy back what you stole from Joey, along with proof by tomorrow lunchtime. Charges will be dropped immediately the money is confirmed and the paperwork is on my desk."

He waited for a moment, checking in his head that everything was out now, that all was said that needed to be said. "Now you may speak. One word. The magic word that will make all this happen."

Paolo looked like a child grappling with the realisation that he was either going to have to eat all the broccoli on the plate or miss his favourite television show. The veins on his neck were bulging, giving the appearance that they had been stuck on with glue. Eventually he opened his mouth to speak, then closed it again and wiggled his jaw. Finally he spoke.

"Sorry," he said.

Satisfied, Elliott stood, knees cracking so loudly that the volunteer who was now arranging flowers on the trestle table turned round. Elliott gave her a smile that would have charmed the angels. He began to leave, then, as if he had forgotten something, turned and leaned over to Paolo.

"In case you were wondering how I found out about the fraud," he whispered, "I didn't. A man far smarter than I gave him credit for worked it out. And you've just confirmed it."

He took one last moment to savour the look on Paolo's face, then walked out of the cathedral leaving Paolo sitting in the pew staring ahead, his face slowly turning blue.

Chapter 29

Wednesday, 8pm

"It is done," said Elliott, sitting on one of the dining room chairs. His back was straight, hands interlocked on the table in front of him, his chin virtually jutting.

"You're not Batman, Elliott," said Lucy. "The fact that you are not going to jail does not mean what you did was right. It was very, very wrong."

"Does not the end justify the means?"

"No. And stop speaking like that. Nobody speaks like that outside of the movies. You got away with this by the skin of your teeth. I'm not sure if you were out for revenge or to change the world, but this is *not* something of which Naomi would have approved."

Elliott glared at his elder sister. Of the two words that made up that phrase it had always seemed to him that 'elder' had taken prominence. Over the years nothing had awoken Alan more often than Lucy and her 'you know I'm right' tone of voice. Trouble was, she only used that voice when she actually *was* right, a stick with which she prodded Alan awake. Over the years it was the same realisation Elliott used to calm himself again. His sister always knew what to do, and what he should do. What was once intensely annoying was something he had learned to accept as fact.

Walking to the mantelpiece, Lucy picked up the photograph of their parents. She held it in both hands and studied it for a moment.

"Do you remember taking this picture?" she asked Elliott.

"No. I've always wondered I'd done to make them laugh. Something stupid, I presume, holding the camera wrong or something."

"What? No, nothing like that. They were laughing at a dog in the sand dunes behind you. It had chased a ball over the edge and was tumbling head over heels. It was ever so funny."

"Oh. I see."

Lucy looked at the photograph again. She was a woman now. Not a sister any more. The thought took him by surprise. What had changed about her to make him see her so differently? He wondered if it was the effect of Joey being in her life.

Twenty years later, as he stood putting flowers on her grave, Elliott would recall that moment and realise how terribly he had always underestimated his big sister.

"Elliott, Mum and Dad were *very* proud of you," Lucy said, looking up. "As am I. Despite what you have just done. I'm still proud of you and what you are and what you have the ability to be. You do know that, don't you?"

"Well, I suppose so."

She returned to studying the photograph. "You were such a shy child. You thought that no one liked you, and you acted accordingly. I had to watch as you made people hate you. I couldn't do anything. Such a frustrating boy. Always right, not as in 'I think I'm right', but actually always right."

The tips of Elliott's ears went red. He would prefer not to be reminded of his childhood.

Lucy stepped back to the mantelpiece where she returned the photograph to its home next to Naomi. She stared at the picture of the vibrant, happy, energetic young woman who everyone had loved. "Do you know what your problem is, Elliott?" she said eventually.

"Yes, I think I do."

Lucy took out two pieces of paper from her pocket and two pens. She placed one of each on the table in front of Elliott and sat at the table opposite him. "Write it down."

"Not another management technique."

"Just do it for me, please."

They both wrote on their squares of paper, Elliott folding his carefully so that the corners matched up. Lucy did the same. They swapped.

Lucy unwrapped her paper, read what her brother had written,

290

then placed it on the table. "Oh, Elliott," she said, looking up at him. He recognised that look on her face. He had seen it before when he used to come home from school with muddy footprints all over his art homework.

Elliott unwrapped his piece of paper and read aloud what Lucy had written. 'You care too much'. He looked up at her, tears now starting to fall onto his lap. "It's true," he said. He took deep, quick gulps in an attempt to compose himself, to be able to speak. "A week ago," he said between gasps, "I would have only noticed the 'You care' bit. Now I think I understand the 'too much' part as well."

Lucy looked at her piece of paper and read again to herself what Elliott had written. "Caring about others so much is both your greatest flaw and your greatness asset, Elliott. It's what makes you who you are. But why don't you just seek a little happiness for yourself before trying to change the world again, okay?"

Elliott tried to agree but instead lost his composure, the tears releasing themselves in great sobs. As his body lurched and jolted it actually felt good to not be in control, to submit to the urges of his body, to yield himself up to uncontained emotion. He had suppressed Alan for so long that maybe he had battened everything else down in that hatch as well. His eyes closed, head bowed not out of shame but as if all the muscles that worked together to hold his body in a bold and upright position had been snipped at the same time. He looked like a marionette waiting for the play to begin, a forlorn, fallen creature without shame or pride, just existing in the moment.

Lucy put down the piece of paper, walked around the table and sat next to her brother. She put both her arms around him and gently guided his head into the crook of her shoulder. He yielded without restraint, his tears now staining her floral chiffon blouse. She said nothing but just held him, tight enough for him to know that he was not alone, loose enough to tell him it was okay to cry. A lifetime of understanding flowed back and forth between them. Elliott's body continued to shudder as the last of the tears flowed. He burrowed in slightly further to the comfort and warmth that can only be provided by the familiar smell of one you truly worship.

On the table in front of them was his piece of paper, upon which was written the words 'I miss Naomi'.

*

"So, how did it go?" asked Elliott. He poured a small whisky and set it in on the low table front of Ian, then picked up his glass of red wine and took the single-seater.

"Yeah, it all went good," Ian replied, oblivious to Elliott straining to not correct him. "Went just as planned, basically. I broke into the building and arranged things so it would look like I'd been there a few days. Put a chair in the room, sat on it and took a piss, put the rope on the floor behind the chair, that sort of thing. Arranged the door so it would look like I'd broken out, not in." He paused before continuing in a halting voice. "I *was* scared, you know. Up there. Really, seriously bastard scared. You left me for hours at a time. I'll never forget that moment when I first woke up as long as I live. One second I'm driving and losing control of my car, next I open my eyes and I'm tied up in pitch darkness. Talk about out of control. Sitting in that outbuilding trying to make it look like I'd been imprisoned there, it brought it home, you know? You had good reason to be pissed off at me, I do get that, but Jesus, Elliott, I'm going to have nightmares about this for the rest of my life."

"I am sorry," said Elliott, misjudging his tone. He had gone for remorse but it came out heavy on the conceit, plus a pinch of hubris. He added quickly, "No, I am, I really am. I'm sorry I caused you so much distress." He should his head sadly. "Still, I'm not really sure I had any other choice but to do what I did, given the opportunity I was presented with."

"You had no choice but to kidnap me? Really? You couldn't have just had a quiet chat? Taken me to a hospital first, maybe? What's wrong with talking to people, for crying out loud? Show them a little respect."

"Would you have listened if I had?" replied Elliott. When Ian did not answer, he continued. "Faced with the person who killed my parents by reckless driving, who was now in front of me, helpless because he had continued to act in the same way, who had clearly learned nothing from the death of my parents and was continuing to endanger the lives of himself and others? Yes, faced with that situation, I think many other people would have done the same thing."

"You actually believe that, don't you?"

"Yes. That there are others in the world like me willing to put themselves in danger to stand up for what is right." Elliott paused for a moment. He tested that statement, rolled it around his mouth like a fine Rioja. He could see the flaw; feel the imperfection in his argument. He spoke before Ian had the chance to, even as the other man started to open his mouth. "The difficulty, of course, is in defining what is right."

He noticed a flash of pique cross Ian's face, a realisation that Elliott was again one step ahead of him in the argument. It was a look that Elliott had seen many times over the last week. He took a further moment to acknowledge to himself that he had actually noticed the effect of his words in another person. He felt a minor shift taking place within his personality, the tectonic plates of empathy and self-awareness moving into a more prominent position.

It was time for the apology that he had been rehearsing in his mind all afternoon, from the moment he had left Paolo. That feeling of something coming to an end that brought with it the ability to look back over what had happened as a whole entity rather than a series of events. Perspective, available to all but used by so few, and with it came the opportunity for explanations and regrets.

"Sometimes what people need is a jolt," said Elliott. "Something to disrupt the ingrained way of thinking, to force them into seeing things a different way and allow the possibility that maybe the change needs to come from them. It is the slap around the face to the hysterical woman, the diagnosis of a terminal illness to the busy entrepreneur who doesn't know his own children. You, Ian, had not changed your way of thinking since the accident that killed my parents. You had buried the incident, put it out of your mind, not confronted it in any way. You needed to be awoken and it needed something extreme to make that happen. I was that something. Not by choice, not by my design, but by fate. I am sorry that it had to happen, I am sorry to have caused you so pain and anguish. But I simply could not allow you to miss your destiny."

"My God," said Ian replied, "you really are a pompous prick. Look, what happened in that room did not change a thing. When I saw that photograph and realised what was behind all this, I saw that you were also a victim. If there was a moment where I *may* have had an epiphany, that was it, not anything you did. If anyone has changed me, Elliott, it is me."

Elliott eyed the reborn man in front of him. Part of him missed the acquiescent Ian from the turret. And yet it was good to talk to someone again, to debate, to be challenged. He got the impression Ian felt the same way – he was sat on Elliott's sofa by choice after all.

"Okay, I'll give you that," Elliott said, "just for the moment. If you are the architect of your own awakening it is because you created me. When you caused the accident that killed my parents you set in motion a course of events that would lead to my intervention and your change. What we are seeing, Ian, is karma in its full glory."

"I still say we could have achieved the same thing over a beer. But that wasn't an option because you acted in anger. Your options were limited by your rage." Elliott felt the sting of the truth. "Lucy told me about Alan."

"Alan," replied Elliott, drawing his shoulders back and picking up his glass with a boldness that bordered on chutzpah, "is someone who will not be influencing me again. Lucy would like to think that he was behind all of this. It is convenient for her to blame something else, to avoid the idea that I did this because I thought it was the right thing to do. Alan may have spurred me on in the very beginning, maybe even have given me the courage to act. But this was not his doing. And he no longer has a role to play in my life. I'm done with Alan for good. All decisions in the future will be mine and mine alone."

Ian finished the contents of his glass. "I'm going home now," he said. "But I'll be in touch. If that's okay? A beer sometime, maybe?"

"I'd like that," Elliott replied. "I'd actually really like that. And Ian?"

"Hmm?"

"Have a safe journey."

Ian laughed. "I'm sure I'll be okay at this time of night," he said. "Not too many slow drivers like you to get in the way."

Elliott looked at his watch, then jumped out of his seat. "Nine o'clock! I need to pick Phoebe up from her judo match." He ran out of the lounge, calling to Ian behind him "Let yourself out, would you?"

*

Ten minutes later and Elliott stood outside the sports hall. He was late. It felt as if something was misaligned in the universe, like the sun had not risen or people were walking round with their heads on backwards. He did not *do* late.

And now Phoebe had already left. He had sent her a text as he was leaving to warn her he was on his way. She had replied as he arrived to say that Mikey had come to watch the bout and would walk her home, but that she had left her belt in the changing rooms and could he pick it up for her?

He walked across the well-lit car park. There were only two vehicles including his. The other was a two-seater sports car with a soft top. He walked over to the main entrance, double glass doors. As he reached forwards a young man approach from within. He had long, dark hair, floppy on top but short at the sides, one long curl falling with precision across the side of his forehead. Pulling the door open wide, Elliott stepped back to let the man through, preparing a large smile for him as he did so.

The young man walked boldly through without so much as a glance, Elliott's smile withering on his face.

"Thank you," said Elliott loudly. Then, "Don't mention it. Oh, you didn't."

The young man stopped and turned to look back at Elliott. He sized him, assessed him coldly, condescension oozing from every pore. A sneer formed, although Elliott guessed the man was unaware of its appearance. His face proclaimed derision driven by deep prejudices. "Oh, do get a life," said the man, before turning and flouncing off. Elliott watched as he sauntered over to the soft-top sports car.

Now unaware that he was still holding the door open, Elliott sighed and narrowed his eyes. He swayed for a moment, hesitating, grinding his teeth, weighing two simple options. Then he drew himself up, shoulders back, and a determination set itself firm in his jaw. Elliott's grip on the door released and he walked briskly across the car park towards the man with the floppy hair.

Acknowledgements

The ideas in this book were discussed over a number of lengthy lunches with fellow writers David Lloyd, Heidi Rhodes and Mick Connaire, each of whom contributed enormously to its development.

For more information on the brainwashing system that Elliott attempts, see the book *Thought Reform and the Psychology of Totalism: A Study of 'Brainwashing' in China* by Robert Jay Lifton.

I am fortunate in the support that I receive from wife, Susie, and children, Ella and George. Creativity requires fresh mental energy, which in itself comes from having space and time, as well being surrounding by open minded and inquisitive people.

For these attributes I am also grateful to my colleagues at Ovation Finance Ltd.

The book is also imbued with the spirit and loving memory of Pru Childs.

My own restless nature comes from my mother. I once told her, as a teenager, that I was bored. She pointed out the window and asked how I could ever have nothing to do. I have never been bored since.

But most of all this book is dedicated to my father, George Budd, who inspired me in so many ways and who passed away in January 2015. I think of him often.

Praise for *A Bridge of Straw*

'Budd's enthusiastic, energetic and empathetic writing style carries you along.'

'I really enjoyed this book…more and more as it hurtled towards its dark conclusion.'

'A Bridge Of Straw is a great debut novel.'

'As soon as I had finished I found myself reflecting on the story.'

'The story reads as though it is written by an established author not as a debut book.'

'I enjoyed it so much I bought it for a friend.'

Find out more about the author at www.cbudd.co.uk
and www.financialwell-being.co.uk

Lightning Source UK Ltd.
Milton Keynes UK
UKOW01f0448171216
290192UK00002B/45/P

9 781781 326176